The Found Child

A Shelby McDougall Mystery

Nancy Wood

Cover design copyright © 2020 by Niki Lenhart
nikilen-designs.com

Published by Paper Angel Press
paperangelpress.com

ISBN 978-1-957146-14-0 (Trade Paperback)

10 9 8 7 6 5 4 3 2

FIRST EDITION

To my parents

ACKNOWLEDGEMENTS

I have written and rewritten this book so many times, with ten major versions sitting in folders on my computer, and many sub-versions in between. Countless plot lines were introduced and discarded. From the beginning, I knew how *The Found Child* would start. I knew how it would end. But it took a lot of rewrites to get from point A to point B!

As so many authors say in their acknowledgements, writing a book truly is a solitary endeavor. Most of the time it was fun. Some of the time, it wasn't! I couldn't have done it without the encouragement of friends and family, who always checked in and asked me how it was going. I certainly couldn't have done it without the help of my wonderful husband, Hans, who not only gently reminded me to get to the computer, but who also came up with several critical plot twists when I was completely stuck. My now-adult kids provided inspiration, good cheer, and much-needed technological assistance.

I'd also like to thank my parents, my siblings, and my in-laws, for reading my books and promoting them. My mother, Alma; my father, Ed; and my mother-in-law, Grace; have special, well-appreciated, talents for book promotion! To all my friends, both here and scattered across the country and the world, thank you for reading Shelby's story and helping spread the word.

I also want to thank my local *Shut Up & Write* group for providing a regular opportunity for socializing and writing. If you haven't found this meetup in your area, start one! You will be inspired.

And many thanks go to my beta readers, Marlene Bumgarner, Mary Flodin, and Andrea Monticue. These women helped me refine and deepen the final version of *The Found Child*. I couldn't have done it without their insight and assistance.

Of course, many, many thanks to Steven Radecki and Paper Angel Press for picking up the entire Shelby McDougall series, giving it a unified look, and producing books that I'm proud to hold.

Thank you all — it definitely takes a village.

INTRODUCTION

This is the third book in the Shelby McDougall mystery series, and, with mixed feelings, I can say it is the last one. I set out to write a trilogy and I'm pleased with what I accomplished. In this book, Shelby's story comes full circle. Shelby has grown and matured and found her place in the world.

I wanted the series to be contemporary and topical, addressing societal issues. The first two books, *Due Date* and *The Stork*, addressed surrogacy, adoption, and synthetic biology. *The Found Child* continues to dig into those issues and also tackles new ones. For example, I used personal genetics — a cheek swab to *Ancestry.com* — as a plot device, allowing Shelby to discover a truth she wishes she'd never known about.

Additional concerns offered themselves up. The pandemic for starters. Urgent, devastating, and unavoidable. There was no way to ignore it, especially because I'd placed *The Found Child* in September of 2020. I had to rewrite almost every chapter to include masks and social distancing.

And just a week after I submitted my manuscript to Paper Angel Press, the devastating CZU Lightning Complex Fire tore through Santa Cruz County, destroying vast areas of the beloved grasslands and redwood forests in the Santa Cruz Mountains. The rural community of Bonny Doon, where Shelby's fictional home sits, was devastated. Rather than change the timing of the book or move Shelby's home to another location, I rewrote yet again. Thank you, Paper Angel Press, for allowing a second submission!

It has been interesting to see how my writing and vision has progressed across these three books. For example, when I wrote *Due Date*, I fudged with places in the county, moving locations around to suit the story, or creating fictitious businesses as needed. I became a bit more grounded in *The Stork,* and in *The Found Child* I tried to place Shelby in Santa Cruz County as accurately as possible. I did take liberties in one area though — I moved Shelby back home to Bonny Doon after the devastating fire much sooner than allowed in real life.

This is my third book published through Paper Angel Press and I am so grateful for the opportunity. Thank you!

Happy reading!

Nancy

1

THE PUNCHING BAG FLEW AT MY FACE. I swung, but not in time. It grazed the top of my head, throwing me off balance. By some miracle, I was able to catch my footing, bounce up, and smash the bag on the rebound, pummeling the teardrop sphere with quick jabs. My shoulders and arms burned. Sweat leaked into my eyes and I grunted each time my glove connected with the target. If I hadn't been wearing a mouth guard, I would have howled instead. My therapist promised it would help.

What helped even more was imagining that the punching bag was Dr. Helen Brannon; the woman who'd ruined my life, the woman I blamed for everything. She was responsible for my multiple miscarriages. The miscarriages that, in turn, had caused my marriage to disintegrate and my financial future to veer off into a chasm.

A piercing whistle signaled the end of the session. I took two more jabs, a right followed by a left, with each swing seeing the woman's arrogant expression and smug smile crumple into a jumble of blood and broken teeth.

Better than therapy any day.

"Take a seat," yelled Tatiana, the instructor. She pointed to the rickety metal bench opposite the boxing ring. "Remember, keep your distance."

I jogged over, wishing I could wipe my face on a towel, but my hands, trapped in the heavily padded boxing gloves, were useless. I found an open spot six feet away from anyone else, leaned over, and rubbed my face on the hem of my baggy shorts. Then I sprawled back against the wall with my legs straight out in front of me. As Tatiana demonstrated the intricacies of a right uppercut followed by a left, exhaustion overcame me and I closed my eyes. Last night's phone call instantly started replaying in my mind. Once again, I'd called my ex. Once again, he'd been polite, but distant. My separation from Cody was going on seven months now. I wanted to get back together. He didn't. My pleading wasn't helping anyone, but I couldn't stop myself.

We'd separated just before the semi-draconian, but absolutely necessary, shelter-in-place order forced all non-essential workers to stay at home to prevent the spread of the coronavirus. With that edict, I lost half my business, all of my already limited social life, my gym outings, and my coffee shop pick-me-ups. Casual friendships tanked and Netflix binge-watching became my new best friend. It had been a long spring and summer, and now, in mid-September of 2020, the nation was still figuring out how to adjust.

Santa Cruz County, where I lived, teetered on and off California's coronavirus watch list. Masks were mandatory. School remained online. Restaurants and cafes were limited to takeout orders or widely spaced outdoor seating. Grocery stores regulated the number of people allowed inside at a time, while retail businesses could conduct only limited service. When on the watchlist, the county's places of worship, movie theaters, bars, wineries, hair and nail salons, and gyms were shuttered. Now that the county's numbers were trending down, all those non-essential, but absolutely necessary services, like my boxing gym, could open again.

My pandemic normal was lonelier than before. And each time Cody brushed me off, like last night, my rage against Helen Brannon intensified. But for her I'd be pregnant. But for her, Cody and I would be living in our sweet home, refinishing it room by room, starting with the baby's room. But for her, I'd still be with Cody, the love of my life.

Back in the locker room, after Tatiana untied my gloves, I unwound the tape from my hands and assessed the damage. Reddened knuckles. Bruising on my right index finger. A purple shadow on my left thumb. Nothing that a bit of CBD oil wouldn't fix.

"Hey, Shelby, how's it going?" asked Bailey, an occasional sparring partner, as she sat on the bench opposite me, wrapped in a towel.

"I used to think I was in shape," I smiled. "I thought I was fit." My daily workouts hadn't prepared me at all for this class. I shook my head. "This is punishing."

Bailey laughed. As she stood to head to the shower, she said, "Julie and I are going over to The Buttery to get a cup of coffee and gawk at the pastries. Want to join us?"

Visions of the tastiest croissants and muffins in Santa Cruz danced through my mind, but I shook my head. "I'd love to, but I have to get to work."

"Too bad. Maybe next time?" Bailey's smile was bright. She was at least ten years younger than me, enthusiastic, optimistic, guileless.

I returned her smile with one of my own. Even though I craved social contact, work always came first. As a sole proprietor and small business owner, there were never enough hours in the day. Between the mountains of paperwork, client meetings, phone calls, court appearances, reports, surveillance, and required continuing education, I always felt pressed for time. Private investigations never stopped. Not even for the coronavirus. Luckily, during the shelter-in-place order, I was able to keep working because my business, Shelby McDougall Investigations, was considered an essential service related to "legally mandated activities." My bread-and-butter contract for background checks for a local tech company continued. Warrants, surveillance for two separate slip-and-fall cases, as well as a worker's comp case, barely kept me above water. In July, an insurance fraud case had occupied most of my time.

I stripped out of my sweaty clothes and left them on the floor as I swaddled myself in a towel. I wasn't shy, but at age thirty-six, with most of the other women in the class in their twenties, I felt a tiny bit self-conscious. Even though I was too thin, gravity was not my friend. My stomach pooched. No matter how many crunches I did, I couldn't get rid of the roll. My hips looked like I wore permanent jodhpurs.

Worst of all, the pandemic had shuttered my hairdresser and my recent cut at the local one-size-fits-all salon made my hair resemble a steel wool scouring pad.

After showering and changing, I shoved my soaking clothes into my gym bag, along with my gear. I walked through the quiet, darkened gym and paused at the office to say goodbye. Outside, squinting in the bright light, I extracted my key fob from the side pocket of my gym bag and clicked open my five-year-old silver Prius. Deep in my bag, my phone chimed. The ringtone, the signature theme from the Harry Potter movies, served as my hopeful reminder of magic, possibility, and miracles. I dug out the phone and glanced at the screen, happy to see that Dexter, my brother, was calling. Dexter and his family had been my lifeline last winter as Cody and I yo-yoed about whether to stay together, separate, keep the house and rent it, or sell it and move on.

And last March, just before the pandemic ravaged our world, when Cody and I decided to split up for good, I parked myself at Dexter's, imposing on him, his wife Megan, and their children. I'd crammed myself into a small utility room on a makeshift cot, trying not to remember how I'd lived with Dexter and his first wife thirteen years earlier; another period in my life when I'd been lost. This time, I had the good sense not to overstay my welcome, moving out after less than a month.

The third time Dexter had rescued me was four weeks ago, in the middle of August, when I had to evacuate because of the CZU Lightning Complex fire that chewed through more than eighty-five thousand acres of Santa Cruz County and neighboring San Mateo County. My neighborhood in the Santa Cruz mountains had suffered multiple structural losses, but where I lived remained standing. Somehow, during the evacuation order, I managed to work, even though I was spending at least six hours a day on Twitter, tracking the fire and the response; staying in touch with my housemate, Erica; and keeping abreast of the neighborhood through our shared email list. Our evacuation order had been lifted only a few weeks ago. The smoky smell still lingered; the meadow and surrounding forest were covered in grainy, black soot; and every morning my car was dusted with ash.

"Hey, Dexter," I said, stabbing the speaker icon and holding up the phone, "how's it going?"

"Good," he replied. "Busy as usual. School started. Finally. What with the delay because of the fire, we were starting to wonder." I mentally kicked myself. Between the pandemic, the fire, and my own personal problems, I'd forgotten to call.

"Annie's in seventh grade, and Ashley is a sophomore?" I asked. Annie, Megan's daughter, was now twelve, and had been born long before Dexter and Megan had met. Ashley, Dexter's daughter from his previous marriage, was fifteen going on twenty-five.

"Yup. Back to school night is in a couple of weeks, so we'll find out everything. All on Zoom."

"How's Max?"

"As fun as ever. He gets to go to preschool. We're all happy about that." Max, Dexter and Megan's son, was an energetic four-year-old. Dexter laughed and continued. "We have a tutor-slash-nanny who comes at noon and works with Annie for two hours after her Zoom classes are over for the day. Then, she picks up Max. Ashley is on her own."

I was so wrapped up in my own world that I hadn't considered the logistics of school life with COVID. Sounded complicated.

"So, what are you up to today?" Dexter continued.

I hesitated, surprised. Dexter never asked me what I was up to on a workday. When we met for lunch, his schedule was always the one that needed working around. He'd been the Director of the Santa Cruz Parks & Recreation Department for two years now. His job was a desk job, with hours of daily meetings.

"Why, what's going on?" I asked.

"Something's come up and I need to talk to you." His voice was quiet.

"Is Megan okay? Mom?"

"Yes, they're fine," he said, but something in his voice made it sound like nothing was fine. "Are you free for lunch?" he continued.

"Yes. I'm in the office all day."

"Great, I'll pick up some sandwiches. I'll be over around noon."

"What's going on, Dexter?" I asked again.

"I'll tell you when I see you. Not over the phone."

As I slipped my phone in my bag, I wondered what was up with Dexter. He was never so secretive.

2

M Y OFFICE IN BRANCIFORTE PLAZA was just a few blocks from the gym, and five minutes later, I pulled into the parking lot. I'd moved to this building from my Santa Cruz Harbor location almost two years earlier, when I bought the P.I. business immediately after my boss, Kathleen Bennett, had retired. This office was less expensive. And it was much easier to park here, always a consideration for coastal Californians. I didn't miss circling the harbor parking lot, waiting for a spot to open up.

Even so, it had taken some adjusting. After the excitement of the move had worn off, I realized how much I missed being able to walk down a flight of stairs to the sand. I missed seeing the vivid winter sunsets. I missed the early morning fog that cloaked the water in a thick, wet mist.

Here, my second-floor office was located about halfway down the hall, with a CPA on my right and a family lawyer on my left. My windows faced the front parking lot and the street. Instead of the nondescript California-style rectangle of my previous office, this building had history in its bones. It had been built in 1929 as a forty-nine bed hospital, and was eventually run by the Catholic Church. After forty years, the hospital moved to larger quarters, and the building sat empty. In the late seventies, it was remodeled into a Spanish Revival style office building, with arched entryways, tile roofs, orange stucco, terracotta, wide staircases, heavy doors, and balconies. Landscaped fountains, palm trees, and abundant bougainvillea completed the upgrade.

Before I'd signed the lease here, I'd heard rumors of hauntings but had never believed it. Someone told me that her friend had once seen a ghost, a specter, float by the front door when she was heading to the restaurant for a late-night drink. I never told anyone, not even Cody, of my sighting. When I'd first moved in and had been working late to organize my desk and files, I'd felt something. A presence. It had followed me as I walked down the hall to the restroom. I'd fisted my keys and whirled around, but there was nothing. Just a visible disturbance in the air, a shimmering. Enough to spook me and cause me to sprint back to my office, grab my purse, and flee. I often wondered who the ghost had been. Perhaps a patient who'd died unexpectedly and her spirit was somehow stuck, doomed to wander the halls for eternity.

Now, the building housed a popular Italian restaurant, Ristoranti Roma, as well as a number of lawyers and accountants, a realtor, two therapists, an acupuncturist, an insurance agent, a rare book and map dealer, a coin dealer, and a tech startup. I was the only private investigator. My office, referred to as a "suite" in the lease, consisted of two rooms. The front room, directly off the hallway, contained a desk, two client chairs, and a low round table for a water jug and coffee pot along with the accompanying necessities: sugar and cream packets, cups, wooden stir sticks. My intern, Lucy Florez, occupied this part of my small domain two days a week.

The back room was mine. My desk, in the middle of the room, faced the door. A round conference table, large enough for three chairs, was in the far corner, below one of the windows. Next to it, opposite my desk, sat a small table with an all-in-one color printer and a stack of printer paper in a drawer below. I'd placed a long low bookshelf, filled with reference books I rarely consulted, beneath the other window. A walk-in closet, large enough for shelves, my safe, and two banks of file cabinets, took up the wall by my desk.

•   •   •

I grabbed my purse and briefcase, exited the car, and locked it. I crossed the parking lot, paused to admire the water cascading down the fountain, and then entered the lobby, empty save for a tenant directory posted on the wall. Once in my office, I opened the blinds, dropped my purse and briefcase on the table, and approached the closet door, a fire-resistant monster I'd had to special order and hire someone to install. I held my right thumb to the fingerprint reader and eased the door open. The two four-drawer file cabinets held client files. The safe held the company laptops, backup hard drives, and cash. Surveillance equipment — cameras, night scopes, binoculars — sat on the shelves.

I continued to follow the security protocols that my previous boss, Kathleen Bennett, had instilled in me. Some habits were hard to break.

But there was one piece of equipment she owned that I didn't. A gun. Kathleen and I had talked about it frequently. Cody and I spent hours discussing it. He wanted me to carry. He pleaded with me to carry. To please him, I went through all the steps — shooting classes and firearms safety classes. We attended gun shows and visited several gun superstores out in the Central Valley. But when it came to purchasing one, I just couldn't. I couldn't imagine ever drawing on someone, let alone pulling the trigger. And I knew that was one of the first rules of gun ownership. Don't carry the thing if you can't use it. Because if you don't use it, it will likely be used against you.

I wasn't naive. I knew all about guns, having been at the wrong end of one several times in my life. I'd seen first-hand the damage a gun could do. But arming myself just didn't seem right.

I turned my attention to the safe, twirling the dial to unlock it. I used to think about forgoing this security measure. Keeping the computers locked away seemed overkill. Each time I powered down the laptop, files were encrypted and uploaded to an ultra-secure server somewhere in the cloud for which I paid an exorbitant sum on a monthly basis. Then, top-secret software wiped the files on the hard drive so that, supposedly, if the laptop ever fell into the wrong hands, no one could discover what we were up to. The reverse of the process loaded files back onto the laptop when I turned it on again.

This level of security was critical. I didn't want any of my work — past, present, or future — finding its way to the internet. Especially because I was investigating more and more cases involving missing children or young adults: runaways, parental abductions, and a few terrifying cases where a child had just vanished into thin air. I shuddered to think of the damage my notes could inflict on parents already crushed by the loss of their child.

After extracting my computer from the safe, I deactivated call forwarding so that calls would now come directly to the landline on the desk instead of my cell phone. I was available twenty-four-seven; I had to be. With missing children, time was critical. An hour could make all the difference.

Right now, my most urgent case involved a missing nineteen-year-old from Santa Cruz. The missing teen, Crystal Bradner, had been in my life tangentially. When she'd been a high school sophomore, she'd attended a Women in Business career day presentation where I'd been a presenter. At the meet and greet following the talk, she'd come to my table and peppered with me questions: *What's it like to be a P.I.? What do you do every day? How do you get cases? What's the hardest case you've worked on? The easiest? How can I become a P.I.?*

I'd been taken by her enthusiasm and curiosity. And her complete innocence. She was astonishingly beautiful, with clear skin, a small rounded nose, enough cheekbone to give her face structure, perfectly arched eyebrows, and full lips. She had no idea how enviously the older women in the room, including me, looked at her side-long, yearning to recapture their younger selves.

We'd talked for a while and I'd offered to meet with her and show her my office; give her an overview of a typical day in the life of a private investigator. That month, she and her grandfather, Stu, had taken me up on my offer and I'd walked them through a few of my cases, using aliases. I'd given her an overview of my security system and equipment. After our visit, I'd arranged for Crystal to do a ride-along with the Santa Cruz police. Cody, then a Deputy Sergeant in the Sheriff's Department, had given her a tour of those offices, as well as the jail. He'd also arranged for her to do a ride along. He'd even tried to enroll her in a two-week summer program for teens who wanted to go into law enforcement, but her stepfather would have none of it. "If it's not a Christian camp, it's not happening," her grandfather had grumbled.

I'd tried to keep in touch, calling her a few times, but had given up when she never returned my calls. I thought of her often and had been surprised and delighted to receive her high school graduation announcement. She'd scribbled a note on the bottom, saying that she planned to live with her grandparents in the fall and attend the local community college. I'd sent her a congratulatory card along with a check.

That was the last time I heard from her.

Two days after graduation, Crystal disappeared, taking a duffel bag of clothes and all the cash in her stepfather's wallet. And now, almost three and one-half months later, she was still missing.

Her disappearance had been reported to me by Stu, not by her mother, Nicole, or her stepfather, Mark. When I talked to them, they seemed just as content that she was gone. They figured she'd run away, and was happily living elsewhere, pursuing what Mark called a "heathen lifestyle."

"Once she got that first tattoo — the tiny moon on her wrist — I knew she had strayed," her mother told me. And her stepfather, a strict born-again Christian, said, "If she hadn't left when she did, I would have kicked her out." I glanced at her mom as he said this; the woman had nodded her head in agreement.

Crystal's grandparents, Stu and Marilyn, had searched and searched, hitting the streets in Santa Cruz and Monterey, and even hiring a private investigator in Portland, where they knew Crystal had friends. I'd helped Stu, pro bono, using my extensive online tools to hunt up any trace of her. I couldn't find anything. She'd simply vanished.

I'd been able to talk to her mom on the phone once, without her husband interfering. Her mom told me that Crystal had been obsessed with money before she'd run off. She'd boasted that one day she'd have bucket loads of money. Enough money to send Stu and Marilyn on an

Alaskan cruise. Enough money to live on her own. Even enough to go to college.

I'd also spent an afternoon interviewing her co-workers at the cafe where she'd worked in downtown Santa Cruz. I'd learned that Crystal liked to run the espresso machine and hated to work the cash register. She had a boyfriend; a sharp dresser who dropped by on a daily basis in the weeks before her disappearance. I assumed the boyfriend was a john and she'd been lured into the sex trade.

Following up on that suspicion, I'd spent a day with Stu in San Francisco's Mission district, searching. It had been a foggy day in early August, and with the pandemic not yet behind us, I insisted that Stu wear a mask and gloves as we trekked one long block after another, showing Crystal's senior portrait in every bar and cafe we stumbled across.

We'd selected that picture because it was memorable. Crystal's thick blonde hair draped across her shoulders and her spaghetti strap pink top was form-fitting, revealing a shapely figure. She sat in front of a dark background, turned toward the camera. Her smile was full-on one hundred watts, revealing perfect teeth. Her makeup was subtle, and she looked much more mature than she had when I'd met her several years ago. She wore a playful look, as if she'd just asked a personal, funny question, and was waiting for an answer.

Not only was she beautiful; she was also inked. As far as I could remember, she hadn't had a single one of those tattoos when I'd last seen her. Tattoos now covered the skin from wrist to shoulder on her right arm. Dragons, fairies, witches, suns, moons, and stars danced in a chaotic maelstrom of blues, reds, greens, yellows, and purples. I knew a full-sleeve tattoo cost a fortune and I wondered where Crystal had gotten the money.

After nine hours of walking that day, showing that picture to hundreds of people, with no one claiming to have seen her, I tried to convince Stu that Crystal was an adult, and that she had left under her own steam. He didn't buy it. Now, with the community college semester about to start, Stu had turned to me out of desperation. He knew I'd help.

And he also knew that once I opened a full-on investigation, I would work until I dropped in order to get results. I wouldn't stop until I had to.

My reputation as a bulldog in missing persons cases was well-known. Because I *had* found missing children, seemingly conjuring them out of thin air. That reputation was hard-earned. Eight years earlier, I had found a child. A child named Justin Boyd. He was one of the twins I'd put up for adoption. Justin had been snatched from his home in the middle of the night. There were no witnesses. No one had seen anything. Even his twin sister, Justine, who slept in the same room, could offer no clues. Finding Justin had been a combination of dogged persistence, a bit of pushiness, and a few extremely lucky breaks.

Since then, Kathleen and I had cleared a dozen cases of missing children. Most were children abducted by the non-custodial parent. A few were missing teens, run off with someone they found on the internet. Only one had ended in tragedy, with the girl's body discovered in a field in the Central Valley. I'd headed down a bad road after that case, but Cody had pulled me back. When Kathleen retired, I continued taking on missing children cases. Seeing the damage that life could inflict on a child, I was determined that when my child was born, he or she would be protected, cared for, and loved. But life hadn't turned out that way for me. Which is why I was taking swings at a punching bag.

Today, in addition to following up on some leads in Crystal's case, I would work on a new case, somewhat atypical for me. A dog breeder, Carla Gray, had contacted me earlier in the month. Carla, an AKC champion cocker spaniel breeder, lived near the inland end of Elkhorn Slough in Monterey County. She was claiming that a newcomer to the business, a Dirk Thompson, had stolen one of her prize females.

At first, it seemed to me that was more a business spat than a concern for a licensed investigator. But as I researched the world of dog breeding, I immediately realized how competitive this profession was. How breeders guarded their breeding females from prying eyes, keeping them under lock and key. How males were rented out at great expense, used as studs to impregnate females. How breeders enhanced the natural process with hormone injections, creams, and potions. How these dogs and puppies were micro-chipped and DNA registered.

Once Coco, her top breeder, had gone missing, Carla convinced me that this wasn't a case of the dog just wandering off. Her security camera had caught a person, in broad daylight, unlocking the gate to the chain-link run holding Coco; choosing Coco from the swarm of drooling, jumping dogs; clipping a leash to her collar; backing out of the run while throwing treats to the pack; locking the gate; and then quickly moving out of the line of view of the camera.

Carla stated, for the record, that the thief would have had to have known her schedule. And of course, as a breeder of champions, she adhered to a strict schedule. Dogs fed at eight in the morning. Exercised from eight-thirty to ten. Trained from ten to noon. And so on. The only time of day the dogs were unsupervised would be from three to five in the afternoon while she was preparing their food for dinner and the next morning: chunks of raw beef mixed with chicken innards. Mashed sweet potatoes and avocados. Freshly ground peanut butter. Nothing processed. Nothing artificial. Carla even made her own dog treats.

So the conclusion was that the thief had to be an insider. But Carla claimed that all her helpers were so loyal that they would have never sold out.

I knew otherwise. The sad truth was that given the right circumstances, almost anyone would sell out. My job was to find out who.

This morning, I'd start background checks on everyone involved.

3

I WAITED AT THE TOP OF THE STAIRS, watching my brother Dexter jog up the wide staircase. He'd aged in the last few years, what with more responsibility as the man in charge of Santa Cruz's parks department. He'd been promoted after the disaster of the previous director, privately nicknamed The Iron Lady, had resigned, leaving department morale in tatters. It had taken at least a year to mend, and then, the pandemic hit. The shutdown had run him ragged, with a scramble to move classes and workshops online and offer support to struggling families. Summer programs for kids had to be completely reimagined. And now, due to the drop in revenue because of the pandemic, layoffs were on the horizon. At one point in June, when I'd chatted with him by video, he'd looked like a candidate for a heart attack. Overweight, florid, short of breath. But he was back on track now — less alcohol, less sugar, less overtime, and more exercise.

I knew that Dexter and his family would eventually have to leave Santa Cruz. All these years, while I'd been working in my dream job, his wife, Megan, was working towards hers. When I'd met her in 2007, she'd been a lost nineteen-year-old, a freshman at the University of California, Santa Cruz, enrolled as a theater arts major. Like me, she'd been a victim of a baby-brokering scam. Megan had kept her baby, while I'd given up my twins for adoption.

That event had scarred both of us, in ways we were still figuring out. Megan had turned her demons into relentless study, exploring genetics, biochemistry, and molecular biology. Now, she was a PhD candidate in Biomolecular Engineering and Bioinformatics. Maybe she could get a job in Silicon Valley or San Francisco, but even that would be a stretch in terms of a commute.

Dexter looked up at me as he approached, carrying two paper bags. His mask dangled under his chin. Though I was part of his family bubble, we still wore masks and abundantly applied hand sanitizer.

"What did you get?" I asked. I leaned in to give him a hug, but he shook his head. "Megan doesn't have the virus, but she does have a bit of a cold," he said. "Best keep our distance." He held up the bags. "One turkey and cheese, one roast beef and cheese," Dexter said. "Plus chips."

"Yum," I replied. "Thank you." Dexter followed me down the hall and into my office.

"No Lucy?" he asked as we passed through the small front room.

"Tomorrow," I said.

Dexter sat down at the small table, placing the two bags in front of him. I moved the bottle of sanitizer from my desk to the table, then reached to open the windows.

"Which one?" Dexter pointed to the food.

"Roast beef, please," I answered.

"This is nice, Shelby," Dexter said, pushing the bag across the table. As he gazed out the window and rubbed sanitizer into his hands, he said, "Your parking lot is much more picturesque than mine. Love those palms." He laughed. "My office is pure government. The desk is from the nineties and the chair is starting to sink. One of the wheels is breaking."

I spritzed my hands, opened the bag, pulled out the sandwich, and then took a huge bite, chomping into the layers of red meat and jack cheese as if I hadn't eaten in days. The morning had gotten away from me. I knew I'd inhaled two cups of coffee, strong and unadulterated, but

I couldn't remember if I'd actually eaten the banana that I'd dropped into my gym bag.

"This is divine," I said. "Thanks." I placed my sandwich carefully on the deli paper and picked up my bag of salt and vinegar chips. "So what's this all about anyway? Why so secretive?"

Dexter fumbled for a napkin and wiped his mouth. He shifted uncomfortably in his chair.

"What is it, Dexter? Do you have cancer? Does Megan have cancer?" The thought made me light-headed. Then, panic seized me and I leaned forward. "Mom. It's Mom. What's wrong with her?"

I always worried about my mom. By some miracle, she'd survived the pandemic so far, even as friends in her retirement community had become infected with COVID-19 and died.

Dexter looked at the table. "Well it's something sort of with Mom." He cleared his throat. "I got a call from her last night."

"And?" I sat back, ready for another lecture about how Mom was getting older, how I should call and visit her more often.

It was true, but I really hoped Dexter was not here to scold me. I popped open the bag of chips, reached in, grabbed a handful. The crunchy texture and oily sheen, the sour vinegar flavor, and the salty finish momentarily distracted me from my worries.

Dexter picked up his sandwich. He was stalling.

I put down the bag of chips and wiped my hands on a brown paper napkin. "Come on, Dexter. What is it?" I tried to soften the sharpness in my voice.

"Okay, here goes." Dexter straightened his shoulders. "You know how Mom has been tracing down the family tree, right?"

I nodded. Family ties had interested our mother for years. Mom was always eager to discover something about her great-great-great-grandmother or her father's grandfather. And since Dad died, she'd thrown herself into this venture with religious fervor. I knew a bit about my family history, but not from my mother. When I'd located Helen Brannon, the woman who'd used my uterus as a science experiment, she'd given my family history as one of the reasons she'd picked me. Her assessment of my familial history was something I'd never forget: no genetic disorders, no drugs, no addicts, no mental illness. No jail time. No TB or pneumonia. According to Helen Brannon, I had well-educated and outspoken ancestors: physicians, professors, mathematicians, nurses, suffragettes. Even so, she'd classified me as "hardy boring stock", as if I were cattle being inspected for breeding purposes. Which, I suppose, I was.

I picked up my sandwich and stared at the oozing bright yellow mustard. Dexter was saying, "Then, Mom decided to spend six months doing research using the *Ancestry* database."

"What's this got to do with me, Dexter?" I asked, lifting the sandwich to my mouth.

"Mom got an email yesterday."

"And? Are we ancestors of Hitler or Mussolini, or the Dread Pirate Roberts?"

"Not quite." Dexter sighed and stretched his neck from side to side.

This was a bad sign. I knew my brother. Dexter only stretched his neck during times of extreme stress. "What is it?"

I stared at my sandwich again, the layers of white sourdough, cream-colored cheese, blood red meat, green lettuce, and pale red tomato not quite as appetizing as it had been several minutes ago.

"What?" I repeated.

"Well, the email was from someone Mom had never heard of. Her username was 'Julia H.' Just that, no last name. You know, you can make up any username you want."

"I know, Dexter," I put my sandwich down, less carefully this time. The top slipped off, revealing gobs of white mayonnaise smeared across the white bread. "So what is it?"

"The email said that she had a twelve-year-old daughter, same age as Annie." He paused a beat then said, "And the same age as Justin and Justine."

Justin and Justine Boyd were the twins I'd put up for adoption. The twins who turned out to be engineered, not made of stardust, but made of altered DNA and chemicals and reagents and enzymes and Helen Brannon's grandiose ego-driven design to create a new race of uber-humans.

"Okay," I said, drawing out the word, not sure where this was going.

Dexter continued. "The email went on to say that she gave birth to the daughter, but she just carried the baby. The egg was purchased from a fertility clinic in San Francisco and fertilized via IVF. The biological father is her husband."

"And?" I asked, squishing my sandwich back together.

"The email said that the woman had done a cheek swab on her daughter, just to see if she could figure out the genetic mother. And of the fifteen million people in the *Ancestry* database, it came up with a twenty-five percent match to Mom."

"What's that got to do with me?" I asked, looking up at Dexter.

"That means that twenty-five percent of the genetic material in that egg came from Mom." He paused. "It means that Mom is that child's biological grandmother." He paused.

"And?" I asked, waiting.

"Shelby, it means that the egg is yours."

4

A BLACK HAZE COVERED MY EYES. I felt like I was about to faint. I began to hyperventilate and wheeze. I couldn't catch my breath. I stared at Dexter, pleading for help, trying to inhale. Panic crossed his face.

Then, I heard the sound of something crumpling and felt Dexter's hand on my back, soothing and reassuring. With his other hand, he handed me one of the brown paper bags from the deli.

"It's okay, Shelby," he said. "It's okay. Breathe into the bag, slowly." Dexter's voice was calm and quiet. The paper crinkled as I breathed in and out, and within a few minutes, my breathing slowed. I smashed the bag between my hands and lifted my head. When I looked at my brother, I felt like I'd aged fifty years.

"What does Megan say?" My voice was small, quiet.

"She studied the report the woman had attached to her inquiry. Mom gave us her log in so we could just sign into her account." He took a breath and blew it out. "There's a high probability that the girl is somehow related to you."

"But that's impossible. I never, ever donated eggs," I protested.

"You did," Dexter stated, still standing next to me. "Sort of. Brannon told you she never used the eggs she took from you."

I froze, ice in my veins. She *had* said that. "But I never said she could use them." I looked up at my brother.

Dexter eyed me, fighting to keep the pity from his gaze. I knew how ridiculous that sounded. As if the woman who'd implanted me with genetically altered embryos would ask my permission for anything.

"And the girl is twelve?" I asked.

Dexter nodded. "Yes. Same age as Annie, Justin, Justine."

"Oh my god." I was quiet, remembering my confrontation with Helen Brannon eight years earlier, as fresh as if it were yesterday. "She did say that, and I never gave it a second thought." A tear leaked from my eye, accompanied by a sudden sharp memory of my most recent miscarriage. The cramping. The metallic odor of blood. Then the doubling-over pain. And the black cloud that never seemed to lift.

"Oh my god," I repeated. "She sold them. My eggs." I looked hard at the floor, then turned my tear-stricken face to Dexter. "And now, someone else has my baby."

•   •   •

After Dexter cleared his calendar for another hour, we left the office and walked downstairs to the restaurant. We found a table outside on the patio, in the sun. Dexter ordered a cappuccino; I stuck to my regular order of straight up black coffee. It was either that, or a shot of tequila with a beer chaser.

I took a sip, grateful for the heat, the bitter flavor, and the nutty aroma. I was glad I'd remembered to grab my sunglasses; they hid my puffy red eyes.

"How are you doing?" Dexter asked, blowing across the top of the foamy milk.

I shrugged. "In shock. No idea what's next."

"Will you tell Cody?"

"I don't know." I paused. "What's the point?" I asked, trying to keep the bitter edge from my voice.

"Did you two ever talk about adopting?" Dexter asked.

"Sometimes. Cody didn't want to adopt. And I wanted to keep trying for our own. I always felt that if I just wanted it enough, I could stay pregnant. That it was something I was doing." I picked up the heavy cloth napkin and wiped my eyes. The smooth polyester cloth slid across my skin. "I think that subconsciously rubbed off on him. I know it's completely illogical." I paused for a beat, then said, "I know that being a surrogate mother with those twins did something to me. I just don't know what. No one knows what."

"Have you heard from the Boyds?" Dexter asked.

Ryan and Lisa Boyd, unable to conceive and eager for a family, had adopted my twins, the babies I'd been carrying as a surrogate mom when I exposed the baby-brokering ring years earlier. Trafficking infants had funded Helen Brannon's grandiose designs. Like me, the Boyds were collateral damage: they didn't get what they'd wished for. Instead of children they could cuddle while reading *Goodnight Moon*, *Pat the Cat*, or *Thomas the Tank Engine*, they'd ended up with children who could read on their own by age two, multiply by age three, and recite pages of the dictionary by age four. Once the true nature of the children had been exposed, the government had stepped in. To observe, study, protect. The family now lived in Virginia and the twins were monitored day and night.

"Yes," I replied. "Had an email from Ryan last week. They're still in Virginia. The handlers seem to be tiring of their jobs. The kids have plateaued in terms of their intelligence. And Justin is getting aggressive. It's bizarre." I felt a guilty shiver as I said that, as if I were part of the frenzied masses now labeling my biological children as freaks. I continued, "Those kids are under lock and key. Treated like science experiments, best I can tell. Ryan has a job now; he works in a motor pool for the Feds. And Lisa was just fired from her job as a medical receptionist at the VA. She can't hold down a job. This entire experience has taken its toll on her. She's fragile, like she has PTSD." I shook my head. "And, she feels like she can't tell anyone who she is. Public opinion has turned. People see them as freeloaders. It's ugly."

"What a mess," Dexter muttered. "From celebrities to pariahs."

"Yup," I agreed. A slight breeze lifted my hair. I slouched down and leaned back in my chair, the sun hitting me full on. A deep-body weariness came over me and I wanted to sleep for the rest of the afternoon.

After a few minutes of silence, I asked, "What happens next? Does the mother want an answer?"

"Yes," Dexter said.

"Maybe Mom should stay out of this. Maybe I should do that genetic test. Who knows, there might be others out there. More kids. Dr. Helen Brannon's perfect revenge." I almost laughed.

"I'm not so sure about that, Shelby." Dexter took a sip of his cappuccino. "You might find out something you don't want to know."

I sat up. "What else could I possibly learn? I know I'm not adopted. I look just like you, just like Mom and Dad. Besides, Dexter," I continued, "what could possibly be worse than finding out I have a child, related to me genetically, created from a stolen egg? I can't think of anything."

•　　　•　　　•

On my way home, after a long afternoon of background checks in the dog-snatching case, of trying to concentrate and repeatedly having to force my thoughts away from *Ancestry.com* and eggs and newly discovered children and Dr. Helen Brannon, I stopped at Pericos, my favorite taqueria, to pick up my newest variation on comfort food: a chicken burrito slathered with sour cream and guacamole. I knew I even had a beer at home to drown my sorrows. Not the healthiest way to end the day, but just what I needed.

As I was waiting for my food, my phone rang. I pulled it out of my pocket, glancing at the screen. "Hi, Megan," I said, swiping.

"Hi. How are you holding up?"

"I'll survive, I guess." I swallowed and felt a tear squeeze out of my right eye. "I'm standing in line at Pericos. I'll call you back in a minute."

After I'd picked up the warm burrito and loaded chips and salsa into the bag and was back in the car, I connected to the Bluetooth and dialed. The phone rang as I backed out of the parking spot and turned right onto Water Street. "Hi Shelby," Megan's voice boomed through the speaker and I turned it down. "How are you?" she asked again.

"Well, I'm not really sure, to tell you the truth." I stopped at the next light by the Town Clock, and watched a homeless man unroll his sleeping bag, wondering if Crystal was doing the same. "How could this happen?"

Megan was quiet. We both knew how it had happened. My eggs were harvested, and, according to the paperwork I'd signed all those years earlier, were fertilized and implanted in my uterus. The extras were destroyed. But, as I already knew, the paperwork lied. And now I had living proof.

Megan said, "I'm so sorry, Shelby. With a twenty-five percent match, it's one hundred percent positive that your mom is related to that child genetically. No doubt."

"How is that possible?"

"It's much more complex than *Ancestry* or *23AndMe* let on. But the gist is accurate. The average DNA percentage shared with parents is fifty percent. The average shared with grandparents is twenty-five percent."

"Maybe Dexter donated sperm at some point?" My voice lilted into a question, and even as I said it, I knew how absurd that sounded. Dexter would never have done that.

Megan replied, "I don't think so. But I can ask him."

I merged into traffic on Mission Street and drove up the hill past the old mission and the park plaza in front of Holy Cross, one of the city's Catholic churches. I made the next light and zipped through it. "You don't need to," I said with a sigh. "I'm sure he didn't." The smell of onions and spicy salsa filled the car, and I was looking forward to unwrapping the burrito when I got home and taking a big bite.

I turned and passed the Abbey coffee shop, housed in a church hall, and then stopped at a stop sign before turning left onto High Street, one of the main arteries leading to the university.

"Are you on the way home? Do you want to stop by?" Megan asked. "I have the sniffles, but we can visit in the backyard for a bit."

I thought about it and almost accepted her invitation. But an image of Annie and Max flashed through my mind. An image of an ordinary family having their ordinary evening of homework and phone calls and TV. I knew I couldn't handle it. Not tonight.

"No thanks," I said, hoping my voice sounded much brighter than I felt. Much brighter. "I have some work to catch up on."

"Friday?" Megan asked. "I'm at the tail end of this cold, so I should be fine by then."

That was one thing about our friendship, I knew. Even though we barely saw each other any more, when things got tough, Megan would be there for me. As she had been since Cody and I split up.

"Sure. Friday is good. Let me know what I can bring," I said.

5

WHILE IDLING AT THE STOPLIGHT by the entrance to the university, I thought about life's odd and circular peculiarities. I now lived in the same neighborhood in Bonny Doon — a rural enclave of homes hidden in redwood groves, with long driveways and tall fences — that I'd lived in when I'd been a surrogate mom thirteen years earlier. Even though I shared a house, and didn't live in a cottage all by myself, it was uncanny that I'd ended up here.

I recognized the landscape had a hold on me: the massive redwood trees with their millions of needles that glinted in the sun, the grassy meadows, the scruffy tanoaks. The explosion of green. The subtle textures of the shrubs and trees. The deer, foxes, and coyotes who inhabited these hills. The bird life. Even with my surroundings blackened by fire, I knew the forest would return. It would heal.

My housemate, Erica Tompkins, was about ten years older than me. Divorced, no kids. Her divorce had made her a rich woman. Her ex was a Google VP and their fifteen years of marriage had left her with several million dollars. Before her divorce, she'd been an elementary school teacher. After her divorce and move to Santa Cruz County, she'd become a potter, making one-of-a-kind giant raku vases — three-foot tall oddly shaped pots that were purely celebratory. Accent pieces. She'd perfected her glazing technique of golds and silvers and blacks and whites. Her vessels, as she liked to call them, gave off light somehow, as if lit from within. They had a presence and seemed alive. Collectors recognized that too. When Erica showed her work, the pieces were snapped up, with a single vase priced at over five thousand dollars.

Erica's house was a forty-acre spread off Pine Flat Road, about a mile from the intersection with Empire Grade and a quarter-mile down a well-tended asphalt driveway. It was eerie how much it felt like where I'd lived before: main house, cottage, meadow, redwood forest. But this house was a two-story updated farmhouse with a metal roof. The house was hemmed by a wide flagstone apron, with a bluestone patio in the back and an asphalt parking area in the front. I'd heard from local firefighters that these precautions had saved the structure.

Three steps led from the parking area to a wide porch and generous front door. The house was more than ample, with a large living room and dining room combo that opened through a broad archway into a well-stocked kitchen that a true foodie would love. A half-bath sat off the kitchen, next to the door leading into the attached garage. The cottage, a few steps away from the main house, served as Erica's pottery studio and classroom.

Erica had remodeled the downstairs, adding a wing off the kitchen, complete with a master suite and an office. My upstairs domain contained two bedrooms and a full bath. The bedrooms were at the back of the house, with windows facing the meadow. I'd moved into the room on the right. A cozy window seat was tucked under a dormer window at the end of the hall. Though Erica kept the second bedroom upstairs for guests, the entire space was basically mine. In the time I'd been here, not a single guest had visited.

One of the selling points for me had been the reliable internet, a must for my job. With no cell service for miles around, I required dependable internet. If I had a missing person case, I needed to work twenty-four-seven. And because I was my own answering service, forwarding the office line to my cell at the end of every day, I needed solid Wi-Fi for my phone.

Most people had hunkered down during the pandemic, but Erica quickly found that she felt isolated. So she'd listed her upstairs room on Craigslist, a brave soul advertising for a stranger to move in. That caught my attention. Before I could set foot on her property, I had to prove that I had no temperature or cough. And before we even got to that point, I'd Zoomed with her three times. I'd sent references and a credit report. I'd even Zoomed with her from my office, showing her my name embossed on the door.

As soon as I talked to Erica, I could tell she was lonely. She loved to talk. And I mean, loved it. We hit it off immediately, with an unspoken caveat on my part. I'd have to have an escape route. And work could always be my escape route. But as it turned out, I didn't have to use that backup too often. Erica was good at reading me, sensing when I was tired or overwhelmed. I hoped that second sense of hers would kick in tonight. All I wanted was to eat my burrito, disappear to my room, and do some research on maternal genes.

I'd never told Erica about my past. She was relatively new to the area, having moved here from Palo Alto after her divorce, just around the time Justin Boyd had been kidnapped. But she never brought it up, leading me to believe she hadn't put two and two together. And if she did know who I was, well, I liked her all the more for never mentioning it.

The shadows were long by the time I turned onto the driveway. Empire Grade at night spooked me. Not just because of my history with this road. Or the two fires I'd experienced in this area — the small one I'd been caught in when I'd first moved up here, and the recent one. Or the one-way ride to nowhere while tied up, minding a catatonic infant. But the pragmatics of the twisty mountain road terrified me. Drunk drivers. Deer leaping out into the car lights. Stray cats or dogs. Racoons. Skunks.

So far, I hadn't hit anything. I hoped to keep it that way.

I pulled up next to Erica's Honda Fit and switched off the car. I knew I could keep it together while I scarfed my burrito. Compartmentalizing was something I excelled at.

When I entered the house, Erica was sitting on the sofa, feet up, an open bottle of red wine on the table, a glass half-full next to it. Her computer was on her lap and I could see that she was watching a video.

"Hey, Shelby," she said as she hit Pause and looked up at me. "How's it going?"

"Good." I lifted up the plastic bag with "Thank you" stamped in red. "Burrito from Pericos." I felt a sudden twinge of guilt. I should have called to ask her if she wanted one. Instead, I improvised. "Want to split it with me?"

Erica shook her head, "No thanks. I already ate. Salad. My diet."

Even though Erica was tall and voluptuous and curvy, she always seemed to be on a diet. But a diet of her own making, something I could respect. She'd rather sacrifice on something else, like lunch, than give up her daily glass of red wine. "Get a glass," she said as she raised hers. "Join me."

"Thanks," I replied. "I'll be back in a second."

"How was your day?" she called after me as I dumped my briefcase and purse at the bottom of the stairs and walked toward the kitchen.

"Okay," I replied. "Busy. I started off with my boxing class at seven."

"Wow," Erica said. "You left here before seven?"

"Hang on, I'll be right with you," I called back, grabbing a plate and wine glass from the cabinet and utensils from the drawer.

Back in the living room, I placed everything on the coffee table and sat down on the sofa opposite Erica. I reached into the bag and pulled out the chips and salsa, then lifted the burrito wrapped in foil, a hefty small log that must have weighed in at well over a pound. I peeled back the foil and the heady aroma of onions and cilantro and salsa wafted up at me. Inhaling, I said, "I left here at six-thirty, actually. We're supposed to be all taped up and ready to go at seven, but usually it's ten after by the time we get started."

I crunched a chip, then carefully cut the burrito in half and folded the foil back over the cut. I knew if I didn't seal it up now, I'd keep picking at it until I ate the whole thing. I hoisted the bottle of wine. A 2013 Pinot from Santa Cruz Mountain Vineyard. Erica loved red wine and never, ever skimped on it. No two-buck Chuck from Trader Joe's for her.

"Help yourself," she said. "It's divine."

"How was your day?" I asked as I poured a glass.

Erica shrugged. "The usual. Yoga, then the studio most of the day. I'm getting ready for a show at a gallery in Sausalito." She sipped her wine and closed her eyes in appreciation. "You really should try yoga with me sometime, Shelby. You'd love it. I practice Iyengar yoga. It's the kind where you hold the poses a long time and you use props to help you get to the pose."

I smiled. Erica was always trying to get me to try yoga. She swore by it. "Maybe sometime," I replied. "You go on the weekends?"

"Saturday morning, ten sharp."

"Sure, I'll try it." Once I agreed, for the life of me, I could not figure out why I had. The idea of yoga appealed to me, in some vague, aspirational way, but actually going to a yoga class had never crossed my mind.

"Great," Erica said. "Looking forward to it." A comfortable silence settled on us.

I broke it, asking, "When's your show?"

"Show runs from November through January. It's a show of raku pottery only. I've seen some of the works of the other artists, but not all of us. There are ten of us all together. Should be interesting."

"How many pieces are you showing?" I asked. I picked up a chip and dipped it in the small container of salsa. I gestured to Erica, but she shook her head.

"Each of us gets five pieces, so I'm trying some new techniques to see if I can get something a bit different. Something that will stand out."

"Erica," I protested, "your work already stands out."

She tipped her wine glass toward me and took a sip. "Thanks, Shelby."

I sawed off the first inch of the burrito and cut it into smaller pieces. The first bite exploded with flavor; the black beans, grilled chicken, rice, sour cream, cheese, guacamole, and salsa melting into a satisfying combination of textures and tastes.

"What are you watching?" I pointed to the laptop.

"I'm looking for a movie," she said. "You in?"

I shook my head. "No thanks. I have some work to catch up on. But I'd love another glass of wine to take up with me when I'm done with this one."

•   •   •

Three hours later, at ten, I pushed my chair away from my desk and stretched, clasping my hands behind my head and arching my back. I'd learned enough. Enough to know that Megan had been right. Not that I'd needed to second-guess her, I just needed to understand.

There was no question that the girl was genetically related to me. In fact, if I submitted a cheek swab to *Ancestry.com*, I knew that my genetic profile and that of the twelve-year-old girl would be a fifty percent match. I wondered if the girl looked like me. Was there a little Shelby McDougall walking around somewhere in this world? I shivered. Not so long ago, I longed for that outcome. Now, I didn't like the idea. At all.

I'd spent my career finding missing children. Children who'd vanished from their regular lives so thoroughly it was as if they'd never existed. Children who'd run away. Or been kidnapped. Snatched. But this child, this twelve-year-old, was something new.

A found child, conjured out of thin air.

I picked up my phone. Mom had called, two hours ago. I'd missed it. Now I vaguely remembered hearing the phone ring and choosing to ignore it. She hadn't left a message. What was there to say? I toyed with the phone, tossing the iPhone in its pink case back and forth, thinking. Besides worrying about me, Mom was probably going through her own confusion and mourning. Another grandchild she'd never know.

I put the phone down and went to floss and brush.

•   •   •

I lay in bed, staring at the ceiling. The forest was quiet. I remembered the owls I'd heard hooting in the forest a few months ago. I'd wondered then how far apart the birds were; sounds would escape the forest behind the house as if from a loudspeaker. I wondered where those owls were now. Erica's house and the meadow behind it had been carved from a dense redwood forest back in the 1940s, when this house had been built. The meadow had once been someone's truck farm, but now trees were colonizing the fields; cones and seedlings creeping into the agricultural zone over the years. Once the original owners had moved out, no farmer had ever moved in again and, before the fire, the land had been slowly returning to what it had once been.

A seasonal tributary to Laguna Creek ran through Erica's property. During the rainy season, she told me, it could be a roaring torrent, but now it was little more than a trickle that created a convenient trail through the redwood forest. I'd always thought about taking a hike along the creek. At this time of year, the thick stands of poison oak would be fading into dormancy, dropping leaves, and looking like innocent branches sprouting from the ground. The sun would filter through the redwoods in a dusky green glow. But now, with the fire, all that was gone. The redwoods were denuded, scarred trunks. The ground was black; still smoking in places.

I rolled onto my side and thumped my pillow. After another thirty minutes of shifting from side to side, trying to sleep, trying to not think about Julia H. and her daughter, I gave up. I sat up, swung my legs out of bed, and snapped on the bedside light.

It wouldn't be the first time I couldn't sleep. And probably not the last.

6

E IGHT YEARS EARLIER, I'd tried to change my internet habit. Truth be told, it was not a habit, but an addiction. My midnight to three a.m. internet compulsion. My therapist had urged me to read instead. She recommended that I study the great books, the ones everyone read in college and never read again. So I tried. I dipped into the Greeks, stuttering through a few pages of *The Iliad* and *The Odyssey*. I opened Plato and Aristotle, managing several stanzas before my eyes glazed over.

I moved on to Chaucer and Shakespeare. I studied Leonardo's notebooks and French philosophers. I read fiction — Jane Austen, Joseph Conrad, Charles Dickens, Virginia Woolf, and James Joyce. But my mind was a sieve. There was nothing I could latch on to. I'd read a sentence, read it out loud even, think I understood it, then tackle the next and the next. It seemed like I had grasped the sentence and the paragraph thoroughly, mastering the words, the sentence structure, the cadence. Then, a page later, I'd be completely lost. Again.

My therapist was sure this new routine would cure me of my midnight internet feeding frenzies, where I'd search for anything remotely suspicious related to surrogacy and babies for sale. To give my therapist some credit, the new routine had worked. Once Cody and I got engaged, life took new and wonderful twists and turns. Instead of Googling "baby brokering" and "baby organs for sale", I was eagerly looking for tips on painting Baby's room and searching out strollers and cribs.

My obsession nosed to the surface after my first miscarriage. I managed to tamp it down, satisfying my urge with a few half-hearted searches before forcing myself to watch puppy videos on YouTube. In desperation, I turned to stretching, deep breathing, and mindfulness meditation. These techniques could calm me for a time, but that urge to "just do something" was powerful. Overwhelming.

By the fourth miscarriage, my obsession had become utter compulsion. And after Cody and I separated, I was back to the internet until the wee hours, forcing myself out of bed to get to work. I wasn't looking for anything specific. I was praying for any small shred of a news story that would lead me to Dr. Helen Brannon; the woman who'd destroyed my life.

Tonight, I decided to start with the *Ancestry* website. The tagline claimed that *Ancestry* was the world's largest online history resource and the largest for-profit genealogy company in the world. Its advertising claimed access to millions of records. I found that terrifying. I'd always known that Mom was interested in genealogy, but I never imagined that she would willingly pay one hundred bucks to basically donate her DNA, something so fundamental and so private, to a database company. What people didn't know about problems with privacy in the digital age would fill a twenty-volume encyclopedia, if such a thing existed anymore.

But me, I *was* concerned about privacy. At home, and when on the road, I ran my own virtual private network, allowing me to set up my computer to appear as if I were located anywhere in the world, from Africa to Europe to Asia to North or South America. I always used a password manager to encrypt and secure passwords. Some would call it overkill; I called it common sense.

I needed my mom's sign in credentials. I knew I could wait until morning and call Dexter for the details, but I was impatient. Besides, it shouldn't be that hard. I knew mom's email address and knew the password combination she'd most likely use: her birthday and the name of her favorite cat, uppercased last letter. I'd discovered this years earlier, in my internet security class at De Anza Community College, when I was a student studying Criminal Justice. One of the assignments in the digital security class had been to audit passwords. I'd asked Dexter, Mom, Dad, my classmates. My parents' passwords, although not as bad as the top password of "123456", were weak. And in spite of my recommendations, which I was sure she saw as badgering, Mom never changed them.

I knew I'd get three tries. I entered Mom's email address, then tried: 07251952chesteR. Mom's birthday and her favorite cat. No go. Next: ChesteR07251952. Again, no luck. One more try. I kept it simple: chesteR. *Bingo.* Once I confessed to Mom that I hacked into her account, I'd have to convince her to create a new password.

I immediately clicked the Messages link. The inbox contained one email, from a user named Julia H. The message read:

Hello Denise M.,

This message will probably come as a surprise; I hope it's not unwanted or a shock. I have a daughter; I'll call her E. to keep her privacy. She was born in December of 2007, using eggs purchased from a fertility clinic in San Francisco, California and her biological father's sperm. I was the carrier. My husband and I have been happily married for 15 years. We tried to have our own children, but after several miscarriages, I found that there were problems with my eggs, so we went the IVF route.

E. has been our delight and joy. She is a beautiful child with a happy, open face; long auburn hair; and a big smile. Lots of freckles. A tomboy. However, she looks nothing like either of us, and she has been asking.

To be prepared for the inevitable question of 'who donated the egg', my husband and I decided to be proactive. We took a DNA swab off her toothbrush and submitted it. We found

you as a twenty-five percent match, which means that you
are likely genetically related to our beautiful E.

I know this is coming completely out of the blue, but we
have a lot of questions. If you are interested in
communicating, please email back. I've attached the report
so you can see it for yourself.

Best,
Julia H.

I couldn't breathe. I shoved back, needing to distance myself from
the email. From the words. From *IVF, egg, auburn hair, lots of freckles,
tomboy.* I slammed the laptop shut.

My child. A found child, pulled out of the misty fabric of the
internet, deposited on my doorstep as a fully functional twelve-year-old.

That should have been my daughter. But this E. wasn't mine. E.
belonged to someone else. To a woman named Julia. Julia had my
child. The one I was supposed to have. The one that was supposed to
grow in my body. The child whose mother I was supposed to be. The
child whose father Cody was supposed to be.

At the time of my surrogacy, I'd been told that a dozen of my eggs
had been harvested. A dozen eggs to ensure two or three tries for a
pregnancy. I'd gotten pregnant on the first IVF attempt and several
months later, went through a pregnancy reduction. I was told that the
remaining nine eggs were destroyed.

Just like everything else about my surrogacy, this had turned out to
be a lie as well. My eggs were never used. And now, the discovery that
some of them must have been sold. A quick way for my nemesis, Helen
Brannon, to make a bundle of cash to fund her research.

A scream, stark and raw, erupted from my chest. I whirled in a
circle, fists clenching and unclenching. My chair clattered to the floor
and for an instant, I thought of Erica, hoping she would not come
bounding up the stairs to check on me. I needed privacy. I needed to
throw something, smash something, destroy something. Instead, I
collapsed on the bed, squinched my head into the pillow, burrowed
under the blankets, and sobbed.

7

I MUST HAVE FALLEN ASLEEP. When I woke, I was still in my clothes, tangled in blankets. Sweat dampened my skin. I sat up, escaped the bedding, and wiggled to the edge of the double bed. I stood, stripped to my bra and undies, grabbed a blanket, and pulled it around me like a robe. I walked to the window and opened the curtain. The smoke had finally cleared and stars glittered across the dark sky. I hadn't looked at the stars since I'd moved in here. In fact, I couldn't even remember the last time I'd noticed the night sky. When I was with Cody, before our marriage took its downward spiral, I slept hard, deep. We were always in bed by ten, with the lights out by ten-thirty. When I spooned with Cody, I could sleep for hours without stirring — he kept my night terrors at bay.

I pressed my nose to the glass. The meadow gleamed in the soft starlight. A few tall grasses that remained looked like burnished spears and the bare redwoods stood in stark silhouette.

As a trained investigator, I always noticed my surroundings. I'd know if I'd seen the same car two times in an hour. I could tell if someone was carrying a concealed weapon. I could sense hostility before it exploded into violence. And I knew my job. In terms of investigations and what was admissible in court, I was one of the best. When I submitted a report, everything in that report had been obtained legally.

But if it wasn't related to work, I felt like I didn't know anything. I didn't know how Cody and I had gone off the rails. I didn't know how, really, I'd ended up here in a rented room, back in Bonny Doon. And staring out into the night sky, I realized how little I knew about the natural world. I didn't know the names of trees, plants, or birds. Other than redwoods, I had no idea what trees grew in the nearby forest. I'd forgotten all about the planets and the relationship of the sun and moon to the earth. I barely even knew my leafy greens. Kale looked like chard which looked like spinach. Learning these things was always on my to-do list. Someday, when I had time, I'd take a botany class or go to the natural history museum. I'd visit the arboretum at the university. I'd learn how to grow vegetables. It never happened though. I never had time.

But I did know something about the stars. Now, staring out the window, I could pick out the North Star and then the Big and Little Dippers. My father had shown me when I was little. Every summer we'd go camping in the Oregon wilderness and he'd lug along his telescope. On those trips, Dad would stay up for hours after everyone else was in the tent. I remember crawling out of my sleeping bag, grabbing a jacket, and slowly unzipping the tent so as not to wake Dexter and Mom. Once outside, I'd always find Dad with his telescope staring at the stars sparkling overhead.

He'd point out the constellations, then zoom the giant telescope in on a swirling pink nebula, on clouds of dust and gas in deep space, on the band of the milky way that looked like a glittering purple ribbon. I missed him. I always assumed there'd be more time. He was only sixty-seven when he died.

Dad had explained to me that the starlight we were seeing was emitted a long time ago. One night, when I was about twelve, as we'd sat wrapped in blankets, he'd pointed to the sky, and tried to explain the concept of a lightyear. My father had told me that light from the three stars in the Alpha Centauri system — stars that were the closest to us, after the sun — was a little over four years old, beamed into space back when I was an eight-year-old pipsqueak. I understood it, but not really. Even now, I still didn't get it. A little over four years ago, my father had been alive. I'd been happy, hopeful. The life I'd dreamed about was just beginning. I'd earned my P.I. license and was preparing, both mentally and financially, to purchase the business from Kathleen when she retired. Cody and I had bought a house. We were fixing it up, room by room, with the baby's room a top priority. We were planning a family.

What had happened?

Keeping the blanket around me, I shuffled over to the desk, plucked my laptop off the surface, stumbled to the bed, and plopped down. I opened my computer. Thankfully, it started; I hadn't damaged anything when I'd slammed the lid down. I was startled to see the time. Only four-thirty. Sleep, I knew, would be impossible. I might as well start the day.

I crept downstairs to the kitchen, plugged in the kettle, and set up the coffee dripper to brew a single cup of coffee. Once it was ready, I snuck back upstairs and set my alarm for seven-thirty. That first sip of coffee was a welcome jolt; the caffeine zipped through my bloodstream and shocked me into wakefulness. I logged into my computer, selecting Amsterdam for my virtual location. I imagined the three- and four-story houses lining the canals, their windows reflecting the water; the bridges; the bicycles.

Then, I opened the browser. My first stop was *Ancestry.com*, where I created an account and ordered a DNA kit. I started to search. This time, if it was the last thing I did, I was going to find Helen Brannon and put her behind bars.

•   •   •

Three hours later, when the alarm on my phone buzzed, I sat back and stretched, feeling not quite as tired as I thought I would. I stood and walked over to the printer, where I'd printed out a sheaf of papers: articles on DNA recombination, genetics, synthetic biology, Crispr, Chinese scientists, and funding streams. Basically, anything I could find about the science behind bioengineered humans and who was paying for the research.

I picked up the stack of articles and leafed through them, stopping on an article published in *Wired* magazine about a reclusive millionaire, a Clark J. Little. Mr. Little had earned his money the old school way, from a chain of grocery stores. He started by buying grocery stores that were in trouble. Over time, he built his empire by buying and selling stores, eventually starting his own private equity firm. He would then run down the operation of his stores, putting them into debt. To top it off, he'd make money by investing in that debt. Plenty of people lost their jobs, their livelihoods, and their retirement in this barely-legal scam. Eventually, he sold the remaining faltering stores to a corporation. At the age of 71, Clark J. Little was worth around five hundred million dollars. What a piece of work.

According to another article I found, published on a website called *Synthetic Biology Watch*, Clark Little had sunk a third of his fortune into GMO foods, believing that GMO would save the world by growing food more densely, thereby reducing the carbon footprint and feeding billions of starving people. I wondered if that was the mark of a true believer or just another publicity stunt. Unlike the *Wired* article, this journalist had managed to get Little to talk.

The interview was mostly what I'd expect, but this particular millionaire had concluded his interview with a bit of boasting that caught the attention of the *Synthetic Biology Watch* journalist. Mr. Little had said: "Something big is coming. I can't talk about it yet, but it's going to be the most amazing announcement in all of human history. We are using technology, inventing new technology, which will allow the human race to reach its full potential. People will be more than they are." The journalist went on to speculate: had Mr. Little figured out a way to grow meat in a lab? Grow rice with protein? Conjure water out of thin air? To me, it sounded frighteningly like Dr. Helen Brannon's claims that she'd created the first in the next race of *Homo sapiens*.

The problem was, after that comment in 2018, Clark J. Little had gone quiet. Vanished, as if he, and that comment, had never existed. I searched link after link using Google, Bing, Firefox, and Safari, but couldn't find anything new about C.J. Little. I clicked into one website,

Genetic Technology Watch, a site midway in my search results. But it took me to a Russian company, with the text in Russian. The translation option didn't produce any English content. Other searches yielded nothing that seemed relevant. No mention of research into super-GMO foods. No mention of his wealth, any fancy homes he might own, no sightings of him at conferences or celebrity events. The man had gone to ground and disappeared. I bookmarked the article, vowing that tonight after work, I'd use all my P.I. resources to find out everything about Mr. Little.

•　　　•　　　•

After another cup of coffee, two pieces of whole wheat toast dripping with butter and jam, and a shower, I plopped onto the sofa in the living room and pulled my phone out of my bathrobe pocket. I held my thumb to the fingerprint sensor, opened the phone app, and pushed my mom's contact. Mom answered on the first ring; she was an early riser.

"Hey darling," she said. Since Dad died, Mom had turned the endearment she'd used for my father to Dexter and me. I loved it. Dexter, not so much. "How are you?"

I took a breath and when I spoke, I could hear the shake in my voice. I didn't even realize it was there. "Not so good," I said. That was the truth. "Not so good," I repeated. "And you?"

"The same."

"Did you tell anyone? Talk to anyone?"

Mom was quiet, then she exhaled. "No. I had a social distancing glass of wine with a friend last night. A new friend, a woman I met in my quilting group. I was about to tell her, but I didn't. It just seemed so," Mom stopped, then picked up again a few seconds later, "so damn complicated, you know?"

I nodded, then realized that Mom couldn't see me. I said, "Yes. I know."

"What do you want me to do?" she asked.

"I don't know," I said. "I've been thinking about it all night. I don't know what to say. No reason to tell this woman the truth. Once she finds out it's mine, she's going to freak out." Once that mother found out that the egg came from Shelby McDougall, the woman who'd given birth to those mutant children, she'd lose it. Who wouldn't?

"I've been thinking about it too," Mom said. "I could just say it's likely I'm genetically related and prefer to remain anonymous."

"Here's another option," I said. "Let's just leave it for a few days. I ordered a DNA kit from *Ancestry* and I'll do the swab. Then I can contact her."

"Oh, honey," Mom replied, her voice so loving it made me want to cry, "you don't need to do that. That seems kind of drastic."

I was sure Mom had immediately jumped to all the *'what-if'*s and I wanted to reassure her. "I know, Mom. It is drastic," I said. "I just want to know. That's all."

"What a year," she said. "The pandemic, the fire, and now this."

"I know," I said. "I know." Searching for something positive to say, I offered, "It's nice to be home. Every time I drive up here now, I give a silent thank you to all the firefighters."

My mother said, "It's true. Amazing people, those firefighters." After a beat, as if she'd run out of conversation, she said, "Okay, darling. I have to go." Mom disconnected the call, a tactic I was familiar with. If she was about to cry, or couldn't think of anything positive or supportive to say, she got off the phone, quickly.

My mouth flattened to a thin, sharp line. I could feel the tension in my jaw and in the set of my lips. Sometimes, I had to massage my cheeks and open and close my mouth like a gasping fish to release the stress. I stared at the phone, suddenly wondering why Mom had asked Dexter to deliver this news to me. Part of me was realistic; knowing that hearing it face-to-face, rather than over the phone would be gentler. Part of me also knew that Mom wouldn't be able to tell me. Our relationship was strained, fractured. We lurched through emotional crevasses, each of us wanting to return to level ground, but not knowing how to get there. My actions, her judgements. Her judgements, my reactions.

Years earlier, when I'd been a surrogate mom and had exposed the baby-brokering ring, I rarely talked to my mother. She'd been so hurt, so disappointed, so sad that her daughter's first-born children were to be handed over to another family. At the time, Dexter's then wife,

Jessica, did everything she could to keep their daughter, Ashley, away from my mother. Though that relationship blossomed once Dexter and Jessica parted company, my mother's disappointment had damaged her relationship with both me and my brother.

Once Cody and I announced our plans to start a family, it was as if my relationship with my mother had come alive again. As if I was only valid to her through any future children I might have. Mom had been so joyful and excited, making quilts and blankets, hats and booties. But with the repeated miscarriages, our relationship had soured. I had my own grief and despair to process. I couldn't process my mother's as well.

•　　•　　•

After the phone call, I brewed another cup of coffee and went back upstairs to my room. I sat at the desk and picked up the remaining papers from the printer. I leafed through them while sipping my coffee, and pulled out an article about Justin and Justine Boyd. It was one I hadn't seen before, dated December 2019. Every year, around the time of the twins' birthday, there was a flurry of articles about the new-species-of-humans Boyd twins. I'd missed this one, so caught up in my own failing marriage, couples counseling appointments, and my latest miscarriage.

I knew from previous years that the articles were mostly inaccuracies. Claims of astonishing physical prowess: not true. Claims of the twins making brilliant breakthroughs in math and science: not true. Claims of mutant children who only ate raw meat: half true. Claims of children who didn't sleep: this one *was* true. Claims of ringed eyes and adult-sized teeth: also true.

The last time I'd seen the twins, three years ago, they were tall, fit, and strong. One of the results of the genetic tinkering was accelerated puberty, so by age nine, Justine already had her period and was fully developed. Likewise, Justin's voice had changed, and he had shot up to a monstrous height of over six feet.

But they seemed to have stalled intellectually. With their photographic memory and ability to read at such a young age, they'd both completed PhD coursework with professors and tutors visiting their house for hours every day. Justin was a math wizard, but had not yet designed a new programming language, figured out time travel, or solved any of the unsolved mathematical Millennium Prize problems. Justine could recite the dictionary backward and forward, every single word, but she had not yet written the great American novel or used her vast knowledge of philosophy across the ages to weigh in on humanity and its future.

The article I held in my hand was a *Fox News* opinion piece that had been picked up and run in dozens of news outlets across the country. A photo of the twins taken at their monthly photo shoot headlined the piece. That photo, I knew, was not casual or accidental. It was staged, with makeup, wardrobe, and a muted backdrop; presumably set up and released by their handlers. I smiled, remembering the photos I'd first seen of Justin and Justine at the Boyds' cramped house in Watsonville; the Sears studio portraits, with the children posing in front of fake fireplaces or oversized crayons.

I read the editorial:

As Justin and Justine Boyd turn twelve, the great experiment of super-humans seems to have fizzled to its logical conclusion. As the youngest in world history to receive their PhDs, the two children have fallen off the map.

The Boyd children, their genetic origin discovered in 2012, and their potential unmasked, have been living under the care of the U.S. government for the past eight years. As the first 'humans' created through synthetic biology, they have come under the domain of the federal government.

They live in upscale suburban Reston, Virginia, with a full complement of professors, tutors, trainers, doctors, nutritionists, housekeepers, massage therapists, and play therapists. Their parents have been given jobs and in addition, receive a salary from the feds, as well as medical care.

The children have produced nothing to prove their worth. There have been no discoveries, no solutions to world hunger or space travel or climate change. In fact, the government has lately been mute on Justin and Justine Boyd. In the last year, there have been no press releases. No information has seeped out. Repeated requests to various federal offices yield the infamous comment: "Sorry, no comment." It's as if the two children have been relegated to the side-show act of human history.

What is happening with this family? As a society, what should we do with these children? Is it ethical to allow them to remain on the dole while others are starving? And more importantly, should they be sterilized?

This author demands full disclosure from the government. If you agree, call your Senators and Representatives.

I knew of the author, Toni Cutler. She was a Fox News commentator, always looking to incite emotional responses, to fan the flames of divisiveness, and to find ways to blame big government for something. Here was a perfectly packaged crisis: a family living off a hand-out, funded by the taxes paid by the average American taxpayer.

I dropped the article on the table in disgust and stomped off to the bedroom to get ready for work.

8

I T WAS ONLY EIGHT IN THE MORNING when I left the house. The driveway twisted through the remnants of a small grove of redwoods, sides of their trunks now burned. Needles still clung to some of the branches; other branches were cracked, broken, and black. At times, the sunlight hit the windshield directly, temporarily blinding me. In other moments, the rays from the sun fell in a broad beam of light, shining through the scorched tree limbs, making them glisten like polished ebony.

The road was empty at this time of day and I didn't see any other cars until I reached the turnout for the private school on Empire Grade, the main artery leading into Santa Cruz from Bonny Doon. Empire Grade ran along the ridgetop separating the coast from the San Lorenzo Valley to the east, and if I followed its seventeen miles from south to north, I'd be driving by state parks, natural preserves, a national monument, and miles and miles of privately held undeveloped land. Rumor had it that the northern terminus ended at a secret military facility. The landscape in all directions had been torched by the CZU Lightning Complex Fire, lending an apocalyptic air to my drive. I breathed a sigh of relief when I reached the city limits.

I activated the Bluetooth and said, "Dial Cody on mobile."

What was I doing? What was the point of telling him about this discovery? This child was in no way related to him. But it was too late to hang up.

"Hi, Shelby." Cody answered on the first ring. This was a good sign. I was sure that sometimes, he just let my calls go to voicemail. "What's up?"

"Are you free to meet today or tomorrow? Lunch?"

Cody hesitated.

"I have to talk to you about something," I pleaded. "Something's come up." My voice sounded small, not the confident, dynamic woman I was hoping to project.

"I don't know, Shel. We've talked it to death," Cody said. "Over and over."

"This is something else." A whiny, begging tone had crept into my voice. "I just need to talk to you. I need you, Cody." Had I really said that? "Please."

Cody sighed. "Okay. Today, lunch. Meet me at the Indian restaurant in Rio Del Mar. Ambrosia. A late lunch, say one-thirty? We can get takeout and eat at the beach. I have to be at work at three."

"Thanks, Cody," I said. "See you soon."

Indian, I thought. Cody had never liked anything spicy. Ever. He'd always been a meat and potatoes guy. Was he trying to tell me something?

•   •   •

By the time I arrived at the office, Lucy Florez, my intern, was already sitting at her desk, her cell phone to her ear. Mask in place, I waved as I squeezed past her. Our rule was simple: we talked on the phone most of the time. When she entered my office, she wore her mask. When I entered hers, I wore a mask.

I unlocked the door to my office and then returned to the outer office after dropping my purse and briefcase on my desk. By then, Lucy had disconnected her call. "Hi Shelby. I was here a little early, so I asked the building manager to let me in," she said. "Was that okay?"

I nodded. "Absolutely." I angled one of the client chairs to face her, pushed it back to keep my distance, and dropped into it. "How are you?"

Behind her mask, Lucy's face lifted in a smile. "Good."

"How are things at De Anza?"

"Great," Lucy said. "Semester starts next Wednesday. I'm ready."

"I remember," I said, wistfully. "Even though it's been years, I still feel that when September rolls around, I should be getting ready for school. What are you taking this semester?"

I knew that Lucy would only be working for me for a short time. Much to her mother's dismay, she planned to follow in her father's footsteps — in law enforcement. But not as a police officer, like her dad, but as an FBI agent. I'd met her at the spring career day at De Anza College, my alma mater, where I set up a booth every year and gave a talk on life as a private investigator. Lucy had stopped by my booth that day and we'd chatted. She'd dropped off her resume, and I learned that she was enrolled in the cyber forensics certificate program, a program that didn't even exist when I was a student. Her grades, her recommendations, and her sunny outlook impressed me. I always hire young women as my interns, knowing that gender discrimination, conscious or not, would follow them throughout their careers. I wanted to give them a good start.

She filled me in on her classes; coursework I'd never heard of: "Network Security, Personal Computer Security Basics, and Ethical Hacking."

My eyebrows rose. "Ethical Hacking?"

"Yup," Lucy replied, "Ethical Hacking."

"You'll have to let me know what that's about." I laughed and said, "Anyway, over here, it's easy street for you today. Background checks."

Lucy smiled. She was one of the few interns I'd ever hired who loved background checks. She approached it as a personal challenge.

"Come on back and get your computer." She followed me into my office, waiting while I opened the closet and safe. I held out her laptop, saying, "I have a few phone calls to make, so I'll see you in a bit." I shut my door, picked up my cell, pressed my thumb to the sensor, and tapped the phone icon. A few swipes later, Kathleen's phone was ringing.

"Hello, Kathleen here." I could feel myself relax as soon as she answered. She'd been my rock for so long. I often checked in with my former boss, for both professional and personal reasons. She always had excellent suggestions when a case stalled. And she always provided helpful insights into my personal problems when I asked.

"Hi, Kathleen," I said.

"Shelby, how are you?" she asked.

"I'm good. Do you have a minute?"

Kathleen laughed. "For you? Always." In a more serious tone, she added, "I just checked in on Evan and am heading back home."

"How is Evan?" Evan was Kathleen's grandson.

Kathleen sighed. "A mess. Yesterday, I was supposed to pick him up after cross country." I nodded; knowing that on good days, Evan ran track. "They were running at Garland Ranch out in Carmel Valley. So I got there, waited with the moms. Chatted with the coach. Watched as all the other kids came in." Her voice dropped. "Evan never showed up. The coach, just a second-year teacher, freaked out.

"I tried to explain that it was okay, but the coach started to hyperventilate, then she fainted. So there I was, worried about Evan, having to play paramedic to this fainting woman.

"Evan finally showed up, back at home in Carmel. He said he got lost and when he finally figured out where he was, it was just as easy to go home."

"Why didn't he call?"

"Who knows?" Kathleen answered. "He's fifteen. To make a long story short, he's off the track team. Coach says she can't have students on the team who just take off." Kathleen sighed, a long mournful sigh that seemed to amplify in the tiny speaker. "He's his own worst enemy, that kid."

"What about Paul and Emily?" Paul was Kathleen's son, Evan's father, and Emily was his wife.

"They grounded him. Little good that will do," Kathleen said. "Anyway, enough about me. What's on your mind?"

"I had lunch with Dexter yesterday," I said.

"And?" Kathleen prompted.

"He told me something disturbing."

"Impossible," she said. "'Dexter' and 'disturbing' don't fit in the same sentence." She laughed.

I forced a light-hearted laugh in return, paused a beat, and plunged in. "About six months ago, my mom signed up for *Ancestry* and sent a DNA swab. After Dad died and she retired, she got interested in genealogy and wanted to do a family tree and all that stuff. Everything was fine, results as expected. But yesterday, Dexter told me that she got an email from someone she didn't know. The woman said that Mom is a twenty-five percent match to her daughter. Which means that my mother is this child's biological grandmother."

Kathleen was quiet, taking her time. "Say again?"

"The email said the couple couldn't conceive and found out that the wife's eggs were the problem. So she and her husband did IVF with eggs they bought from a fertility clinic in San Francisco."

"Oh no," Kathleen said.

I continued. "The only thing we can figure out is that the egg must have been one of the ones taken when I was a surrogate." I couldn't hide the bitterness in my voice as I said, "It was stolen. Stolen from me."

I stared into my phone, wishing Kathleen were in the room with me. I missed her. She always knew what to say, what to do. But now she seemed at a loss for words. I'd never seen her speechless, even during my interview with her years earlier, when I'd told her the complete story of my surrogacy. No matter what was thrown at her, Kathleen was always solid. But this, I could tell, this had thrown her.

"Wow," Kathleen said. "I'm so sorry, Shelby. So sorry."

9

WITHIN SECONDS, Kathleen had switched to her problem-solving mode. According to successful private investigator Kathleen Bennett, every problem had a solution. There was always an answer, no matter how impossible a task seemed.

"Obviously," Kathleen was saying, "selling a donor egg without the donor's consent has got to be illegal, right?" She continued, "We'll have to take a look at the contract you signed." She paused and added, "You do have a copy of that contract, right?"

I found myself shaking my head, even though I was on the phone and Kathleen couldn't see me. "I was so angry, so beside myself," I said, "that I destroyed anything that had to do with that year of my life."

Before Kathleen could continue, I said, "My guess is that Helen Brannon, wherever she is, has a copy of it. And there was probably a copy of it in the cabin where I found Justin, so whatever law enforcement agency ended up with all those papers might have it." Dr. Helen Brannon had all kinds of incriminating papers in the remote cabin where she was hiding and studying kidnapped uber-human Justin Boyd.

"Do you remember reading the contract?" Kathleen asked.

"Yes, it was simple. Probably too simple," I said. "It said that my eggs were going to be used. They weren't. And I think it said that any eggs that weren't used would be destroyed. Obviously that didn't happen either.

"Now, I'm thinking she sold my eggs to generate income."

I could hear the turn signal in Kathleen's car, and the sound of the engine as Kathleen slowed to a stop. I suddenly craved a cup of coffee.

"Any idea how many eggs were taken from you?" Kathleen asked.

"They told me twelve at the clinic. At the time, twelve was the optimum number to ensure a successful pregnancy, or something like that. Now the number is fifteen. Back then, it could have been more, could have been less."

I heard Kathleen's car accelerate. "So the contract is null and void in any case," Kathleen said, "since it was broken on her end. I wanted to see it for the fine print. In case you'd signed something that gave away your rights to those eggs."

I said, "I don't know. I don't remember."

Kathleen paused, and then said, "Here's my idea."

Five minutes later, I hung up.

•   •   •

After a quick trip to the restaurant downstairs where I picked up a latte for Lucy and an extra-large black coffee for me, I buried myself in my office. I told Lucy to hold all phone calls for the next several hours. I needed to concentrate.

Kathleen had suggested I create a broad timeline, month by month, of the events to date. It was the same advice she always gave when a case got confusing or too big: "Go back to the beginning, Shelby. Start at the beginning."

So I started, making a table of significant dates and events. It was slow going. I remembered the events in a single stream, a long flow of fluid developments punctuated by terror and despair. It wasn't easy to parse out what had happened and when.

I started with the events in 2006, fourteen years earlier. After an hour, with breaks to wipe away the tears streaming down my cheeks and search for dates on my phone, my table looked like this:

Spring 2006	Graduate from University of Oregon with an art history degree. Start looking for a job.
Summer 2006	Live at home, work at YMCA camp teaching art. It's not my thing.
Fall 2006	Ad in the back of *Rolling Stone* for a surrogate mom catches my eye and I apply, assuming nothing will come of it.
Late fall 2006	I meet intended parents Jackson and Diane Entwistle. Within two weeks, I get a phone call, telling me I've been selected.
Early 2007	I sign the contract with Jackson and Diane and move to Santa Cruz. I stay with Dexter, his first wife, Jessica, and his daughter Ashley.
February 2007	I start hormone shots for the egg retrieval process.
Mid-March 2007	A dozen eggs are retrieved.
End of March 2007	The fertilized eggs are implanted in my uterus.
Mid-April 2007	Pregnancy confirmed with a due date of January 5, 2008.
Mid-May 2007	Pregnancy reduction to reduce the number of viable embryos to two.
Early September 2007	Jessica kicks me out and I move to the cottage on Jackson and Diane's property. It's in Bonny Doon, well out of town. I don't have a car and am dependent on Dexter and Diane for groceries and rides.
October 2007	Dexter gets suspicious; he doesn't like Diane and thinks something is off, especially after he finds that Diane had hired a P.I. to follow me.

That should have tipped me off. But she seemed so sincere, claiming that after her previous surrogate had broken the contract and run off, she was worried, suspicious, not sure I was who I said I was.

I continued:

Late November 2007	Dexter hires an acquaintance, cop-on-suspension Frankie Browning to look after me.
December 2007	Frankie disappears. I think Jackson and Diane have discovered his role and done something to him. I search the property and break into a locked storage shed. I find trophies; hand-knit caps, crocheted baby blankets, a quilt. Evidence that Jackson and Diane never intended to keep my babies. Proof that they'd done this multiple times before.
	I follow Jackson to an isolated out-building on the property where I think they are hiding Frankie. Instead, I discover another pregnant woman, Megan Fitzgerald, locked in a cage. We escape, but at a cost. Megan is shot in the leg. Her baby is delivered that night. My twins are born a week later. She keeps hers, I put mine up for adoption. Frankie shows up while I am in the hospital. I go home to Portland to recover.
Winter 2008	I become obsessed with finding other scams. I am sure that there is someone behind what happened to me. I am positive that Jackson and Diane were not operating alone.
March 2008	I move back to Santa Cruz where I look up Frankie. We date, I fall in love.
May 2008	After dating Frankie for three months, I'm ready to change my life for him; to forgo graduate school and stay in Santa Cruz forever. But I'm contacted by the cops who have been watching Frankie. They think he is my mastermind, who I've nicknamed The Stork. I think that is ridiculous and say I'll

snoop, but only to prove them wrong. But I find evidence linking Frankie to Diane.

Frankie discovers me, and I realize that Frankie is also part of the baby-brokering ring. He is working for Jackson and Diane, transporting babies from bogus intended parents to their new lives. Frankie finds me snooping and takes me on "one last delivery". I manage to escape and keep that baby alive. I go back to Portland, again, to recover.

January 2009	I move back to Santa Cruz, get a job.
Fall 2010	I enroll in the De Anza Criminal Justice - Law Enforcement certificate program.
Summer 2011	I start working for Kathleen as an intern, chipping away at the 5,000 hours of experience required for my P.I. license.
June 2012	I meet Cody in the parking lot at the harbor.
July 2012	I get the fateful call from Lisa Boyd, mother to Justin and Justine Boyd, the twins I gave up for adoption. Justin has been kidnapped. I meet the Boyds and learn that twins are super smart. Not just genius smart, but beyond genius. Savants. Wizards.

In my quest to find Justin, I take Megan (my now BFF) along with me on a scouting mission. Later that day, someone thinks Megan is me and takes her. She is beaten so severely she has to drop out of school for a semester.

Later that night I get run off the road and am kidnapped. I escape from my prison, only to end up captive again. But I end up in captivity with Justin. Justin had been taken by ...

My cell rang, interrupting my train of thought. I almost ignored it, but then glanced at the screen. Cody. I picked it up and swiped eagerly.

"Hi," I said.

"Hi," Cody replied.

"What's up?" I asked.

"I was wondering if we could meet at one instead of one-thirty," he said.

"Sure, that's fine," I said. "Same place?"

"Yes," he said.

"Everything okay?" I asked, hoping my voice sounded bright and positive, hoping to mask my despair.

But Cody had already disconnected.

I picked up my coffee cup, only to realize that I'd already finished the entire twelve ounces without noticing a sip. I'd been so preoccupied, caught up in these memories. Honestly, if it hadn't happened to me, I wouldn't be able to believe it.

I reviewed the events. Quite a list, I thought, though I wasn't sure what this exercise would accomplish. It wasn't like I'd get the recompense I deserved. My fertility restored. A child with Cody as the father.

I decided to continue; I had a few more hours until my meeting with Cody. I might as well complete the table now. I'd come back to the July 2012 entry later. I'd never forget what happened then.

December 2013	Dexter and Megan get married. I was so happy for them, and a bit jealous. Cody and I were living together at the time and were planning to get married. I was ready. But Cody wasn't.
June 2014	Cody and I get married. I don't change my name. It is my business name after all. And the name that had brought me fame and notoriety. I am thirty and Cody is thirty-three.
May 2015	We buy our sweet starter home, a fixer upper in Live Oak. I love the house, a two-bedroom, one-bath with an overgrown yard that needs work.
December 2016	I get my P.I. license. I'm thirty-three. I am so proud.

Fall 2017	Cody and I decide to start a family. I'm thirty-four, almost thirty-five, and Cody is thirty-seven. We consult an OB and several geneticists. I call the doctor I'd promised to contact if I ever decided to get pregnant, but he'd retired. I can't find anyone who will talk to me. My OB says it should be fine. A whole army of geneticists clear me. They know my history and still clear me. I feel healthy, confident, strong.
December 2017	Megan's daughter, Annie, and the twins I put up for adoption, Justin and Justine, turn ten. The events with Jackson and Diane Entwistle happened ten years ago. So hard to believe.
January 2018	I'm pregnant!
Mid-February 2018	Miscarriage #1
May 2018	I'm pregnant again.
Mid-June 2018	Miscarriage #2
October 2018	Pregnant
Mid-November 2018	Miscarriage #3

I paused for a minute to wipe a tear away. I'd never put it in writing before. The facts were grim.

December 2018	Kathleen retires. I buy the business and change the name to "Shelby McDougall Investigations". I move the office from the harbor to the current location at Branciforte Plaza.
June 2019	One miscarriage this year, in June. We can't afford IVF or hiring a surrogate and Cody is dead set against adoption. He's seen too many drug addicted infants. Marriage counseling doesn't help.
February 2020	Cody and I separate and sell our house. I move in with Dexter and Megan.
Mid-March 2020	COVID

End of March 2020	I move in with Erica.
Mid-August 2020	CZU Lightning Complex fire devastates Santa Cruz Mountains. I evacuate to Dexter's.
September 2020	Return home after the fire is contained, our house is inspected, the power is back on, and the roads are cleared. Here I am.

•   •   •

It was only noon when I finished my list, but I was so exhausted that I left early, asking Lucy to hold down the fort. When I reached the restaurant, I backed my car into a parking spot so I could see the arriving cars. I hoped Cody would be able to find a spot; this was a popular place to eat, with the rich Indian sauces and the perfectly steamed long-grained rice. But instead of keeping watch, I found myself dozing, unable to keep my eyes open. The parking lot was in full sun, and even with the window cracked, the interior of the car grew stuffy, lulling me to sleep. I set my alarm for ten minutes before our meeting time, so I'd have time to wake up, brush my teeth, and freshen my makeup. Instead, I was woken by a sharp rap on the window.

I inhaled sharply, rubbed my face, and turned to look, squinting through the glass. Cody, dressed for work in his green uniform, was leaning over, left hand raised into a fist, knuckles protruding, as if to rap on the glass again. He had his game face on, his work face. A mask of serious concern, covering an attitude of suspicious detachment. Since I'd last seen him, he'd cut his already short hair into a Marine-style buzz cut. A pair of mirror sunglasses masked his eyes. His usual smile was gone, replaced with a steely jawline and compressed lips.

I'd seen this expression before. I knew if he took off his glasses, his eyes would be flat. Cold. Distant. As our problems increased, I'd seen this expression more and more frequently.

Even so, my heart skipped. We were still married and I still loved him. I glanced at his left hand. He still wore his gold band. Thankfully. I still wore my small diamond. I rubbed my face, trying not to imagine what I looked like. I hadn't even glanced in the mirror when I'd used the restroom before I left the office — I assumed I'd have time to freshen up before seeing Cody. I probably had dark, puffy circles under my eyes. My face was likely bloated. I was sure my eyes were bloodshot. But not having any choice, I opened the car door. Cody grabbed the top of it, pulling it toward him.

"Hey, Shelby. What's up? What's so important?" he asked as he stared down at me.

"I just wanted to see you, that's all. I have something to tell you." I said, swinging my legs out of the car and pushing myself up.

"What is it?"

I wanted to give him a hug, but that would involve wiggling around the open door that stood between us like a barrier.

"Do you want to go order?" I pointed at the building.

Cody shook his head. "No. First I want to know why I'm here."

I stared at Cody, trying to keep my voice level and my eyes flat. "Okay." I took a breath. "I had lunch with Dexter yesterday. He told me that our mom had done a DNA kit on *Ancestry*. She got an email."

Cody didn't say anything.

"The email was from a mom who carried a child to term through a donor egg purchased from a fertility clinic in San Francisco. The child is now twelve. The child's genetic profile shared twenty-five percent of genes with my mom, meaning that she's this child's biological grandmother."

"What's that got to do with me?" Cody asked.

"Cody, it means that the eggs they took from me when I was a surrogate were stolen. They were sold to someone else. I have a biological child out there. At least one, if not more." I searched his face. Had his jaw tightened, the tiniest bit? With those sunglasses on, I couldn't tell what he was thinking. He made no move to touch me, to give me a supportive, friendly hug, to tell me that he still loved me. That we'd get through this. Together.

Instead, he staggered back, losing his balance as if he'd been hit by a fist. He landed on the hood of my car, legs splayed out in front of him, hands behind him. His glasses were knocked loose and fell to the pavement.

He turned to look at me, where I stood, fixed in place next to the driver's door. Tears clouded his gaze. "I'm sorry, Shelby," he said. "I can't do this right now. It's too much. Later, okay?" He leaned over, picked up his glasses, and checked them for scratches, avoiding me. "I'll call you tomorrow."

Keeping his head down, trying to keep his emotions in check, he said, "See you." He hurried back to his truck, climbed in, closed the door, and drove away.

I sank back into the driver's seat and wept.

10

W HEN I REACHED MY BUILDING, I slunk in, stopping by the restroom. Luckily, the three-stall bathroom was empty, and I was able to take a hard look at my reflection in the mirror. My eyes were red and bloodshot. The skin around my eyes was puffy and the tip of my nose was red and raw from crying. I sighed, splashed cold water on my face, dabbed it dry with paper towels, and then fiddled with my makeup for a good five minutes.

When I entered the office, Lucy greeted me and wanted to show me something on her screen, but I begged off, pointing to my wrist. The universal sign that allowed me to make a graceful exit. Once in the cocoon of my office with the door shut, I sagged into my chair and dropped my purse on the floor. I was so distracted when I'd left for lunch that I'd forgotten to follow my own security procedures with my laptop. But it remained on the desk where I'd left it.

I spent another hour on the events of July 2012. I then reviewed the file, saved it, and emailed it to Kathleen. I didn't know what Kathleen could do to help me. Completing my history in concise format and sending it along made me feel like I had done something, even though I'd just spent four billable hours doing something unbillable. To make up for it, I started in on the dog breeder's case with a zealous fervor, determined to push everything else out of my mind.

I heard Lucy leave her desk and return, probably a simultaneous restroom and coffee break. She didn't knock on my door or buzz me, so I just kept on with what I was doing, reading about the razor-thin margins and cutthroat world of dog breeding. Not a cheerful topic.

At four, Lucy did interrupt me. She knocked, waited until I'd pulled on my mask, then placed the laptop on my desk, saying, "Hey, boss. I finished all the background checks. They're all uploaded. You okay?" she asked, eyeing me with concern. "You look a bit under the weather."

I mumbled, "Bad night's sleep. It's catching up to me." I added, "I'll review your work tomorrow and send them in." We usually chitchatted for a few minutes, but today I didn't have the energy. "So I'll see you Tuesday?"

"Sounds good," Lucy said.

"Any phone calls today?" I asked.

Lucy shook her head. "Sorry, boss."

I gave a small smile. "That's okay. We've got plenty to do. Have a good weekend."

"You too." Lucy turned to leave.

"Lock the door behind you, please," I called as she walked out.

"Sure thing," she replied.

I turned back to my computer just as an incoming email pinged. It was from Kathleen, saying that an emergency had come up with her grandson. She'd read what I'd written tonight and she'd see me tomorrow for lunch. We'd started our monthly lunches when she retired. It allowed her to keep her finger in the business, but now, for me, it was invaluable. I felt like I should pay her as a consultant. She always had a new angle to consider, something I hadn't thought of.

I pushed my chair back from my desk and walked to the window. I could see the traffic on Soquel Avenue, one of the main roads leading from the westside of Santa Cruz through downtown, to the eastside and Live Oak, the unincorporated area of the county between Santa Cruz and Capitola. As usual, traffic was already backing up. I clicked the blinds shut. It was only four-fifteen, but I realized I hadn't eaten anything since the toast I'd had for breakfast. I was famished. I glanced at the laptops and file folders sitting on the desk. The Word file with my personal history was open. Lucy's computer was off; the folder she'd populated with her background checks would have already been uploaded to the cloud, encrypted, and deleted from the laptop.

I'd be gone for just a few minutes. I glanced over at the closed closet door, with the safe hiding inside. I'd have to open the closet and the safe to put the laptops and file folders inside, then open it again to take them out. Too much trouble. Lucy, I knew, would not approve. "Security measures only work when you follow them," she'd tell me. But Lucy wasn't here and I was so hungry. And there were two locked doors between these laptops and the hallway.

I closed my laptop, picked up Lucy's and stacked it on top of mine, then placed them square in the middle of the desk. I didn't activate call forwarding; if anyone called, I'd get the message when I returned. Picking up my purse, I slung it over my shoulder and exited my office. I made sure the door was locked behind me, then pulled the outer door shut and checked that it too was locked. I jogged down the stairs. Once outside, I fumbled for my sunglasses in my purse and turned to the left. Shopper's Corner, a full-service family-owned grocery store was just a block away.

I wandered the aisles, ignoring the mom with her two kids and the couple looking for picnic items. The label on a bottle of red wine caught my eye. I knew next to nothing about wine and tended to base my selection on the label and price. Both met my criteria — the label was no-nonsense with the name of the winery stamped in a large font overlaying a grape arbor. And the price was just under twelve dollars. In the deli section, I ordered a cheese sandwich on sourdough with avocado. While waiting, I picked up a container of potato salad, a large bag of chips, a chocolate bar, and a six pack of Belgian beer from the cooler. Just to be sure.

Back in my office, I put my purse and the bottle of wine in the bottom drawer of the desk and placed the bag of food and the six-pack container on the small table. I grabbed a bottle of beer, walked to my desk, located a bottle opener in the center drawer, and popped the bottle open. After a long sip of the refreshingly cold liquid, I sat back and eyed the laptops. Hadn't I left them square in the middle of the desk, Lucy's sitting on top of mine? Now, it seemed like they were a bit to the right of center. I sighed, sure I was entertaining paranoid fantasies.

Beer in hand, I walked over to the two black low-slung canvas chairs by the table and plopped down. I levered the blinds open and stared out the window while taking a second sip, a long one. Holding the bottle up to the window, I admired the golden hue and delicate bubbles. Three more generous swallows and the bottle was empty. I deposited the empty back in the six-pack carton and unpacked the food. The sandwich bulged in its deli paper and the potato salad glistened under its plastic lid. I unfolded the paper around the sandwich, then folded it back up and opened the chips. I took a handful of chips, opened another beer, and sank down into the comfy chair. I pulled the other one close and put my feet up. In my mind's eye, I saw Cody's face crumple in pain as he staggered back.

I drank this beer more slowly, relishing the cool liquid followed by the bite of the salty chips. I wiped my hands on a paper towel and removed my phone from my pocket, held my still greasy index finger to the sensor. My smart phone wallpaper was a picture of Cody and me at Glacier Point in Yosemite standing in front of the view, arms slung around each other. Taken last December, almost a year ago now. After the last miscarriage, when we were in the midst of therapy, trying to adjust to a childless future.

I took another sip of beer, ate another fistful of chips. We'd splurged on that trip and had booked a room at the Ahwahnee, now called The Majestic Yosemite Hotel. A ridiculous name for the grand building, the rename forced by a copyright dispute with the company that used to hold the concession in the park. I stared at the image, partially hidden behind a spray of colorful icons. Cody's hair had been as long as regulation allowed, to the top of his collar, and I loved how it curled the tiniest bit and framed his face. My hair was shoulder-length, just long enough to pull into a ponytail. That day, it had flowed out from under a bright pink wool beanie; the reddish hue of my hair an eye-catching contrast to the shocking pink. I could almost see the ghosts of a toddler and a preschooler by our knees. The family we would have had if everything had gone according to plan.

The beer tasted good as it slid down my throat. Light, refreshing. Bubbly. I put down the bottle, held my phone with my left hand and then with my right, accessing the Settings screen. I swiped to the Wallpaper setting and with a few deft swipes, changed it back to the swirl of colors, the generic, soulless home screen. It suited me just fine.

Another long pull on the beer. Another handful of chips. This time, I wiped my hand on my blouse, smearing grease across the silk, not caring about staining the delicate fabric. A few stabs and swipes later, the *Synthetic Biology Watch* article I'd bookmarked about Clark J. Little appeared on the screen. I read it again, the man's quote in the last paragraph once again jumping out at me: "Something big is coming. I can't talk about it yet, but it's going to be the most amazing announcement in all of human history. We are using technology, inventing new technology, which will allow the human race to reach its full potential. People will be more than they are."

What could that possibly mean — except for engineering new humans?

11

I LEVERED MYSELF UP, TOTTERED TO THE DESK, picked up Lucy's laptop, and wiggled mine free. I set it on top of hers and flipped it open. The computer always took a few minutes to wake up and as I usually did, I lifted my index finger to my mouth and started chewing at the nail. From habit, I'd always kept my fingernails short. Or rather, my mother had. For piano at first. Then, for softball. Of late, I'd emerge from a trance to find my index finger or my pinkie in my mouth, with me diligently chewing on a hangnail.

The laptop sprang to life, and I opened the browser, Googling variations of "Clark J. Little", trying "Clarke" with an "e" and just the name, no initial: "Clark Little". I tried "Clark John Little", "Clark Little GMO". And on, and on.

For such a bold statement and such a wealthy man, the internet didn't serve up much on Mr. Little. I would have found more articles about me, if I'd cared to look.

I sat back, swiveled in my chair, noticed the light reflecting off the bottles of beer on the table. I rolled over in my chair and pulled another one out of the six-pack holder. I picked up the bottle opener and pried off the top. Number three. The lucky charm, isn't that what they say? Cody and I had said that the third time I'd been pregnant. The third time a test showed a positive result.

I took a long, deep sip, practically inhaling a quarter of the bottle's contents. A huge burp bubbled to my throat, and I belched, big and loud and satisfying. I giggled.

I opened Facebook, then LinkedIn. My Mr. Little was a ghost. I searched for the grocery chain he started, Food King. Nothing. In an obscure filing to the SEC in 2000, which I could barely decipher, I learned that Mr. Little had sold the remaining stores for a cool one hundred and twenty-five million to the Safeway Corporation. From articles on sites like *Street Spirit*, *Mother Jones*, *Supermarket News*, and *Progressive Grocers*, I learned that hundreds of workers had lost their jobs. For those who remained on, wages were cut by one-third. The union was gutted and pensions disappeared.

I reread the *Synthetic Biology Watch* article, and this time, carefully examined the three photos that accompanied the article. In one photo, Mr. Little was on his yacht, aptly named Rascal. But Little was not standing proud with his arms outstretched. Instead, he was ducking into the cabin, face hidden behind a folded newspaper. The second photo must have been from the sales brochure for the yacht, as this was no ordinary watercraft. The boat's blue hull sparkled in turquoise waters, the likes of which were only found in Bali, Fiji, or the British Virgin Islands. Its two-tiered deck, topped by navigation equipment, looked a little like a wedding cake. A hot tub and small motel-sized swimming pool adorned the deck on the bow, and a full bar complete with lounge chairs graced the sitting area on the stern. The yacht could easily hold ten or twelve, and likely had master suites and full bathrooms and guest rooms and salons.

It probably came with its own staff as well. A quick Google search revealed that superyachts of this size sold for around twenty-five million bucks in 2020 dollars. When Mr. Little sold his grocery chain twenty years ago and presumably picked up this yacht, it would have cost around fifteen million, I guessed. And thanks to the glories of the stock market and margin calls and hedge funds, Mr. Little's fortune was continuing to grow, leaving him plenty of cash to pursue his dream that GMO foods would save the world.

But was that really his dream, or was it something much more sinister?

Rascal was originally owned by a small privately-owned LLC called Cottonwood City. Cottonwood City, in turn, was owned by a holding company called San Antonio Holdings. I discovered that a holding company exists only to own, or hold, stocks in its subsidiaries. A control mechanism. I also discovered that finding out anything about a holding company, like the name of an actual person affiliated with that company, was virtually impossible.

The third photo interested me the most. It was a picture of a chemistry lab. Mr. Little, a ten-gallon hat resting on his head, stood in the middle of a standard-looking lab in front of counters filled with equipment: beakers, scales, Bunsen burners, centrifuges. Behind him, a few lab assistants in white coats worked at counters. What looked like metal boxes with glass hoods sat on tables along the far wall.

I hit the Print icon. As the article and photos printed, I picked up the bottle of beer and realized that I'd drained it. All gone. But I didn't feel fuzzy or drowsy or even drunk. I just felt energized. Without thinking, I reached for the six-pack container. Number four. The bottle was wet on the outside; it had been sitting there, unrefrigerated for several hours. I glanced at the clock on my computer. Eight o'clock.

I located the bottle opener next to the six-pack carton and popped the beer open. Not quite as sparkly as if it were crispy cold, but tasty enough. Absently, still staring at the results from my last search, where I'd typed in "San Antonio Holdings Delaware", since I knew that Delaware had tax implications favorable to corporations, I pulled the cheese sandwich toward me and unwrapped it. I broke off a corner of the sandwich and put it in my mouth. Not bad. It was squishy and rich with mayonnaise and extra avocado. Before I knew it, I had taken another bite and another, washing each down with a swig of amber beer.

When I finished eating, I realized too late that I didn't have a napkin or a paper towel. Glancing down at my shirt, I noticed the smear of grease already there from the chips and used my shirt for a napkin again, wiping my fingers across the front at my waist. The fact that no one was here to care made me giggle.

I liked that I was alone and could do whatever I wanted.

But when I stood, realizing with sudden urgency that I needed to use the restroom, I found myself swaying and stumbling, wishing I had someone with me to help me down the hall. I caught myself on the corner of the desk. Maybe I shouldn't have drunk that last beer.

Four beers was a lot of beer. I'd never, ever drunk that much beer in one sitting, even when at my lowest. But then, when at my previous lowest, I'd always had Cody to help me.

Well, he wasn't here and I'd have to manage by myself.

In spite of the beer messing with my head, I stuck to my training, and picked up my keys off the desk. I slowly walked to the door, tripping from one piece of furniture to the next, grabbing onto the back of a chair and lurching into the wall for support. I squeezed past Lucy's desk, leaning on her desk chair, then stumbled across the small space to land in one of the client chairs. The room spun and I closed my eyes, feeling nauseous. But nature called. I fought the dizziness and stood, then stumbled to the office door. I clutched the door jamb for support, slammed the door behind me, checked to make sure it was locked, and held onto the wall as I walked down the hall. I reached the restroom just in time.

As I washed my hands, I stared at them. Were they really mine? They looked old: worn, creased and calloused. With my short, chewed nails and almost stubby fingers, my hands looked like those of a person who labored outside. I had always wished for my mother's hands — long, graceful fingers with well-manicured nails that tapered to a slim, attractive point.

My diamond glinted in the fluorescent light, and using my right hand, I spun the ring around so the gem was hidden. I tried to pull the ring off, but it stopped at the knuckle. I sighed and tenderly twisted the ring back in place. In spite of everything, I wasn't ready to let it go.

I turned the hot water back on, tested it, and when it was lukewarm, I splashed it on my face. It felt like a balm, calming me, returning me to some sense of equilibrium.

Dabbing my face dry with a paper towel, I examined myself. Dark puffy bags hung under my eyes. My hair frizzed. My makeup was long gone, and my skin looked pale and ghostly, almost as if I didn't exist. As if I weren't real.

I wished the events of the last twenty-four hours weren't real.

But what could be more real than finding a child out of the blue that you never even imagined existed?

It changed everything, I thought. Everything.

12

B ACK IN MY OFFICE, STILL FEELING UNSTEADY, I lifted another beer out of the six pack carton. The bottle was warm to the touch and it felt wet and slimy. I let it slip out of my hand and it fell, bouncing as it hit the floor and rolling under the table.

I remembered the bottle of wine. Where had I put that? As I looked around, I felt like I was on a see-saw; the room was moving in a dizzying kaleidoscope of colors and shapes and light and shadow. I plopped into my office chair and put my head on the desk. And, as if in answer to my prayer, the bottle of red wine, the crimson liquid bewitching, was right there, next to my purse in the open bottom desk drawer.

I fumbled in the drawer where I kept pencils and notepaper and found a wine bottle opener. A fancy one, left there two years earlier, when Cody and I had celebrated the move to my new office with a bottle of bubbly, a slab of brie, and slices of crisp, tart apple; followed by a very expensive bottle of red. With the help of the guide on the corkscrew, I twisted the mechanism into the cork and pushed down the levers. The cork released with a satisfying pop and I leaned over to sniff. The label claimed that the wine was "fruity with a hint of chocolate and blackberry, and a whiff of cherry." What a crock, I thought. No one can tell me they smell cherry.

Lacking the energy to get up and find a glass, I took a swig straight from the bottle. The wine was smooth and tangy, and I loved the rush I felt as it slid down my throat. I held the bottle up to the light, admiring the rich red tone of the liquid. It looked mysterious. Seductive. I took another sip and set the bottle down next to the mouse.

My hand hit the keyboard and the monitor turned on. I entered my password. The words "San Antonio Holdings Delaware" glowed in the search box, with a list of results below.

I lifted the bottle to my lips as I tried to remember why I'd typed in that particular search term. I squinted at the other tabs open at the top of the browser. I saw the Google "G" icon and variations on the name "Clark". And I remembered. C.J. Little. He was the key to finding Helen Brannon.

San Antonio Holdings was the name of the holding company that owned his yacht. Why did that matter? I held up a finger and said, slurring my words, "When you're stuck, start at the beginning and try everything." Kathleen's mantra. I wished she was here to help me.

I tried to concentrate on the list of results. Nothing was a perfect match. There were links to San Antonio, Texas, and to the state of Delaware. Links to SEC documents for other holding companies in Delaware. Delaware, that tax haven. But there was no link to a shiny website for a corporation called San Antonio Holdings. After paging down a few times, I jumped to the end of Google's list of results, where I found a link to a book about the golden age of railroads and how the railroad came to San Antonio. Not at all relevant.

I sipped the wine again and placed my hands on the keyboard. I'd try one more search before calling it a night. The obvious one. "Clark J. Little Helen Brannon". They had to be connected. Little's boastful claim about people being more than they are could have just as well been spouted by Helen Brannon. He had to be connected to her. In my drunken state of mind, I was as sure of that as anything.

I tried to type, but my right hand was off by one key, and I ended up with a mish-mash of symbols and letters. I giggled, moved my hand over, and with the serious intent of a toddler, picked out the correct letters. Again, no exact matches. I peered at the screen, willing the letters to stop jumping around. I increased the font size on the screen, which helped. Page after page of nothing.

The time on the bottom right of my computer read "12:30 AM". Impossible. Where had the time gone? How could I have been surfing the web for seven hours and come up with nothing? I picked up the wine bottle and stared at it. One-third gone already. I'd sucked down four beers and at least one glass of wine. Almost sixty ounces of fluid.

I pulled out my phone and held a shaky finger to the sensor. I tapped the email icon. At the top of the list was a new email, one with the subject line: `Justin`. It was from Ryan Boyd, the twins' adoptive father. I squinched my eyes and tried to read it, but the text kept wiggling, as if alive. Besides, it was way too long. Later. I concentrated, trying to remember why I'd opened my phone in the first place. I couldn't.

Moving my eyes back to the laptop, I saw a screenful of random text that had nothing to do with what was in the search box: "Clark J. Little Helen Brannon". The time on the computer now told me it was almost one in the morning. I glanced to my left and right. Ah-ha, the wine bottle. I remembered why I'd picked up my phone. I swiped open the calculator. Sixty ounces was seven and one-half cups. That was equal to the almost eight cups of water I tried to drink every day.

But this was alcohol.

Carefully, I set the wine bottle on the desk. I stood, gingerly holding the edge of the desk. I lurched over to the small table holding the printer and grabbed the pages from the printer tray. I flopped into the chair next to the small table and dropped the pages on my lap. Suddenly nauseous, my head pounding in a sudden storm of a headache, I felt woozy, as if a migraine, the flu, and a serious case of food poisoning were descending like a hurricane.

I was drunk. All those college expressions rolled through my mind: *Drunk as a skunk. Sloshed. Smashed. Three sheets to the wind. Hammered. Blotto.* The ever-so-friendly *shit-faced*. The kinder term, *drowning your sorrows.* Not wanting to think about my sorrows, my many, unjust, unfair sorrows, I opened my eyes. The *Synthetic Biology Watch* article I'd printed and dropped in my lap swam into focus. I picked it up. The letters were moving, looking like ants on a scouting mission. After a few minutes I gave up and studied the picture. Maybe Megan could tell me what that jumble of equipment was all about. That would be a place to start, I thought, as I drifted off, a place to start.

•   •   •

Hours later, I tried to roll over. But my arm hit something hard and sharp, and a hot flash of pain shot up my neck, taking my breath away. I opened my eyes. Or rather, pried my eyes open. They seemed glued shut, cemented shut with goop. I gently massaged my right eye and opened it and repeated the process with my left. It was pitch dark. A spinning, whirligig of darkness, as if I were on an out of control merry-go-round. I leaned forward, resting my head on my thighs, closing my eyes. I kneaded the back of my neck. A chill spread down my back. Where was I?

Sitting back up, I took a breath and willed the spinning to slow, to stop. I opened my eyes. And then I remembered.

Cody, unable to look at me. Unable to talk to me.

Four beers and at least a third of a bottle of wine.

The contours of my office loomed out of the gloom, illuminated by strips of light that crept in through the blinds. My desk and chair. Two closed laptops on the desk. The six-pack carton with one empty and one full bottle. The open bottle of wine. An open, empty greasy chip bag next to a wad of crumpled deli paper. The unopened plastic tub of potato salad. The article I'd been looking at when I fell asleep. Two empty bottles of beer on the tabletop, another on the floor by my foot. The full bottle that had rolled under the table.

I groaned and pushed myself up.

I baby-stepped across the room to my desk and flopped onto the chair. I opened the laptop and checked the time. Five a.m. I'd been asleep in that chair for hours.

My immediate needs demanded my attention. I stood up quickly, too quickly; the room tilted around me. Grabbing the back of the chair for support, I took two deep breaths, leaned over my desk, and searched for the keys. Once my fingers closed in on the brass keyring, I palmed it and slowly made my way to the door. I slipped out and, knowing that the building was completely empty at this hour, left the door wide open and slipped my keys into my pocket.

I staggered down the hall to the women's restroom, trying to carefully place my feet on a floor that seemed to be shifting and slanting beneath me. More like the deck of a ship than a solid plane. Little's yacht, I remembered. Rascal. A better name for a dog than a boat, I thought, as I stumbled and caught myself on the door.

Cody and I had thought about getting a dog. A rescue dog from the shelter. We even went to look one Saturday, but after talking to one of the volunteers and falling in love with each and every dog in the room, we decided we couldn't. We were never home. But in the glories of hindsight, maybe a dog would have kept us together. Maybe.

Five in the morning. I had to get home. Before the workday started, I had to get home, shower, change, drink a gallon of coffee, and sober up. Maybe I could even get to my boxing class at seven, though that seemed a bit ambitious.

I knew I couldn't drive. But there was Lyft or Uber. The drunkard's savior.

I exited the bathroom and slid down the hall, one slow step at a time. I could see my office doorway down the hall, just a few quick steps when I was sober.

But now, the door seemed unattainable, like a shifting mirage.

One step, then another and another. I felt a cold breeze on my neck.

I whirled around. The hall stretched off to emptiness. An overlight light flickered and then went out.

I heard a faraway snick, the sound of a door closing.

I picked up my pace and tripped over my feet as I lurched for my office door.

But my office door was now closed. Hadn't I left it open?

I tried to remember as I fumbled with the key, the brass keyring clanking like a jailor's. I was sure I'd left the door wide open. I'd decided that no one but me was in this building and it would be safe to leave it open.

Why would I have my keys if I had left it open?

Shivering, I finally got the key in the knob and twisted. The door opened and I crept in as quietly as I could. But after I whacked my toe against Lucy's desk and cussed, loudly, I decided I was alone. I looked around, concentrating as best I could. Everything seemed to be in place. Two laptops. My purse. The pages I'd printed out.

Then, it was time to pack up and figure out a way home. I spent an inordinate amount of time concentrating, focusing like I'd never done these routine activities before — placing my thumb on the reader to open the closet, opening the safe, depositing the laptops and file folders. I knew that activating call forwarding would be way outside of my abilities right now. I'd be back in a few hours anyway.

I focused carefully as I closed the office door, checking it and double-checking. I careened down the stairs, holding on to the bannister for dear life. Pushing the heavy front door open took all my available strength. I let it slam shut behind me. The fresh air hit me hard, like a snowball, and for an instant, I didn't feel drunk. I felt clear and alert, convinced I'd be perfectly able to pick up my phone, find the Uber or Lyft app, and request a ride.

But it was dark. And I was completely alone. Maybe I should have thought about this before leaving the safety of the building.

The light above the door shone on me like a spotlight. Though the parking lot was well lit, with light poles at the beginning, middle, and end of every row, I felt exposed. Naked.

I could see my car, my silver Prius, across the lot, parked under a light. If I could reach my car, I could lock myself in and call an Uber. I walked down the steps to the small plaza with the fountain, gripping the rail for support. I stopped at the bottom of the steps, swaying. My car doubled into two vehicles — two identical silver Priuses parked right next to each other. I closed my eyes and opened them again, shaking my head. As I shuffled across the sidewalk, carefully navigating the drop at the curb, I felt as tenuous on my feet as if I were on a tightrope. Keeping my eyes fixed on my car, I dragged one foot after the other, making sure the soles of my feet were always in contact with the ground.

About halfway between the building and my car, I heard the roar of an engine. It filled my ears, as if it were right next to me. I stopped, glanced around. I didn't see anything. Running was out of the question; I'd topple like a bowling pin. I took another step, then another.

I sensed headlights to my left. I tried to lift my feet and move faster, but I felt stuck, like a mouse on a glue pad. I wasn't moving.

I put my head down and took another shuffle-drag step. Then another.

I kept staring at my feet. If I didn't acknowledge that car, it didn't exist.

Another shuffle-drag step.

Suddenly, it was dark again. And quiet.

I froze.

The car, a black pickup, had parked on the far side of my car.

Maybe I should turn around and run back to the building. Scream? Should I scream?

I turned around. The building loomed like a fortress across the parking lot, a million miles away. In my impaired state, I'd never make it.

The only thing to do was to face what was coming.

I planted my feet. Swaying slightly, I held my ground and stood tall.

The door to the truck on the driver's side opened and slammed shut.

A figure walked around the front of the truck and in front of my Prius, now dwarfed by the monster vehicle. He stopped under the streetlight. He was tall, with a puffed-out chest and hard-toed shiny black boots. His hands were fisted at his sides. He studied me, his gaze flat and direct and unflinching.

I stumbled back.

13

H E CONTINUED TO ADVANCE, one heavy step after another, staring right at me, his features now obscured.

I stepped back again.

He stopped a few yards away, looming as large as Andre the Giant. Just staring, toying with me, a flat expression above a black mask.

"Who are you?" I asked. My voice shook.

"Shelby," the man said, putting his hands palms out. His voice was gentle. "Shelby, it's me, Cody."

The angular lines resolved into familiarity and I sagged with relief. It was Cody, still wearing his uniform. A black mask, stamped with the Sheriff's Department logo, covered his face. His tan shirt was tight over his bulletproof vest and a small radio was clipped to his collar. His duty belt, heavy with a billy club, taser, handgun, handcuffs, flashlight, fit tight on his waist. The large pockets on his green pants bulged.

"Shelby?" he asked.

Still swaying, I lifted up my hand, thumb outstretched, and pointed it at my torso. "Dat's me," I slurred.

"Are you okay?"

"Sure," I replied. "Dandy." After a beat, I added, "Right," I paused, searching for the expression, "as rain."

"Have you been drinking?" Cody asked.

I held my hand up again, thumb and index finger an inch apart. "A little," I giggled. "Just a teeny-tiny bit," I added, pitching my voice high, hoping I sounded girlish. Cute. Adorable. Coquettish. Not smashed to the gills.

"You weren't going to drive, were you?"

I shook my head vigorously, with all the certainty of a drunk.

Cody walked toward me.

I was trying to form the words. The words to tell him that I was going to get in my car, summon an Uber, and wait in the safety of the locked vehicle. The words to tell him that I had to get home before people started arriving for their workday. The words to tell him that I loved him and needed him. But the words wouldn't come.

So I just stood there. Waiting. Watching.

"Can I give you a lift?" Cody asked. "I drove by here a few hours ago and was surprised to see your car still here. And I just got off and decided to check again before heading home." He stared at me, a peculiar longing etched on his face. "I'm worried about you. I'm sorry I walked out on you this afternoon," he said. "I'm sorry. I'm sorry for all of it." He shifted and cleared his throat. "I drove down to the beach and sat in my truck for a long time. It wasn't that this latest bit about a child that could be yours was so bad. Given everything else that's happened, that seems like a small thing.

"But everything together, all of it. It's too much for me. Between the pandemic, the fire, and now this." His voice grew heated as he said, "I just can't take anything else."

He stared, eyes searching mine. "I wish things were different. In the world. And between us. With us. I love you, Shelby. But right now that's not enough."

He shifted from one foot to the other again. His voice was rough as he added, "I'm sorry."

I stood still, fixed in place, barely breathing. He loves me, I thought. He loves me.

"Are you ready?" he asked quietly. "I can wait while you get a shower and then bring you back. Because you definitely need a shower."

I smiled and nodded, pausing, concentrating, before I managed to say, "Thank you."

He loves me.

"Come on," he said, reaching for my elbow. "I'll help you into the truck."

He carefully took my elbow and steered me across the parking lot. He opened the door for me, took my purse, and stood behind me as I climbed into the cab, something I'd done countless times before. Once in the truck, he carefully pulled the seat belt over my chest and reached across me to fasten it. I sat, frozen as a statue, inhaling him. The sharp scent of deodorant, which he applied as often as he could while working, mingled with that Cody smell. Laundry soap, dryer sheets, body wash, shampoo.

He stood back, asking, "All set?"

I gave a sloppy thumbs up.

He slammed the door, walked around the front of the truck, and climbed in. Once the car was on, he opened his window all the way. "You can't fall asleep on me, okay? I need directions to your place. Bonny Doon, right?"

I nodded again. Other than the directions, I wasn't going to say anything. I didn't dare say anything. I needed to remember exactly what Cody had said. He loves me.

But what else had he said? What was it? That this new information seemed like a small thing? Maybe it was. Maybe, he was saying, I was getting all out of whack for nothing. So what if Dr. Helen Brannon had sold my eggs. So what?

I shook my head. Cody, I wanted to say, you don't get it. You haven't thought it all the way through. Helen Brannon stole my fertility, I wanted to tell him. She'd manufactured the DNA in the eggs implanted in me. I knew *that* was the cause of my miscarriages. She stole my future. Our future.

On top of it, those eggs she'd harvested from me were mine. They could have been saved for me. For us. They could have been used to produce our child.

"Cody," I muttered.

But he put his hand up, palm facing me.

"Let's not talk about anything right now. Just directions, okay?"

I bit my lower lip. Even though he loves me, I thought, we're right back where we were.

•   •   •

Cody had to jostle me a few times to wake me for directions, but we eventually arrived at my house. The lights were off; Erica's car was in the driveway.

I handed him the keys and put my fingers to my lips in a *shhh* motion. "Erica," I managed. I clasped my hands together, held them to the side of my face, and placed my face on them, as if I were sleeping.

Cody nodded as he unlocked the front door. He turned on the overhead light in the living room before shepherding me in.

As I lurched across the threshold, I waved my hand toward the kitchen. "Coffee is over there," I said in an exaggerated whisper. I was just about to collapse on the sofa when Cody said, "Nope. You need a shower, okay? Fresh clothes. Brush your teeth."

He steered me to the bottom of the staircase and stood watching as I staggered up the stairs. I was having moments of clarity now, where the room snapped into focus and my thoughts were crystal clear. But they slid away quickly, and the world became murky and fuzzy and bile would rise to my throat.

Thirty minutes later, after I'd stood under the steady stream of hot water for a good fifteen minutes, dried my hair, downed three Advil, brushed my teeth, and pulled on my comfy flannel robe that Cody had given me one Christmas, I walked down the stairs. Even though my head still pounded, and I thought I might still be drunk, I was upright. And somewhat functional. Thank goodness it was Friday.

Cody was standing at the kitchen sink, mug in hand, watching the sun lighten the charred meadow.

I grabbed a mug from the cupboard, picked up the carafe off the stand, and poured myself a cup. I slipped into one of the hard-backed upright chairs at the small kitchen table, grateful for the support.

"Thank you so much," I said. "Thank you."

"Feeling better?" He turned to face me, relaxed, one hand cupping the mug and the other resting on the lip of the sink.

I held out my hand flat and wiggled it back and forth. "I think I still might be a little bit drunk," I said.

"Probably," Cody commented. "What did you drink?"

"Beer," I replied. "Four of them."

Cody winced. "That's a lot. And you don't even like beer," he pointed out.

"I know. Plus almost a half a bottle of red wine."

"Good golly, Shelby. I can't believe you're even standing."

I smiled. I took a sip of the coffee and it slid down with a jolt. So perfect. The coffee I made never tasted this good. Even though I'd watched Cody make coffee a zillion times using this exact coffee maker and had done it myself a zillion times, his always, always, tasted better.

The light outside the kitchen window was now golden, creating a halo around Cody. I stood up and walked toward him. "Look," I said. He turned and together we watched the light, an active presence, as it kissed the tops of the blackened and stubby meadow grasses. Across the field, branches hung from fire-scarred redwood trees.

"It's amazing this place didn't burn down," Cody said.

"I know," I replied, cocooning the mug, warm to the touch, in my hands. "All the concrete around the house helped. And Erica had hired someone to come out every week to water the meadow and mow. Before we evacuated, we laid out all the hoses. She was always worried about fire and had very specific instructions about the ... the ..."

I paused, trying to grab the right word, but Cody supplied it for me. "Defensible," he said.

I nodded, continuing, "... the defensible space around the cottage and the house. It worked. It's a miracle." I looked at Cody. The sun was rising now, dripping golden light across the meadow into the kitchen, making sharp shadows on the wall.

"Thank goodness for the firefighters," I added, shaking my head. "If it weren't for them, everything in this area would have been torched. It still smells pretty bad, but it's getting better." I paused, then asked as I sipped my coffee, "How's your place working out?"

Cody shrugged. "I'm not there much. I pick up as much overtime as I can. I share with another officer. Our neighborhood is very tidy and very quiet. Once someone knows that two deputies live on their street, they are very, very careful." He grinned, then yawned and wiped his face with his hand. "Tired," he said.

"Me too," I replied. "Me too."

14

I FOLLOWED CODY INTO THE LIVING ROOM. He sprawled out on the sofa and closed his eyes. He looked uncomfortable with all that equipment still attached to him, but I knew he wouldn't take it off until he could lock it up safely at home. And I knew if someone tried to lift something from him, he'd be awake in an instant. That man could sleep anywhere and leap to full functioning consciousness in the blink of an eye.

I sipped my coffee and stared. His silhouette was striking, the lines on his face clean and visible, illuminated like a Dutch portrait, with his high brow, feathery eyelashes, long nose, angular cheeks, full lips, strong jaw, the cleft in his chin. And those dimples. Those dimples I used to trace with my finger after we kissed. Now that he was so thin and sinewy, he looked like a cross between the marble statue of David, without the curly hair, and Rudolf Nureyev, the Russian ballet dancer.

With a sigh, I finished my coffee and placed my mug on the coffee table. Back in my room, I tossed my filthy clothes in the hamper and pulled out a new set. A pair of black sensible pants, just in case something came up and I had to go out on a job. Black flats. At least my shirt could be feminine. I picked a teal short-sleeved silk blouse with a scooped neckline, a pair of silver earrings that dangled from my ears in a flower shape, and a thin silver chain with an emerald pendant. As I picked it up, I remembered that Cody had given it to me on our fifth wedding anniversary.

He loves me.

But I placed the necklace back on the dresser, and chose a necklace of fresh-water pearls instead. In the bathroom, I brushed my teeth, again.

Even though the room still spun slightly, as if I were sitting in a swing, I felt as ready as I ever would to face the day.

•   •   •

At seven in the morning, Cody pulled into the parking lot at Branciforte Plaza and stopped next to my Prius.

I lifted my purse from the floor to my lap. "Thank you," I said. "Thanks for everything."

Without turning off the car or turning to face me, Cody nodded his head. "I'm glad I came along when I did," he replied. "Have a good day."

"You too," I said. I turned to open the door and twist out of the car. Closing the door behind me, I resisted the urge to kiss my fingertips and wave, something we always used to do. Throwing love at one another, yelling "Love you, love you," until the other person's car had vanished from sight. Our once-abundant love, now only a memory.

Cleaning my office took all of five minutes. I hid the empties and the remaining unopened beer, along with the six-pack container, in one of the Trader Joe's reusable shopping bags I kept in my office. I picked up the chips bag and tossed it in the trash along with the sandwich remnants, then bundled up the trash bag and marched it to the trash chute. I grabbed a spray bottle of cleaner and a roll of paper towels from the kitchen, strode back to my office, and cleaned off every surface, from the table to the chair arms and seats, to the top of my desk. Then, using the small hand vacuum I kept in the closet, I hoovered the floor, erasing all traces of last night's debacle. My last chore was to pick up the half full bottle of wine, hide it in a plastic bag, walk to the bathroom and dump the remaining liquid down one of the toilets. I flushed then rinsed out the bottle, letting the water in the sink run until all the evidence had been erased.

I added the empty wine bottle to the Trader Joe's bag, set it on the floor, and took stock. My mother would be proud. I picked up my keys, but before leaving the office, I cancelled the nighttime call forwarding so calls would come directly to the landline. I exited the office, strode down the hall, out of the building, and to my car. I shoved the Trader Joe's bag on the floor in the backseat and threw a towel over it. Evidence hidden.

Food was the next item on my agenda. I walked briskly across the mostly empty parking lot to the Italian restaurant. Once inside, I slid into a booth and immediately turned my coffee cup over, signaling coffee. I practically salivated when the hostess, Trish, filled my mug.

"Your regular?" she asked.

I shook my head. "Not today," I replied. My regular, two poached eggs and sourdough toast, didn't seem quite substantial enough. "How about two pancakes, two eggs over easy, and two pieces of whole wheat toast?"

Trish arched her eyebrows, then nodded, and smiled. "Rough night?"

Now, it was my turn to smile. I'd always liked Trish, the daughter of the couple who owned the restaurant. She was able to read me like an open book. I shrugged.

"The pancakes gave it away," Trish confided. "All those carbs soak up the alcohol.

"And your car out there at four in the morning when we got here," Trish laughed. She picked up the menu, lifted the coffee carafe high in the air, and walked to the next table.

No secrets around here, I thought.

I sipped the coffee, relishing the bitter flavor and the jolt to my nerves. I could feel my strength return with each swallow. The headache receded; my vision seemed to grow clearer. I extracted my phone from my purse. I browsed to the *Synthetic Biology Watch* website, read the article again, then Googled the journalist, a woman named Leslie Smith. Leslie Smith was a real journalist with real credentials. She'd received her degree in journalism from Northwestern, and had landed her first job at the city desk for the *Cleveland Plain Dealer*. After five years, she'd moved to the *Chicago Tribune*, then after another five years to the *San Jose Mercury News*, taking a plum job in science and technology. But then, the dot.com bubble burst, and Leslie Smith had disappeared for a while, resurfacing as an investigative journalist in the synthetic biology/DNA/human genome arena. With all my research into this topic, I was surprised I'd never heard of her.

Satisfied with the journalist's credentials, I returned to the article, reading it one more time, reading and rereading Little's closing quote: "Something big is coming. I can't talk about it yet, but it's going to be the most amazing announcement in all of human history. We are using technology, inventing new technology, which will allow the human race to reach its full potential. People will be more than they are."

If that wasn't an announcement about synthetic humans, then what was? In the United States, the number of scientists and funders working in the banned field of human engineering had to be small. Little and Brannon must be connected. I knew it. If I could find Little, I would find Brannon. And once I found Brannon, I could mete out my revenge. As I tucked into my syrup-laden pancakes, I made a list. First, I'd save the images from the article to my laptop: the photo with Little hiding behind a folded-up newspaper as he slunk onto his boat, as well as the one with Little flanked by two lab workers.

Suddenly I smiled. I loved my job. Using my high-res photo imaging program, I could blow up the images and scan through them looking for clues. Any photos, certificates, or awards that might happen to be on the walls of that lab. Any clue to lead me to someone who worked there. And tonight, when I saw Megan and Dexter for dinner, Megan would be able to identify all that lab equipment.

I couldn't wait to get back to my desk.

•   •   •

But my workday started with a bang and didn't let up. By the time I returned to my office, I had three messages: The first, a call from the dog breeder, wanting an update. The second, a call from an Arjun Patel, requesting a callback. He was at work, but would be able to pick up between ten and eleven. And a call from Crystal's grandfather, Stu, with an update on Crystal's case. He was calling to say that he'd received a postcard from her. From Vegas. The fact that he'd heard something was remarkable. But the origin was not reassuring.

Stu had read the brief message: "Dear Grandpa and Grandma, Sorry I haven't contacted you. It's been a rough summer. But I have moved to Las Vegas now where I am waitressing in a restaurant. I share an apartment with three others. So far, so good. I have put off community college for a while. Love, Crystal."

Stu concluded with, "I know it's a long shot, but Marilyn and I would like you to find her. We'll pay whatever you want."

I returned the phone to the handset and sat back in my chair. Las Vegas? The chances of finding a person in Las Vegas were next to nothing. With six hundred thousand people in the city proper, two million in the metropolitan area, and an estimated forty million visitors a year, it was nearly an impossible task.

But this was Crystal, after all. A friend. After suffering harsh rejection from her parents, she must have felt that her only option was to flee. I hoped that she'd found protection in Las Vegas, but I knew that Sin City was called that for a reason. It was not an easy place to make your fortune.

I listened to the voicemail from Arjun Patel again. He'd left the message at 7:30 a.m., and had sounded very much awake and very agitated. His number was in the 650 area code. Palo Alto, Atherton, Daly City, Foster City, Mountain View. From Silicon Valley to just south of the San Francisco Airport. I jotted a reminder to call back right at ten.

Before launching into my phone calls, I checked my email. I remembered I'd received one from Ryan Boyd last night, but at that time, hadn't had the mental acuity to look at it. I read it anxiously:

Hey Shelby,

How are you? I hope life is well in Santa Cruz.

I wanted to fill you in on the latest, before you saw it in the news. Justin is in protective custody. He attacked one of the officers.

He took the guy out, Shelby. Justin is now almost seven feet tall. He's angry most of the time but knows he has to control it. Math problems soothe him, and he spends twenty-four hours a day working on the six still unsolved Millennium Prize math problems. These are epic problems that no math genius has been able to crack. He wants to solve all of them by the time he's fifteen. So in three years. He's never met a math problem he couldn't figure out, but these seem to have him stumped.

He mutters to himself, doesn't shower, only eats meat. The rawer, the better. Rants and shouts.

And, last night, it seemed like he just snapped. He attacked an armed marine stationed at the front door. Justin almost tore his arm off, Shelby. It was like he was possessed.

Now Justin is in a military prison at Quantico. I went to see him and brought him a stack of textbooks. No thank you, of course, not that I expected it, but he just handed me a list of what books he needed. And a request that Justine come and visit.

Can you call me? I'm at my wit's end.

Ryan

I knew that the family had had guards, twenty-four-seven. Supposedly to keep the whackos away from the family, but now, part of me was wondering if it was also to keep Justin and Justine in. I immediately Googled "Justin Boyd" but nothing new came up. A

Wikipedia page, a list of articles, with the most recent six months ago. The handlers were keeping this latest development under wraps. Military secrets.

I thought about calling Ryan, but it would be Friday at lunchtime in Virginia. He would be at work and I didn't want to talk to Lisa. Conversations with her had become increasingly difficult, as if she were harboring something. As if she felt that I should have known about Justin and Justine. That I'd given them up for adoption because I had known about them and wanted to get rid of them. But I hadn't. I only knew that with no job and no place to live, I couldn't care for two children.

I sighed, shook my head and decided to call tonight, when I knew Ryan would be able to answer.

Then, I extracted the dog breeder's file from the safe, flipped through it quickly, picked up the handset and dialed. The background checks on her employees had turned up nothing. And without cause or a warrant, I couldn't search the property of her competitor, Dirk Thompson. I had run a background check on him, and other than a long-ago DUI, his record was clean.

Carla answered on the first ring. "Elkhorn Cockers," she said in a bright cheery voice.

"Hi Carla," I said, "this is Shelby."

"What have you got for me?" she demanded.

"It's a very challenging case," I began, but Carla interrupted me.

"Just tell me what you have," she said.

"Basically, nothing." I said, then blurted, "Yet." I shook my head; when under stress, I was a blurter. After all these years, I still hadn't learned. Kathleen had schooled me in never, ever promising results.

"What do you mean, nothing?" Carla asked.

"Well, I've run background checks on all your employees. You'll be glad to know that nothing turned up. Dirk's background check turned up a few things, but nothing pertinent to this case. He and his operation are in good standing with the AKC and he's been breeding cockers for five years now with no complaints from either the Better Business Bureau or the AKC." I glanced again through the file. "He's an upright citizen in Carmel Valley, as I'm sure you know. He has two young children who attend the local elementary school. His wife works part-time as a bookkeeper and also keeps the books for the dog business. She's on the PTA at the school and volunteers at the library. He's a volunteer firefighter and a member of the Chamber of Commerce." Continuing, I said, "I emailed his references, and everything checked out. Great dogs, good temperaments. One person was even showing one of the dogs."

"What's the dog's name?" Carla snapped.

"Hang on." I sifted through the papers in her file. "That dog's name was Prince Lucky."

Carla sighed. "What a ridiculous name."

I added, "I even hung out at the deli and the supermarket in Carmel Valley, trying to waylay Dirk or his employees. But no one would talk to me."

"And what do you mean his background check showed a few things, but nothing pertinent to the case?" she asked.

"I'm not at liberty to say," I replied. "If I thought his past record had a direct impact on this case, like he'd been arrested for dog snatching in the past, I would, of course, tell you. But this was something else."

Carla snorted. "Yes, but I'm paying you and his past actions could inform me, as well as implicate him by bad-decision making or by character association. Please tell me what they are."

"I'm sorry, Carla," I said. "These infractions are over fifteen years old. I'm not at liberty to say."

"Look, Ms. McDougall, I'm paying you a lot of money, and I want results. I need my dog back."

Knowing I would not get anywhere with Carla, I told her I'd review everything again, no charge, and see what I could find. I got off the phone as quickly as possible. Those hours of reviewing everything would be on my personal time, not billable.

I hung up the phone and rubbed my temples. So far, thirty minutes into my workday, my headache was holding steady.

15

AFTER ENDING THE CALL, I glanced at the time: only eight-thirty. Too early to call Arjun Patel, and Stu could wait for another hour. I opened Carla's folder, pulled out every scrap of paper, and arranged it in chronological order, starting with the day Carla had first called our office. It had been a Friday morning. September 4th to be exact, at nine in the morning. She'd discovered her dog Coco missing when she'd gone out to feed the pack on Thursday evening at five. She'd spent the evening frantically looking, knocking on all the neighbors' doors, calling the cops, who wouldn't do anything, driving up and down farm roads, calling and yelling. Later that evening, she'd discovered that her security camera had captured an intruder.

I'd driven out to her house that afternoon, seen a photo of Coco, who, to my untrained eye, looked like all the other dogs on her property. I watched the security footage several times, and while I was at Carla's house, I'd emailed a copy of the video to myself.

Carla's house was in Prunedale, an unincorporated area of the county. Her five-acre property was off the delightfully-named Strawberry

Road. When I'd gone to her place that first time, I remembered thinking how strawberries were like gold around here, with the harvest season from May to October. No one was picking the day I was there, but I'd often seen strawberry pickers bent at the waist, filling plastic clamshells with the ruby-colored berries. As I drove, I could see the red globes dangling from the bushes, and I was sure the pickers would be in these fields in the next few days. Strawberries were grown in precisely-placed raised beds covered in black plastic that seemed to stretch for mesmerizing miles down the hillside toward Elkhorn Slough.

I remembered thinking too, how a dog could easily get very, very lost in all those strawberry fields. I reviewed the notes I'd taken when visiting the neighbors. Two of them had answered their doors and corroborated Carla's story. Both agreed that she had indeed stopped by, very upset, looking for her dog, wondering if she could walk their property and look. They'd thought that was the end of it.

I pulled my chair close to my desk, interlaced my palms, and stretched my arms out in front of me. Then, I shrugged my shoulders, feeling a long stretch up through my back that released the tension in my neck. Finally, I took a long drink from my water bottle and sighed, pushing away the image of Cody on my sofa, drinking coffee. Turning my attention to my notes, I started reading, remembering the long and open driveway, with the dog pens visible from the main road. Anyone could have known that Carla was breeding dogs. Of course, there was also the sign on the road: Elkhorn Cockers. But if you were going to steal a dog for breeding, you'd have to steal the right dog. And I remembered the swarm of black and white and gold jumping and barking. You'd have to know which dog was her champion breeder.

Carla's property abutted the agricultural fields under conservation easement that surrounded Elkhorn Slough, a seven-mile-long tidal slough about thirty minutes south of Santa Cruz. Carla lived on the far side, so the drive had taken me around Moss Landing, the small town at the mouth of the slough, and then along small winding roads to Strawberry Road. A forty-five-minute journey one way.

My notes then recorded my initial meeting with Carla. How she'd seemed a bit high-strung, but with ten incessantly barking dogs, I could see how that would be the case. I hoped that her cocker spaniels didn't go out into the world with their bark reflex always on. She was very upset. Crying, gasping, trying to keep herself under control. She told me she had ten to fifteen dogs at any time, some always available for sale. Puppies at various ages.

Coco, her champion breeder, was ready for her next litter. A breeder from Fresno was bringing his male over in ten days. If all went well, in about two months, Coco would have eight to ten puppies that would sell for around eight hundred to one thousand dollars each. Coco was a top-notch breeder Carla told me, with her average of ten puppies per litter, all AKC-certified. This was her second litter, and she could produce two more before retiring. Carla had assured me, more than once, that she was a responsible breeder who put her dogs first. She followed the AKC breeding guidelines.

Carla had also explained that per AKC guidelines Coco was insured. The insurance could not be collected for four months after a dog went missing or until a corpse was discovered. If she never got Coco back, Carla would at least receive some compensation. At this, Carla teared up again.

I always kept my original notes, and saw that I had jotted a question mark next to the insurance questions. When I'd asked her which insurance company, she'd waved a stack of papers at me, but I never did see the original document.

Carla had introduced me to Earl, her morning dog handler. Earl had been working for Carla for five years. He checked out clean. He lived in the area and used to breed Irish setters, but had gotten out of the dog business. Too expensive, he'd confided in me, but he still loved the dogs. He'd been a dog breeder for twenty years, AKC-certified, without a single complaint lodged against him. And, my interview with him assured me that he had absolutely no interest in getting back into the business as a breeder. I could look at him again, but I wasn't sure I'd get any different results.

Carla's afternoon handler was a high school senior who lived a half-mile down the road. She checked out clean also. Squeaky clean. Straight As, debate club, now applying for college. She went to school, came over to Carla's after school, Monday to Friday, and on Saturday afternoons.

Without any hint of wrongdoing, I didn't feel the need to dig any further into either of her employees.

I reviewed the security footage again. I'd looked at it initially, stopping it and starting it multiple times to see if there was a clear photo of the thief. There hadn't been. But I decided to check one more time. There were two things that had bothered me. How would the person know which dog was Coco? And why would the dog so willingly go with the person? Had the person offered a special treat? Maybe now, three weeks later, I'd notice something I hadn't seen before. I started the grainy footage. There was one camera, attached to a tree branch outside the dog run, offering a direct view of the gate. The fisheye lens was set up to capture the full area, from the path leading to the gate to the end of the pen.

At exactly 5:15, after the high school student had left for the afternoon, the camera showed a figure enter the field of view and stop at the front of the pen. The person, wearing black tennis shoes and socks, black jeans, a plain black sweatshirt with a hood and no logo, and black gloves, was so completely covered as to be almost a caricature of what someone thought a thief would look like.

He or she extracted a key from the front right pocket of his or her jeans, opened the monster padlock, and wiggled it off the chain. With a practiced motion, the person gracefully swung the chain through the fence, letting it dangle. He or she then latched the clasp of the padlock through the fencing. The dogs were frenzied.

I watched the figure, distorted in size due to the fisheye lens, wade through the swarm of dogs to the far end of the enclosure, where he or she reached down and picked up a squirming, licking, squiggly black and white dog. The person was confident and the dog was equally confident. There was no hesitation; the thief knew exactly which dog to nab. And the dog didn't shy away or put her head down or flatten her ears. It was as if they knew each other.

The thief then extracted a pink leash from the depths of the front pocket of the sweatshirt and clipped it to the dog's collar. Placing the dog on the ground, the person slowly backed up, sliding his or her feet along the ground carefully so as not to step on a dog. Once the person reached the gate, he or she crouched down, so only the top of the sweatshirt hood appeared in the video.

Then, the person turned around, opened the gate, crouched, and duck-walked out of the pen, leashed dog in tow. Once outside, the person turned their back to the camera, stood, and locked the pen, ignoring the swarm of leaping, jumping, and barking dogs. And then the black-clad person was gone, sidestepping out of the frame, the precious Coco in hand.

I froze the last frame, catching a dog mid-leap, its legs splayed and mouth open. Why would someone dress in black at 5:15 on a summer afternoon, when the sun wouldn't set for at least three hours? And why was the leash pink?

I went through the footage again, this time in slow-slow-motion, so the three-minute clip extended to fifteen minutes. It was astonishing how the thief knew exactly when to turn and hide from the camera. Astonishing and almost too good to be true. A theory was developing in my mind and I turned it over as I reviewed the footage a second time.

From the back, the person looked as if he or she were trying to hide their gender, though if I had to guess, I'd settle on female. Even though the sweatshirt was pulled down in the back, I could see the swell of a classic feminine bottom. Not a Marilyn Monroe backside, but feminine all the same.

I watched as the person, I wouldn't call her a woman just yet, took quick steps toward the gate. I stopped the footage and zoomed in on the shoes. The tennies were all black: uppers, laces, soles. No Nike swoosh or racing stripe. No pink laces. They looked brand new, as if bought specifically for this purpose. While I had the video paused, I zoomed in on the jeans. The sweatshirt almost covered the back pockets, but I could see the stitching on the bottom edge of the back right pocket. A pattern of silver thread with wide stitches. Girl jeans.

So our thief *was* female.

As the woman stood at the gate, unlocking it, I pegged her height to be about five-five, based on the height of the enclosure, which I knew to be six feet. As she walked in slow motion toward the back of the pen, I picked up something I hadn't seen at full speed. The woman was reaching out and patting some of the dogs on the head. It was a quick movement, so quick as to look like she was just waving her hands in the air to calm all those dogs. But she was actually touching them as they leapt up.

I sat back and thought as I downloaded the video to my phone. I'd run my theory by Kathleen, and then call Carla to set up another appointment.

16

I SAT BACK, DRANK MORE WATER, AND STOOD. I wished Lucy was in. Someone I could procrastinate with. I wasn't looking forward to my call with Stu. Finding a missing teen in Las Vegas was as unlikely as finding a four-leaf clover in a desert. Las Vegas took people in, chewed them up, and spit them out. If they were lucky. Otherwise, they'd get stuck there, dragged down into the morass.

After a bathroom break, I pulled out the file I'd started on Crystal back in August, and sunk into my seat. I dialed and Stu picked up on the first ring.

"Hi Stu," I said. "Shelby here."

"Hi there," he replied.

I could hear weariness and strain in this voice. "I got your message," I said.

"We got the postcard yesterday," he said, "and we talked about it for hours. Should we let her live her own life or try to help?" His voice caught. "I've known that kid since she was a baby," Stu continued. "And how lost she became when her mom remarried that …" His voice trailed off, but after a beat, he said, "My daughter basically chose that husband of hers over her daughter. She drove her own daughter away. Couldn't accept her if she didn't sign that Purity contract and wear a Purity ring." His voice was bitter.

"Purity ring," I said. "What's that?"

"Where you agree to abstain from sex before marriage."

"Oh," I replied. In my world view, teaching respect and contraception was a much more realistic avenue. For a tiny instant, I was thankful I wasn't the parent of a teenage girl. For just an instant though.

Stu paused, and I could only imagine what was going through his mind. "Anyway," Stu's voice was stronger as he continued, "we decided that we want you to go to Las Vegas for us. Find her. I can pay you this time, Shelby. We can pull some money out of our retirement. We just want her to know that we love her and that she can come here anytime."

He was quiet, then said, "If you won't do it, we'll find someone who will."

I clutched the handset. "First of all," I said, "no one is pulling any money out of their retirement for this. I can't let you do that."

"But ..." Stu said, and I cut him off.

"I'll start by doing some online legwork, and we'll take it from there." My voice softened. "This might be a dead end, you know."

"I know." He took a breath and his voice was shaky. "But if we don't try, we'll always, always wonder. And that would kill me. I don't want to go to my grave feeling like I should have, could have, done something.

"I'd go looking myself," he continued, "but you remember how tired I got that one day in San Francisco. My knees and my heart aren't what they used to be. And I can't drive around a city like that and deal with the heat. Marilyn can't do it either," he added. "And with the virus ..." his voice trailed off.

"I know," I said. Even though I had my doubts, I knew I was Stu's best chance. And Crystal's too.

Las Vegas. I hated Las Vegas. I sincerely hoped I wouldn't have to go there. An image of The Strip passed through my mind: the gleaming buildings, the wide boulevard, music blaring from every open door, the sharp light, the heat, and the crowds of people jostling each other, laughing, staggering down the sidewalk while keeping their super-sized cups of booze upright. And what would Vegas be like now? I was sure the city would be open for business as usual — pandemic or not. A twenty-four-seven Mardi Gras or Brazilian-style Carnival, with packed crowds of non-stop party-goers.

Cody and I had passed through Las Vegas on our way to Zion and Bryce one spring. We stayed just one night, landing on the fiftieth floor of the Mandalay Bay resort, with a dazzling view of The Strip and the desert beyond. We'd wandered The Strip, gawking, neither of us fully believing that such a place could exist. Even then, the crowds, the alcohol, the glitz, and the lights overwhelmed me. Cody's takeaway wasn't the excitement; it was the stress. For someone in law enforcement, the anxiety would be constant; the shifts terrifying. There would always be crime and guns and violence.

When we drove away, to the east, I felt an immeasurable sense of relief. I'd felt on my guard in Vegas, unable to relax. As if I were a small scrap of trembling, skittish prey, with an apex predator lurking around the corner. Waiting for me to let my guard down. Waiting to pounce. A lost, vulnerable teen would be an easy mark there.

I sighed and said, "Listen, I'll contact the missing persons department in Las Vegas. Her tattoos are quite memorable, so we have that going for us. Give me until this afternoon to do some research and make some phone calls. I'll call you back before the end of the day."

He thanked me and we disconnected. I placed the phone back in the cradle and walked over to the window. The sun was slanting in through the blinds and I levered them shut, throwing the room into sweet, mellow dusk.

I sat down to jot down notes about the call. I was thankful I'd be seeing Kathleen soon; I knew she'd be able to give me good advice.

•   •   •

At five minutes after ten, I called the number Arjun Patel had left. He picked up on the first ring, as if he'd been waiting. After I introduced myself, he said, "Hang on, let me get to a private area."

I heard the snick of shoes on a hard floor and the sound of a door opening and closing followed by a crisp, "Hello, this is Arjun."

"Shelby McDougall returning your call," I said. "What can I help you with?"

Arjun enunciated his words. "I want my fiancée followed. We're getting married in a month, and I think something is going on. Her bachelorette party is next weekend, Friday through Sunday, in Las Vegas. I want to find out what she does."

Vegas? A plan began to form in my mind, while I was also turning over what Arjun was saying. Follow his fiancée? I'd heard this before, plenty of times, though it usually came after a wedding, not before. Suspicion. Mistrust. Doubt. I would not be the person to broach the elephant in the room — the fact that if he was having these feelings, now, maybe he shouldn't be getting married. Instead, I said, "Can I ask why?"

He snapped, "No. I just want to know what happens over the course of the weekend. All of it, from the minute they get on the plane in San Jose to the minute they get off, back home."

"It won't be inexpensive," I said, "and it may not give you the information you're looking for. For example, I won't be able to follow her into a private hotel room." I didn't need to add anything else; I'm sure he knew what dangers lurked in Las Vegas.

"I know that," he barked. "Money is not an issue." Without missing a beat, he asked, "Will you take this job or not?"

"I'll need a bit more information before I'll be able to make a decision and offer a contract," I answered. But, as I outlined what I'd need from before accepting or rejecting the job, I already knew that I'd take it. It would let me get to Las Vegas where I could kill two birds with one stone. Little did I know that a third bird would peek up, loud and raucous, demanding my full attention.

•　　　•　　　•

After I disconnected, I slipped into one of my comfy chairs and leaned my head back, thinking. I could extend my Vegas stay and spend a day or two hitting the streets in search of Crystal. Kathleen could help me figure this out. I had an hour and a half before lunch, and I set my alarm before sliding down onto the chair. As I drifted off,

I had an image of replacing the two canvas chairs for a small sofa. Or a futon chair.

When the alarm chimed, a no-nonsense bing, I sat up and shook my head, not quite sure where I was. As I picked up my phone and turned the chime off, I remembered. Lunch at Lillian's with Kathleen. We always ate at Lillian's, an Italian restaurant within easy walking distance of my office. It was loud enough so our conversation could be anonymous, but quiet enough so we could still hear each other.

17

I ARRIVED AT LILLIAN'S FIRST. After aiming a thermometer at my forehead to take my temperature — another change due to the virus — the waitress, wearing a mask, seated me in a back corner against the open window, facing the door. Tables were widely spaced now, a bonus for private conversations. Out on the street, a couple walked right past me, no masks, pausing so the man could light a cigarette. Cars idled at the stoplight. I watched a teen, no mask or helmet, step off the curb on my side of the street, toss his skateboard down to the pavement, and twist between two idling cars.

When the waitress came over to drop off the now-disposable menus, I declined. We didn't need to look; we always ordered the same thing: roasted beet salad for Kathleen and minestrone soup for me. Herbal tea for Kathleen and black coffee for me. I ordered the coffee and tea, and ignoring the sign at the door — no cell phones — along with the pointed looks of diners at a nearby table, I activated my phone and happily played Solitaire.

I looked up when Kathleen arrived, wishing I could give her a hug. "How are you?" I asked.

She sat and hung her small purse on the back of her chair, placing it on the side of the chair next to the wall. In Kathleen's world, everything had to be secure before she could relax. "I'm okay," she said. "I think."

I picked up my mug and stared at her over the rim. "You think?"

Kathleen shrugged. Since retiring, she'd stopped dyeing her hair and it was now a silvery gray. Her subtle makeup highlighted her features rather than masked flaws. Every time I saw her, she seemed more muscular, more fit, more alive.

"Evan. My grandson." She sighed. "You remember what happened, with him ditching out of track?"

I nodded, cupping my hands around my mug.

"Turns out he didn't even show up for online school yesterday. His mom told me that he was on the computer in the morning like usual, but he never signed in to any of his classes."

"Not good," I said.

"I know. I'm going to stop by there on my way home. We'll see." She smiled again, this time, fuller and more engaged. Her face was small and her chin round. When she lifted her neck, she had a determined look. "How are you?"

Now it was my turn to sigh. "I'm okay. Cody doesn't want to hear about it. I'm not sure what to do."

She picked up the menu. "I received your file, your chronology. I'm sorry, but with everything going on with Evan, I haven't had a chance to look at it yet."

"That's okay," I replied.

"Anything on your end?" she asked.

I shook my head. "Not yet. I haven't worked up the courage to email the woman back. I don't think Mom has either. I should get my DNA kit soon."

"Your what?" Kathleen's eyebrows shot up in surprise.

"My kit. From *Ancestry*. I decided to do it and see if I get a match."

"Shelby." Kathleen's voice was low. "I don't think that's a great idea."

"Why not?"

"What if you find out things you don't like?"

"Like what?" I couldn't imagine what could be worse than knowing there was a child out there who was biologically related to me. Who wasn't mine.

"Like more kids you didn't know about?" Her eyes were fixed on mine.

I slumped back in the chair. The thought had not occurred to me that there might be more than one. My intent with *Ancestry* had been to derail the idea. To prove to this Julia, that no matter what the results said, there was no way a child could pop up from the sheer landscape of the three hundred and thirty million people in the U.S. and claim to be a genetic match. Kathleen's point, that there might be more, was absolutely possible.

I blew out a breath, slouched down further in the chair, and shook my head. "No," I said, "that hadn't occurred to me."

I took a sip of coffee, hoping it would soothe my nerves. It didn't work; the hot liquid burned my throat and stung my esophagus as it travelled to my belly. Shrugging, hoping to jolt myself out of the anxiety-induced stupor I felt closing in like a clamp, I said, "I have some work things to check in about."

Kathleen shot me a look. "I know you don't want to talk about it, but if you do, I'm here. Okay?"

I stared into my coffee.

"Shelby?"

I took another sip and managed a weak smile. "Thanks."

The waitress approached to take our order, placing two baskets of warm bread along with plates of olive oil and balsamic vinaigrette on the table. I tucked into a slice of bread, pulling off a small chunk and drowning it in olive oil. Warm bread — the elixir of the gods, a balm. And today, another carb to soak up all that beer still sloshing around in my belly.

Kathleen asked, "So what else is new?"

"I heard from Ryan Boyd," I said.

Kathleen's eyes grew wide as I filled her in on Justin attacking the marine. "Holy smokes," she said, shaking her head. "That is really bad."

"I know," I said.

Kathleen looked at me slowly, a look of what I'd almost interpret as fear. But Kathleen wasn't scared of anything.

She started, stopped, and started again. "What if," she asked, "what if," she repeated, then blurted, "What if the child your mom found is also engineered?"

I dropped my bread on my plate and looked down. The blob of dark balsamic vinaigrette pooled in the golden olive oil looked like blood.

"Oh no," I said, shaking my head. "No way. That is not possible. Brannon would not let one of her creations loose like that." I stared at the plate, thinking, sorting through the possibilities.

"Maybe it's her control," Kathleen said.

I looked at her. "But it couldn't be," I said, shaking my head. "The child's genetic material was the match. If the eggs were tinkered with, there wouldn't be the twenty-five percent match with Mom. Helen didn't use my eggs for that," I said firmly. "She sold them."

Kathleen put her hands up in defense. "Just a thought," she said lightly. She picked up her mug and blew on the still-hot liquid.

I sat back and picked up the bread, trying to tamp down the unsettled feeling.

Kathleen shifted in her chair, knowing it was time to change the subject. She asked, "So what else is going on?"

I toyed with the bread, tearing it into smaller and smaller bits, arranging them on the edge of the plate. I said, "I had a phone call this morning from someone named Arjun Patel. He wants me to follow his fiancée, who is having her bachelorette party in Las Vegas next weekend."

"How did he find you?" Kathleen asked, eyeing me over her raised mug.

"No idea," I shrugged. "I forgot to ask. He's sending me the details this afternoon. He was calling from a 650 number," I added.

Kathleen raised her eyebrows.

"Palo Alto, I'd guess," I replied. "He had to go into a conference room, somewhere private, to talk. He was definitely in an office. Could be tech."

Kathleen shook her head. "That is rough. Not even married, and he's having her followed? That doesn't seem like it's going to work long-term."

My lips compressed. "I know. That is trouble."

I picked up my coffee. "Remember Crystal?" I asked.

Kathleen nodded.

"I got a call from her grandparents," I said. "They got a postcard from her, from Las Vegas. She said she was living there and waitressing. They want me to go to Las Vegas and find her. It sounds impossible." I turned my hands up in a gesture of resignation. "But Stu said if I didn't do it, he would find someone who would. He's ready to raid his retirement account. I can't let him do that. He's my friend." I sighed. "Since I'm already being paid to go, it seems like I should figure out a way to help him."

Kathleen thought for a minute. "You could tack on a day or, at the most, two days. That would keep expenses down, and I think you would know pretty quickly what the landscape was looking like."

"But I have no idea how to start," I protested. "A missing young woman in Vegas? There must be thousands of them."

Just then, our food arrived. Steam wafted from the bowl of soup, and Kathleen's salad glistened with purple beets and goat cheese. After the waitress topped off my coffee, we turned our attention to our food. Kathleen took a few bites and looked up, saying, "I love this salad."

I nodded, stirring my spoon idly in my soup, waiting for it to cool.

"I have an idea." Kathleen leaned across the table. "Before you started working with me, way back in the dark ages ..."

I smiled.

"... I had a case that took me to Las Vegas. Insurance fraud. The person was claiming back problems that kept him in bed. But lo and behold, he ended up in Vegas, shooting craps. I had help from a private investigator. I can call her if you want."

"Thank you," I said. "How can she help me?"

"Think about it," she said. "She's probably done this kind of work before. As you said, lots of runaways end up in Vegas."

"True," I nodded. "So, say I do find her. What if I find out that Crystal just wants to be left alone? That would break Stu's heart."

Kathleen shook her head, stabbing a forkful of beets. "No. Not at all. That would be the biggest gift you could give to her grandparents. They'll know that she's alive. And she'll know that they love her. Even if she refuses her grandparents' offer, at least they'll know they did everything they could."

My appetite returned. I was suddenly famished. I slurped, inhaling the restorative scent of rosemary and broth. As we ate, we launched into a discussion of how this trip could work. Kathleen's suggestion was simple: allow Arjun to make my hotel reservation and my flight to Vegas. I could book the return myself. Arjun would pay for the flight to Vegas; Stu could contribute to the return. I could write the rest of the trip off as a loss. Kathleen then proposed that after the bachelorette party left on Sunday morning, I move to a less expensive hotel and work on Crystal's case through Tuesday.

I liked her plan and nodded in agreement.

She asked, "What else is on your plate?"

"Carla. The dog breeder." The waitress cleared our plates and refilled my coffee, while Kathleen ordered a latte. "Remember Carla?"

Kathleen nodded. I'd run this case by Kathleen several times now. "Anyway, Carla called me this morning, wanting an update. I called her back and told her there wasn't any new information. She hit the roof, so I offered to comb through everything one more time, no charge." I grimaced as I said this. Kathleen had trained me to avoid do-overs. They made the firm look wishy-washy, she'd told me, and made an investigator look like she hadn't done her job well the first time around.

Kathleen compressed her lips and shook her head.

"I know, I know. It is bad form," I agreed. "I couldn't think and I panicked. I did spend an hour already reviewing the tapes." I leaned in and dropped my voice to a whisper. "I think I have an answer to Carla's case."

"Really?" Kathleen lifted her eyebrows in surprise.

"I think Carla did it. I think it's an insurance scam." I picked up my phone and scooted my chair around the small table to sit next to her. I swiped to my files and started the video in slow motion, then clicked the Pause button, reaching for my coffee.

"Why would she give you the tape if she'd done it?" Kathleen asked.

I shrugged. "Obviously, she didn't think I was smart enough to figure it out." I took a sip, set the mug down, and started the video.

"So, here's why I think the thief is Carla." I stopped the video when the person stood in front of the gate to dog run. "Notice the design on the back right pocket of the jeans. I'm pretty sure these are jeans that a woman would wear."

Kathleen nodded.

"Now, watch, how easily she unlocks the pen and hangs the lock and the chain from the fencing." The video played, and I added, "See how practiced that is? As if she'd done it a million times. And look at her height. The pen is six feet tall; I think that puts our thief at about five-five, just about Carla's height.

"The other thing I found curious is how excited the dogs are to see her." We watched the figure wade through the swarm of dogs. "And she knows exactly which dog she's getting. To me, they all look the same."

"To me too," Kathleen said. "They're all black and white and gold. They're all jumping. They're all barking."

"And look how she pulls that leash out of her pocket and snaps it on the dog's collar. No fiddling. No turning the collar around to find the metal loop. Again, as if she's done it a million times before.

"There's one other thing," I added. "The pink leash. When I was at Carla's, she took me to the shed where she kept all her records, prepared the food, stored her equipment. Dangling from pegs on the wall," I paused for dramatic effect, "dozens of pink and blue leashes.

"When I was at the site, I asked her about an insurance policy. She said the dog was insured. She did not show me the policy and I didn't push. It seems like it wouldn't be too hard to find that information if we need it."

"Good work, Shelby," Kathleen said. "You might be on to something. So what's your next step?" she asked.

"Thought I'd go back and see if I could find the dog. A dog that answers to the name of 'Coco'. When Carla isn't at home of course."

"I have a better idea," Kathleen said with a twinkle in her eye. "I'll give her a call and stop by. I'll pretend to be a client."

I smiled. "Thank you." I sat back, eyeing her, thinking. "That is a great idea." I added, quickly saying, "I'd be happy to pay you for your time." I said.

She waved her hand. "My pleasure. I'll call her after lunch, maybe stop in this afternoon."

"Keep me posted," I replied.

The check came and I picked it up. I pulled my credit card out of my wallet and placed it on the tray.

As we walked outside, Kathleen asked, "Do you want me to call the P.I. in Las Vegas for a referral?"

I nodded. "Sure, and thank you."

18

B Y THE TIME I RETURNED FROM LILLIAN'S, Arjun Patel had emailed me the information I'd requested: his full name and his fiancée's name, flight, name of the hotel, and dates, as well as his fiancée's details, including social security and passport numbers. He also sent a brief paragraph explaining that the wedding was in one month and that he wanted to be one hundred percent sure of his wife-to-be, even though they'd already signed a prenup.

I sat back and shook my head. Cases like this came across my desk on a regular basis. Usually, though, the couple was already married. The wife wanted the husband followed. Or the husband was sure the wife was having an affair and wanted her followed. In one case, she'd actually been going to a therapist's office twice a week, likely to work on her marriage.

Cases like this always brought back my wedding day. How happy we'd been and how impossible it seemed that anything would ever go wrong. The June afternoon, in Highlands Park in the San Lorenzo Valley, had been sunny, sparkling, and blessed. As we stood in the gazebo surrounded by redwoods, we could see the sun glinting off the San Lorenzo River in the distance. The river was still high, swollen with water from the late spring rains and we could hear the water chuckling over stones and past boulders. Cody's friend, Steve, from work, had registered as a Universal Life Minister for one day so he could marry us.

Our wedding had been small, and I could still remember each person, as clearly as if the ceremony was just yesterday. Mom and Dad. Dexter, Megan, Annie, and Ashley. Megan's mom and her partner Tracy. Friends from Cody's work. Cody's parents and a few friends from the police academy. His uncle and aunt and cousins. Kathleen and her husband.

Truth be told, even though at that point I'd lived in Santa Cruz for seven years, I didn't have many friends. My friends from De Anza, where I'd earned my criminal justice degree, had scattered to other parts of California for work. In my day-to-day life, I was too busy for friends. I had Dexter and Megan. And Cody,who'd been my all. On my wedding day, that had been plenty.

I sighed, pulled myself back to the present, and put my hands on the keyboard. If you didn't trust your partner before your wedding day, the situation surely wouldn't improve after.

Within an hour, I'd discovered the pertinent facts. Arjun and his fiancée, Tessa Jones, were in tech. He was a senior director at a hardware company that made solid state drives, while his fiancée worked at a venture capital firm as an administrative assistant. Arjun was the higher earner, pulling in two hundred and fifty thousand per year, while Tessa made eighty thousand. He lived in an apartment in downtown Mountain View, where rent topped out at four thousand a month for a two-bedroom apartment. Tessa shared a two-bedroom apartment with three young women in Sunnyvale, where she paid only seven hundred and fifty a month.

Background checks didn't turn up anything out of the ordinary, other than the fact that Arjun was twelve years older than his fiancée. Arjun had grown up in the Central Valley, where his parents owned and operated a string of motels. He'd attended Stanford, then earned a masters and doctorate in computer science from Berkeley. Tessa grew up in New Jersey and went to Rutgers. No advanced degree.

Their Facebook profiles went back through college. Tessa's showed a young woman, always dressed to the nines. Her blonde hair was shiny, curling to her shoulders. She was cute, always dressed in matching yoga pants and top or flattering slacks paired with a business-casual top. Her makeup was flawless. She was a mystery to me: on the one hand, she'd graduated with honors and a business degree from Rutgers. On the other, most of her Facebook posts were of a social nature: parties, drinks, dinners, yoga retreats. Once she'd met Arjun, her photos included him. They were a striking couple: Arjun, tall, black-haired, dark-eyed; Tessa, petite, blonde, and blue-eyed. Tessa had five hundred Facebook friends and more than three hundred contacts in her LinkedIn network. Impressive. I had no more than one hundred LinkedIn contacts. And Facebook? Maybe fifty, which was probably good considering I never, ever posted anything on Facebook. Clients relied on my discretion.

Arjun's social media presence wasn't quite as robust. He kept up with LinkedIn, with over two hundred in his network. But he hardly posted on Facebook at all; his last post was the announcement of his engagement, one year earlier. No photos of him with his bride-to-be. No photos of the engagement party. Surely Tessa had tagged him in photos; he just hadn't bothered to post them. He had updated his profile with details of high school, college, graduate school. No details about interests or activities outside of work. It's completely possible that his work was so demanding that he had no time for anything else.

Further digging took me to Instagram, where I found that Tessa was a swimsuit model. The skimpier the better. As far as I could tell, Arjun wasn't even on Instagram, and I wondered if he knew of her account.

My phone chimed as I was drafting Arjun's contract. As it had ever since I started back to school almost a decade ago, my phone kept me organized. It was my life. I always wondered what someone would think of me if they discovered my calendar. I recorded past activities, including my work days, so I'd know how much time, down to the fifteen minute mark, I'd spent on an activity per day, including time with clients. I recorded my workouts, my workout goals, my weight. I entered phone calls to my mother so I could look back and see the last time I called her. When Cody and I were trying so hard and so unsuccessfully to conceive, I had an ovulation app that linked to my calendar. We'd have sex according to the calendar. At first it had been a fun adventure. Then, a chore. And finally, a despair.

I'd deleted the app months earlier.

"Hello," I said as I tapped the phone icon, "Shelby here."

"Hi, Shelby." It was Kathleen. "I wanted to let you know that I contacted the P.I. in Las Vegas, Amy Begay. She'd be happy to help you out. And," she added, her voice rising in excitement, "I'm going to see Carla tomorrow morning."

"Wow," I replied. "Thank you. Call me as soon as you can, okay?"

"I will," she said. "Enjoy the rest of your afternoon," she added, promising to email Amy Begay's contact information. "And have a good weekend."

"Thanks," I replied. "You too." I ended the call.

Other than dinner with Megan and Dexter tonight, I didn't have any plans for the weekend. Saturday and Sunday yawed in front of me, empty and merciless.

At four, I finished the contract for Arjun and emailed, explaining that he should book the flight to Vegas, but that I would take care of the return. Then, I reported Crystal as a missing person to the Vegas police department and called Stu and told him I'd take the case. I explained that I'd be in Las Vegas for another job, and that I would add on a few days to look for Crystal.

"I'll send you a contract as soon as I can," I said, thinking to myself that at least I'd be able to fill a few hours over the weekend, drafting a contract.

"Thank you, Shelby. I can't thank you enough. This is our last chance," Stu said, his voice breaking. "Do whatever you have to."

We hung up, and I added to-do items as calendar reminders, so I could tick them off when I was done. My calendar items linked to a take-a-note app where I could jot down notes that I could import into Word to create my reports. I'd spent a long time figuring out this workflow and was particularly happy with how seamless things were now.

Before turning off my computer, I browsed to the *Synthetic Biology Watch* website. It looked real enough, with articles and videos and essays on human genetics. The "About Us" page told me that the website was started two years ago by a graduate student in journalism at Berkeley, Matt Haver. He'd started it in response to the news, in 2018, about a Chinese scientist using Crispr technology to create the first gene-edited babies. Well, not exactly the first, I thought. I remembered that story, when it hit the news cycle, and remembered wondering why no one had compared that bit of news to the birth of Justin and Justine Boyd, born just about ten years before.

I kept poking around. It was a pretty website, with a perky theme, a bold san-serif font, large Shutterstock images of needles, test tubes, labs, and pregnant women. I found a page that listed all the articles published since the site launched. I noted all the articles relating to Clark Little:

"Clark Little Lab Promises to Provide Insect-Resistant Food"

"Clark Little Lab Develops Promising Technology to Prevent Colony Collapse Disorder"

"Clark Little Lab Develops New Technology in Race to Deliver GMO Rice to Africa"

The titles were odd. Insect-resistant food had been around for decades. And colony collapse disorder, as far as I knew, was related to insecticides carried back to the hive from foraging. GMO rice delivery to Africa had more to do with politics than technology. But I printed them out anyway.

Then, I opened the photo of Clark Little in his lab and printed it out at regular size, eight and one-half by eleven inches. I opened the photo in my photo magnification program and printed it out again, quadrant by quadrant. Each quadrant was the same size as the full-sized photo I'd just printed. I could tape it together when I got to Megan and Dexter's. Megan could help me decipher it.

I resisted the urge to open up my mother's *Ancestry* account and find out as much as I could about Julia, the mother of my genetic child. Going down that path would only lead to heartache.

It was almost five by the time I finished for the day. I locked the computer in the safe, placing it on top of Lucy's. I remembered my security breach the other night, when I'd left both computers sitting on the desk while I went to the grocery, then later in the evening when I'd staggered down the hall to the restroom. No one would have to know, I thought.

My head had cleared somewhat from last night's binge, and even though I was fatigued, I decided that a walk along the water would be just the thing to wake me up before going to Dexter and Megan's for dinner. By some miracle, on a Friday afternoon in September, I found a parking spot on Westcliff Drive, the road that curved along the edge of the Monterey Bay on the western edge of Santa Cruz. The walking and bike path followed the cliffs for two and one-half miles from the Dream Inn on one end to Natural Bridges State Park on the other.

I exited the car and opened the hatchback, then reached into my gym bag for my tennis shoes. I held my nose; I'd forgotten to remove my now-stiff and stinky clothes from the bag. I pulled off my flats and slipped into my sneakers. After grabbing my sunglasses out of my purse, I swung it over my shoulder, slipped the keys into my pocket, and pulled on my mask.

On this glorious mid-September Friday late afternoon, everyone on Westcliff was walking with someone else. I passed a group of moms pushing strollers, dressed in exercise pants and tops, chattering excitedly with each other. A family cycled by, a girl and a boy concentrating on staying upright, with their parents, one ahead and one behind, coaxing them along. Groups of older women, in twos and threes, strode past me, some deep in discussion, others laughing, another crying. Two young men jogged by. A group of teens zipped by on skateboards. You'd never know we were in a pandemic that had infected millions of people and killed hundreds of thousands.

I thought about listening to a podcast, but it seemed like too much trouble to fish out my earbuds and fiddle with my phone. Instead, I concentrated on the waves, the surfers, and what was around me. I heard snippets of conversations from "I can't, Mama. I'm too tired," to "Jesus, did you hear what he said?" to "I know the wedding is next week, but he adores me and I can't let go of my boy toy." That morsel made me stop. I turned around and gawked. The speaker was a young woman, in her early twenties, with long, glossy black hair, a rounded bottom in tight pastel-pink leggings, and toned arms. She waved her hands as she talked and walked, giving me a bird's eye view of her manicured red nails. Her friend kept her head down, and I couldn't help but wonder what she was thinking.

I continued on for twenty minutes and then turned around, wanting to arrive for dinner on time.

19

DEXTER AND MEGAN LIVED on the lower westside of Santa Cruz, not far from the bay. Their house was in the middle of The Circles, a neighborhood laid out in concentric rings around a church, recently sold for redevelopment. Dexter and Megan lived on the innermost circle, a quiet street that few drivers ventured into for fear of getting lost. It was a small three-bedroom one-bath bungalow, fronted with a quaint porch hidden behind a curtain of red bougainvillea and yellow trumpet vine. The front yard was a hodge-podge of sunflowers, nasturtium, and daisies. "Whatever grows," is what Megan said.

The house was crowded. Ashley, Dexter's daughter from his first marriage, yo-yoed between her mom's house on the eastside and Dexter's. Ashley occupied a garden shed that had been converted into a bright and comfortable bedroom. When I'd been evacuated from the fire, I'd stayed there. Annie, now twelve, commandeered one of the tiny bedrooms, while Max, just four, slept in the small utility room I'd occupied in March, when Cody and I had split up. Now, the space was all boy. Legos and cars covered the floor, with clumps of clothes and cast-off shoes pushed to the corners. A tower of blocks spilled out into the hallway. Dexter and Megan had managed to squeeze a single piece of furniture into the room, an ingenious bunk bed-dresser-ladder-slide combination.

Dexter and Megan were crammed into the largest bedroom. It was still like living in a matchbox, however; their queen bed and two dressers filled the entire room, leaving little space for maneuvering. The closet was original to the house and didn't even hold half of Megan's clothes. The rest of her clothes, along with Dexter's uniform of khakis and blue button-downs, were in a wardrobe in the living room. Close quarters, but it worked. I tried not to show my envy.

Max was in the front yard when I arrived; Annie sat on the top porch step, reading. A neon orange Hot Wheels track swooped from the porch railing down the steps and along the straight cement sidewalk, ending in front of the gate. A turquoise car just missed my foot as I pushed the gate open.

"Aunt Shelby," Max called as he ran to me in excitement, throwing himself at my legs.

I dropped my purse on the ground, adjusted my mask and knelt down, holding up my hand in a high five. "Hi tiger. How are you?"

He waved a small yellow race car at me. "Look," he pointed. "Look at what Annie built."

"It's beautiful," I said.

He ran back to the porch. "Watch," he ordered. His face was serious as he placed the small car in the starting gate. Before pulling the launcher to release the car, he looked at me to make sure I was watching. I gave a thumbs up. The car shot forward and blurred down the track until it reached the finish line. Max leapt down from the porch and followed the car as it slowed to a halt on the bumpy sidewalk.

"Very cool, Max," I said. Looking at Annie, I asked, "How are you?" I reached over to give her a hug, happy I was part of their family bubble.

"Good," she picked up a book sitting on the porch next to her and waved it at me. "I'm already ahead in my reading list for school."

"Excellent," I replied. "That's great. What are you reading?"

"It's called *Stars Beneath Our Feet* and it's about some kids in Harlem who like to build things. It's good," she added, "but I like adventure books better."

"That sounds interesting," I said. "How's school going anyway?" I asked.

Her tone grew serious. "It's okay," she sighed.

"How's Olivia?" I asked.

Annie scowled. "She's fine, I guess." I sat down next to her and put my arm around her. Max barreled past, turquoise car in one hand, yellow in the other.

"Watch, Aunt Shelby, watch."

I smiled at him, while saying to Annie, "You want to talk about it?"

Annie bit her lip and shook her head in fury.

"Auntie Shelby, you're not watching," Max called.

"Hang on a second, Max," I said as I leaned in toward Annie. "What happened?"

A tear traced down Annie's cheek, and she muttered, "Nothing." She stood and stomped across the porch into the house, slamming the door behind her. I watched her leave, wishing I hadn't asked.

"Look, Auntie Shelby, look," Max called.

I sat and watched Max race the two cars, delighting in his enjoyment and excitement, at the same time, worrying about Annie. Something had happened with her best friend and it was only a few weeks into the year. Olivia had been her bestie since kindergarten. Even in the easiest of times, middle school was a horror I wouldn't wish on anyone.

"Hey, Max," I said. "I'm going in."

"Look," he shrieked, pointing. The yellow car had flown off the track and had landed by the gate.

"I better go in before I get beaned," I said laughing. "Hello," I called as I stuck my head into the living room. I left the door open so I could keep an eye on the four-year-old.

"Hi Shelby," Megan hurried out of the kitchen, pulling the door behind her. She held a blue and white dish towel in her hand. "Dexter's talking to Annie," she said. "Something about school."

I said, "Seems like something's going on with Olivia."

Megan sighed. "I know. Olivia got invited to a sleepover tonight with some new friends. A sleepover, can you imagine, with the virus? Annie wasn't invited. Even if she was invited, we wouldn't have let her go." Megan sat on the sofa, defeated. She waved me into the room. "Sit, Shelby. You can take your mask off," she said.

I slipped into the sagging easy chair across the room, dropped my pack, and removed my mask.

"How did she find out?" I asked.

"Annie Facetimed Olivia this afternoon and could hear girls chattering in the background. Olivia told her where she was, what she was doing, and then hung up." Megan sighed. "It hurts. I thought this stuff might happen. But already, when school's barely started?" She looked at me, her eyes cloudy. "It makes me so sad for my baby girl."

"I'm sorry," I said. "Maybe she can come have a sleepover with me some time," I offered. "Small compensation, but it might help." I thought of my empty Saturday night and hoped Megan would take me up on it.

"That is so nice, Shelby." Megan replied, "Let's get it on the calendar."

"Tomorrow?" I asked.

"No can do," she replied. "Already have plans. We've decided to do a family night once a weekend, where we all watch a movie together or go on a picnic."

Blindsided, I sat completely still. Hurt and hurting. Obviously I wasn't enough of family to be included in that circle. Managing to recover before the silence grew too long and too awkward, I said, "Oh, that's a good idea. Another time, then?"

Megan smiled. "Definitely. Annie would love that." She sighed, heavy and deep. "We haven't seen Olivia since the middle of August. Those two used to be inseparable. Facetiming every day. Going on bike rides around the neighborhood. Hanging out in the backyard. They were really good about social distancing," she mused.

I nodded, still fighting a sharp pang, as real and tender as if I'd just been shoved in the chest, hard.

"I think Olivia made some new friends somehow, because Annie said she started to talk about these two girls all the time: Maddison and Emma. I think Olivia must be hanging out with them. Plus, Olivia's into soccer. Annie isn't. You know, music and reading are her interests. The soccer coach is holding online workouts with extended social time. So, I guess this split was inevitable."

"I hope she makes new friends," I said quietly, trying to push that surprising, sharp ache away. Back in its compartment.

"Me too," said Megan. She looked at me then, saying, "Shelby, how are you? You've had a hell of a week also," she pointed out. "What a thing." She shook her head.

"There's no mistake?" I asked. "No possibility?"

Megan shook her head. "I'm sorry, but there isn't." I knew Megan was right. As a PhD candidate in biomolecular engineering, I knew that Megan knew all about the human genome. About DNA and genetics and genetic ancestors.

"Maybe Mom gave up a baby for adoption, and the egg was donated by that daughter," I said.

"Not likely," Megan replied flatly. "She would have told you."

"I know." I knew better than to suggest that Dexter had donated sperm to a sperm bank. That would be way, way outside of his comfort zone. Besides, he was always the sensible one. He went to community college and transferred to the University of Oregon as a junior. His loans were minimal and paid off. Unlike me. I'd wanted to follow my passion. I'd spent hours arguing with my parents. They wanted a sensible college major. I wanted art history. I had no artistic talent, so art history was the next best thing. I should have listened to them. My passion had led to a huge college debt, which in turn led me to a surrogacy arrangement, which in another twist, had led to this. A found child.

"So how are you?" Megan asked, again, interrupting my chain of black thoughts.

Now it was my turn to shrug. "Not great. Trying to figure out what to do." I didn't tell Megan about Kathleen's response, still weighing on me, that there might be multiple children out there who were genetically related to me. Nor did I tell her that I'd ordered a genetic testing kit.

"Hey," I said. "I'd like you to help me with something."

I could hear Dexter's voice from the kitchen, a comforting low tone, along with Annie's occasional protests and muffled sobs. But instead of reaching for my purse, I turned to Megan. "You better go in there," I gestured to the kitchen. "I'll hang out with Max."

"Thanks, Shel," she said. "See you in a minute." She stood up and hurried toward the kitchen, pulling the door open and slipping in. I could hear Annie weeping. Poor girl, I thought. I remembered seventh grade. Luckily, I had softball to fall back on. Hopefully, Annie's love of music and reading would carry her through.

Outside, I sorted through Max's plastic tub of cars and track, and picked up a bright red truck with fire decals on the sides. "Hey Max," I said. "How about this one?"

He held out his hand. "Give it to me," he ordered. He skipped down the steps and picked up the cars at the end of the course. Scampering back to the porch, he shouted, "Watch, Aunt Shelby. Watch." His joy was infectious and within minutes we were constructing another track.

Twenty minutes later, Megan came out on the porch, saying, "Dinner in ten. Time to put that away, pumpkin."

"Mom," Max replied, completely absorbed. "Wait a minute. Watch."

Megan said, "We can set it up again tomorrow. I have to go in and help your dad get dinner on the table, okay?"

"Hey, Max," I said before he could object. "One more race and then let's put it away."

Megan blew me a kiss as she went back inside.

Five minutes later, after I'd taken at least fifteen photos of Max and the complicated loops and crossovers we'd constructed, we disassembled the track and dumped all the parts back in the tub. Max crouched, and pushing with his entire body, managed to shove the tub to the corner of the porch.

"Thanks, big guy," I said. "Let's go eat." I held out my hand.

Inside, Annie was sitting on the sofa with her mom's tablet, watching a movie. Bright cartoon flashes animated the small screen. Max immediately sat next to her, and without thinking, Annie pulled him onto her lap. The eyes of both children glazed over, as if they had been injected with a drug.

"*Frozen*," Megan said as I maneuvered in the small kitchen. "Still Annie's favorite movie." She sighed. "I'll let her watch as many movies as she wants tonight. Damn Olivia."

"Hey." Dexter's voice was sharp. "It's no one's fault. Olivia is making new friends, that's all. It's just going to take Annie a little longer."

"I know, babe," Megan said. I startled; even though they'd been married for almost seven years now, it still caught me off guard to hear my brother called "babe." He wasn't a babe, in any sense of the word. Megan continued, "I just don't like to see my girl so sad."

"I know. Me neither," said Dexter. "At least we know what's going on and we can help her."

After dinner, Annie picked up the tablet and retreated to her bedroom, Max trailing her. Megan started to clear the table; Dexter said, "I'll get it. You cooked."

Megan threw him a grateful look. "Thank you. It's been a long week." She turned to me. "Now, what was it you wanted to show me?"

20

AS WE MOVED TO THE LIVING ROOM SOFA, I picked my purse up off the floor and pulled out the photo printouts. The sofa groaned under our weight and Megan laughed. "We got this thing when we first moved in together. A Goodwill special. Probably time for a new one, but until Max is no longer using this as his sailboat or fort, it doesn't make sense."

The sofa faced a set of windows that looked out on the bedroom-garden shed and the overgrown backyard. A security light glared over the weed-studded patio and the crabgrass lawn that was littered with balls of every imaginable size, from golf balls to basketballs. Half-dead juniper bushes lined a sagging redwood fence.

Megan smiled as she said, "Every weekend we think we're going to fit in a couple hours of yard work, and every weekend slips by without us even venturing out there.

"So what's on your mind?" She turned to look at me. Her eyes were clear and focused. She'd grown her hair out in the last few years, and it now hung straight to her shoulders. Her earrings were small studs, and I suspected that was now a habit, started when Max was little. He used to grab for anything shiny and loved his mother's dangly earrings.

I handed her the photo of the lab. "What is this?"

She studied the picture. "A chemistry lab," she said. "Pretty standard, but there is some high-end equipment."

"What's the equipment for?" I asked.

She picked up the photo and examined it closely, then pointed to a glass box with a hood sitting on a table. "That thing is a polymerase chain reaction workstation. A PCR workstation. It's used for cloning and amplifying RNA and DNA."

In response to my questioning look, she explained, "Gene amplification. It's used to replicate the number of copies in a gene sequence. Basically, it copies genes so that you can get a large enough sample to work with."

"Why would you do that?" I asked.

"Well," Megan said, "you can use it to clone genes so that you can diagnose hereditary diseases or analyze DNA. It's used quite a bit in cancer research." Returning to the photo and pointing to one of the desks, she said, "There's a lot of equipment here: a pipettor, two gene sequencers, an electrophoresis unit for doing gel electrophoresis. That lets you sort DNA strands by their length. The autoclave, here, cleans things."

She sat back, then twisted to look at me. Her voice was flat. "What's this for, Shelby? What are you up to?" She stared at me. I couldn't tell if she was curious or worried. Probably both.

I shrugged. "Just working on something. That's all." I reached into the folder. "Look, I blew up the picture in case you needed a close up." I offered her the four sheets of paper, but she didn't take them.

She stared at me, hard. "I can't imagine what you're going through right now," she said gently. "That child has to be your genetic relative. It must be very, very difficult." She leaned toward me. "But there's nothing you can do about it. It's over. I'm so sorry," she said. "So sorry."

I returned her gaze and then dropped my eyes. I'd start to cry if I wasn't careful. I was exhausted and still hung over. I felt as fragile as a glass figurine. I wasn't about to tell her what had happened since I'd received the news from Dexter — my meeting with Cody, my bender, his gallant early-morning rescue as I lurched across the parking lot to my car, and the painful truth that love wasn't enough to get us through this. If love wasn't enough, what was left? But I couldn't go there, not even with Megan, my best friend and sister-in-law. Someone I shared everything with.

"I know," I finally replied. "I just want to know more. See how it was all done. Maybe if I understood it, from a practical standpoint, it wouldn't be so overwhelming."

Megan nodded. "That makes sense." She pointed to the photo. "So here's what would happen in a lab to sequence a gene." As she talked, my mind wandered, and I wondered what else was buried in the photo. Any clue to where the lab was located? Any personal touches?

"Hey, Shelby," she said, noticing that I was staring out the back window. "Are you even listening?"

"Sorry," I replied. "Yes. You were just talking about gene sequencers."

"Good. A gene sequencer is an amazing piece of equipment. Looks like this lab has two of them. One older, and one completely state of the art. I've only seen that one in high-end private labs. It doesn't require that you amplify the gene first; it uses a completely new third-generation sequencing technology." She paused. "I wonder why they have both; maybe to verify results. Different equipment can produce different results. That new machine costs upwards of a million dollars." She angled the photo toward the light.

"Could the equipment in this lab be used for creating new DNA?"

Megan threw me a look.

"Just wondering," I said.

She nodded, sighing. "Yes. It could. More likely this equipment is used for genetic testing or cancer research. Though the technology for tinkering with DNA — you've heard of Crispr of course — doesn't require special equipment. Just special proteins." Megan paused and placed the photo in her lap. "But, Shelby, what that scientist did to create Justin and Justine was way beyond Crispr. Even now, no one knows exactly how she did it. Sure, there have been plenty of theories, and lots of papers from Russia, China, and the Ukraine, claiming to have done it again, but there's nothing definitive. No more next-human-species babies.

"Thankfully," she added. Then, after a beat, she asked, "Why are you going down this rathole again?"

I stared at the photo in her lap. "There has to be a reason."

"Reason for what?" Dexter emerged from the kitchen, wiping his hands on the striped apron tied around his waist. "What are you looking at?"

I kept my head down, praying that Megan wouldn't tell Dexter. At least not now, while I was still in the room. I knew she'd tell him later, but that was all right. Thankfully, Megan said, "I was giving Shelby a primer on genetics, that's all."

She deftly handed me the photo and I slipped it back into the folder. I threw her a grateful look. "Hey," I said, eager to change the subject, "I'm going to Las Vegas next week."

"Vegas?" Dexter asked. "Vegas? Why would you want to do that?" He slipped into the easy chair across the room.

"Work," I replied. "A guy called me today, wanting me to follow his fiancée on her bachelorette party next weekend."

"Ugh," Megan said, "that sounds awful. Especially Vegas of all places. Is it safe?" she asked, just as Dexter was saying, "If there are problems before you get married, it's only going to get worse after you tie the knot."

"I know," I said. "I'll take my mask," I added, "and be careful."

Megan warned, "It's not over, Shelby."

"I know," I said.

"How are you going to watch her?" Dexter asked.

"Follow her around," I replied. "With disguises. Different outfits, sunglasses, hats."

"When do you go?" Megan asked, absently plucking a thread on the arm of the sofa.

"Friday," I said. "In a week. I have a second job tacked on after that," I added. "Missing teen."

Just as I was about to tell them about the postcard Crystal's grandparents had received, Megan yawned. My cue to leave.

"I'll be back the following Tuesday night. I'll text you." I stood and put the photos back in my purse. Dexter slipped onto the sofa next to his wife, putting his arm around her.

I stood. "Have a good weekend, you two. I'll go say bye to the kids." Down the hall, through the closed door, I could hear the strains of "Let It Go," the signature song from *Frozen*. The lyrics didn't get by me.

I knocked and pushed the door open a crack. "Bye, love you," I waved. A chorus of "Bye, Aunt Shelby," followed me down the hall. I heard a patter of footsteps and was tackled by Max from behind. I spun around and knelt down to give him a hug. "Bye, tiger. Be nice to your sister this weekend."

21

B Y THE TIME I ARRIVED HOME, it was dark and the house loomed at
the end of the driveway like a Victorian mansion out of a horror
movie. I turned off the car and the headlights flicked off. During the
day, and with the lights on, the peaked roof, attic dormers, and
wrap-around porch were inviting. At night, they turned into hiding
places for slithering goblins and ghouls.

Erica was often out at night. Had I known that ahead of time, I
might not have moved in, but here I was. I always got spooked when I
drove up and all the lights were off. It was involuntary, and no amount
of reasoning or logic could will away the uneasy feeling. I grabbed my
purse off the passenger seat, slid out of the car, and hurried to the door,
clicking the car locks with my key fob. Once inside, I locked the door
behind me, turned on every light in the living room as well as the porch
light, and beelined to the kitchen where I checked the back door. Also
locked.

The uneasy feeling lifted once I'd brushed my teeth, closed the
door to my room and locked it, and then firmly closed the curtains. I

plugged in my phone and turned on my laptop. A connection to the outer world would help calm my fears.

The first email in my inbox was another from Ryan Boyd, with the subject line of: `Justin (cont'd)`. He'd sent it this afternoon.

Hey Shelby,

Wanted to let you know that Justin won't be returning home, ever. They are holding him somewhere in Quantico. They say he's not a prisoner, but they also say he's not free to come and go on his own. We are allowed to go see him once a week. No contact. He's locked in twenty-four-seven. In a suite, like a hotel suite, but it's a cell with a lock and a key.

Strangely enough, when we saw him tonight, Justin seemed relaxed. It's almost as if he's no longer stressed. Maybe they're giving him something to calm him down; I don't know. I talked to a lawyer this afternoon. He said that if we wanted him back home, we could fight it since Justin is under eighteen. But he also said that we would likely get resistance. Laws apply to people. Technically, 'Justin is not people,' the lawyer said. In reality, neither Lisa or I want Justin home. He's too terrifying to live with.

So, he sits in his suite and works on math problems. Same as he did here really. All other contact, except for Justine and me and Lisa, is by video. He meets with his professors by video, with the doctor and the psychiatrist also. Even the personal trainer has to see him by a video link. His food is delivered through a slot in the door. His meds must be mixed into the food somehow.

It's all monitored of course.

Lisa and I are adjusting. Our stress level has gone down, but Justine is more distant. We did hear that the Marine will recover. Eventually.

Give me a call when you can,

Ryan

It was eight California time, eleven in Virginia. I was sure Ryan would still be up. If he didn't answer in four rings, I'd try tomorrow.

But Ryan answered on the first ring. "Shelby," he said, "thank you so much for calling. I guess you got my emails?"

"I did," I replied. "What a thing."

"It's awful. The Marine needed over a hundred stitches."

"What?" I asked. "A hundred stitches?"

"Yes. You heard right. Justin was biting him. I couldn't pull him away. He had his jaws clamped around the guy's bicep." Ryan sighed. "Jesus."

"Did Lisa see it?" I asked.

"No, thankfully. I'd just gotten home from work. Lisa was still out. The kids were upstairs, and suddenly Justin came roaring down the stairs, saying he had to get out, get out, get out." Ryan paused, and I heard him swallow. He then said, "In the last month, Justin has grown six inches. I'm not kidding. He doesn't work out, but developed this hulking superhuman strength ..." He paused and gave a small, pitiful laugh. "I know, he is superhuman, right?"

I didn't laugh. I held the phone in front of me, rubbed my ear, and put it on speaker phone. "This is terrible," I said.

"It gets worse," Ryan continued. "The Marine stood in front of the door, you know how they do, with legs planted. He held his rifle or AK47 or whatever it's called across his chest. Any normal person would have melted into a puddle on the floor, seeing that.

"But Justin kept charging. I saw the Marine lift the gun and I realized, 'This guy is going to shoot.' They have orders to shoot these kids. Then the Marine yelled, 'Justin, stand down, stand down.' But Justin ignored him, and the Marine pointed the gun at him, and then Justin jumped. Landed on the guy and started biting. Eating, almost. Like a monster." Ryan's voice caught. "Like a monster."

"Oh, Ryan, I'm so sorry. So, so sorry," I said. I could see it unfold, all of it. "How did you separate them?"

"The Marine must have had an emergency beacon and been able to activate it. Within five seconds, two more Marines had manhandled Justin into a pair of handcuffs. The injured Marine was squirming on the floor, blood pouring out of his arm. Justin's face was dripping with blood. It was like *The Walking Dead* or something.

"Then another Marine came in and injected Justin with something and he dropped. It all happened so fast.

"When it was all over, I turned around, and there was Justine. She'd been watching the whole thing. And she snorted. And then giggled, the littlest bit."

I froze. That piece of information was as terrifying as the rest of the story. Though I hadn't seen Justine for years now, I could imagine her. Statuesque, contemptuous, aloof. Her indifference had likely morphed to arrogance, and I wondered if she had developed a fondness for casual cruelty. "What's going to happen to them?" I asked.

"Justin stays where he is. But he and Justine won't function well apart from each other."

I was quiet.

"Any suggestions for me?" Ryan prompted.

"I'm thinking," I said. "I'm thinking. Maybe you and Lisa could take a vacation and go on a cruise or something. See what happens while you're away."

"Oh," Ryan said, surprised. "Oh. That's a really good idea. I hadn't even thought of getting away."

"How will Justine be on her own?" I asked.

"I'm sure she'll be fine. Someone will be with her all the time." I heard some background noise, and a hushed whisper. "I better go, Shelby. I woke Lisa up."

"Think about a break, okay?"

"I will," he said. "I will."

After we disconnected, I dropped the phone on my desk and rubbed my temples. I was astounded. A giant twelve-year-old with the strength of a linebacker.

I hoped that Ryan and Lisa could get away. I didn't want to think that by adopting the twins I'd given birth to, I'd created a life for them that resembled a prison.

I lay in bed, completely awake, only relaxing enough to sleep when I heard Erica come in around one in the morning.

22

I SLEPT LATE ON SATURDAY MORNING, waking at nine. I stumbled downstairs, surprised to find Erica still in the kitchen. Usually on Saturday mornings, she'd be off to yoga, out on a hike, or working in her studio. I was jolted into wakefulness when she handed me a mug of coffee, saying "Good morning, Shelby. I was just about to wake you up. You're still on for yoga, right?"

I stared at her blankly.

"Remember? We talked about it on Wednesday."

I sipped the coffee, working my way back through the week. Wednesday was the day I found out. The day my life changed forever, when Dexter met me for lunch and told me about my biological daughter. I must have been numb when I agreed to attend a yoga class with Erica, for I had absolutely zero memory of it. Nothing.

"It's at ten," Erica continued, unaware of my frozen mind. "We need to leave around nine forty-five. See you then." She waved at me as she exited the kitchen. I heard the door to her room open and close.

I stared after her. Yoga. Why not? The idea of contorting myself into noodle-like poses and holding them seemed a bit out of my league, but it also seemed like something I ought to do. Something that might calm this rage inside me, this unrelenting fury that threatened to consume me.

I went upstairs to change.

The yoga did calm me. So much in fact that I almost crawled back in bed when we got back home. Erica was energized though, and talked non-stop on the ten minute drive back to the house, telling me about her latest boyfriend, older and thoughtful and interested in her pottery; two of her students, ten-year-old best friends who came to the studio twice a week as part of their homeschool program; her community work, volunteering in the local elementary school, doing clay hand-building with kindergarteners. I envied her full, enriching life.

When she asked me what the rest of the day held for me, I pushed aside the vision of the bedcovers and binge-watching Nextflix. "Going into work," I said.

She laughed in reply, saying, "The joys of being a small business owner. Twenty-four-seven." I laughed in return, wishing her comment wasn't really true.

Because I did work most of the time. Even when Cody and I had been together. More once we split up. If I wasn't working, I was there in my head, working on my most recent case, or imagining ways to drum up more business. Cody never noticed. He worked all the time too. Between his overtime, his visits to the firing range, and his community service, he averaged an easy sixty hours a week. As we grew distant, work was his excuse for crashing in the dorm at the station. When he was home, he slept. We'd never had the conversation about cutting back on work once the baby was born, because I never got far enough along in my pregnancy.

I checked my email as I savored my second cup of coffee, along with a piece of whole wheat toast with jam. My bitter and sweet jolt to jump-start my system. Nothing new from Ryan. I tried to imagine an almost seven-foot-tall Justin, a perfect human specimen who'd attained that physique effortlessly. I remembered him at five years old: a stocky child who could barely run. I wondered what gene combination had activated during his very early puberty, turning him into a strongman.

•   •   •

It was after twelve by the time I reached the office. The day was warm and sparkling, and, I had to admit, the yoga had done my body wonders. Once I showered and changed, I discovered I was filled with a heady serenity, a peaceful focus I wasn't sure I had ever experienced before.

After pulling out my computer and logging in, I discovered that Arjun had emailed me the digitally signed contract and had sent the retainer to my Google Pay account. He'd also booked my flight to Vegas and the hotel. The Southwest flight left San Jose at ten in the morning on Friday. Tessa and her friends were returning Sunday morning at eleven. Barely forty-eight hours. The bachelorette party was staying at the Bellagio, a luxury hotel with rooms starting at three hundred and fifty a night. I did a mental calculation: Arjun had already spent almost one thousand dollars on this case for me to track his fiancée. I wondered if I'd get the results he was hoping for.

As I checked the Vegas weather, in the mid-nineties, I started a list of what I'd need for this portion of the trip. Over the years, I had assembled a collection of surveillance outfits. Rather than taking them home, I stored them at the office. I walked to my closet, mulling over what would work for Vegas. I figured on five outfits. I eyed my shortest pair of shorts; the cutoff jeans that rode almost to my underwear. Not so flattering, I knew, but they would make me anonymous. I pulled out four pastel spaghetti strap shirts. A sundress. A hat, big sunglasses, sandals. A pink sweatshirt and a sweater for the inevitable over air-conditioned indoors.

And, I knew I had to bring my one cocktail dress. Megan called it my "Bond girl" outfit. The dress was made from a shimmery silver fabric that lay tight against my skin. I was proud of that find: ten dollars at Ross. I completed the outfit with a black shrug and a matching silver clutch that was big enough for my phone, ID, and room key. A pair of black stiletto heels finished off the look. I could totter around inside, in a casino, for a few hours in those shoes, but that would be it. The entire ensemble had put me out only forty dollars. A bargain.

I'd only worn it once before, on a surveillance case tracking a wandering spouse. That time, I'd stayed at the Fairmont in San Francisco. The woman who'd hired me did not get the results she'd been anticipating. She was the mistress and wanted the husband followed; he'd promised to divorce his wife. Instead, I found him with a third woman, someone new.

The equipment was easy. By this point in my career, I had my list of go-to items for surveillance. A camera with a telephoto lens. A small wide-angle camera the size of a button, along with a backup and backup batteries. It ran on a programmable timer. I could hide it in a plant or stick it on a table leg to watch the entrance to Tessa's room. In addition, I packed a travel laptop, a battery pack, extra camera cards and batteries, a small foldable tripod, and binoculars. I decided against the night scope; Las Vegas was lit up twenty-four-seven. It was never, ever dark. Save for the laptop, I packed all these items inside a heavy-duty backpack, which I then tucked inside my carry-on.

For the second part of my Las Vegas trip, searching for Crystal, I didn't need anything special. Just a sturdy pair of walking shoes, since I knew I'd be doing a lot of old-fashioned legwork, shopping her photo around. A hat and sunscreen. I made reservations at a smaller, off-Strip hotel for the remainder of my stay, one that averaged a mere seventy dollars a night.

I tossed in three cloth masks and three pairs of disposable gloves, along with a small pouch of disinfectant wipes and a travel-sized bottle of hand sanitizer. Even though states had reopened, I wasn't taking any chances. It was one thing to be in Santa Cruz, where residents mostly paid attention to the stay-at-home order. It was another to be in Vegas, with hordes of people in a casino, breathing recycled air.

As I was completing my car rental reservation online, the desk phone rang. "Shelby McDougall Investigations," I said into the handset. Even now, every time, I got a small smile when I said that. Cody used to joke that I was easily amused.

"Hi Shelby, Stu here," Stu's voice was measured. "We're rethinking."

"Why?" I asked, surprised.

"We don't want to seem like we're intruding," Stu said quietly.

"I don't think that finding her would be intrusive," I said quietly. "I think she'd like to know that someone went to all this trouble because they loved her. Assuming I do find her. Las Vegas is a huge city," I reminded him.

"I know," Stu replied. "We go back and forth."

"Stu," I said, "since I'll already be there, I'll see what I can do. Okay? You won't need to pay me anything. I'll spend two days and show her photo around. Just like we did in August, in San Francisco. I'm contacting a local P.I. for assistance."

"I don't know, Shelby." I could imagine him in his office, wearing the signature overalls, blue work shirt, and ballcap he'd likely worn every day in his life as a farmer in the Salinas Valley.

"I'm going to be there anyway," I said.

Stu thought for a moment. "When you find her, just follow her for a while and see how she is. And then call me. Okay?"

"Sure, I can do that," I replied. My heart ached; the chances of me finding Crystal were slim to nothing.

After a beat, I said, "I'll need a signed contract, along with a form that gives me permission to work with a Las Vegas P.I. and share information with her, including photos."

Stu sighed, weary. "Okay."

"It'd be good to get it out of the way soon," I said. "Should I email it?"

"You could," Stu replied, "but my computer's down and I can't print it."

I had an idea. "What are you doing this afternoon?" I asked. "How about we meet in Salinas, say at three? Bring any additional recent photos you have and the postcard. I'll bring the contract along with a consent form."

"You sure?" Stu asked, his voice thick. "Thank you."

We made plans to meet at a Starbucks at the northern edge of Salinas. It would be about an hour's drive for each of us. Stu and Marilyn would be driving from the south, from the small farming community of Greenfield, where he'd retired several years ago as one of the last asparagus farmers in the region. None of his children had wanted to take over the ranch, so he'd sold most of the acreage to a large agricultural conglomerate.

Back at my computer, I booked a return flight home for the following Tuesday afternoon, giving me all day Monday and part of the day Tuesday to search for Crystal.

After a bathroom break, I sat back down at my desk. I thought about calling Kathleen, but knew she would call after she'd seen Carla. Carla, I knew, would be no match for my former boss.

I prepared a packet for Stu, with the contract and the additional form. Then, I rummaged in my purse and pulled out photos of Little's lab. I moved to my client table and laid out the four blow-ups; each eight-by-eleven representing a quadrant of the room. I was now looking at a sixteen-by-twenty-two version of the photo. The original sharpness of the photo had been retained when I'd blown it up. So it was clear, and I could see details I hadn't noticed in the eight-by-eleven. Labels on bottles, stickers with barcodes on test tubes, Post-it notes stuck to shelving above workstations, a safety poster on the wall.

I didn't need to leave for another thirty minutes. I decided to look at the photos in a systematic fashion.

23

I PICKED UP THE TOP PHOTO, the image that I'd downloaded from the *Synthetic Biology Watch* website. Banks of fluorescent lights covered the ceiling and the room was bathed in a bright light. There were no windows. Four workbenches stood along the back of the room, holding the high-end equipment Megan had pointed out, the polymerase chain reaction workstation and the two gene sequencers. The room was large, with plenty of space between the work benches and the equipment. Three of the four lab workers had their backs to the camera, but one worker, a young woman, peered through a gap in the shelving above her workstation, looking curiously at the commotion.

I picked up the blown-up images, arranging them to complete the room. Shelves stuffed with books and file folders lined the left wall. Across from the bookshelves were four workbenches and shelves organized with blue- and yellow-capped plastic bottles of solution, test tubes and pipettes in bright blue plastic trays, glass beakers and flasks of different sizes, and Tupperware tubs. Microscopes and scales sat on the countertops, along with hot plates, Bunsen burners, mortar and pestles, wire grates and brushes, and a tub filled with safety goggles. Each workbench contained a stainless-steel sink.

The front of the room was dominated by C.J. Little. He'd planted himself there, in a leather jacket, tan slacks, cowboy boots, and a tan ten-gallon hat with a black band. Master of his domain. His face was heavy. He was large, not overweight, but a substantial person. Forceful. Power radiated off him and I guessed he was a man used to doing things his own way, regardless of the consequences.

I retrieved my magnifying glass from my desk, and zeroed in, trying to pick out words on the bottles, test tubes, boxes, and bins. A spiral-bound book next to the gene sequencer was labeled "GeneWorkbench P25"; it must be an instruction manual. Blue-topped bottles labeled "Saline" lined one shelf. Bottles of a mysterious magenta liquid, no label, sat on another shelf. Test tubes in a rack on a corner of a workbench were barcoded. A stack of red binders, spine face out, sat on the shelf above. They were labeled "GS125-10", "GS125-11", and so on, probably referring to a run of an experiment.

Shipping boxes sat on the top of a lab workstation shelf in the back of the room. The text on the mailing label was blurry, but I could make out the abbreviation of the destination state: NV. Nevada? I opened the photo on my laptop, and increased the zoom, hoping that the text wouldn't dissolve into meaningless pixelated squiggles. I got lucky. I could read the full address:

```
Little Lab
Goodsprings Bypass Rd.
Goodsprings NV 89019
```

As well as the return address, from a Fischer Scientific location in Pittsburg, Pennsylvania.

I read the address again. Little Lab? If the man was trying to hide something, he wouldn't get very far with that name.

I immediately Googled "Little Lab Goodsprings Nevada" and unearthed links to the town of Goodsprings, with no mention of the lab. Then, I opened Google Maps, trying to tamp down my growing excitement. If it was near Las Vegas, I might be able to squeeze in a drive.

And I got lucky. Only thirty minutes south of Vegas, and twelve miles north of the small town of Goodsprings, Nevada, a small community with a church, elementary school, and a truck stop. I played with the street and satellite views for a while on Google Maps. The only street view was taken from the window of a Southwest flight. The satellite view showed a rugged dry terrain, with the town nestled at the base of an alluvial plain that stretched up to a north-south mountain range. The highest peak was called Shenandoah Peak, a name that brought to mind lush green forests and chuckling streams. Not a wind-blown, dusty mountaintop with boulders the size of semitrucks.

I continued to examine the photo on the computer, zooming in and out. The woman I could see peering through the shelves looked curious, nothing more. Granted, with those safety goggles masking her expression, it was hard to tell. I zoomed in on a particularly cluttered shelf, above a section of one of the workbenches that was stacked with papers and file folders. Someone was hunched over a microscope to the left of this mess, and I wondered how the lab operated. Were individual scientists assigned to specific areas, or was the lab completely collaborative, with everyone moving between areas, depending on what equipment they needed? Did everyone order their own supplies, or was there a lab manager orchestrating things? Did the mess bother others in the otherwise pristine lab?

Someone had taped personal items to the shelf in the particularly cluttered area. A postcard of a tropical beach. Another of an alpine forest, with a snow-capped peak off in the distance. A yellow sticker with a sketch of a birthday cake and the wish: "Don't grow old. You'll live to regret it." And next to that was a small black and white image cut from a newspaper. An image I'd seen before. An image that caused tingles up and down my spine.

It was a photo of Justin and Justine clipped from a newspaper. This photo of the twins had been plastered in the media years earlier when Justin had been kidnapped. It had accompanied every news story, every online post, every TV clip. The photo had been taken at Sears, about a month before Justin disappeared. The two five-year-olds, dressed in preppie outfits, stood next to each other. Their imperious expressions bordered on arrogance, even at that early age. No little kid cuteness. No chubby cheeks or wispy hair. Just those predatory ringed eyes, a know-it-all expression, and a full set of teeth.

Why would someone clip that photo? An inspiration? Or a warning?

24

I CONTINUED TO SCAN THE PHOTO, hunting for other clues. Maybe I could find a notebook with "Manifesto" written on the spine or a test tube with a "Justin Boyd" label slapped on it. But no matter how much I picked over that photo, nothing else emerged. I was unable to identify any additional details that would help me understand what I was seeing.

As I sat back, I tried to figure out why a photo of five-year-old twins Justin and Justine, obviously clipped from a newspaper, had shown up in a lab, supposedly a GMO foods lab, in the remote outlands of Nevada. It didn't make sense. Nothing made sense at this point. Shaking my head, unsure where this was taking me, I glanced at my phone, checking the time. I'd been at this for over an hour. Leaving the photo on my desk, I stood up and stretched, again, wishing it was a day Lucy was in. Wishing for a distraction. I walked to the window; at this time on a Saturday afternoon, the parking lot was completely empty. I cranked the window open a notch. I could hear traffic noise out on the street and a group of children, yelling and laughing, playing in a nearby backyard. Kids outside on a warm, sunny Saturday afternoon. In another lifetime, Cody and I …

I willed the thought away and returned to my desk. Time to leave to meet Stu.

•   •   •

I arrived at Starbucks early and slipped into a parking spot that had just opened up. This mall was vast, with over one hundred stores and three big-box stores: Costco, Target, and Best Buy. And the parking lot, on this glorious afternoon, was full. Row after row of cars glittered in the sun. I'd done my turn around a mall or two when I was in middle school, but I'd outgrown mall hopping. I'd much rather read or hike or visit or watch a movie or, well, do anything, than shop on a Saturday afternoon.

Paying attention to the taped marks on the floor, I stood in line at Starbucks, waiting, while the woman in front of me ordered two complicated drinks, whipped, foamed, half caff, blended, with two percent in one, and macadamia milk in the other. Her order came to over ten dollars. I ordered a black coffee, straight up. Mine was two-fifty.

While I waited for Stu and Marilyn, I put in my ear buds and scrolled through my news feed, a random collection of sources I'd curated over the years. Cody had set me up with a YouTube channel of cute puppy and kitten videos. On the days immediately following our breakup, those videos were the only things that kept me going. I softened as I watched a pile of kittens play fight and then dissolve into a pile of fluff and fall asleep. Cody had also introduced me to fail videos. Videos of cars driving into sinkholes. Videos of people stepping on the working end of a shovel or a rake so that the handle flew up and hit them square in the face. Videos of misplaced or misspelled signage. Videos of architectural fails. In spite of myself, knowing I was often laughing at someone's misery, I liked them.

"Hi Shelby," Stu said, interrupting my focus. Not that what I was watching, a movie trailer for the next big action movie, required any focus at all. I removed the ear buds, stopped the video, and stood, adjusting my mask. "Hi Stu," I said, "thanks for coming."

"No, thank you," he insisted. "This is perfect."

"Is Marilyn here?" I asked.

Stu shook his head. "No, she was busy."

"Coffee?" I gestured toward the counter.

"No, thanks. I'm of the age where if I have coffee after noon, I can't sleep." He smiled, but it was a forced smile, and I could tell he was tired. "I keep thinking about that postcard," he said. "Marilyn and I have been talking about it all morning. Why Las Vegas?"

I shook my head and sat, watching Stu fold himself into the seat across from me. "Who knows the mind of a young adult?" I picked up the cardboard cup of coffee and cradled it between my hands. "You sure you want me to do this, right?"

"Yes. Marilyn is not so sure now, but I am. She thinks that looking for Crystal might send a message that we actually don't trust her." He reached for the visor of his Salinas Rodeo cap, tugged it down on his forehead, then reset it to exactly the same position.

"Stu," I said, leaning across the table, "I think it will show her that you love her and care about her."

He nodded, his face drawn, and gave a shaky sigh. "I agree with you. Let's hope so. And besides," he added, "you might not even be able to find her."

I kept my face neutral. I wasn't going to agree with him, even though that was likely true. Given the statistics, my chances of finding Crystal were slim to none. But I had found other children before, against all odds.

I slid the file folder across the table toward him, reached into my purse, and pulled out a pen. A Shelby McDougall Investigations pen with the phone number. Cheesy, I knew, but the dark blue pen with the bright red italic lettering was eye-catching. And memorable. When Kathleen had first retired and business had been slow, I'd ordered a lot of one thousand of those pens. I'd planted them all across the county, casually leaving them in coffee shops and libraries, doctor's offices, therapist offices, hotel lobbies, and restaurants. I knew of at least one client who'd found me via those pens, so I figured the investment paid off. But in truth, I'd spent much, much more on search engine optimization, hiring an expert to help me get my listing to the top of web results for private investigators.

"Why don't you read that over? I have to run to the restroom."

Stu opened the folder and picked up the two-page contract.

When I returned five minutes later, the folder sat closed on the desk, with the pen on top of it. Stu had pushed it back to my side of the table. His hands were folded in front of him and he was staring at them, as if in silent prayer. "Everything okay?" I asked as I slid in across from him.

"Yes. I signed it and wrote a check and put it in there."

"Stu," I said looking at him. The creases in his face were deep, and his eyes were recessed.

"Just take it, Shelby. Please?"

I nodded, knowing that to argue or protest would embarrass him. I didn't have to cash it.

"You'll call me as soon as you know anything?"

"Yes," I replied. "Did you bring more photos? The postcard?"

"They're in an envelope in there. Please bring them back to us. Senior picture from high school." He shook his head as he continued, "All those tattoos. Reminds me of the kids from juvie who used to come out and work at the ranch."

He returned my questioning look. "A long time ago, Juvenile Hall used to have a program where the kids would help out on ranches in the valley. Until a group of them ran away. Not from our place, but a neighbor's. Of course, the program got discontinued. Most of the kids were really sweet inside, with a tough exterior. No support at home." He paused and repeated the gesture with his ball cap, tugging it down and then repositioning it on his forehead. "Kind of like my daughter and her knuckle-headed excuse of a husband." He added, "Marilyn isn't quite so kind in her description."

He sighed and stood. I rose. "I'll let you know before I go if I have any questions," I said. "The earliest I would get hold of you would be week after next, as I have the other case in Las Vegas before yours. I'll start looking for Crystal a week from Monday, and take it from there."

"Thank you, Shelby. Like I said, if you find her, just let us know, and we'll decide what to do."

After Stu left, I opened the folder. Stu had written his check carefully and had paper-clipped it to the envelope of photos. It wasn't much, but I knew it was more than they could afford.

I opened the envelope and shook the photos onto the table. That same senior photo was on the top. I'd have to memorize those tattoos; they might be the only recognizable thing about her. She could have lost or gained weight. Cut or grown out her hair. Changed the hairstyle or color. If she was using, she might be strung out and thin, with sores on her face.

My phone rang as I was gathering my things to leave. I picked up the phone, delighted to see that Kathleen was calling.

"Hi there," I said. "Can I call you back in five? I'm just about to get in the car. I'll call you when I get on the highway."

"Sure," she said. "I'm driving too. Talk to you in a few."

25

A S SOON AS I HIT 101 NORTH, I voice-dialed Kathleen. She answered with a cheerful, "Hey, Shelby."

"You sound pumped," I said as I moved into the left lane to pass a slow-moving older model Toyota Corolla.

"Well, I had a great visit with Carla," she replied. "Those dogs are cute. But a bit overwhelming. She has a lot of them. And she is chatty."

A pickup truck pulled up behind me and the driver flashed his lights, once, twice, three times. Playing nice, I put on my signal and moved to the right.

"Anything about a missing dog?" I asked.

"Not a peep," she said. "She even introduced me to a dog she called 'Coco'."

"What?" I said, surprised. "She did?"

"Yes, she said this dog was her breeder. To me, she looked like all the other dogs. The dog didn't seem to be responding to the name."

"How many dogs were there?" I asked, moving over to the left again to pass a truck loaded with stacks of empty palettes.

"I didn't get a complete count, but at least twenty."

"Really?" As I put my blinker on and moved back over to the right, I took in the tall, graceful eucalyptus trees lining the highway. "I think the day I was there, there were only ten dogs. I'll have to look at my notes." I paused a beat. "Were they all in the one pen out in the back? The one in the security footage?"

"No." Kathleen sounded surprised. "None of the dogs were in the pen. They were all running around. When I drove in, they massed around the car like vultures on a dead sea lion. I thought I was going to run them over."

"Strange," I said, surprised. "When I was there, they were all in the pen. Did they all look the same? Like cocker spaniels?"

"As far as I could tell." Kathleen's voice sounded like it was coming from a wind tunnel. I turned on my signal to exit the highway onto San Miguel Canyon Road, the fastest way to reach the coast from Highway 101. It would take me through the small community of Royal Oaks, a rural enclave of ranchettes, barns, fields, and warehouses surrounded by tall razor wire fencing. I was just about to ask her what she suggested next when the call dropped.

Suddenly, I realized this route would take me close to Carla's place. All it would take was a left turn in a few miles, and a short drive toward the upper reaches of Elkhorn Slough. Another fifteen minutes and I'd be there.

I tried Kathleen again. She picked up, but her voice was fading in and out.

"I think I'm going to pay Carla a visit," I said. "I'll call you when I'm done."

Now it was Kathleen's turn to be surprised. I could hear it in her voice. "Why?"

"She's hiding something," I said flatly. "And this latest thing with all the dogs just doesn't make sense. She steals her own dog to collect the insurance payment because she needs the money and then takes in ten more when she already told me she had financial problems?"

But the call dropped again, and this time, when I redialed, nothing happened. No service.

As I drove, I tried to pay attention to what was in front of me and get my mind off Carla. The afternoon was sunny and clear, and the lush agricultural fields of the Pajaro Valley glowed with prosperity. I passed acres of grapes and could occasionally glimpse green or purple globes dangling from a vine. Black netting, to prevent feasting birds from making away with the produce, covered acres of raspberry and blackberry bushes. As I drove farther from the highway, I passed fields of strawberries, the low-lying green plants snug in their raised beds.

Ten minutes later, I turned left onto Strawberry Road, following the inland edge of the slough. Elkhorn Slough was the last tidal wetland in this part of California and its inner arms spread for five miles, the fingers of the marsh appearing and disappearing with the tide. I remembered kayaking there with Cody, early on in our relationship. We'd rented sit-on-top boats from the concessionaire at the mouth of the slough, paying more attention to each other than to the safety instructions. We paddled into the upper reaches of the slough, exploring the narrow channels through the pickleweed. The tide was so low that the mud banks loomed above us and our world was reduced to blue sky, mottled green pickleweed, the three-foot mud bank, and the brown, slow-moving muddy water.

We'd startled more than one Great Blue Heron, awed by its proximity and size, and its blue-green feathers that sparkled in the sun as it spread its wings and jumped into the air. Red-shelled crabs scuttled into mud holes in the bank of the channel as we approached. Small fish jumped. In one channel we disturbed a clutch of rays that reminded me of aquatic bats as they slowly swam along the bottom, the lazy movement of their fins forming small whirlpools in the water. We popped back into the slough's main artery at the upper reach, watching a freight train lumber along the tracks that cut across the channel on a levee. When we turned around to head back, the tide and the wind were against us, making our return journey twice as long. We'd had a good laugh about that, later, when we knew each other better.

But it had been worth it. On the way inland, we'd passed the sea lion rookery where baby sea lions, looking like small, shiny sausages, sunned themselves on the sand spit. A flock of pelicans took off as we rounded another sandbar, lifting up on an air thermal just over our boats. Their wings sounded like fans as they bit into the air. One of the pelicans was missing a hunk of flight feathers, as if something had taken a mouthful from its open wing.

I reached the turn that led to Carla's place, and followed the road a few miles through the strawberry fields. But when I arrived at her driveway, a chain had been pulled across it. An orange cone sat in front of the chain, and a makeshift sign had been taped to it: "Closed. Open by Appointment Only."

I clicked my Bluetooth to give Carla a call. No service.

Another day then. I'd call her on Monday and set up an appointment.

But just at that moment, a truck drove up behind me and in one swift move, parked broadside, blocking me in. It was Carla's truck. I turned off my car, picked up my phone, and put my hand on the door handle. As I pushed down on the latch, Carla appeared from the driver's side of her truck. She was waving a wooden baseball bat. A dog started to bark, rapid, high-pitched and insistent.

Carla yelled, "Coco, hush."

I froze. Coco?

The dog continued to yap in the same unrelenting tone.

Carla repeated, "Coco. Be quiet."

No mistake. If I could get her to say it one more time, I could record it. I quickly swiped into the phone and turned on the recording function. I wondered what I could do to make sure that dog kept barking.

I slowly scooted to the edge of the driver's seat.

"Who are you? What are you doing, trying to get on my property?" Carla yelled. I could see in the rearview mirror that she'd lifted the bat to her shoulder like she was standing at the plate. Hearing her loud, aggressive voice caused the dog to bark even louder.

"Coco," Carla roared. "Dammit. Shut the hell up."

Coco completely ignored her and went ballistic, running behind her, then darting toward my car and back to Carla, almost as if spinning.

But I'd recorded it; I was sure of it.

Now I had to decide what to do. I could either pretend I hadn't heard her say "Coco" three times or I could confront her. Seeing as how she had my car blocked in, and was carrying a baseball bat, I decided to play dumb.

I left my phone on the console, with the record function still running, opened the door, and stood, raising my hands.

"Carla," I said. "It's me. Shelby. I was just driving back from Salinas and thought I'd stop by."

Carla looked confused for an instant, and it occurred to me that she might be having a serious mental episode.

"It's me. Your private investigator."

She still clutched the bat to her shoulder, gripping it as if her life depended on it. The dog circled her feet and then sat down next to her. They made an odd pair: the small black and white dog; and Carla, dressed in jeans and a blue sweatshirt, holding a bat on her shoulder, as if waiting for a pitch.

"Shelby?"

"Yes, it's me. I had an errand in Salinas and thought I'd stop by. I tried to call, but my phone doesn't have service out here."

Carla shuddered and dropped the bat. It hung in her right hand. "Oh, Shelby. Hi."

"Hi Carla. It looks like this is a bad time, so if you'll move your car, I'll head out and call you on Monday."

But Carla's eyes narrowed, and I could see that she was thinking about what she'd said and if I'd heard it. I had to escape before she realized her mistake.

I slipped back into the car, turned it on, and backed up until my rear bumper was almost touching the side of the truck bed. Then, I angled forward toward the chain. Even though it was just a foot away, I did have some maneuvering room. I kept angling back and forth, checking my mirrors, watching Carla just stand there, with that dog sitting by her side.

Watching Carla watch me.

As soon as I had my Prius parallel to her battered rusty Ford, she knocked on my window.

I didn't roll it down, but I stepped on the brake and looked at her.

She stared at me for a good long moment, and said, "I'll move my truck."

I watched her walk back to her truck, toss the bat into the passenger's side, gesture for the dog to jump in, and then pull herself in and slam the door shut. She backed up and I turned, slipped in front of her, and turned right, wanting to get to the main road as quickly as possible.

Once I'd put several miles between Carla and myself, I stopped. I picked up the phone, turned off the recording function, and then listened to it. I had gotten it. All of it. The dog barking. Carla yelling at the dog to shut up, using the dog's name and swearing along with it. Our brief confrontation. The beeps from my Prius indicating that I was backing up.

I would not be going back to Carla's property. I'd send her the recording as well as the transcription along with my final invoice. I'd call Kathleen when I got home, and be done with it.

26

ERICA PLACED THE WOK of steaming stir-fry veggies — cabbage, broccoli, carrots, peas, and red onion — down on the table next to the large bowl of brown rice. I'd called her on my way home, checking in to see if she needed any groceries. Even though we usually purchased our food separately, I was happy to pick up anything she needed. I was in town a lot more than she was. Today, she said that if I picked up ingredients for stir fry, she'd make it. I was all in.

Just as she sat down, I stood. "Water?" I asked.

Erica shook her head. "I'll just stick with the wine," she said. She picked up the wine glass, tilted it in my direction, saying, "You're sure you don't want any?"

"No thanks," I replied. I was still steering clear of alcohol. At least for a few more days.

"How was your day?" she asked.

"Good," I replied. "After yoga, I went into work for a few hours. I ended up driving to Salinas to meet a client and I stopped by another client's on my way back home." I winced, remembering I'd forgotten to call Kathleen and update her on Carla's case. "Yours?"

Nodding, Erica scooped a large spoonful of brown rice onto her plate, and said, "Good. I was finally able to get a tree person to come out and give a bid to take down and haul off all the burned vegetation around the house and along the driveway. They won't be able to do it for another month, but at least we're on the list." She wrinkled her nose. "And someone's coming out next week to help me figure out how to get rid of that persistent smoke smell."

"It's not too bad," I said, as I took a sip of water. In truth though, everything stunk now, the odor reminding me of an ashy campfire.

"No," she replied. "It's not. And compared to other homes, we are so lucky."

I nodded, saying, "I know."

"Anything exciting happening at work? Any new cases?" Erica asked.

"No. Same ones," I said, sipping my water. "Missing dog, wandering fiancée, and missing teen."

I didn't tell Erica much about my cases. I didn't know who she knew. In truth, even though Santa Cruz was a town of fifty thousand, it seemed much, much smaller. I was often crossing paths with people I'd met in different contexts: at the gym, at Cody's work, at Trader Joe's or Shopper's Corner, at a workshop, at the doctor's office, at the police station or the county courthouse, even while walking on the beach.

I knew that Santa Cruz was a hotbed of progressive politics, but in my time here, I'd managed to stay well out of that world. As a small business owner, getting my nose stuck in local politics seemed a particularly bad idea. Erica, I knew, was heavily involved a few local causes: Grey Bears, a food pantry, thrift store, and support network for seniors; Arts for All, an artist activist organized around the belief that if everyone rose to their full artistic potential, all would be right in the world; the Women's International League for Peace & Freedom, a political progressive organization close to my mother's heart.

My politics were more nuanced. Owning a business meant I always had to think about taxes and the bottom line. As a private investigator and married to a Sheriff's deputy, I spent a lot of time thinking about law and order. As someone who'd been at the wrong end of a gun too many times, my concerns were also focused on the criminal justice system. And anything having to do with reproductive technology and human engineering would instantly grab my attention. These weren't the usual issues that concerned someone in their mid-thirties.

"Rice?" Erica asked, turning the handle of the spoon in my direction.

"Thanks." I placed a large spoonful of brown rice on my plate and then topped it with a scoop of the glistening vegetables. I took a bite and said, "This is yummy." In truth, it wasn't that flavorful, and I longed to rummage in the fridge for the bottle of soy sauce.

But Erica beat me to it. Saying, "Hang on," she leaned back, opened the refrigerator, and pulled a brown bottle off the shelf. She doused her vegetables, took a bite, and said, "Much better." I followed, and agreed with her assessment.

As we ate, I told her about my upcoming trip to Las Vegas, keeping the details on the skimpy side. "We should talk about me quarantining when I get back," I offered.

Erica waved her hand. "If we eat together, we can go outside," she said. "And in the kitchen, we can wear masks and sanitize surfaces. If you show any symptoms, you can get a test. Otherwise, I think we're safe. We're pretty separate here."

"Okay," I agreed.

"Did you read that story about the Crown Prince of Abu Dhabi donating up to twenty million dollars for testing so Vegas could open up? I guess he missed his 'entertainment'," Erica said, air-quoting for emphasis. "They spun it as reopening the economy, but all you have to do is read between the lines. I hate Vegas," she said.

She then told me about her last trip to Vegas, right before she and her husband split up for good. "Neither of us were in our right minds," she said. "I'm not sure why we even decided to go there. He suggested and I agreed." She took a sip of her wine and then ran her hand through her thick hair. She laughed as she continued her story. "We decided to go for broke. We got a room at one of the fancier places. Tony had so much money at that point, we didn't even have to pay attention to the cost. We got there, got to this incredible room, with a bed the size of your bedroom, gilt and decorative curlicues everywhere, mirrors with fake Louis the 14th frames. You know, those heavy gold frames with the embellishments and swirls and the arched top that draws your eye upward." She laughed. "I remember just standing there, staring at myself while Tony was in the bathroom, thinking, 'This is not me at all.'"

She sighed. "When Tony came out, I told him I was going home and moving out." The smile left her face and she sighed again. "I got a taxi back to the airport, flew back to California, spent two days packing, moved most of it to a storage unit, and then moved to Santa Cruz, where I'd always dreamed of living.

"The funny thing is," she said, "that wasn't Tony either. At least when we got together. He was one of the first engineers at Google. Just a guy who loved to write code. And go climbing on the weekends. And throw pots. Then he changed."

"What's he doing now?" I asked.

"Still at Google. Runs some division. Remarried, of course. Someone younger. He's fifty now, she's your age, I think. They have a kid and live in Palo Alto." She shrugged. "I guess that's what he really wanted."

Raising her glass, she added, "I got what I wanted. Perfect house. Potting studio and a place to teach."

She took a few bites and then pushed her plate away. "Ugh. This really is terrible food," she said. "It's kind of oily."

My plate was clean by this time, and now, it was my turn to shrug. "I liked it," I said.

"You're not that good of a liar," Erica said, laughing. "Oh, you got a package. Sorry, I opened it by mistake. It's from *Ancestry*?" Her voice lilted to a question as she pointed toward the living room. "It's by the front door."

"Thanks," I replied.

"You're going to do that?" she asked, as she carried her plate to the sink. "Willingly contribute your DNA to a universal database?"

"It's complicated," I said slowly, reaching for another scoop of rice. Erica knew nothing of my history prior to my separation from Cody. "My mom did it, so I thought I'd do it too."

As she scraped the remnants on her plate into the compost bucket by the sink, Erica said, "Well, if your mom's already done it, the cat's out of the bag, I guess."

I nodded. "I guess." That was one way to put it, I thought.

"Did she find anything unexpected?"

At that moment, Erica's phone rang, saving me.

27

A FTER A LATE-MORNING BOXING CLASS on Sunday, I decided to stay in town, sit at a cafe, and read the latest news about human engineering. I searched my news feeds for stories of Justin; but there was nothing about the attack on the Marine. The military had kept the event under wraps. Before heading to Bonny Doon, I stopped by the grocery, then ran into my office to pick up my surveillance clothes and equipment for my upcoming trip. When I arrived back at home, Erica was in the kitchen, assembling a tray of cheese, crackers, and sliced apples. A bottle of Martinelli's cider sat on a tray with two glasses.

"Hey, Shelby, how's it going?" she asked. "How was boxing?"

I nodded as I pulled a carton of milk, one percent, out of my reusable Trader Joe's bag and put it into the fridge. "Good," I replied. "We worked on our upper cuts."

Erica laughed, clear and uncomplicated. "Better than yoga?"

I laughed in return. "Not a chance." I'd liked the yoga class more than I was willing to admit.

"What are you up to this afternoon?" she asked. She was placing the apple slices in an overlapping chain around the wedge of oozing Brie.

"Not sure," I replied. "Just hanging around, I guess. You?" I put my tub of fake butter on the shelf in the refrigerator next to my milk, along with a jar of organic jam and a tub of plain yoghurt.

"A friend's coming over to throw some pots. I'll be out in the studio for the rest of the afternoon."

"Sounds like fun."

Erica picked up a clamshell of green grapes, rinsed them under the sink, and set them on a towel, dabbing them dry. Then, picking up a pair of scissors, she started cutting the giant cluster into small tendrils of three or four grapes each.

"Need help?" I asked as I stole a small bunch and popped a grape into my mouth.

A knock on the door interrupted our conversation. Erica laid down the scissors, wiped her hands on a towel, and barreled past me, saying, "Hang on, coming."

I could see clear to the front door through the wide-open arch that separated the kitchen from the dining room, and watched, a bit enviously, as Erica greeted her friend. The woman trailed Erica back to the kitchen, where Erica picked up the scissors again and returned to trimming the grapes. Her friend slid into a chair at the round kitchen table.

"Shelby, meet Mary. Mary, this is my housemate, Shelby." Mary was an older woman with iron-gray curly hair and kind eyes. She wore a heavy canvas floral print apron over blue jeans and a pink sweatshirt, and a mask made from a sunflower patterned fabric.

"Nice to meet you," I said, pulling on my mask.

"You too," she replied.

"Mary has been throwing pots for at least fifty years," Erica explained, excitement in her voice. "She's a wizard. Wizard-ess? In any case, she's a master. She's going to show me some techniques this afternoon."

Mary laughed, an infectious tinkly laugh, making me wish she was my friend. "You flatter me, Erica," she said.

Erica placed the last of the grape clusters on the tray and picked it up. "Ready?" she said.

"You want me to carry the drinks?" I asked, picking up the bottle of cider and the glasses.

"I'll get them," Mary said. "You can get on with your day."

"See you later, Shelby," Erica added.

I handed Mary the bottle and the glasses, and watched as they walked away, their voices lifted in excited chatter. Their giggles were abruptly cut off as Erica closed the door behind them.

•   •   •

I went upstairs to my bedroom. Afternoon sun streamed in, burnishing the hardwood floor and shining off the surface of the silvery laptop. The room was stuffy, quiet. I opened the window and heard a crow squawk, followed by a chorus. Three crows were dive-bombing a hawk, flying in close as the hawk cut across the meadow and disappeared into the denuded forest. I picked my phone out of my back pocket and swiped through to Spotify, but none of my playlists appealed to me. I'd named them with optimism, finding just the right music for each mood or activity: Happiness, Romance, Family, Remodel. Now, they just reminded me of Cody and our house. Our lazy weekends. Our intimate dinners. I tossed the phone on the bed, plopped into my desk chair and swiveled to face the room. My life was here now, small and immediate. The double bed Cody and I had shared, covered by a quilt my mom had made. A closet full of work clothes. A few little-kid pictures from Max tacked to the wall. A bulletin board of reminders and nature images torn out of *National Geographic.* A dresser from Crate and Barrel; the top cluttered with jewelry suitable for work, not for fun or romance.

I turned back to the desk, opened the laptop, and checked my email. Nothing new from Ryan. Nothing from Cody. Or Dexter and Megan. I'm not sure what I was expecting. Restless, I stood up, made the bed and fluffed the pillows. Then, I flopped on the bed and squirreled my back into the pillows with my legs straight out in front of me. I crossed my ankles and adjusted the computer in my lap. An all too familiar position. I spent a few unenthusiastic minutes searching for anything new on Mr. Clarke Little, Helen Brannon, or Justin and Justine Boyd. Nothing. I thought about calling Cody, but I wasn't sure what that would accomplish. I tried my mother, but the phone just rang and rang. Kathleen didn't answer either.

The sun shone and it was a glorious afternoon. Sunny and warm, with a breeze. T-shirt weather. I could go for a walk at Henry Cowell, the nearby state park. The fires had largely bypassed the main part of the park, several miles down the ridge. But on this beautiful afternoon, the park would be busy. And a walk in the redwoods was something you did with a friend. Not alone.

Instead, I decided to spend the afternoon indulging in guilty pleasures: binge watching one of my favorite shows, *Parks and Recreation*. I put in my ear buds and got to it. The sheer ridiculousness of the story, the pure comedy, the precise editing, and the pitch-perfect acting made me giggle.

•   •   •

My phone rang as I started episode five, and I turned it over and glanced at the screen. Mom. I paused the show and swiped the phone.

"Hey Mom," I said, "How are you?"

"I'm good, honey, and you?"

"Okay," I said. "I got my DNA kit yesterday. I'm going to send it in tomorrow."

"Shelby, are you sure?" I could hear my mom's voice dip into worry. "You don't need to do that, you know. I'll pass on anything else I find out."

"I know. I'm curious," I said. "Any more emails?"

"No, nothing. I'd let you know," she said.

"Just call or email me directly this time, okay? You don't need to go through Dexter." As I was talking to her, something occurred to me. I wondered if my mom had done her own search, looking for genetic relatives. Rather than having people find her, did she find people? I added, "Would it be okay with you if I opened your account and did some poking around? Just to see how it works?" I didn't let on that I had already hacked into it.

"Sure," she said. "Please don't send any emails without telling me though."

"Thanks, and I won't," I added.

After she gave me her *Ancestry* sign-on credentials, which I already had, our conversation drifted to Dexter and Megan, to Annie's problems at school, to Max and his Hot Wheels, to my upcoming Vegas trip.

"Your father and I went to Vegas once," my mom said.

"You did?" I asked in surprise. I know my parents liked cruises, but Vegas seemed a bit over the top for them. They weren't heavy drinkers, gamblers, or shoppers, or fond of glitzy shows. "Why?"

Mom was quiet for a moment. "We went for our anniversary one year. You and your brother were teens, so it must have been our twentieth. It was in the summer and you all stayed down the street with the neighbors. It was ghastly hot and people were wandering around sweating and drinking. Inside, it was freezing. Way over air conditioned." She paused for a moment, then said, "I think we were supposed to stay for five days and ended up coming home after three. Never again, we both agreed."

I laughed. "That's not a good report, Mom. I'm going for five days as well."

"At least you're getting paid for it," she joked. I was happy to hear my mom joking. She'd had a rough time since my father died. Downsizing and moving into a retirement community in southern Oregon, followed by the pandemic and the massive fires in her area, had aged her.

"I'll keep you posted," I said. "Love you."

"Love you too," she replied.

After we disconnected, I imagined Mom in her small one-bedroom apartment in The Village, a complete senior community with activities, a dining hall, a med center, assisted living, and a nursing home. It had been two years since she'd moved there and she was now happy and active. She'd lost weight, restyled her hair, upped her wardrobe, and basically reinvented herself. She swore she'd never meet another man as good as "your father," as she put it, but I secretly hoped she would. Though the ratio of women to men in her new home seemed to be about ten to one.

The pandemic had been rough on retirement living. She'd been confined to her small apartment for months, but had kept up with people over Zoom: coffee hour in the morning, social distancing happy hours in the afternoon. Quilting bees and exercise classes. The restrictions on social activity had given my mother the time to explore family history. Mom viewed family as a tether, an anchor in a chaotic storm. I sometimes viewed family as a heavy chain, pulling me down. That made me smile. Typical of me, to crash headlong into something I had a visceral, negative reaction to. Though I hadn't sent in my DNA kit.

Yet.

28

I ARRIVED AT MY OFFICE after boxing class on Monday morning, showered and ready for work. Not refreshed, not rested. I hadn't felt refreshed or rested since long before Cody and I split up. In truth, not since my third miscarriage. I'd still had hope after the first two.

I knew that this constant state of edginess wasn't good for my health, but short of completely reinventing my personality, I wasn't sure how to make a change. Yoga had helped. Mediation might help, also. That was another thing my mom had started: a daily meditation, guided by an app on her smartphone. Neither fit with the Mom I'd grown up with.

My first order of business for the day was to call Kathleen. She picked up right away, saying, "Hey, Shelby. I checked in on Evan. All good. How are you? I saw you called yesterday, but we were busy with family."

"You won't believe what happened," I said.

After chiming in with the appropriate *"you're kidding"*'s and *"no way"*'s as I was telling my story of Carla and Coco, Kathleen laughed. "That is a first, Shelby," she exclaimed. "After I left, she must have gone to get the dog from wherever she was hiding. And that confirms my suspicion that the dog she was trying to pass off as Coco wasn't Coco at all. What a piece of work." I could imagine Kathleen shaking her head and smiling. "What are you going to do?" she asked.

"I'm going to transcribe the recording and send it off to Carla with a final invoice."

"Do you have a video?"

"No," I replied. "Just the audio. Anyone listening can tell it's Carla."

"Is it clear?"

"Yes."

"Would a voice expert be able to confirm they're the same voices?"

I paused. My phone had been inside my car when I'd made the recording. "I guess so," I said doubtfully. "I assume so." It was Carla, after all. "And besides," I added, "this doesn't have to hold up in any court. This just has to hold up enough for Carla to know she's busted and for me to get paid."

"True," Kathleen's voice cut out and then returned. "… owe you?"

"What?" I asked. "You broke up."

"How much does she owe you?" Kathleen repeated.

"She's paid the standard retainer. I've put in more time than that. I interviewed the neighbors and did background checks. I tracked down the so-called competition. And then, I did that half-day review of the case for no charge." I sighed, then added, "But, if I hadn't done that, I probably wouldn't have figured out she's the thief." I knew that Carla owed Shelby McDougall Investigations a sum at least equal to the retainer, if not more.

"I hope you get it," Kathleen said.

"Me too." I didn't operate on a shoe-string budget, but it was close. Rent on my office and the cost of business insurance took up at least one-third of what I made every month. On top of that were office supplies, subscriptions to databases and services of all stripes, journal subscriptions to keep abreast with law enforcement and investigative advances, car maintenance, and gas. Since the official start of the pandemic in March, the number of inquiries had dropped by half. When I was living with Cody, my money seemed to go a lot further.

And god forbid, if we ever divorced, I'd have to pay for my own health insurance. I needed the money Carla owed me.

"When are you going to Vegas?" she asked.

"Friday," I said. "I work on the fiancée case until Sunday, and on Monday, switch over to Stu's case." I didn't tell her that I had reserved Sunday afternoon for a trip out to Goodsprings to track down Little's lab.

The phone cut to a hollow emptiness, signaling that the call had completely dropped. Kathleen lived in Carmel Valley and the road to her house was twisty and windy, through a canyon. She'd call back when she could.

Even though the transcription of the recording was something Lucy could easily do tomorrow, I decided to do it myself. It gave me a peculiar pleasure to nail the unpleasant woman, and I knew my glee in this particular job was justified. After I finished the transcription, I crafted my final invoice, composed a courteous, if abrupt, email, and attached the transcription and the recording. Usually my invoices were a thirty day receipt, but I put Carla's on a fifteen day turn-around. I wanted my payment from her sooner, rather than later. With grim satisfaction, I imagined how it would play out: me threatening to expose her if she didn't pay. But it probably wouldn't matter. I suspected her business was ruined one way or another.

My next item for the day was to start a case file for Arjun Patel. My record-keeping system had evolved over the years, and now I had a system that worked for me. I'd tried everything, from yellow legal pads to subscription case management systems. What I ended up with was a hybrid. I created a folder for every client. The most important item was the spreadsheet, where I recorded time spent, down to fifteen-minute increments, as well as expenses. I transcribed it from my calendar at the end of every day. Those weeks I'd been at my worst, after Cody and I had split up, I'd jotted my time on random pieces of paper and stuffed them in an envelope. I'd let it go for weeks, and trying to reconstruct my days had been almost impossible.

I also kept a daily file for every day I worked on a client's case. As I made notes, I added categories so I could do a quick search if a client had a specific question. For example, in Carla's case, I'd added categories of BACKGROUND CHECKS and NEIGHBORS and

SEARCH and COMPETITION. Sometimes, when I was in a hurry, I used the recording function on my phone and Lucy would transcribe the recordings. I'd add in the keywords as I thought of them. Lucy was an excellent editor. She'd ask questions that would help me categorize my notes in ways I hadn't thought of.

And Lucy was always on the lookout for ways to improve my business. Once, she'd tried to roll out her own system that used open source software, so I wouldn't have to keep up my subscription to Microsoft Office. Another time, she'd talked to a bookkeeper friend of hers to help me streamline my accounting services, but that didn't pan out either. Kathleen and I had been using a local bookkeeper, Josie May, for years. She knew our system, did payroll, paid quarterly taxes, and prepared everything for the tax preparer in a timely fashion.

Before I left the office, I cracked open my DNA kit, swabbed my cheek, dropped the Q-tip in the provided plastic bag, placed it in the provided envelope, and sealed it. I'd take it to the post office on my way home.

•　　　•　　　•

I dialed Ryan Boyd as I walked to my car. My primary contact had originally been Lisa — she'd called me in hysterics after Justin was kidnapped, asking me to help. But since then, even though Ryan claimed that Lisa was always the person who wanted to get in touch with me, Ryan and I were the ones who communicated.

Ryan picked up on the first ring and said, "Shelby, thanks for calling. How are you?"

"I'm good," I said. "Work is busy, going to Vegas this week for a job." I hadn't told him about my split from Cody. They'd never met. By the time Cody and I were truly a couple, Ryan, Lisa, Justin and Justine had been moved from Watsonville, California to the carefully ordered suburb of McClean, Virginia, living in a government-owned suburban house, a place that was more like a prison than a home.

"Vegas," Ryan said. "Lucky you. Lisa and I went to Vegas for our honeymoon."

"Did you like it?" I asked, smiling. Everyone had a Vegas story.

"Not really. Lisa more than me. You remember her infatuation with Thomas Kincaid?"

"Yes," I said. I remembered their small home in Watsonville, the walls of the living room hidden behind dozens of Thomas Kincaid paintings of thatched cottages, golden sunbeams, snowy villages, purple sunsets, and soft-focus Disney characters.

"At the time we were there, it was the height of Kincaid's fame. She found the Kincaid gallery, a massive store in one of the casinos, and spent almost our entire trip budget on Kincaid paintings. She watched the associate finish each painting with a small fleck of precisely-placed gold paint. Just so they could say it was hand-painted." He snorted and said, "What a crock."

I knew what he was talking about. Back in my former life as an art history major, I'd worked in a Kincaid gallery and had done exactly that. Sold paintings and placed the gold fleck just where it needed to go. Just for the "hand-painted" tag. I had liked that job though; loved it. Still, all these years later, for whatever reason — my sentimental nature, my yearning for love — seeing a Kincaid painting gave me a hit of pleasure. Kind of like that first sip of wine at the end of a long day.

"I think that store is gone now," I said.

"Probably. I heard the empire crashed and then the guy died," he said. "Or maybe it was the other way around."

"So how are things?" I asked. I was leaning against my car, feeling the afternoon sun on my skin. I felt relaxed in a way I hadn't in a long time.

"Better," he said. "Curiously better. The tension in our house has been dramatically reduced. Justine barely comes out of her room. Only to eat and use the bathroom. Her professors say she's doing just fine; that she has the mind of a brilliant scholar. I have no idea what that means or what she does. Read, read, read. Write, write, write. She doesn't talk to us much anymore."

After a beat, he added, "Sometimes Lisa and I talk about just leaving. Moving back to California. But now, it's so expensive there and I don't think we could afford to buy a house. Here or there, it's the same, though. Those kids aren't really ours anymore. Maybe they never were."

He paused, and I felt a grief telegraph though me, a feeling so strong it threatened to bring me to my knees.

"What a thing," he said quietly. "What a thing."

I found myself wiping a tear away and said, "Yes, it is."

29

T HE SOUTHWEST TERMINAL in the Mineta San Jose Airport was
spacious, with high ceilings, wide seats, bright lighting, jumbotron
ads, techy art installations, metal sculptures, and the usual offering of
coffee, fast food, books, and magazines. Uptempo music filled the
terminal. This was my first flight since the easing of travel restrictions
after the pandemic and people were embracing life with gusto. The fear
seemed to be gone, although about half the people I saw were still
wearing masks. Some even wore gloves. A group of high school students
zipped toward their gate, leaving their anxious chaperones behind.
Parents herded their kids. Couples meandered along the concourse. It
was easy to spot who was travelling for business: black roller bag with
matching black briefcase and earbuds attached to a phone in hand.

I found my gate and picked a seat in a row of benches that faced
out toward the concourse, where I could watch the activity. l sat down
on the end, resisting the urge to spread out, wanting to put my purse
and briefcase on the seat next to me and my suitcase in front of that
seat. I still had the social distancing urge. Besides, the last thing I

wanted to do was engage in small talk after an early hour-long drive in rush hour traffic. I fumbled with my laptop and set it on my lap, keeping an eye out for "the girls" as I'd started to call them.

I felt as ready for this trip as I could be. I'd completed all my outstanding business. I'd procrastinated returning the DNA kit, but had finally dropped it off at the post office. I'd regaled Lucy with the story of my encounter with Carla and she'd howled in appreciation, just as I'd hoped she would. We talked about the background checks she needed to work on while I was away. I knew she'd finish those quickly, and I hoped that something would come up between now and then to keep her busy in my absence. We discussed security protocol — with me out of the office, she wouldn't be able to access the safe with the laptops. We decided that in this one case, and this one time only, she would take her laptop home, guarding it with her life.

I checked in my briefcase once more, making sure that I had the envelope with the photos of Crystal, as well as the pictures of Mr. Little's lab in Goodsprings, Nevada. I had my week mapped out in my head. Today and Saturday, I'd follow the bachelorette party. Sunday morning, I'd trail them to the airport and see them through security. I'd pick up my rental car and switch hotels. Sunday afternoon, I'd collapse and then start my report for Arjun. In the early evening, I'd drive to Goodsprings to see what I could of Little's lab. Monday morning, I'd meet with Kathleen's P.I. friend. Monday afternoon and evening, as well as Tuesday morning, I'd hunt for Crystal. It would be a busy week and I'd have to take careful, copious notes.

I received an update from Arjun yesterday. Tessa would be traveling with five other women, he told me. They were flying priority boarding, meaning that they had the privilege of being the first on and off the plane. Arjun was sure they would just breeze in at the last minute and claim their spot in line. When I asked why Southwest instead of an airline where they could all fly first class, he'd said, "Finances, of course. Money does not grow on trees, you know." I thought about what the background check had revealed. For Arjun, money actually did grow on trees. His salary equaled approximately five thousand per week, which, last time I checked, was more than most people saw in a month.

Just as I was thinking of getting out my laptop, a group of five women arrived at the gate. They ranged in size from small and petite to voluptuously plump. They all pulled roller bags and carried large Coach purses. Every last one of them was wearing leggings and pink or black close-fitting T-shirts with plunging necklines, paired with feminine hoodies. Some wore heels, others, chunky tennis shoes. Earrings dangled from their ears below glossy swept back hair. Their masks were shiny and rimmed with sparkles. They laughed, giggled, hooted. Noisy.

They didn't sit, but clumped around the boarding area. As far as I could tell, based on the Facebook pictures I'd seen, Tessa was not in this group. Two of the women talked to each other; the others scrolled through feeds on their phones, swiping and flicking with quick gestures.

Five minutes later, Tessa arrived. The other women flocked around her, taking her into the circle, hugging, laughing. I couldn't catch their conversation, but from their animated motions, I could tell they were talking about clothes, jewelry, makeup. After they stood back, I could study Tessa openly. She had long, thick blonde hair, high eyebrows, thick black eyelashes, and expertly applied bold makeup. I imagined bright red lips under her pink mask. She wore heels, black leggings, a pink crop top that revealed a taut, tanned belly, over which she'd layered a light blue jeans jacket decorated with sparkly studs. A pair of large sunglasses rested on top of her head. Silvery drop earrings swayed from her ears and diamonds, which I assumed to be fake, sparkled around her neck and wrists. Her friends jealously *ooh*ed and *ahh*ed. In short, she was drop-dead, head-turning gorgeous, and obviously used to being the center of attention. Her friends looked like props, dressed down on purpose to make her stand out. Once the greetings subsided, she moved to the outside of the group and took up her spot at the head of the line, resting one hand on her shiny hard-sided roller bag. I knew those ran over one thousand dollars; I'd researched them thinking how perfect that would be for all my equipment. I ended up with a Costco knock-off.

When the agent announced that it was time to line up, Tessa and her friends were first. Arjun had put me into an early boarding slot, but I still ended up at the end of the first group to board the plane. By the time I boarded the plane, Tessa was seated in row one, on the left side of the plane in the aisle seat. Her friends occupied the rest of the first row; six of them all together. In terms of following the group, the only thing I had going for me was that it would take them a long time to get anywhere. They'd need two taxis for any excursion. If they all wanted to sit together at a restaurant, they'd have to wait in line. I was soon about to find out how naive my assumptions were. Money could buy you anything, especially in Vegas.

I slowly walked past them, dragging my suitcase behind me, studying the floor and the shins and shoes of the woman in front of me. Out of the corner of my eye, I saw a man in the row one behind and to the left of Tessa lean forward, just to get a glimpse of her. How the world moves for the beautiful, I thought.

I dropped my briefcase onto the first open aisle seat and shoved my bag into the overhead bin. I inhaled two small cups of coffee on the flight and then took a nap, knowing I'd need all my resources, mental and physical, once I arrived in Vegas. I hoped I'd be able to exit the airplane quickly, following the girls as they found taxis, and be in line behind them as they checked in, so that I'd know what rooms they occupied.

But luck was not on my side. Once the plane landed, I grabbed my luggage and pushed my way forward. In the terminal, I glimpsed Tessa ahead of me and hoped that someone in the party would stop and use the restroom. But they didn't. They barreled ahead as a group and walked quickly toward the arrivals area. Once outside, they moved as a unit to the private taxi area. My heart sunk as I watched them climb into a black stretch limo. At least I was able to catch the license plate. I repeated it to myself, fumbled in my purse for a pen, and scrawled it on my hand. I wondered why Arjun hadn't told me this important detail, and I hoped there weren't others he'd accidentally forgotten.

An hour and fifteen minutes later, I arrived at the Bellagio. The line for the taxi had been interminable. I'd tried Uber and Lyft, but both apps told me the wait would be at least an hour. The woman coordinating taxis told me that she could guarantee forty-five minutes, which she did. When we drove into the grounds of the Bellagio, up the sweeping drive jammed with people watching the water show in the huge lake in front of the hotel, it was almost one in the afternoon. I made small talk with the driver, but once I learned that he was from Somalia, where he'd been an economics professor, I grew quiet, at a loss for words.

After I checked into my room, another thirty-minute wait, I called Arjun.

No greeting, just an annoyed, "Why are you calling?"

No joy from me in return. "Look," I said. "You didn't tell me that Tessa would have a private limo."

"Of course she would," he snapped. "No one uses taxis in Vegas. Too long to wait."

"Well," I countered, "I wish you would have told me. I had to wait." I paused, waiting. Either he didn't pick up on my pointed silence or he just didn't care. "I'm going to have to invoice you for that as well," I said.

"Fine," he replied.

"Have you heard from her? Any idea what room she's staying in?" I asked.

"That's your job," Arjun snapped as he hung up.

Wow. I looked at the phone and shook my head. I didn't have time to point out that the delay had cost me valuable hours. In this hotel of thousands of rooms, I had no idea which one Tessa was staying in.

I changed into my Vegas day outfit: oversized sunglasses, floppy hat, the short shorts, one of the spaghetti strap shirts, with a pink sweatshirt draped around my shoulders. I studied myself in the mirror. The furrows next to my mouth pulled my lips down into what I thought was a permanent scowl. The crow's feet on the sides of my eyes were worry lines and the wrinkles across my forehead made me look anxious. I thought about makeup to cover those lines and bring out my cheekbones, which a counter makeup artist had once told me were my best features, but I knew it was almost ninety outside. Anything I put on my face would just melt. After slathering myself with sunscreen, I grabbed my camera, phone, hat, as well as a notepad and pen, and stuffed them in my bag. I'd have to return later to change for the evening; I assumed the women would return as well at some point. Now, to find them.

But I got lucky. I thought I was entering the same bank of elevators I'd come up on, but I ended up in a different place, in the casino. I almost stepped back into the elevator, to see if I'd pushed the wrong button, but as I scanned the room, I glimpsed Tessa. She stood in the same clothes she'd worn on the plane, leather bag over her shoulder, eyeing a group of young men at a roulette table. Her friends were nowhere to be seen.

I exited the elevator and strode across the casino floor. It was a noisy place. Electronic *bings* and whistles and *ka-chings* and jingles came from the slot machines; a tad louder than the piped in easy-listening music that reminded me of the Lawrence Welk tunes my dad used to whistle along to. Someone sitting at a slot machine laughed. Ice cubes rattled. Cards clicked as they snapped onto the felt of the blackjack table. A metal ball clacked against the chutes of a roulette wheel.

I slipped into a chair by a slot machine where I could watch Tessa on the sly. I fumbled in my purse for my credit card. I had to make this look authentic. The machine had so many options, I wasn't sure where to start. But I didn't have to. Tessa accepted a drink from a waitress in short shorts, stilettos, and a skimpy top, revealing generous breasts. A shout from the roulette table took Tessa's attention. She walked to the table and stood behind one of the men. He turned around to look at her, she smiled and cocked her head. Was she flirting?

A few minutes later, the other five women burst out of the elevator, chattering, laughing. They immediately spotted Tessa and hurried over to her, their voices tumbling over one another in their excitement. Tessa laughed and pointed to the roulette table, but one of the other women grabbed her arm and they moved toward the lobby of the hotel.

30

BY THE END OF THE DAY, I'd sat outside more luxury stores than I knew existed. The group started in the Via Bellagio mall, located on the second level of the hotel. They visited the Coach, Gucci, Aramani, Prada, Chanel, the Dale Chihuly shops, emerging with pink, orange, black, and red shopping bags. I loitered on benches outside, playing word games on my phone, and snapping photos as they wandered, trying to avoid the attention of security guards who must have been as bored as I was. The group ducked into a few casinos, and turned heads, but never stopped to gamble. They hit a high-end bar around six. I followed them inside, found a booth near their circular table, and watched. Tessa ordered a cocktail that came with an umbrella. Her friends ordered wine, beer, cocktails. They raised their glasses to her. I couldn't catch a word, but I did manage to get a few photos. They repelled advances from groups of men who offered to buy them drinks.

When they returned to the hotel around seven, I was able to squeeze into the same elevator, pushing myself to the back wall as it filled with women, perfume, boxes, and bags. Tessa and three of the women exited the elevator on the fifth floor; I followed them and feigned confusion as I stood in the hallway. Rooms 500-550 to my left; 551-599 to my right. Tessa and company went left; I followed. The rooms were laid out in a square, with a hollow core in the middle of the building. I could stand against the railing and look all the way down to the lobby, to the top of a priceless Dale Chihuly glass sculpture suspended from a complicated set of wires.

I let Tessa get a few steps ahead and followed her with a purposeful stride. I got lucky. She stopped at room 515, in the middle of the corridor. Even luckier, a potted palm was placed against the balcony railing directly across from her door. I strode past her, keeping my eyes averted.

My turn-around was quick. Twenty minutes later, I was back in the lobby, dressed in my evening outfit: silver dress, heels, sweater, clutch. I had put on makeup, which I knew would smear under my mask. I waited in line at the concierge's desk and made arrangements for a driver for the evening. Another cost for Arjun. After a long two hour wait, the women appeared from the elevators, dressed in skimpy, glittery dresses, fit for a red-carpet gala. Tessa's dress was short and hugged her curves. She carried a small black clutch and a black shrug. The women were exquisitely coiffed, dripping with sparkly jewelry, faces heavy with makeup, hair coiled and curled. None of them were wearing masks.

I trailed the group to the lobby; overhearing one snippet of conversation I found interesting. "Tess," one of her friends asked, "where did you get that dress? Does Arjun know you have it?"

Tessa laughed. "Oh no, he wouldn't approve. He likes to keep me all to himself." She lifted her hands over her head and shimmied. "But he's not here, is he?"

The women hooted. Tessa strode to the front door and slipped something to the valet. I stood behind them, asking the valet to contact my driver. Quickly. My ride pulled up just as the women climbed into their luxury vehicle.

"Hello," I said as I slipped into the car, "please follow that car." I leaned forward and pointed. "Don't be obvious and don't lose them."

The driver eyed me curiously in the rearview, and his look said it all. I was a jilted girlfriend or wife, following my man's mistress to see what she was up to. Didn't I know the saying: what goes on in Vegas stays in Vegas?

Ignoring him, I looked out the window. Throngs of people crowded the sidewalk around the Bellagio fountains, watching laser lights and jets of water pulse to amplified show tunes. People laughed and took photos. A group of kids ran up and down the sidewalk, playing tag, while their parents completely ignored them and talked in a circle. The limo turned right, onto The Strip, then right again, and hit the freeway, heading south. After a few miles, we exited the highway. We kept to a main six-lane boulevard that stretched for miles, gaining elevation. In fifteen minutes, we turned to the right, onto a road that led through suburban streets.

"Where do you think they're going?" I asked.

The driver replied, his voice muffled behind his black mask, "It gets real exclusive up here. After this development, there are only a few houses, but they are killer. I think a movie producer lives in one, a hedge fund manager in another."

It dawned on me that they were going to a private party. A ritzy private party. Just as I figured that out, the limo turned into a gated driveway, where a security guard sat in a lighted kiosk.

"What's the address here?" I asked.

The driver recited it to me, and I noted it in my phone, as well as dropped a pin on my Google map. "Okay," I said, "take me back."

"That's it?" He looked at me in the mirror. "You're not going to go in there?"

I shrugged. "No invitation."

"A pretty girl like you doesn't need an invitation," he said as he glanced into the mirror. "In that outfit, you'll be able to waltz right in there. There'll be so many people, you'll never meet the host."

I paused, wondering what I'd learn by trying to bluff my way in. "You think?" I asked.

"Of course," he said.

Now he turned around to look at me. He was an older man, likely in his sixties. His eyes were kind behind his heavy dark-rimmed glasses. "What's your name?"

I paused, thinking. "Let's say it's Angel. Is that a good Vegas name?"

"Sure," he said. "I'll get you in. Put a fifty in your palm just in case. But you have to promise me something," he added.

"What?" I said, as I fumbled in my purse. A fifty? All I could manage was two twenties and a ten. Only people who went into banks or had people who went into banks carried fifties. I wasn't one of those people. The ATM was my best friend. Another divider between them and the rest of us.

"You look like a nice girl. Things can get rough in parties like this. I've seen it before. Any sign of trouble, text me, and I'll come in and help you, okay?"

"Okay, sure," I replied as we exchanged numbers. My palms started to sweat, and I felt anxious. "What do you mean by rough?"

"If there aren't enough girls, then the ones who aren't there to get paid end up doing the same type of work, you get what I'm saying?"

I shuddered. "I won't be there that long."

A horn behind us caused the driver to turn around. "Yeah, yeah," he said. "I will be waiting for you. The valet will move me. You want me to chat up your friends' driver?"

"Sure," I said, eagerly. "That'd be great."

He rolled forward to the kiosk. Rolling down the window, he thumbed in my direction, and said, "Angel here for the party."

The guard typed into the computer, frowned, and said, "I'm sorry, no Angel on the list."

I unrolled my window, offered my hand with the money rolled up in my palm, and said, "Late addition."

The guard looked at me, at my hand, and then back at my face. "Sure, Miss, uh, Angel," he said. He took my hand and I felt the money slide out as he palmed it. He waved us along. "Enjoy the festivities."

The driver carefully navigated the long driveway until we reached a glass and concrete monstrosity with two-story floor to ceiling glass windows, a deck that stretched the length of the second story, outlined by a corrugated metal railing that gleamed dully in the lights from the windows. Dozens of people spilled out onto the deck. More people were squeezed into a great room downstairs, where purple, red, blue and yellow lights pulsed in time to the throbbing techno-music.

I drew in my breath. "That's a lot of people," I said.

"Yup. A Vegas party. No masks. You better take yours off if you don't want to stand out." He glanced at his watch. "Here's how it's done. When you're ready to leave, you come out, slip the valet a twenty, give him my number, and he'll text me. That's the most efficient way. If you text me directly, it will take hours to get out of here, since I'll be boxed in by other cars. Only the valet can get all those other cars moved."

He pulled up to the valet and I put my hand on the door. The limo containing Tessa and company had already disgorged its passengers and been shunted off to the parking area.

"Thanks for the tips," I said, blushing. I was glad to have this stranger keeping an eye out for me. I might need it.

Reluctantly, feeling like I was risking my life, I removed my mask, put it in my clutch, walked up the steps, and entered the door. A wall of sound enveloped me. A young woman in a red bikini that shimmered with silver medallions slid up to me with a tray of drinks. She pointed and smiled; her smile genuine enough, but not reaching her eyes. I shook my head and she slid off on what I now noticed were four-inch high black stilettos. She couldn't have been more than twenty. I wondered if she was a runaway, like Crystal.

I stood by the door and eyed the packed crowd. My driver had been right; I did fit in. My dress was spot-on Vegas. Showy, glittery, a bit gaudy, with a touch of tacky. I slid through the shoulder-to-shoulder bodies. Some people seemed to be trying to talk, yelling at each other with abandon. A man to my right was wearing shorts, Teva sandals, and a yellow T-shirt that read "Resist". He had a mop of wild hair that stuck out in all directions, like those memes of Einstein. Either a tech genius or a hanger-on. Another waitress, in a black shimmery bikini, tottered by on red stilettos, earning the interested glance of the man in the "Resist" T-shirt.

I needed to find Tessa and her friends. I fought my way through the crowd into a smaller room, just as packed. The sound of the music receded into a dull thump, the bass reverberating through the floor and into my spine. A staircase snaked upwards over the corner, and I pushed my way over to it, walking up a few steps to turn around and look over the crowd.

But the sight took my breath away. Out the window, the lights of Vegas stretched down the alluvial plain in a glittering, showy stream, just like the Milky Way. I could see all the way to The Strip, at least ten miles off, where laser lights of all colors crisscrossed the sky, leaving traces of red, yellow, white, green, and blue. Gaudy neon lights pulsed. White headlights and red taillights streaked across the blackness.

I heard someone come down the stairs, then stop. A smooth voice, male, said, "Beautiful, isn't it?" His accent was British, and his voice reminded me of the actor who introduced the Masterpiece Mystery episodes. Cultured, but playful.

Without turning around, I said, "Yes, it is. Never seen anything like it."

The man came down one step, then another. He was standing next to me. I could feel his presence, his energy. "The lasers are amazing. Do you see the pattern they make?"

I squinted, as if that would help. "What pattern?" I asked.

Before I knew it, the man had put his right arm around my shoulders and had drawn me close. He was pointing with his left hand. I tried to wiggle away, but his grip was firm. Solid. "Look," he said. "See the red one? It's drawing a heart." He traced a pattern in the sky, following the track of the laser beam. "And the yellow, that's a star." Again he traced a pattern against the sky.

I leaned away, then ducked down and out from underneath his arm. He caught my wrist and turned to look at me. It was the man wearing the "Resist" T-shirt.

"Hey," he said, "don't go. I'm Barry. You are?"

I scurried down the stairs away from him, slipped through the crowds in the smaller room, and then pushed my way through the crowds of gyrating dancers to the front door. I didn't see Tessa anywhere. She would stand out in a crowd. All of the women in that group would. After I took a few breaths, I plunged back in, this time shoving my way up the stairs to the second floor, a large open room with a deck overlooking the view. I wormed through the crowd to the deck. The view was as breathtaking as before, but the six women were not there, admiring it. Where had they gone?

Back downstairs, I circled the dance floor one more time, then slipped into the smaller room. Then, I saw Tessa. She was dancing, leaning in close to a young man dressed in tight jeans and a form-fitting T-shirt that showed every ridge in his six-pack abs. The other women clustered nearby in a group, watching, flirting with anyone who came near. I squirreled my way close and was able to get a photo. Tessa leaned in, putting her arms around the man, pulling him close. He towered over her, and moved his hands down, to the swell of her bottom. They moved in unison. I got another photo, the flash from my camera phone just another bright light in all the chaos. I risked a video.

After ten more minutes, the man took her hand, and they twisted through the crowd, up the stairs. One of Tessa's friends whistled. I trailed them up the stairs, but by the time I reached the second floor, they'd vanished. They must have disappeared behind one of the closed doors. I waited for fifteen minutes, fending off interested glances from both women and men, and finally decided to call it a night. Outside, I gave the valet a twenty along with my driver's cell phone number. Five minutes later, I was back in the car.

"How was it?" my driver said.

"Too many people," I replied. "But the view was spectacular."

As he swung the car onto the six-lane boulevard and started back north, I asked, "Did you get a chance to talk to the driver?"

"No," he said. "He was Somali. They stick to themselves. He was already huddled with his buddies. Not a chance of me breaking in."

I nodded. "Thanks for trying."

I'd formulated a plan by the time we reached the hotel. I'd place my button-sized camera in the plant across the hall from Tessa's door, and let it do the stalking for the rest of the evening. I could write my notes from the day, then kick back, order room service, and browse the internet, researching C.J. Little, Helen Brannon, *Ancestry*, and synthetic biology.

· · ·

When I woke on Saturday morning, I checked the feed from the camera I'd attached to the lip of the blue ceramic vase. The vase held a six-foot potted palm, and as long as the plant people didn't come for watering or plant-fussing in the next twenty-four hours, I was golden. The wide-angle camera was motion sensitive. Whenever there was movement in its frame, it turned on and started recording. It recorded until thirty seconds after the motion stopped.

It caught plenty of hotel guests on their way back to their rooms. Some stumbled, some strode with purpose, one even ran, as if she couldn't get to her room fast enough. A few single women, dressed to the nines, prowled the floor. Tessa returned at two in the morning. At two-thirty, three men strode into the camera's field of view. A young blond man was wearing a fireman's outfit. A redhead wore a police uniform. And a third man, with black hair, was dressed from head to toe in camo.

The door opened.

An hour later the men reappeared. They turned right, looking as vigorous as when they'd gone in.

Strippers? Hookers? Both? Who'd arranged the show? I wondered what Arjun would say.

31

AS I WATCHED TESSA AND COMPANY stride toward the TSA PreCheck line at Vegas McCarran airport at ten on Sunday morning, every muscle in my body ached from stress and exhaustion. My knees creaked, my lower back throbbed, and my head pounded. But Tessa and her friends looked as fresh and energetic as they had on Friday morning. And no wonder, they'd spent all day Saturday being pampered at a luxury spa that advertised hot rock massage and cucumber-lemon verbena facials in the window. They'd then visited a high-end hair and nail salon. Saturday night took them to a Celine Dione show, followed by dinner and drinks at Spago, the Wolfgang Puck eatery in the Bellagio. They must have made their reservation months ago, something else Arjun failed to mention. But I loitered in the lobby, hiding behind a magazine for the three hours they'd spent inside the restaurant. The women returned to the hotel by midnight and fanned out to their separate rooms. My camera didn't record any nocturnal visitors to Tessa's room.

Once the women entered the security line, I made my way to the car rental, where I picked up my tiny white Mitsubishi Mirage. I then drove to my new hotel, near the airport. It was a low-budget, quiet, family-oriented place, with rooms facing the interior courtyard, complete with a pool and lounge area. A group of kids was playing Marco Polo in the pool, while the tweens skulked by the vending machines, hoping someone would take pity on them and buy them a soda. I was sure that high-price escorts would not be prowling the halls of this hotel in the wee hours.

After a quick walk to the nearest Starbucks, I returned to my room and opened my laptop. My first task was to update my billing spreadsheet. Once that was done, I turned my attention to my report. By now, Tessa would be climbing off the plane in San Jose, with Arjun none the wiser. I was glad I wouldn't be in the room when my report hit his mailbox.

Three hours later, I had a first draft. I transferred videos and still photos from my phone and referenced them from my report, edited the videos for brevity and impact, verifying that the date and time of the recording was readable. Like I always did, I saved the file and emailed a copy to myself so I'd have it in case of computer failure. I always wrote the first draft of my report as quickly as possible after an investigation, in order to record every single detail. Then, I let it simmer for a while, mulling it over in my head, making sure I hadn't missed anything or reported events inaccurately. When I returned to the office on Wednesday, I'd review it once more, prepare an invoice, and send it along.

Draft saved, I set my alarm for an hour later, tucked into my bed, and fell into a deep, nourishing sleep.

•   •   •

I slept through the alarm and it was seven in the evening when I woke. My room sat on the second floor and fronted the long balcony, so I'd closed the blinds when I arrived. But I knew it would be dark by now. A perfect time to go sleuthing. I'd picked my nondescript white sedan just for this purpose. I secured my small camera to the door handle on the passenger's side of the car using double-sided tape, hopped into the car, set the GPS, and cracked the window as I drove south.

The air here, dry and warm, was nothing like the air back home. It rolled off my arms like a balmy shawl, caressing my skin in a light heat. Even though it was dark, the sky sparkled with light, from the Vegas signature laser lights to headlights and taillights, streetlights, billboards, and flashing jumbotrons. I quickly navigated onto the freeway and set the cruise control for seventy. The traffic was steady, but light, and I let my thoughts wander.

Thirty minutes later, when I turned off Interstate 15, I opened the window all the way, smelling the sharp tang of creosote mixed with sage. I pulled over at the turn onto 161 north and exited the car. I remembered the satellite view from Google Maps — miles of rangeland tilting to alluvial plains and mountains. Now, knee-high scraggly bushes stretched out as far as I could see, rippling in the slight breeze. The moon was almost full, and each shrub cast a wavering shadow, turning the desert floor into what looked like a living, moving creature. To the east and west, the land sloped gently upward, until it lifted, miles away, into steep, sharp mountain ranges. The steady stream of cars on the nearby interstate was somewhat comforting, but I shivered, realizing I was out in the Nevada wilderness, alone, and that no one knew where I was. Cody and I used to share our location with each other, but when we split up, that was one of the first things he did. He stopped sharing his location with me. So I did the same.

I reached the small town of Goodsprings a few minutes later and passed the truck plaza to continue north onto Goodsprings Bypass Road. I pulled over at the intersection, checked that the camera was still in place, then picked up my phone, and activated it.

The road I was on continued for miles, eventually ending at a quarry. As far as I remembered, the lab was the only structure on this road. After ten minutes of driving at forty miles an hour, I was beginning to wonder if I was heading in the right direction. But then, after I rounded a curve, I could see a large metal structure to my right. It sat in the middle of an immense parking lot, surrounded by a chain link fence at least twenty feet high topped with razor wire. The building looked like a cross between a bunker and several 1940s-era Quonset huts welded together. A guard house by the gate was lit by a small bulb. I could see the silhouette of a person in it. Five cars were parked in the lot, clustered under the single streetlamp.

I slowed, knowing that I'd only get one shot at this. I put on the blinker, angling the car so that the camera could capture the parking lot, the kiosk, and the building.

The guard put down his phone and looked up as I approached. He opened the door and stood, then turned on a flashlight that he pointed into the car, aiming it directly into my face. I stopped outside the gate and turned off the car.

"Help you?" he grunted. With the light in my face, I couldn't see a thing, but from his voice, I could tell he was young-ish, probably pulling a night shift to earn extra cash.

"I'm lost," I said. "Can you put that light down?" I asked.

He dropped the angle of the light, pointing it away from my face toward the ground next to the car. "Where are you heading?"

"Came from Vegas. Thought I'd come out in the desert to watch the sunset, but once it got dark, I got all turned around."

He leaned down. "It's easy. Turn around and go straight. You'll get to Goodsprings. Once you're in town, look for the lights of the truck plaza and then 161. It will take you all the way back to the interstate. Head north on the interstate and you'll get back to Vegas in about thirty minutes."

"Oh," I said in a small voice, putting on my best damsel-in-distress act. "I got way lost. Just in Vegas for a conference," I added. "It starts tomorrow."

"Well, you better get going then."

"Wow," I said. "I came a long way out of the way."

"You did," he replied, switching off the light. It was then I noticed the camera dangling from the roof of the kiosk. The small blue light indicated that it was on, recording. Well, I decided, I might as well go for broke.

"Where am I?" I asked.

"This here is a work site," he replied.

"Oh," I said, and continued with a bit of confusion in my voice. "A work site?"

The guard nodded. "Yes. And you better be going."

"Okay," I said, deciding not to press it. "Thanks for your help." I waved.

He watched me. Instead of backing up and pulling out onto the highway going in the correct direction, I wanted to give my camera one last shot. I backed up, drove past the security kiosk on the shoulder to the end of the fence, then made a dramatic U-turn, and sped away.

•　　　•　　　•

By the time I reached the hotel, it was almost ten. I'd driven about ninety minutes for a minute-long video. I hoped it was worth it; I knew I couldn't go back there again. I thought about the plain, nondescript building. It could have been anything. A light manufacturing plant. A pipe-fitting enterprise. A distribution center. Why was a research lab there, in the middle of the desert? To hide? Or because of its proximity to Vegas, one of the most anonymous places in the world?

I removed the camera and carefully dropped it in my pocket. Once in my room, I transferred the video to my laptop, then took one quick look before dropping into bed. The camera did capture it all, but it was grainy and, because of the wide angle and the distance, the cars in the parking lot and the building were relatively small. It would take some finessing to actually see anything. But I was pleased with my night's work.

32

S IX-THIRTY CAME EARLY, and I fought the urge to hit the snooze button on my phone's alarm. I knew it would take at least thirty minutes to drive across town to reach the P.I.'s office and I didn't want to be late. I stumbled into the shower, then made my way to the hotel's restaurant for a plate of scrambled eggs and a cup of watered-down coffee. I'd have to factor in time for a Starbucks drive-through.

The investigator I was scheduled to meet, Amy Begay, worked out of her home in Henderson, sixteen miles south of Vegas. The drive was against traffic, so even with my Starbucks stop for a black coffee, I arrived fifteen minutes early. Rather than sit outside the perfectly landscaped split-level home in the McDonald Ranch subdivision, I decided to take a short drive. But the streets were cookie-cutter suburban, and after a few turns, I found myself lost. The cream-colored stucco homes with street-facing garages and small porches, red tile roofs, white gravel with carefully placed creosote shrubs and wispy acacia, looked identical. The streets were empty. No cars were parked along the curb. No one was out driving. There was no evidence of any kids: no bikes or strollers parked in front of houses. No basketball hoops. No skateboards or ramps. I wondered if this was an over-fifty-five community.

I stopped and checked the map on my phone. My destination was just three streets over and two blocks back, but it took me a good five minutes to find my way there. The lack of street signs didn't help.

When I reached 2250 Driftwood Court, I parked on the street, even though the driveway was empty. The pavement looked as pristine as the day it had been poured. I took my last sip of coffee and crunched a couple of breath mints so I wouldn't have coffee breath. One of the downsides of wearing a mask, I'd discovered, was the odor of your own stale coffee breath. I checked in my briefcase for my file on Crystal and exited the car. The sounds of the closing car door and the beep of the key fob echoed in the empty street, announcing my presence as efficiently as a doorbell.

I walked up the walkway to the house, past the carefully tended landscaping. The door was already open and P.I. Amy Begay stood in the shade of the foyer.

"Shelby?" she asked.

I nodded and she said, "Come on in. Welcome."

I glanced at her as I stepped inside. She was an older woman, well into her fifties, with expertly coiffed hair and few wrinkles. I couldn't see half of her face due to her mask, but I could tell that she wore an open, friendly expression. I reached to shake her hand, then pulled back. No one shook hands anymore.

Her house was cool and dim. Everything had its place and everything matched. The chair and small side table in the hallway matched the furniture in the living room, to the right. It was a light, bright collection, with a dusky orange sofa and oversized chairs, a Navajo rug, tasteful large prints of desert sunsets and sunrises. We walked past a long wooden farm table in the dining room. A vase of sunflowers sat on the table in a tall glass vase. Six open-backed wooden chairs were placed around the table. Very inviting.

When I reached Amy's office, something clicked. Across the room from her desk, in a locked glass cabinet, was a collection of woven baskets and small ceramic pots. Her last name, Begay, was a Navajo name. I only knew that from reading Tony Hillerman's Navajo

Tribal Police mystery series. But with her blonde hair and blue eyes, Amy looked as Caucasian as I did.

She saw me glance at the cabinet. "I have a Masters in Social Work from the University of New Mexico," she said. "I lived on the reservation for several years, working as a social worker, but soon realized that social work wasn't my thing. I met my husband there. Now we live here and I switched careers. He's a detective with the Las Vegas police."

I surprised myself by saying, "My husband is in law enforcement too." I stumbled. "I mean my ex. Or sort of. We're separated." I forced myself to stop talking, appalled by my unexpected sharing. Not at all professional, I thought.

But her voice dropped, and her eyes fell, as she said, "I'm so sorry. These careers do take their toll."

I nodded in agreement, completely aware that our jobs were not the whole reason Cody and I were no longer together. But Amy and I exchanged a look and I knew that if we lived closer to each other, she would be a good friend. I immediately felt like I could tell her anything and everything. And she'd understand. The stress that came with being in love with someone in law enforcement. The challenges of being a P.I., with a twenty-four-seven job. The difficulties of being a woman running a small business. I wondered if she had children.

As if she could read my mind, she said, "No kids on this end. You?"

I shook my head. "Long story. But no, no kids."

She smiled. "We decided early on, no kids. I was already thirty-three. Tony, that's my husband, has nieces and nephews on the reservation who need financial and emotional assistance. So that's what we do."

"We tried and tried. Too many miscarriages," I replied.

A sudden realization crossed her face. It was as if a light went off and she snapped her fingers. "Oh," she said, drawing out the two letters. "You're *that* Shelby McDougall?" Her emphasis on the word "that" didn't escape me.

I laughed. "Yes. That one. The one and only."

She clapped a hand to her mouth. "I am so sorry. That was so rude of me."

I chuckled in return. "No worries. I get that a lot. Though not as much lately."

She gestured for me to sit in a chair facing the desk. "Do you want some coffee, water?"

"No thanks," I said. "I just had a cup of coffee on the way over." I picked up my briefcase and pulled out the file. "I submitted her photo to the Vegas Missing Persons Department, but haven't heard anything yet," I said.

"I showed the picture to my husband and he ran it through his databases, but there was no match. That particular young woman has not come to the attention of law enforcement," she said. "Yet. But he did give me some ideas of places we could check."

"The Strip?" I opened the manilla file folder. Crystal's eight-by-ten prom photo was at the top of the small pile of papers.

She shook her head. "No. That area is controlled by johns who run high-end escorts. She wouldn't be there so soon, if at all," she said as she picked up the photo. "Do you know if she's ever done sex work before? Back home?"

I shrugged. "It's her grandparents giving me all this information, so I don't have any way of judging what's accurate. Her parents won't talk to me. Her parents are quite conservative, and believe that once she got that first tattoo, she was lost. They pretty much rejected her at that point." I picked up the photo and handed it to Amy, then said, "She's now nineteen, and her grandparents have offered to have her live with them and pay for college."

"Generous," Amy commented, as she stared at Crystal's photo. I'd examined the photo many times — the young woman wore a deep-blue off-shoulder gown that complimented her blonde hair and blue eyes. Her makeup was perfect; with eyebrows plucked to a thin line and cheek lines accented. Her hair had been styled, falling to her shoulders in perfect curls. She wore a yellow orchid wrist corsage. Her date stood behind her, tall and solid, brown-haired and blue-eyed. He wore a tux complete with cummerbund and red rose. Save for the full-sleeve tats, it was a photo that could have been taken any time in the last twenty years.

"Wow," Amy said. "You just sent me the senior photo before. She's beautiful. And those tattoos are something. Even so, how did she go from this," Amy waved the photo at me, "to a runaway in Vegas?"

"From what the grandfather tells me, the parents are very strict evangelical Christians. Very restrictive. Purity contract and all that …" I stopped myself just in time. For all I knew, Amy could be even more conservative than Crystal's parents.

But, to my relief, Amy said, "That's a bit much. Can you imagine putting that on a teen? It's not realistic."

"So true," I said. "Anyway, the home life was unbearable, apparently. The mom married this very strict religious guy after getting a divorce from someone who cheated on her multiple times. The mom, Stu and Marilyn's daughter, was somewhat religious before the divorce, but after she met the new husband, she did a one-eighty and is now what they call a fanatic. Their words, not mine."

"How old was Crystal when all this happened?" Amy asked.

"Twelve."

"Any reason to suspect abuse from the parents? Beatings? Emotional abuse? Sexual?"

"I don't know," I admitted. "Stu never said anything. I asked, but he never replied."

"Well, I'm just going to make the assumption that there is something. Kids sometimes run away because they have a curfew, but to stay away for this long and end up in Vegas?" Amy shook her head. She picked up the postcard that Crystal had sent to Stu and Marilyn. She read it, then leaned in to examine it more closely. "Look at this, Shelby," she said, pointing to the stamp and angling it in my direction. "The postmark is from San Jose. Not Vegas."

"What?" I picked up the postcard and stared. The postmark read: "13 September 2020 San Jose CA". I sat back, wondering how I could have missed something so obvious. "What do you think that means?"

"Maybe someone mailed it for her," Amy replied. "You're sure it's her handwriting?"

"Stu didn't say it wasn't," I said, puzzled. "But I'm here now and we might as well stick to our plan. Thanks for helping me," I added. "How do you know Kathleen anyway?"

"When I was first starting out, I worked in an insurance agency as an investigator. She contacted us; she had a case that needed some legwork here. Slip and fall case. She had dug through someone's trash and found an airline receipt for a flight to Vegas. When the claimant was supposed to be on complete bed rest. It was a pretty easy case, and we became friends after that." She paused, then added, "When did you start working for her?"

"About nine years ago. Seems like forever. When she retired I bought the business from her."

Amy broke in. "Kathleen? Retired? She told me she'd work until she dropped."

We spent a few minutes catching up, and then ventured into the financial side of the arrangement. I'd pay her her hourly rate for eight hours. Given that I'd be completely on my own otherwise, not knowing anything about Vegas, it was worth it. I didn't mention my time was *pro bono* and that I'd be paying her out of my own pocket.

"So, how do we start?" I asked.

"I think we should avoid The Strip completely, for reasons I said earlier. We could start by walking along the old strip, Fremont Street, and check out 'The Fremont Street Experience'," Amy said, using air quotes for emphasis. "It's a five-block indoor mall. We'll cruise along just to get a feel for things. The whole area is supposed to be family-friendly, so there won't be any sex workers there, but we will see guys handing out advertisements for strip clubs and bars. We can start by seeing if she's in any of those photos."

"Do you have any inside info from your husband where we can find sex workers?"

She nodded. "He gave me a few likely locations. But that's all I could pry out of him. We have an agreement. We don't talk about our work to each other. There are too many potential legal gray areas. We would both hate to have cases thrown out because of off-the-record conversations. My husband would lose his job, pension, medical benefits, etc. And his reputation. I'd lose all my clients, people's good faith in my work, and my reputation also. Not worth it."

"That makes sense." I winced, thinking about all those late-night conversations Cody and I used to stray into.

"Besides," she added, "I think it's a moving target. The girls get driven in and dropped off. They get into the john's car for five minutes or whatever. No office needed."

I shuddered. "How much do they make?"

"Not much at all, as far as I know," Amy said. "The type of sex worker we're talking about, barely anything. As part of their arrangement, they get a place to stay and food. And drugs. Voluntary or not. Something to keep them hooked. Nasty stuff."

An image of the men entering and exiting Tessa's room crossed my mind, and I took a breath. "Well, we should go."

"Let me change," she said. She eyed my outfit: jeans, T-shirt, floppy hat. Big sunglasses and straw bag. "You look perfect. Touristy. We'll look like two women out on a lark, rather than two P.I.s searching for someone. Or worse yet, two undercover cops." She stood and said, "Feel free to use the restroom down here before we head out. I'll go change."

I picked up Crystal's photo and the postcard and put them back in the file folder, then slid the file back in my briefcase. I glanced at the framed certificates and awards hanging on the wall as I stood up. Amy's license was proudly displayed, with a dollar bill stuck inside the frame on the left-hand bottom corner. She also had commendations from the Henderson Police Department as well as the Las Vegas Police Department. I wondered what those were for. In addition, she'd served on a search and rescue team and was trained as a first responder. I wished I had time to get all that training. If I were still living with Cody and had a bit more disposable income, I might. But I couldn't let my thoughts wander down that path, and I mentally clamped down, putting those feelings into an iron vault at the back of my mind. I snapped it shut with an enormous rusted padlock, like the kind on a pirate's chest, and mentally threw away the key.

I used the restroom and was ready when Amy trotted down the stairs, wearing a skirt, a short-sleeved blouse, and a pair of sandals. She'd fluffed her hair and freshened her makeup. She looked like a well-to-do woman on a holiday.

"Ready?" I asked.

She nodded. "Ready."

33

BY THE TIME WE HIT THE STREETS, it was mid-morning and sizzling hot. I was grateful for my hat, but the mask smothering my face made me itchy and irritable. We started our walk at the east end of Fremont Street, weaving through the jostling crowds mobbing the sidewalk. Less than a quarter of the people wore face coverings. A man carrying a cup the size of a 7-11 Big Gulp bumped into me and sticky liquid sloshed on my foot. He gave me a bleary smile and muttered, "Sorry," as he pushed his way past me. I caught up to Amy at the next crosswalk. She already had three postcards in hand. One displayed a full-body image of a young woman posing on a stripper pole, while the other showed a series of provocative headshots, with "Girls, girls, girls," in bold italic script across the bottom. The third postcard showed images of young men's naked torsos.

"Where did you get those?" I asked. I hadn't seen anyone handing out anything.

"You just have to know where to look," she replied. We ducked into the portico of a casino and stuck our heads out. "See that guy in the sweatshirt looking at his phone, with his foot against the building? Baseball cap turned back? Watch."

Within a second, the man had pulled a postcard out of the front pocket of the sweatshirt and offered it to a man trailing behind his wife and two young children.

I turned to look at Amy, surprised. "Well, that takes some guts," I said.

"Vegas," she replied. "What happens in Vegas stays in Vegas."

We continued down the streets and within five minutes, I had identified five more touts. They all wore sweatshirts, which should have been an obvious give-away. No one would willingly wear a sweatshirt in this weather. All sported a forced nonchalance, pretending to be absorbed in a phone call or a YouTube video. But once I started looking, I noticed how they watched people, and only handed out the cards to men or single women. Never women with kids. Ever. We escaped into a hotel-casino and found chairs in the lobby. Amy handed me her collection of cards, and I handed her mine. Plenty of young women, but none were Crystal.

"Pit stop?" Amy angled her head to the restroom.

"Nope," I said. "Let's keep going."

When we reached The Fremont Street Experience, the air-conditioned indoor mall, I wanted to linger and cool down, but it was relatively empty at this time of the morning. We hurried from one end of the five-block stretch to the other, melting when we exited back into the punishing heat. An hour later, sweaty and tired, we decided to take a break. We'd walked the entire length of Fremont Street, both sides, and were almost back where we'd started. In that short time, we'd collected twenty-five cards. As we slid into a booth at an all-day breakfast diner, Amy handed me her stack. "As far as I can tell, she's not pictured on any of these," she said. "How about yours?"

We examined the collection, trying to keep the lot hidden from the family at the table next to ours. When our food arrived — black coffee and English Muffin with butter and jam for me, and a two-egg omelet for Amy — we tucked in, happy for a respite. It was hard to think of the women behind the images. All these lives. Maybe by choice, but to me it seemed like a difficult, unpredictable way to make a living. I was sure these glam photos of happy, smiling girls hid a much darker pool of manipulation and power and abuse.

"So, what have we got?" Amy asked.

"A lot of photos," I said. "A lot of 888-girls type phone numbers. And a smattering of addresses of bars and clubs."

"Well," said Amy as she balanced a bite of omelet on her sourdough toast, "I guess that's where we head next."

But that starting proved to be an ending. The first club we went to was closed, not open until six in the evening. The second was in a rough neighborhood where Amy's banana-yellow VW bug couldn't have drawn any more attention to us than if we stood on the corner shouting. We talked our way past the bouncer and dodged our way into a third club where it was pitch dark save for the spotlight on the stage where two very young women, wearing only pasties and thongs, gyrated. Neither were blonde and neither sported sleeve tattoos. It was true, Crystal could have dyed her hair, but these women were shorter and rounder than Crystal. One had a long, straight nose, unlike Crystal's small button nose, and the other woman's nose was larger. Much larger. Amy handed Crystal's photo to the bartender, but within a second, a bouncer appeared and escorted us out. Which was fine by me.

As the bouncer led us to the door, Amy held up the photo, but he put his hand over it, saying, "I'd love to help, Ma'am, but our rules here prevent me from identifying any of our girls."

She cocked an eyebrow and smiled. "Ma'am?"

The bouncer, practically a caricature of a bouncer, short, burly, muscled, tatted and gold-chained, with a turned back cap on his head, smiled and shrugged. "Ms.?" he added, and Amy laughed.

We continued for the remainder of the morning and kept going through the early afternoon. Of the people who would look at Crystal's photo, no one had remembered seeing her. One young woman, a hostess at a strip club, commented that her tattoos were unusual, that she'd remember someone with those kinds of tattoos. Out on the street, a young man shook his head saying, "My boss would never hire her. Those tats are too memorable."

By three, we were done. The last club we visited was on a side street in a seedy, hot neighborhood of North Las Vegas. We'd passed one crumbling building after another, and had ducked into a few bars heavy with smoke and loud music.

We climbed into Amy's cramped car. Within minutes, the air conditioner blasted us with cool air. I resisted the urge to yank off my mask and put my face right next to the vent.

She pulled out into the empty street and did a U-turn. "I think we should drive along Fremont Street tonight. In a taxi — you look out one side and I'll look out the other. You never know. And then we can drive to a few locations where we'll find groups of women. There's one place under a highway bridge. Another place by a dry canal. So how about we head back to my house? You can pick up your car and head back to the hotel for a rest. I'll pick you up around nine tonight? Sound good?"

I was still fanning my face. "Sure. I'll be waiting in the lot. What's our outfit?"

Amy thought for a minute. "Something that makes you approachable. Something that will make the girls want to talk to you. We definitely don't want to look like law enforcement or investigators."

"Agreed," I replied.

34

A FTER A SHOWER AND A QUICK NAP where I didn't actually sleep, but spent the time perusing Google News, my go-to brain candy, I opened my laptop and played the video I'd taken last night in the lab's parking lot. The license plates on the five cars were completely indistinguishable. Rounded blobs that could have been letters or numbers. I looked up the format of a standard Nevada plate and found that there were two types. One with a blue sky for the background, a mountain range in desert orange, the word "NEVADA" at the top, and the numbers below. The updated state motto, "Nevada Means Home", was in a chunky, friendly font along the bottom. The old Sunset plate, issued from 2000-2017, sported a blue mountain range covering most of the plate. "The Silver State," the previous state motto, was stamped at the bottom edge.

Four of the cars in the lot were definitely registered in Nevada. But one of the cars, the one closest to the building, an older Honda Civic, had a white plate with blue lettering. A smudge of red ran across the top and the bottom. A California plate. Maybe, just maybe, this

217

was the link I was looking for. I knew it was too much to hope that it would actually belong to Helen Brannon, but, in spite of myself, I felt a prickle of excitement.

I uploaded the video to our secure cloud locker. I emailed Lucy to tell her what I wanted. With her tech skills and a bit of luck, she could decipher the plates in the morning and have registrations for me by the time I returned to the office on Wednesday. I was already looking forward to home. Hotel life and Vegas were getting to me. When I left my room, the stale smell of smoke wafted toward me from the ashtrays sitting on the balcony railing. The shouts and screams of kids in the pool had become grating and shrill, and the hot, still air and bright sun made me feel like I was cooking in a heat chamber.

I dressed sensibly, in the clothes I'd wear home tomorrow on the plane. I carried my purse, empty save for Crystal's photos and my ID, cash, room key, and a credit card tucked in the small inside zip pocket.

"Hey Amy," I said as I pulled open the door to her car. She looked me up and down, appraising me. "Perfect outfit. How's mine?" she asked. She wore a black skirt, round-toed shoes with webbing, and a loose T-shirt. She lifted a small leather purse.

"Perfect. I think we should say we're her aunts," I said.

Amy shook her head. "No way. We don't look anything alike. You resemble her more than I do. You're her aunt and I'm your sister's best friend."

"Great story," I said. Amy slid into the driver's seat. As I started to get into the car, I asked, "Should we take my rental instead? Since we're doing a lot of driving, it might be easier. Plus, an obvious rental fits better with our story."

"Oh, that's a good idea," Amy replied.

"Go park," I said. "I'll let the desk clerk know you're using a spot."

Five minutes later, we were in the car, heading toward Fremont Street. "Another idea," I said. "Instead of getting a taxi that's going to cost an arm and a leg, I'll drive slowly up and down the street. You look."

"Okay," Amy agreed. "That's a good idea. Why spend the money if you don't have to?" She seemed tired, her bubbly enthusiasm from earlier in the day gone. I felt the same way. This seemed like a needle in a very, very large haystack. Impossible. I dreaded having to tell Stu we couldn't locate Crystal anywhere among the thousands of teen runaways in Vegas.

As I moved into the right lane, Amy rolled down her window. "Go slow," she ordered. "There's a lot of people out there."

I slowed as much as I could and ignored the annoyed honks from the drivers behind me. At a light, a car zipped up next to me and the driver gave me the finger, which I ignored. I could practically hear them swearing at the clueless tourists.

Amy smiled and shrugged. "Whatever," she muttered.

We passed casino after casino, with marquee lights flashing; disco, metal, or country blaring from outside speakers; security guards and bouncers stationed at every door. Groups of casino-crawling tourists trolled the streets. No girls. No groups of obvious runaways. At the end of the street, where I was positioned to make a U-turn, Amy muttered, "This is a waste of time. We're not going to find her here. We better branch out. Don't turn around," she said. "Turn left instead. We'll go to the highway bridge first."

We drove in silence. Amy pointed out turn after turn. When we merged onto I-15 south, Amy said, "We're going to exit in two miles. We'll be driving in some rough neighborhoods," she warned. "Doors locked?"

I glanced down at the driver door handle. "Yup."

A few minutes later, Amy pointed to the exit and said, "Get off here."

I left the highway and we were in a neighborhood similar to those we'd visited this afternoon. The streets were dimly lit. We passed small houses, tucked between bars, warehouses, and empty lots. After a few blocks, Amy instructed me to turn to the left and then to the right. Any semblance of life vanished; replaced by one story brick buildings that housed businesses: a welding supply company, a fabrication shop, a junkyard, a laundry service. We drove through block after block of razor-wired lots, utility trucks, with streetlights winking on and off, as if subject to mini power surges.

"It looks like the end of the world out here," I said.

"It's the real Las Vegas," Amy replied. "This is what most of the city is like, outside of the glitz and glamour. Middle to low income neighborhoods interspersed with miles and miles of small industrial businesses, all hanging on by a thread."

I slowed the car as we drove past a junkyard; I could see the shadowy profiles of two German Shepherds prowling the fence line. One of the dogs jumped up against the fence and snarled.

"Good deterrent," I muttered.

I drove for a few more blocks, finding myself just slowing at the corner stop signs instead of coming to a full and complete stop. At one intersection, two young men ran toward the car, jumping and flinging up their arms. As I hit the gas, Amy said, "High as a kite. We're getting close."

"They sell drugs there too?"

Amy looked at me. "Wow, you really are from the sticks," she said, shaking her head. "Stop up here," she instructed.

I stopped the car about a half-block from a bridge underpass. It was as dark as the inside of a cave.

"So, here's what we're going to do," Amy said, leaning over toward me.

A minute later, we exited the car, holding only the photos of Crystal. I used the key fob to lock the car and slipped it into my pocket. We'd left our bags in the car by design. Nothing to keep us hostage if things went south. As we approached the underpass, we held our hands loosely at our sides. Amy had warned me to look relaxed. "These folks are masters of the tell. They excel at reading people."

A few of the girls approached, wobbly on three-inch tall heels, but as soon as they realized we were women, they stopped in their tracks. Two young men walked toward us with a swagger. The one on the left wore a blue Raiders sweatshirt, the one on the right, a black one. I didn't know much about sports, but you'd have to be almost blind not to notice the Las Vegas Raiders signs plastered all over the city. They were just a few games into the season, playing to empty stadiums because of the pandemic, and already on an epic losing streak.

Up close, I could see a characteristic bulge in the front pocket of the blue sweatshirt. Some kind of pistol.

"Look," I called out, "we don't want to cause any trouble. We're just looking for someone. A girl. My niece. Can I show you her photo?"

Blue Sweatshirt held his hand out but didn't say a word. He glanced at the photo and shook his head. "Can you look?" I appealed to the other man. He peered over Blue Sweatshirt's shoulder and shook his head also.

"Can I show it around?"

Blue Sweatshirt eyed me and nodded slowly, obviously deciding that my request didn't pose enough of a threat to get excited about.

He followed me as I walked to the knot of women watching us. They were young, too young, and my heart ached for them. But their faces were hard and wary, and I knew that my sentiments would get me nowhere. I held out the photo, and the girl closest to me snatched it. "Who is she?" she asked.

"My niece." The lie rolled off my tongue. The girl shook her head and passed it to her right. Out of the corner of my eye, I could see Amy across the street with her photocopy, approaching individual women standing on the curb. The two sweat-shirted men were watching us: Blue Sweatshirt's eyes were on me; Black Sweatshirt's on Amy.

A pair of headlights turned onto the street, coming from the direction opposite to our car. "We're done here, ladies," Blue Sweatshirt said. He whistled and all the women walked to the curb and took up various poses. A hip jutting out here, a long leg, slinky in black fishnet extended over there. He turned to me and pointed down the street toward our car. "Go," he said. "Consider this a courtesy, but don't come back."

I met up with Amy by the car. She sprinted toward me, turning around to look at the women positioned on the curb like models on a runway. She motioned toward me to unlock the door. "Get in, get in," she said breathlessly. "Let's get out of here."

I looked at her. "What," I asked, "what happened?"

"I'll tell you in a sec."

Amy pointed, "Make a U-turn and turn left at the first block." She turned around as I drove, looking back toward the bridge. "Go, go," she urged.

As soon as we were a few blocks away, Amy sat back and said, "You leave tomorrow, right?"

"Tomorrow afternoon," I answered.

"Good, good," she replied.

I looked at her again, worried now. "You're scaring me. What happened?"

Amy sat back. "That bulge was a gun, right?"

"Yes, had to have been."

"While you were fixating on that, I noticed the other guy taking a picture of the car and of us. I don't think he could pick up a license plate from that distance, but …"

"Wow," I said. "I'm really glad we brought this car and not yours."

"I know. They probably won't go to the trouble of trying to find out who rented the car, but it was definitely an intimidation tactic. I did get one of the girls on my side of the street to talk to me. Hopefully, they won't figure that out."

We reached the highway on ramp, and Amy pointed. As I accelerated, I asked, "And …?"

"She told me a couple of things," Amy spoke quickly, wanting to spit it out as fast as possible. "Number one: That if we knew what was good for us, we should leave. A-sap. 'These two are ruthless', she said. And she repeated it: 'Cold and ruthless.' And, number two: She said that a girl like that wouldn't last long on the streets. She'd be picked up and moved somewhere else."

It took a moment for that to sink in. I put on the blinker and moved to the left lane. "What did she mean?"

"I think she was saying that pretty, clean, young women like Crystal don't end up under highways bridges. They're trafficked, sold." Amy blew out a breath and shook her shoulders, releasing tension. "But she might just have well been messing with me. She had a flinty look to her. And her hand out for some cash."

My heart sank. "Did she say anything else?" I asked.

"No. At that point the car drove up, so it was all business."

"We have to go back," I said. "Have to talk to her again." I pulled to the right lane.

"Oh no," Amy said. "Not happening. That is A. Really. Bad. Idea. Shelby, these guys are low level, they're out there waiting to prove themselves so they can move up in the ranks and get into more action and more money. We would provide them with just that opportunity. Do not go back there," she repeated. "And that's an order."

I sighed, but agreed, saying, "Yes, ma'am."

Thirty minutes later, I was back in my room, having said goodbye to Amy. We agreed to call each other in the morning at nine. As much as I wanted to return to that underpass and question the young woman again, I knew Amy's instincts were correct. It would only be asking for trouble.

But trouble found me.

35

THE NEXT MORNING, after a leisurely cup of coffee in my room and a long hot shower, I walked through the lobby on my way to the hotel restaurant. When I passed the main desk, the clerk called out, "Ma'am? Hello?"

I stopped and turned, not sure if she was referring to me. "Me?" I asked, pointing at my chest.

The woman waved me over. She was solidly middle age and the name tag clipped to the pocket of her snug blue uniform shirt read "Barbara." She leaned across the counter as I approached. "We've been letting all our guests know that there was some trouble in the parking lot last night."

"Trouble?" I asked. "What kind of trouble?"

"Tire trouble," she replied. "We had ten cars with slashed tires and one car with broken windows."

"Which cars?" I had a sudden sinking feeling.

"Most of the cars were in the back of the lot, where it's not so well lit. But they hit a couple on both sides of the building too."

"Are the police here?"

"They're on the way."

"Has anyone reported that it's their car that got vandalized?"

"Not yet. It's going to be a long morning, that's for sure. All the managers are on their way in, as is the head manager, who's responsible for all the hotels in this chain in the Vegas area."

"I better go check my car," I said.

"That would be a good idea," she said.

I exited the lobby and turned left, toward the corner of the building. My heart sank as I rounded the corner. My car was two cars down, and I could tell something was wrong. The sun hit the two cars closest to me with an even light, but the light reflecting from the roof of my white Mitsubishi Mirage was not even. It was puddled. I ran and stopped, pulling up short.

Both the windshield and the passenger window had been bashed in. Viciously, as if someone had hit them twenty times with a baseball bat. The two front tires had been slashed and the car listed forward like a too-heavy wheelbarrow.

I reached in the pocket of my jeans for my phone. I took photos of the damage. The roof was caved in. Shards of glass littered the ground. The glove box was open and, with a pit in my stomach, I realized that the rental contract was missing. With my business name and business address, my phone number. The receipt with my credit card number had been stapled to the contract. All gone.

I walked briskly around the lot, looking for the other cars. Wondering. Was this a hit on rental cars to get IDs? Was it random, kids out on a joyride, making trouble? Or was it just my car?

Along the back of the building, the rear tires on five cars had been slashed. No other damage. There didn't seem to be any distinction between rentals and non-rentals. On the other side of the building, more tire-slashing. But my car was the only one that looked like it'd been hit with a bomb.

I needed to call Amy. And Lucy. And I needed the police.

•   •   •

By the time I'd talked to the police at length, emphasizing my personal safety due to my missing persons case and our excursion last night, and contacted the car rental company, the credit card company, both for the missing card and the insurance coverage, I was ready for more coffee and food. My flight out wasn't until four in the afternoon, which would give Amy and I plenty of time to discuss what had happened.

While I waited for Amy in a window booth in the hotel's restaurant, I called Lucy. I caught her just as she was starting her day. She answered with a cheerful greeting, "Shelby McDougall Investigations. How can I help you?"

"Lucy, it's me, Shelby." But before I had a chance to launch into my story, Lucy cut me off. "I'm so glad you called," she said. "I was just about to call you. Someone has hacked into our computers."

"What?" My vision squeezed down to a pinpoint. "What did you say?"

"Shelby, I have an alert that pings when our computers have been infected. I know you have yours with you, right?"

"Yes," I replied.

"Have you turned it on yet this morning?"

"No," I said.

"It's a pretty sophisticated hack. I'm not seeing any weird ads or pop-ups. No clue unless you know what to look for. I'm running a scan now to see what I can find out. If you can help it, don't turn on your laptop until I look at it. You'll be back in the office tomorrow, right?"

It was taking me a minute. "You mean someone has access to all my searches and emails and reports and photos?"

"Probably," Lucy said.

I started to hyperventilate and my hands started to shake. "This is bad," I said. "Really bad. How could this happen?"

Lucy answered, "I don't know."

But suddenly, I did. I knew exactly what happened. The day I'd left my computer out, and on, when I'd gone to the grocery, and later, when I'd lurched down the hall to the restroom. The day I found out about the found child. I remembered how I sensed that things had been shifted around. In my absence, someone must have installed a virus on my computer, which, in turn, had infected files uploaded to our secure locker. When Lucy downloaded those files, her computer would have been infected as well.

"Thanks, Lucy," I said grimly. "Let me fill you in about what's happened here," I continued. "What a morning." I explained what had happened, starting with my Sunday night excursion into this morning. I tried to compress the story, but it took a good five minutes. "If you can run that plate in the video …" but my voice trailed off and I realized that would be impossible now. If someone was monitoring our computers, I didn't want them to know what I was up to. Not safe for Lucy or for me.

I said, "Scratch that," just as Lucy said, "I could. Whoever is spying on us already knows you went to that lab, took a video, and asked me to run the plates."

My voice was firm. "Better skip it for now. See if you can figure out what happened with our own security, and we'll talk about it later."

Lucy agreed, saying, "Okay. I'll call you later. I'll be in tomorrow instead of Thursday to clean your computer. I'll be in around ten."

We hung up and I rubbed my temples. I wished it was later in the day; I was craving a shot of something warm and soothing and highly alcoholic.

I held my head in my hands, feeling my lungs constrict, making it hard to breathe. Feeling an all-too-familiar panic and despair surging in my chest. But Amy slid into the bench across from me at just the right time. She grabbed my elbow and the warmth of her touch radiated through me. "Shelby," she said. "Shelby. Listen. They're just trying to scare you. No one is going to come after you. I promise." She jiggled my arm. "Look at me."

I lifted my head. Tears filtered down my cheeks. "I'm scared, Amy. Really scared."

"You didn't go back there last night, did you?" Her blue eyes were wide and open, searching mine.

"No, no way," I shook my head. "No how. I listened to you." I took a shaky breath and wiped my eyes, trying to shake off the tears. "I parked the car. Walked into the hotel, went into my room, locked the door, and climbed into my jammies. That was it."

She looked at me closely. "I'm going to call my husband. He can tell us everything he knows about where we were last night. Okay?" She dropped her hand, wiggled forward in her chair, and picked up her phone.

My coffee arrived, piping hot. As I took a sip, hoping my hands would stop shaking, she stood up and walked away from the table. I cupped the mug in my hands, relishing the warmth and the reliable flavor.

Amy came back to the table saying, "Love you too, honey. See you soon." She slid into her seat and placed the phone by her coffee mug. "He'll call me back as soon as he can," she said.

"Did you tell him last night what we were doing yesterday?" I grabbed a napkin from the holder and blew my nose.

"No," she replied. "Like I said we don't talk about our work. No overlap. But this one is personal. We have an agreement that when it gets personal, we need to let our partner know." Amy looked at me intently. "Don't worry," she repeated. "No one is going to follow you a thousand miles to Santa Cruz. It doesn't make sense. The only thing I can think of is that these guys needed to show who was boss."

"You don't think anyone followed you, do you? To your house?"

"No," Amy replied. "I'm one hundred percent sure of that."

"But how can you be so sure? We didn't see anyone follow us back here, and someone clearly did."

"True," Amy said. "But here's my thinking. As I pulled out of the lot, I watched my mirror, just to make sure that you got out of your car and didn't drive back to where we came from. I saw you exit your car and watched you turn the corner to the front of the hotel. At that point, I left, keeping an eye on the rearview.

"No one left the lot after me. I kept my eye on the mirror all the way down the block, and I even stopped at the corner and watched the hotel entrance and exit."

"You don't trust me that much?" My eyes narrowed, and I tried to keep the offense out of my voice.

"It's not trust at all," Amy explained. "It's safety. That's all."

I filed that away to review later.

"And after about three minutes, I left. No one followed me."

"Do you think they got a photo of you or your license plate?"

Amy shrugged. "It's doubtful. But I'm not too worried. Our house is alarmed to the wazoo. I do carry."

"You had a gun all day yesterday?"

"Of course, Shelby. It was in my purse. I wouldn't go into those neighborhoods unarmed. I just assumed you were carrying also."

I shook my head. "No," I sighed. "I'm one of those few P.I.s who don't carry. I don't even have a gun." I paused. "My ex never could understand it either."

Amy looked surprised. "He let you out and about without a firearm?"

I shrugged. "It wasn't his decision," I said.

"I know, but with your history …" Her voice trailed off and I could sense her struggle with what to say next.

But I stopped her, putting up my hands. "Well, maybe I should reconsider." As I said that, I knew I never would. I was just trying to placate her.

Amy's phone rang, and I picked up my mug again. I downed the coffee without even noticing what I was doing, and I signaled to the waitress for a refill. Amy stood and walked away from the table. I could hear her *"uh-huh"*s and *"okay"*s and *"I got it"*s as she listened to her husband on the other end.

Her face was serious when she returned. She slid in and picked up her mug, taking a big sip, as if fortifying herself. "Here's what my husband said. That spot under the bridge where we went has been a pickup spot for years. And for years it went largely unnoticed. None of the girls were undocumented immigrants. None of them were minors. There didn't appear to be rampant drug use or violence. Just a spot where a man could drive up, a girl jumps in the car, the man drives a few blocks away, and sometime later, he drives back, deposits the girl with the money.

"A little-known fact is that prostitution is only legal in some parts of Nevada. It's illegal, here, in Clark County, but is legal in some of the more rural counties. So the cops know about this place and let it slide. It's like whack-a-mole. If they shut it down here, it will move somewhere else." She paused and took a sip of coffee.

"Anyway, this spot came on the radar a few months ago for drug distribution. Heroin. The cops have not busted anyone. They've just been watching. So my guess is they assumed we were undercover cops. And my second guess is that when they found the rental contract in your car, they found what they were looking for. A woman who lives in California, looking for a runaway niece.

"What name was on the rental contract?" she asked.

"Business name, address, credit card. But you're right, I could still be someone's aunt and a P.I. as well." I set down my mug. "Thank you for talking me off the edge. Thank you. Something about seeing that car with the smashed windshield and window, and the empty glove box just triggered a panic attack." I tried to smile, but I suspect it appeared more as a grimace.

"I can see why that would be," Amy replied. She stood up and glanced at her phone. "It's almost noon. I can drop you at the airport on my way home."

"That would be great," I replied gratefully. "Maybe I can get an earlier flight."

•   •   •

At the airport, I was unable to switch to an earlier flight without paying an exorbitant fee. By the time I made it to my car in the off-airport parking lot near the San Jose airport, it was almost seven. I decided to stop in Scotts Valley on the way home and eat at my favorite restaurant, a Thai place with the best pad thai in the county. I could always count on the warm noodles and the crisp vegetables glistening with peanut sauce and a dusting of finely chopped peanuts to lift my spirits. At this late hour, I was the only person in the outdoor patio, and enjoyed spreading out, flicking through my news feed to see what had happened in the world while I was away.

According to the president, the pandemic was officially over in the United States. No matter the rising number of cases and spike in fatalities. It was time to reopen the economy, full scale, and get our children back in school. Across the globe, countries were trying to pick up the shattered pieces of "normal" life that remained. The optimists of the world had hoped for regime changes, the death of capitalism, and tectonic shifts in power structures. But so far, dismal realities of repression and control had become the norm. In India, Modhi had set up camps for Muslims. The civil war still raged in Syria. People in North Korea were still starving. Here, the pundits were starting to worry that our sitting president would not exit the White House if he lost the election in November. Locally, those who had lost their homes were suffering and our homeless population had spiked. I decided to look at puppy videos instead.

I'd called Lucy as I'd waited by the gate for the plane. She was still working on running scans and scripts to remove the virus from her laptop. She'd heard from the security company who'd set up the system; they claimed there were no traces of how a virus had wormed its way into her computer and wreaked havoc. She'd changed the password to her computer and had sent it to me on WhatsApp, which she regarded as the holy grail of encryption.

As I'd fallen into a restless sleep on the plane, my mind wandered to the smashed windshield on the rental car and my stolen rental contract. The destruction could be related to where Amy and I had explored. As the engines roared and the plane grew stuffier and stuffier, another thought occurred to me. Could it have something to do with my field trip to Little's lab?

$$\bullet \qquad \bullet \qquad \bullet$$

Erica, my housemate, was out when I arrived home. I unpacked, showered, sorted through my laundry and clothes. Once in my pajamas, I flopped in bed, thinking I should just watch some TV and try not to do anything of consequence. But I had to write down the events of the day while they were still fresh. I used my personal computer for the task, hoping it didn't have a virus as well. Nothing strange had popped up. No ads for Viagra or vitamins or jewelry. No random emails. It seemed fine, as fast as ever. To be on the safe side, I'd take it in tomorrow so Lucy could look at it.

I opened a file and jotted down what had happened this morning, then, turned to the more serious work of recording what Amy Begay and I had done yesterday. Using my Google timeline, I recorded every bar, street corner, alleyway, club, or liquor store where we'd stopped to ask after Crystal. We'd covered six miles yesterday on foot, in the heat. It had yielded nothing, except to verify that no one remembered seeing Crystal. The one telling comment we'd received is that she'd be hard to hire as she was too memorable with all those tattoos. In our nighttime wanderings, we'd driven thirty miles all told, with not one clue to show for it. I hoped Stu would understand why I had to curtail my search.

36

I WOKE THE NEXT MORNING BEFORE THE ALARM, tired, and feeling hung over, even though I hadn't had any alcohol to drink for days. I headed downstairs for coffee and breakfast, glancing out the windows. A flat, overcast day. A gray sky hung low over the charred landscape.

The door to Erica's bedroom was now closed, so I assumed she'd come home sometime in the middle of the night. After my morning ritual of black coffee, toast with jam, and email, I went back upstairs to shower and get ready for the day. I scoured my email again, hoping for something from Cody. It seemed like ages since I'd seen him, but in reality, it hadn't even been a week since the night he'd rescued me. I tried not to let disappointment cloud my day.

•　　•　　•

An hour later, I stopped by the Italian restaurant on the first floor of my building to grab a cup of coffee. I plopped into a chair at a table by the door, dropped my purse on the floor, and adjusted my phone in the back pocket of my jeans so it wouldn't poke me. Within seconds, Trish, the owner's daughter, placed a steaming mug of coffee on the table. She sat down across from me, setting a coffee carafe down on the polished wood surface.

"Long day already?" I asked, smiling. It was only eight, and I knew that Trish worked breakfast and lunch, went home for a few hours, and then returned for the dinner hour. She was all of twenty-five, and I had no idea how, or if, she had a social life.

"Yes. On Wednesday mornings we get our orders for the weekend. So I'm here early with my dad to make sure we get what we ordered. Mom doesn't have to get here until six to start cooking."

I took a sip of coffee. I don't know how they did it, but the coffee here, even the coffee brewed by the jug, had a deep, rich, flavor. So much more so than the stuff I brewed at home.

"Magic," I said. "Thank you."

Trish stood up and picked up the carafe. "Hey, did your friend find you?"

I glanced at her, puzzled. "What friend?"

"Some guy stopped by about an hour ago. Said he was a friend of yours from Vegas."

"Vegas?" A pit formed in my stomach and the coffee turned to acid.

Trish shrugged. "I sent him upstairs. Maybe he's waiting for you now." She noticed the look of alarm on my face and asked, "Did I do something wrong?"

I elbowed past her, almost knocking the coffee carafe out of her hand. Heads turned as I sprinted through the restaurant, slammed down the release bar on the door, and ran outside. I tore around the corner, sprinted down the sidewalk, leapt up the outside steps, and shoved the heavy front door open. I took the stairs two at a time, panting. My breath came shallow and quick, and all I could think of was the stolen rental contract with my work address on it.

If someone wanted to get my attention, they were doing a good job.

At the top of the stairs, I flew down the carpeted hallway. Everything looked like it was supposed to. Doors were closed; lights were off. But at the end of the hall, on the left, I could see a light. My office. Lucy had said she'd be in early. I hoped, I prayed, she wasn't in yet, and that she'd simply forgotten to switch off the light when she'd left last night.

When I reached the door, it was ajar, hanging open. Enough for the light to creep out. But not enough for me to see what was inside.

I tried to muffle my loud ragged breathing, and just for an instant, I put my hands on my thighs and dropped my head. I took one deep breath, and blew it out in a steady, controlled exhale. I straightened up and stepped to the door. I gently put all five fingers of my right hand on the frosted glass, just under the gold italic text I'd chosen for my business name, and pushed.

The door swung open. The outer office, Lucy's office, was empty.

An open laptop sat on the desk, with Lucy's black purse dropped next to it. Lucy's 'Life happens, Coffee helps' mug was on the desk next to the purse.

Lucy had been here.

"Lucy?" I called. I circled the desk. The laptop screen was blank, as if it hadn't been started up yet, or had shut itself off.

The chair behind the desk was misplaced, moved almost to the wall separating Lucy's area from mine. One of the guest chairs sat between the small coffee table and Lucy's desk, cockeyed, with the back of the chair facing the desk.

I still held out hope. Maybe Lucy had run to the restroom. Maybe she'd eaten something that had disagreed with her, dodged around the desk, using that chair for support. Maybe she'd run down the hall to the ladies', leaving the out-of-place chair in her wake.

I sprinted through the hallway and shoved open the restroom door. "Lucy," I yelled. "Lucy?"

No answer.

One by one, I elbowed the doors to the stalls open. She wasn't there.

Just to make sure, I checked the men's bathroom across the hall. Empty also.

The small kitchen was deserted, as was the common room with a printer, copy machine, fax machine. No one was around.

I ran back to my office and dodged around the desk, banging my fingers on the laptop keyboard to wake it up. It switched on and displayed a beautiful picture of the Grand Canyon, overlaid with an entry box for the password. Lucy had likely been getting started for the day when the visitor from Vegas arrived.

I typed in the password, but it didn't work.

Suddenly, I remembered that Lucy had changed the password because of our security breach. I pulled my phone out of my pocket, held my thumb to the sensor to wake it up, and swiped to WhatsApp. I found the password, a long string of letters, numbers, and special characters. I got it right on the second try. The screen opened to a Word file, a plain white rendering of a piece of paper with a toolbar and ruler at the top.

It displayed two words in all caps: HELP GU

With shaking hands, I dialed 911.

•   •   •

Four hours later, I'd repeated my story three times to three different police officers. Trish, the only person who'd seen the man, had given her description several times. Tall, lanky, well-dressed. Good-looking. A sketch artist was on the way. Without seeing an image, I knew it was not one of the two men Amy and I had seen on Monday night. Those men had been powerfully built, like wrestlers, not possessing the lithe physique Trish had described.

I'd called Kathleen right after my 911 phone call. She had dropped everything and had met me at the Santa Cruz police station. I'd been fingerprinted for crime scene elimination purposes. Now, we were sitting in a small interview room at the police station, waiting for the detective to return with the image created by the sketch artist.

I looked at Kathleen. "What can I do?" I asked, my voice small. I wished I could yank off my mask. It felt oppressive.

All indications pointed to the fact that Lucy had been taken. The open door and the out-of-place chairs. The words on the screen. Her coffee and purse still sitting on the desk; the tattered remnants of a regular, normal morning.

Kathleen shook her head, her eyes serious above her cheerful blue mask, such a contrast to this windowless, claustrophobic room. "You know you're on to something to cause this kind of reaction," she said. "My guess is that the man was hired to toss your office. He was supposed to go in, break the interior window, unlock your office door, and destroy things. To scare you off. But Lucy was there, so he took her instead."

"Who? And why?"

"Let's run through the scenarios." She paused, rummaged in her purse, and pulled out a tissue. "It might be the same person who bashed in your rental car in Vegas. Who didn't like you asking about a girl." Kathleen shook her head. "That doesn't really make sense though. Even if someone had wrecked your car because you were trying to find Crystal, there's no way they would have followed you here."

"I don't even think Crystal was in Vegas," I said. "Amy noticed that the cancellation on the postcard was from San Jose, not Vegas."

"Weird," Kathleen said. "I'll have to come back to that." She leaned in. "So, let's go over it again," she said. "Start from the beginning."

"When is the beginning?" I asked.

"Let's start when Dexter called you and told you about your mom's *Ancestry* email."

I stood and walked across the room. When I reached the far wall, I turned and leaned back, gazing at the worn linoleum flooring, thinking. My mind was on overdrive. The found child — a girl who happened to be the same age as Justin and Justine Boyd. As Megan's daughter, Annie.

A lab outside of Vegas owned by a man named C.J. Little. The equipment in that lab, along with the photo of the Boyd twins, pointed to genetic testing. In turn, this led me to suspect a connection between C.J. Little and Helen Brannon.

This scenario opened up another possibility for my wrecked rental. Someone from C.J. Little's lab had followed me back to the motel. They'd waited for twenty-four hours and then destroyed multiple cars in the parking lot just to send me a message. But how would they have known I would be staying in Vegas and where they could find me? The infected computers, of course.

I pushed myself off the wall and started pacing. "So two weeks ago," I said, "the night after Dexter told me about the found child, I started doing more research."

"And?" Kathleen asked.

"Long story short," I replied. It took me five minutes to fill her in on how I'd found the lab, discovered the address, and driven to it and filmed the outside of the building. How I'd captured the license plates of five cars and emailed the video to Lucy. "Then, yesterday," I continued, "when I called the office, Lucy told me that she thought our computers had been hacked. Tracking software. Something that allowed someone to access all our files, our searches, our email, photos, videos. She spent all day yesterday working on it, she said, and was going to continue today. On Wednesday. Not the day she usually works. She said she'd be in around ten, but obviously came earlier than that.

"She wanted to scan both my work laptop and my personal one." I reached the opposite wall and turned. "I took my work laptop with me to Vegas. I typed up the report for Arjun and emailed it to myself for safekeeping. I copied the video of the lab parking lot to the laptop and then uploaded it to the locker. Then, I emailed Lucy to tell her it was there."

Kathleen said, with excitement, "So the computers had spyware on them. As far as you know, the phones are clean. So whoever was asking for you didn't know that Lucy would be in on a Wednesday. They assumed she was just in on Tuesdays and Thursdays. He didn't expect Lucy to be there."

I spun toward her and pointed at her. "Exactly."

"Could the computers have been infected before you left on Friday?"

I stopped and slid back in the rickety chair across the table from Kathleen. "Yes," I said. "There's something along those lines I have to tell you." I leaned forward in my chair and crossed my arms across my chest. Then, I took a breath. "The night before we had lunch, Thursday night, I went on an all-night binge. I saw Cody that afternoon, to talk to him, and tell him what was going on. He didn't want to talk about it. He was so upset." My voice was shaky and I was about to burst into tears.

But I took a long breath and thought about Lucy. I needed to be in control for Lucy. "I walked to the grocery, loaded up on food and alcohol, and spent the night in my office, drinking. I left my computer and Lucy's computer out a couple of times that night when I went to the bathroom. I may have left the office door unlocked."

Kathleen looked at me in surprise. "You did what?

I put my hands up in self-defense. "I know, I know. I made a mistake." I stood and started to pace again. Faster this time. I was talking out loud. "So, let's say someone installed tracking software on my machine and Lucy's machine that night."

"Why then?"

"Opportunity?" I asked.

She gave me a blank stare. "Someone would have had to be following you to know you were there, alone, at night, drinking, leaving your computer unattended."

I sighed. "I know. None of it makes sense."

"Besides, how would they get past your password? Please don't tell me you left it on."

"I was such a mess, I probably did." I paused and looked up at the dingy white ceiling tiles, thinking. "Someone would have known that I'd found the lab. That I'd blown up the image of the lab and figured out what the equipment was. Someone would probably have figured out that I'd seen the picture of Justin and Justine on a shelf and found the address of the lab on a box." I started to pace again. "And someone would have known I'd taken the video outside that lab."

I worked through the timeline. "So whoever was doing this would have known that I knew about the child who appeared on *Ancestry*. And they would have known I'd done searches trying to connect Helen Brannon with C.J. Little." I reached the wall, placed my palms flat against it, and leaned in. "Because I know that woman stole my eggs." My voice cracked as I tried to keep my composure. "She stole my fertility, Kathleen. And because of that, Cody left me.

"If it's the last thing I do …"

I saw, in my mind's eye, Helen Brannon's face purpling, her lips turning blue, blood vessels bursting in her eyes, as my hands squeezed her neck, choking the life out of her.

I should have done it when I had the chance.

"Shelby? Shelby?"

Kathleen's voice came to me from close by. Her hands were on my shoulders, rubbing, gently massaging the back of my neck.

"You can't do anything about that now, okay?"

At that moment, the detective entered the room, holding a piece of paper encased in a plastic sleeve. She handed it to me. "Does this person look familiar?"

It was a sketch artist's rendering, based on Trish's description. I reached for the paper, half-wishing I knew who it was and half-terrified I would. Neither scenario was good.

I stared at the sketch, taking in every detail. The man's face was long and thin. A shock of brown hair peeked out from under a Giants baseball cap. Everything about his face was thin: long, perfectly straight nose; thin lips; thin, symmetrical eyebrows. His jaw was square and strong. His expression was intense, with the lips drawn straight and the jaw a bit clenched. He was good-looking, in a Tom Cruise-Mission Impossible sort of way. The details put him at over six feet, wearing a pair of jeans, a black T-shirt, and a gray sport coat.

But I'd never seen him before. I shook my head, saying, "No. I don't know who this is."

The detective sagged, the tiniest bit. "We'll put out a BOLO and start interviewing everyone we can find who might have seen him in the restaurant this morning. Let me know if you think of anything, anything at all. We have a call in to Lucy's parents; they should be here soon." She continued, "You are free to go. We've taken Lucy's computer and purse from your office and dusted for fingerprints. I'm sorry it will be a mess to clean up, but you know the drill."

She stared at me, hard. "Do not, and I'll repeat, do not investigate on your own. I promise, I will call you as soon as I know anything."

37

I COULDN'T LET IT GO.

Kathleen tried to convince me, unsuccessfully, to take the afternoon off. I knew that would be impossible. At the very least, I could talk to Trish, the woman who'd seen the man who'd presumably snatched Lucy. I could knock on office doors in my building to see if anyone had heard or noticed anything. And I could burn off excess energy by cleaning up.

It was mid-afternoon by the time I left the police station. The parking lot at my office building was full. Business as usual, for everyone, except me. I detoured to the restaurant. The lunch hour was winding down, and Trish was standing at the hostess podium, flipping through the reservations book. She looked up as I entered and gave me a tired smile.

"Any news?" she asked.

I shook my head. The phone rang and she held up a finger as she picked it up. "Ristorante Roma," she answered, "How can I help?" After a pause, she said, "Two for six o'clock. Name?" She scribbled in the reservations book, thanked the caller, hung up, then, reaching down behind the podium, handed me my purse, saying, "I picked this up after you took off."

I thanked her, then asked, "Is there anything else you can think of about the guy? Anything at all?"

She paused and shook her head. "I told the police everything I could think of. Shoes to baseball cap. The sketch is a dead ringer for him."

"Anything look unusual? Could you see a bulge in the waist of his pants? Like for a gun?"

She narrowed her eyes, thinking, then smiled quickly, her gaze falling on a person standing behind me. "One minute, please."

"Not that I noticed," she said. "Why don't you go sit at the bar for a minute? Get a glass of something? I'll be over in a few."

Five minutes later, as I was staring into a glass of soda water, Trish returned and slid on to the bar stool next to me. "Here's what I remember. It was about seven forty-five. I had just seated someone and returned to the front desk and he was standing there. He said, 'I'm looking for an old friend of mine. Her name's Shelby. Do you know her?' I remember thinking it was weird that he would be asking here, in the restaurant, instead of in the office building, but I figured maybe he'd already seen that your office was locked and was hoping to catch you here." Trish took a breath and continued. "I nodded, and he asked, 'Is she here now?'

"I thought that was weird too, because if he knew you, he'd know what you look like. But you can't see all the seats from the front of the restaurant, so, I figured he didn't want to go wandering around." Her eyes took on a far-away look, and I could see her replaying the scene in her head. "Now that I think about it, there was just something off about him." She turned her gaze to me. "Something creepy. Anyway, he said, 'Tell her her friend from Vegas stopped by.' And that was it. He turned on his heel and left."

I shook my head. "It doesn't make any sense. Why would he announce that to you? If I had been up there, and he had taken me, no one would be any the wiser. Lucy wouldn't have figured out until much later that I was AWOL.

"It's as if he knew I wasn't in the office yet, that I wasn't anywhere nearby, for that matter."

"I'm so sorry, Shelby," Trish said. "I feel terrible."

I shook my head. "It's not your fault," I said.

"The police were here all morning," Trish continued. "They had a warrant to search through the receipts, to track down anyone who paid with a card. So they could interview them." She shivered. "My parents agreed, of course, but they're worried that if it gets out, people will be freaked out because they turned over receipts to the cops. They're terrified their reputation will be ruined."

"I'm so sorry," I said.

After saying our goodbyes, I left the restaurant and returned to my car. I opened it with the key fob and dropped my purse on the driver's seat. I grabbed the flashlight out of the glove box. Time to do an inspection. As I was talking to Trish, a thought had occurred to me. How would anyone know that I was not in the office unless they were following me or knew where I was all the time?

It didn't take long to find the GPS tracker installed in the wheel well of the rear right tire. It was cleverly hidden, attached with a magnet to the interior of the hubcap. On careful inspection, I could see the corner of the small black device peeking from behind one of the holes in the hubcap. I pried the hubcap off and, using the tissue, lifted off the tracker. If only Lucy were here, she could probably figure out when it had been attached. Maybe even determine who was reading the data. I carefully set the tracker on the ground and replaced the hubcap. Then, I pulled a plastic bag from the stash I always kept in the kit in my car and dropped the tracker into the bag. I labeled the bag with the date and time and had absolutely no idea what to do with it.

Once inside the building, I slowly walked up the stairs, looking around, carefully checking the ground. Nothing was amiss. No crumpled pieces of paper that Lucy may have dropped, no earring backs, no nothing. I knocked on doors, quizzing anyone I saw. But people were only asking me questions. No one had seen anything.

Yellow crime scene tape covered my door, and I carefully unlocked it, trying to avoid the black fingerprint dust. I used my hip to gingerly open the door. Once inside, I flicked on the light switch, shoved the door closed, and checked to make sure it was locked. The place was a mess. The doorknobs, desk, and chairs were covered in black powder. The computer was missing as was Lucy's purse that I'd seen on the desk this morning. The drawers had been opened; the contents rifled through.

The door to my office, the inner room of my two-room suite, was wide open. I turned on the light. I set the tracker on the desk, deposited my purse next to it, and reached into the central desk drawer for the pair of latex gloves I kept there. I also picked up the heavy-duty flashlight I kept for power outages. I would go over everything once again and then clean it all up. I was sure I wouldn't find anything the cops hadn't, but it was worth a try. And it would make me feel like I was doing something.

I walked back to the front room and switched on the Maglight. At a foot long, when fully loaded with batteries, it weighed almost a pound, making a serviceable weapon.

Where to start?

I surveyed the small room, all one hundred and twenty square feet of it. I knew that because every month, my rental statement gave me the square footage and the price per foot. The front office, for some reason, cost a dollar more a square foot than the back office. I decided to start in the back left corner and complete a sweep, foot by foot. Maybe I'd find a stray piece of paper or some other clue.

I picked up the flashlight and dropped to my knees, playing it along the baseboard, wondering if Lucy had managed to hide a message there. I tried to imagine the instant Lucy had looked up from her computer, politely asking the intruder if he had an appointment, then watching, in shock, as he pulled out his handgun. I could imagine her fear, her horror. The first time a gun was aimed at me, I had no training, and my terror stopped me dead cold. I remembered, in living technicolor, the tiny barrel, the round hole, the cold hard sound of the safety clicking off. I shivered. The second time a gun was aimed at me, I'd had firearms training. Years of it. But it still didn't prevent that instant quaking full-body fear.

I shivered, shaking off the memory. Thinking about that wouldn't help me now.

I lowered myself to my hands and knees and examined the rug, inch by inch. I found a straight pin embedded in the low weave and wondered how long it had been there and how it had gotten there. I stood up and stretched when I reached the client corner: the two low-slung chairs and the small long table with a one-gallon water crock, a stack of pint-sized paper cups, a coffee pot, a small bowl of sugar and creamer packets, wooden stirrers, and a stack of cups for hot drinks. A now stale carafe of coffee, missing one cup's worth of liquid, sat on the heating element. Lucy must have been accosted just a few minutes after she poured her first cup of coffee.

I searched under the table, under the seat of the chairs, even under the table legs. Nothing out of the ordinary.

Then, I hunkered down on the floor under the desk, shining the light below the bottom of the piece of furniture. It was a heavy piece I'd inherited from the previous owner. At five feet long, it took up most of the small room, giving it a cramped feeling. But it had been free, so I'd agreed to keep it. A dark, imposing piece, I'd thought it'd be perfect for the front office. Now, it felt too heavy and formal to be welcoming, but I'd tried to sell it with zero interest. I'd even tried to give it away, listing it multiple times on Freecycle. There were no takers, so I was stuck with it.

Next, I turned my attention to the desk itself. I'd done a cursory search this morning, to see if anything was out of place, but in my panicked distraction, I hadn't noticed anything unusual. I sat in Lucy's swivel chair, switched off the flashlight, and put it on the blotter. I opened the top drawer on the left side of the desk. Pens and pencils. Paper clips. Post-its. Rolls of tape. The drawer below was a utility drawer where I found cartridges for the printer, batteries, envelopes, scissors. The file folders in the bottom drawer were all in place as far as I could tell. Nothing sensitive or confidential was kept there, just bills. Most of my bills were paid online, but I insisted on a paper trail, so every month, Lucy dutifully printed out all my bills and receipts and filed them. The drawers on the right side of the desk yielded very little. Again, pens and pencils in the top drawer. Random office clutter in the drawer below. And the bottom cabinet was completely empty; Lucy hadn't even had time to deposit her purse.

The black plastic trash can was empty. The forensic tech must have already emptied it. I pulled out the keyboard tray. Nothing. I picked up the keyboard and shook it over the desk. A shower of crumbs littered the desk blotter. I swept them into a pile and stared at them, as if they were tea leaves or tarot cards. No hidden messages there. I carefully moved the black in-and-out basket and the container of pens and pencils off the blotter, picked it up, and dumped the crumbs into the trash. There was nothing underneath.

My continued meticulous search turned up absolutely nothing. Not that it was a waste of time — I'd learned that the only clue Lucy had left were the words on her computer.

I sat back in her chair and swiveled slowly, taking in the room from floor to ceiling. From my vantage point, I noticed something I'd missed on my previous sweep through the room. The coffee pot was plugged into a six-way adapter. I'd replaced that coffee pot several months back. I'd plugged it into the wall, not into an adapter. I was sure of it.

Within seconds, I had the adapter in my hand. It looked normal enough. Maybe Lucy had picked it up for some reason. But maybe not. I pushed through the door dividing the two offices and put the adapter on my desk while I rummaged through my desk drawers for a screwdriver. I was going to take it apart, just to be sure.

And as soon as I'd unscrewed it and removed the outer casing, things suddenly started to make a bit more sense.

Nestled inside the adapter was a round flat disc, as small as a pencil eraser. A tiny SIM card was attached to it, as well as a memory card and tiny black plug, which I assumed was a microphone. If Lucy were here, she'd be able to tell me exactly what it was.

I dropped the device on the desktop and shoved back from the desk. I stood and started pacing, shaking my head. Sweating. My office was bugged. Someone had been listening to our conversations. For how long? I got down on my hands and knees, crawling along the perimeter of my office. And plugged into the wall socket under the table was an identical six-way adapter. I knew I hadn't put it there.

I was just about to yank it out of the wall when I stopped myself. Maybe there would still be fingerprints on it.

Quickly, I picked up my phone and walked to the hallway. I pulled the detective's card out of my pocket. When he picked up, I filled him in on my discovery. He said he'd send out the forensics team to pick up the devices and do another sweep of the office.

Fuming, I paced up and down the hall. Who would want to bug me? It had to be the same person who'd put the GPS tracker on my car. I thought about the sketch of the man I'd never seen. Had he done it? Violated my private space? My office? Why?

I suddenly realized that what Kathleen had said about Lucy being in the wrong place at the wrong time had been just that. Lucy had said to me, over the phone, that she'd be in around ten. Whoever was listening would have heard that. But Lucy had obviously decided to come in earlier, when the office was supposed to be empty. Maybe the person had been coming to toss my office as Kathleen had suggested. And Lucy was collateral damage.

I'd picked up that coffee pot at least six months ago. I could determine the exact date by checking my receipts. For argument's sake, I decided that someone had bugged our offices shortly after I got that coffee pot. Whoever was listening would have known everything. They'd have known details of all my cases for the last six months, including Crystal's. They'd have known that Cody and I were separated. They'd have heard my conversation with Dexter about the found child. My incoherent mutterings the night I'd been drinking and researching Helen Brannon and C.J. Little. They'd have known I discovered the lab in Vegas.

And then, it hit me. Helen Brannon was stalking me. She was keeping tabs on me. She knew about my miscarriages. She knew about my failed marriage. Maybe she'd been bugging me for more than six months and I'd been blissfully unaware. She could have been doing this for years. Maybe this six-way adapter was just the latest in a long string of listening devices that had been installed in my office. A string of bugs I'd never known about.

I slid down to the floor by my office door.

This time, I had to find her. I had to stop her. I had to make her pay for what she'd done to me.

Was I crazy? Losing my mind?

Just as I was about to call Kathleen, to see if my reasoning was the least bit sane, my phone chirped its incoming text notification. I tapped. A text from Erica.

"Pick me up two burritos from Pericos: one veggie, one carne asada?"

I sent back the message "Two?"

She sent back a heart in return, and I knew just what that referred to. Erica's new love interest must be in the house. I sent back a smiley face and a thumbs up, along with the message that it would be a while.

The two forensic techs, a young man and woman, arrived, interrupting my second attempt to call Kathleen. I showed them the devices and they quickly took photos and bagged them. As I explained how I'd found the adapter to the young man, the woman walked around the perimeter of both rooms, holding up a device designed to search out bugs or hidden cameras. Both rooms came up clean.

"I've read about these," the woman said, "but have never seen this specific model. We'll be able to give you all the specifications soon, but as far as I can tell, the microphone is strong enough to pick up any conversation in the room. The audio is recorded. The person who planted this can call into the SIM card and listen to the recording or download it."

The other technician broke in. "You could probably make it yourself," he said.

"Did you ever notice that the door to the office had been tampered with?" the woman asked. "That someone tried to break in?"

I shook my head.

"That's an old-style lock," the man added. "Easy enough to jimmy."

I almost smiled. Lucy would get a kick out of that. For all the security we had in place with the computers, the safe, and the fingerprint-sensored closet, we'd forgotten to upgrade the old-fashioned lock on the office door.

38

I FOUND MYSELF KEEPING AN EYE on my rearview mirror as I drove home. Usually, I found the drive soothing, the curves of the empty road mesmerizing, calming. But today, I saw sinister cars at every turn, waiting to cut in front of me or smash my bumper into oblivion. Both had happened before. And as I knew in this line of work, just because something had already happened didn't mean it couldn't happen again. And yet again.

I tried Kathleen several times, but she hadn't picked up. I needed her input. I needed to run my thoughts by her. There was no way I could take this to a detective without more evidence. Without at least talking it through with someone I trusted.

I was eager to get home, get through the niceties with Erica and her new boyfriend, and then sweep my room for spy equipment. I was also going to download software and do a full security check on both my personal computer and my phone. Whatever this was, it had to stop. Now.

Even though it wasn't yet dark, the porch light was on when I arrived, casting a warm, friendly glow. Two cars were in the driveway, Erica's white Honda Fit plus a silver Lexus. Erica was moving up in the world. Usually her dates, as she called them, drove battered pickups with cabovers, or ancient rattling Subarus with at least two hundred thousand miles on the odometer. I parked, extracted myself, and reached for my briefcase and the plastic takeout bag. The stress of the day suddenly released in a woosh, making my knees shaky. I felt like I'd just slugged back a few shots of whiskey.

I staggered up the steps. "Hey, Erica," I called as I opened the door. No answer. I dropped my briefcase on the sofa and threw my keys on top of it. I carefully set the takeout bag down next to my briefcase as I reached into my purse for my phone. I flipped the light switch on the wall. Even in the brightest daylight, the front room was always dim as the windows were shaded by the porch and didn't let in much light. The overhead light, a mere forty watts, flooded the room in a yellowish cast.

I called out again, "Erica? You here?"

Again, no answer.

The house was chilly. I pulled on my fleece jacket that was hanging on a peg by the front door. Maybe Erica and her friend were in her room, but if that were the case, she'd have some music playing, so I knew not to wander too close. I slipped my phone into my back pocket, picked up the bag of food, and walked toward the kitchen, yelling, "Hey, Erica." But there was no response. The house was completely quiet.

I glanced at the woodstove as I made my way toward the back of the house. The utensils were lying on the brick apron, instead of leaning against the squat-legged stove as they usually did. The shovel was there, as was the broom and the oversized tongs, but the poker was missing.

I shifted into high alert. Should I leave the house, get in my car, and drive off? But go where? And get who? Instead, I put the bag of food on the top of the stove, slipped my phone out of my back pocket, pressed the side button to turn it on, and held my thumb against the sensor. I composed a text to Kathleen, typing:

```
SOS. At home. If u don't hear from me in 15,
call cops.
```

I pressed Send and stared at the display, waiting for confirmation. Instead, I saw the message "Waiting for connection" and I looked at the notification bar at the top of the display. The Wi-Fi was off.

Now I knew something was definitely wrong.

I stuck the phone back in my pocket. I quietly picked up the shovel and hefted it. It was a flimsy thing, more for show than practical use. I lifted the tongs, appreciating the weight. They were about two feet long, weighing in at about four pounds. The tongs themselves were lined with small razor-sharp teeth. I made my way through the dining room, eyes focused on the kitchen. The door was open, but the room was in shadow. If someone was in there, and watching me, they would have seen me pick up the tongs. My element of surprise gone, I brandished the tongs and strode into the kitchen. The room was empty. Erica was not sitting at the table, and no shadowy figure jumped out at me from the corner. I dropped the tongs to my right side and switched on the light. Three place settings were arranged on the kitchen table.

Slowly picking my way through the kitchen, I yanked open the door to the back patio. It was empty. I turned toward the door that led to Erica's room, her master suite on the first floor. The door was ajar, and I strode to it, holding the tongs in front of me like a sword. I shoved the door open and barged in, ready to slash to the right or left. But both the bedroom and bathroom were empty. Breath wooshed out of me and my arms shook as I dropped the tongs.

Erica and her friend must be in the studio or out on a walk. I sank down on the foot of her bed and stared blankly across the room. My eyes landed on her desk, a jumble of books and paper, boxes of clay, hand-thrown pots and mugs. The router sat next to her computer monitor. Instead of displaying an array of flickering green lights, it was dark. I wiggled it forward.

The power cable had been pulled out of the back of the device.

I plugged it back in and sat on the edge of her bed. What was going on? A chime from my phone interrupted my thoughts. I glanced at it and realized that the message to Kathleen had gone through. Just as I was about to text her to cancel it, I heard a muffled scream from upstairs.

I dropped my phone and heard it smash on the floor. Glass crunched under my feet. Without a second glance, I ran out of the bedroom, through the kitchen and living room to the staircase. I took the stairs two at a time, careening to a halt when I reached the second floor. I wasn't going to surprise anyone here; they'd have heard me coming. I hurried down the hall and yanked open the bathroom door; I didn't even have to turn on the light to tell that no one was hiding in there. The hall closet, lined with shelves holding towels and sheets, was no place to hide anyone, but I pulled the door open quickly, glancing in as I slid past. My room was just as I'd left it this morning. Bed unmade. Curtains drawn. Clothes on the floor.

I hurried back out of my room and stared at the guest room across the hall, where a crack of light snuck out from below the door.

I lifted up the tongs, holding them like a baseball bat. "Erica?" I called. "You in there?"

No answer.

I pushed the bottom of the door with my right foot and stepped in.

And then, I froze.

Erica sat upright on the edge of the bed, back ramrod straight, wearing only a frilly pink bra and a pink thong. Her eyes were wide, as if she was trying to communicate something critical. She worked her jaw, but a gag prevented her from saying anything. She slid her eyes to the left. But it was already too late. As a dark figure blurred into my vision, dodging out from behind the door that opened into the room, I took it all in, in one terrifying glimpse. Erica's feet were planted solidly, soles on the ground. Her ankles were bound. And she was shaking, in a full-on body convulsion, as if she were sitting in a walk-in freezer.

A crack, a sudden, jarring pain on the side of my head, and I dropped, whacking my head on the floor as I fell. Everything went dark.

39

I SURFACED TO A ROCKING, THROBBING MOTION, like I was in the engine room of a ship. The sickly-sweet smell of gasoline swirled around me and I felt like I was about to puke. Still half-out, I tried to roll over and escape the odor, but as I turned, my shoulders and knees slammed against a hard surface above me.

I pried my eyes open. Blackness.

I blinked, lifting my right hand to my face to wipe my eyes. A chain clanked and my movement jolted to a halt. I jerked both hands to my face and was thwarted again. A coldness seared my skin above the top of my jeans, as startling as a burn.

I started to hyperventilate. With each shallow breath, the surface above pressed down. Blackness drilled down. Sweat dripped into my eyes. The nauseating odor of gasoline and oil was making me choke. I desperately needed to cover my mouth. I tried, again, to touch my face. Again, my hands jerked to a stop inches from my nose.

Finally, I realized I was handcuffed. With terrifying clarity, I understood that the handcuffs were attached by a short chain to another chain encircling my waist.

I was shackled.

I blinked and blinked again, squeezing my eyes shut and opening them several times.

Think, Shelby, think.

My childhood prayer, the one I'd relied on in years past flashed through my mind. "Please be okay. Please be okay. Please be okay." I could recite that for hours, I knew. It might soothe me.

But it wouldn't change any of the facts. And it wouldn't help me get out of here.

A bolt of adrenaline coursed through me, starting in my gut and rising up through my lungs and my throat. I screamed. The sound reverberated and bounced back at me. I screamed again. And again, and again.

The shrill sound rocketing through my prison jolted me awake.

I shook my head, willing away the fuzziness. Willing my eyes to see. Even though it was still pitch-black, my jail cell snapped into focus in my mind's eye. I could imagine it as clearly as if I had a flashlight. I was wedged on my side, curled in a fetal position, with my kneecaps almost hitting my chin. My wrists were handcuffed and shackled to a chain around my waist. My hips dug into a hard surface below and my shoulder grazed a hard surface above. I was barefoot.

Even though I still wore my fleece jacket, I was cold. Chilly air blew against my back, travelling up and down my spine. I listened, straining to hear what was around me. I could feel steady vibrations through the floor of my coffin. The engine noise slowed and quickened.

I had to be in the trunk of a car.

Then, I began to hyperventilate again. Sweat streamed down my face.

I needed to breathe. Wasn't that what the yoga teacher had said? We'd started class with deep breathing, counting our breaths. I counted now, inhaling to the count of two, and blowing air out to the count of three. Over and over. I don't know how long it took, but finally, the terror subsided and I could think.

I was alone in this small space. Thank goodness for that. I hoped that Erica was still at home, that Kathleen had received my text and had called someone. For now, I'd operate under that assumption. There was nothing I could do about it, in any case. Other than escape.

The car swayed, as if it was moving from one lane on the highway to another. I was flung from side to side in my small space, shoved violently, as if I were playing Crack the Whip and was the last, unfortunate, person in the chain.

Whoever had taken Lucy had come for me. Erica was bait.

To soothe myself, to tamp down the increasing panic, I started counting out loud. "One-Mississippi, Two-Mississippi, Three-Mississippi …" until I reached sixty, when I started again. After thirty cycles, I lost track of how many times I counted to sixty. Maybe twenty minutes had passed. A few minutes later, I felt the car slow, sliding into a right-turning arc. My body shifted.

The car turned to the right, followed by a left turn after the count of five. The car picked up speed, but after the count of ten, turned to the right again, slowly bumping over what I assumed was hard-packed dirt. Where were we? I must have been out, unconscious, as the person wrestled me into the car and started the long drive to the highway. I had no idea where we could possibly be. Hopefully still in the six hundred or so square miles of Santa Cruz County.

A few minutes later the car stopped. The driver turned off the engine. I heard a car door open, and felt the car spring up as someone exited the car. The person slammed the door. Not worried about stealth, I assumed. The chirp of the key fob indicated that all doors were locked. I heard the person walk away.

I yelled. I beat my hands against the floor of the trunk. I kicked as best I could, curling into as small a ball as possible to keep the chain slack. When no one came, I scooted around in the trunk, trying to run my hands along the carpet. My hands found a smooth plastic circle in the surface, but any latch or dial had been removed.

I almost gave up, ready to resign myself to whatever was coming next. I could feel the panic returning.

But a little voice, from somewhere, my voice of self-preservation, started talking. It was Cody's voice, then Dexter's, then Kathleen's, followed by Megan's, Lucy's, Erica's, my mother's. Even Amy Begay. Over and over, in each voice, it repeated, "Shelby. Don't. Give. Up. Don't. Give. Up."

Again, I breathed, counting my breaths.

I started to shiver. Even though it was only the end of September, the nights were growing cool, and I realized that I'd been sitting in a cold tin box for the better part of a few hours. The temperature was probably in the mid-fifties and my prison felt like a walk-in refrigerator. Cold seeped in underneath me and where my feet and head touched the metal sides of the trunk. A chill tickled my neck. I didn't think I would die from this cold, but I was uncomfortable.

And I needed to pee.

Suddenly angry, furious, righteously pissed off that I was here, stuffed in a trunk, and left to rot, I decided to do something about it. I scraped my fingernails along the carpet, making sure I was leaving enough DNA for identification and also inserting bits of fiber under my fingernails in return. As small as I made myself, and no matter how I twisted my head and swung my hair around, I could not reach a single strand to pull out and leave behind. I yanked a button off my blouse and stowed it underneath me, hoping it would be lost in the darkness, when, if, I ever got out of here. And then, I peed, the warm liquid comforting for a few minutes until I grew cold and it chilled me even more.

I waited, harnessing that anger. Someone would come eventually, and when they did, they would get an earful.

I continued to count, "One-Mississippi, Two-Mississippi, Three-Mississippi ..." The mantra kept my mind clear and my anger intact. When I reached "Five-hundred-Mississippi," I heard footsteps and the sound of voices approaching the car. The key fob chirped and the trunk popped open. A light played in my direction and I was temporarily blinded.

"Dammit. She peed herself." A man spoke, disgust rippling in his tone.

"My car," another man shouted. "Goddamn. My brand-new car." I then knew I was in the silver Lexus I'd seen in the driveway at home. The car driven by whoever had tied up Erica. Maybe the same car as the one driven by the man who'd taken Lucy.

Then, his voice came out in a low pitch as he muttered, "You little bitch." I could hear the menace, the threat, the tone: a promise of something more to come. A tone designed to stop someone in their tracks.

But I could not allow that. If I didn't do something now, it would all be over. So I spit.

And I screamed. A full out, long, shrill, horror-movie scream.

Something slammed into my cheek, and before I passed out, all I could think was how much I hoped someone had heard it.

40

THIS TIME, IT WAS NOT SO EASY to come out of the fog. My head pounded. Every shallow inhale made my head feel like I'd been clobbered again. My neck was stiff and my shoulders burned. My back was on fire. My feet were blocks of ice. My knees ached, my shins were cramping, and my arms, cuffed behind my back around a pole, trembled. I sat on a frigid, unforgiving surface. I shifted positions, drawing my legs in close to my chest and hunching, but that put more strain on my shoulders. I forced myself to breathe, remembering to count each inhale and exhale. "One-Mississippi, Two-Mississippi, Three-Mississippi …"

But a quiet voice, small and hesitant, squeaked out from a corner of the room, interrupting me. "Hello? Who's there?"

I snapped my head in the direction of the sound. "Hello?" I asked.

"Shelby?" The woman's voice was hesitant.

"Lucy?" I sagged, tension spilling from my shoulders. "Lucy, is that you?"

"It's me." The voice was ragged, but unmistakably Lucy's.

"Thank goodness," I said. "I was so worried. Lucy, you're here. You're alive." I bit back a sob as I said, "I am so sorry."

I could hear Lucy shift positions. "I don't really know what happened," she said. "I can't stop thinking about it. I was in the office, getting my laptop set up and then this guy appeared at the door. I asked how I could help him and he pulled out a gun. I couldn't do anything," she said, her voice a plea. "I froze."

"Lucy," I replied. "You did do something. You left us a message on the laptop."

"But I froze, Shelby." Lucy started to cry. "I was so scared, too scared to run. Too scared to push past him and run away." Her sobs grew louder and I could hear the anguish in her voice. "I just froze. I thought I would react better."

"Shh, shh," I said, trying to keep my voice low, calm. "Lucy, you reacted just fine. You're alive. You did what you had to do to stay alive. When someone is pointing a gun at you, you do what you need to do to survive."

She cried even harder.

"Lucy," I said, trying to cut through her sobs. "Lucy. Shh, shh. It will be okay. We'll get out of this. Okay?" I shifted and sat up straight, twisting around to face her. "Let's take an inventory."

My eyes had adjusted to the dark now and I could make out her shape against the blackness. She was huddled against the wall, one arm behind her, with her knees to her chin.

"Are you handcuffed?" I asked.

Something clanked and I could see that she was yanking her right arm straight forward. But her range of motion was restricted, and her movement jerked to a stop. "Yes," she said. "My left hand is cuffed to a pipe."

"Your right hand is free?"

"Yes," she said.

"Can you stand up?"

She answered, "No," but didn't say anything else.

"My hands are cuffed behind me," I told her. "Around a pole. Did you notice it when they brought you in?"

"No," she replied. "I was blindfolded when they brought me here. When they took me to use the restroom earlier, they put a hood over my head."

"Have they brought you any food?"

"No," she said.

"Did anyone hurt you?" I asked.

She was quiet for a moment and then answered, her voice strained, "Let's not go there."

I clenched my jaw and swore. I would find whoever had harmed Lucy and … but I held my reaction in check. I needed to get free first.

"We will get out of this," I vowed. "I promise. Okay?"

Lucy was quiet for a long time. She squirreled her knees to her chest and dropped her head. Her hair covered her face, as if she were trying to shut out the world. When she spoke, her voice came out small, like a child's. "It seems impossible, Shelby." It wasn't a question. Just a statement.

"Lucy," I snapped, "don't say that. Don't even think it. We are together. We are still alive. We are talking to each other. We will figure something out. We will get out of here."

I squirmed, sliding my butt on the ground, inching over the smooth cold concrete. I tried to lie down, to extend my feet and bridge the gap between us, but she was too far away.

I repeated, "Lucy. We'll be okay. I promise."

Silence.

I continued, "We should probably try to get some rest. Are you able to slide to the floor and stretch out?"

"No," Lucy replied. "My arm is up and behind my neck. There's only one way I can sit without too much tugging, but it hurts."

I lowered my wrists to the ground and pulled my feet up, curling around the pole. "Well, if it's any consolation, I'm in the same boat. I'm contorted around this pole. My knees are starting to throb. These handcuffs are too damn tight and my wrists hurt. My shoulders are killing me. And my feet are freezing. They took my shoes."

Then, I chuckled. "And, I peed my pants on the way here, getting pee all over the trunk of the guy's car. He was ticked. But now, I'm paying for it. My undies are riding up and my butt is starting to chafe."

Lucy gave a small laugh. That was a good sign.

"Night, Lucy," I said.

"Night," she replied.

I tried to sleep, but it proved impossible. My options for trying to get comfortable were nonexistent. I could either stand up with my hands cuffed behind me, around the pole, or sit on the floor, leaning against it with my hands behind me. I tried to stretch by leaning forward and easing the strain on my shoulders. That helped, but within seconds, the burning started again. I twisted again, trying to find a position that was the least bit comfortable.

We needed to act. Somehow, we needed to take matters into our own hands and control the situation.

41

"LUCY," I HISSED. "Wake up. I have an idea."

I pushed myself up, standing as tall as I could. My legs protested. I could hear Lucy move, pressing her back to the wall, sitting up. Then, she froze, as if paralyzed.

We heard a rattle outside the door as someone inserted a key into the lock. Hinges squeaked as the heavy metal door was opened. Dim yellow light spilled in from the hallway, silhouetting the figure standing in the door. I quickly scanned the room to get a visual. I was positioned near the center of the room. I looked up. The pole I was chained to looked like a gray PVC sewage pipe. But it was too slender for sewage. It was attached to the ceiling with a black plastic fitting. I twisted and looked down; below me, the pipe fed into the floor, held in place by a sturdy metal collar.

Lucy sat against the far wall, arm over her head, chained to a pipe that ran along the length of the wall at waist height. She was hunched over and refused to look up.

I glanced around the room. A stack of boxes stood in a corner. Save for a utility sink and a shelf, the room was otherwise empty.

A figure approached, wearing a tight-fitting T-shirt and a pair of blue scrubs.

"Who are you?" I asked.

No answer.

"Who are you?" I repeated.

"No one," he replied. "I was told to bring you this." He swung a bucket up in the air and I flashed back to when I'd been a prisoner years earlier. How a bucket of pee had helped me escape. I wondered if it would work again, but, chained up as I was, immediately dismissed that idea.

"I'm not going to be able to use that," I said. "You've got us tied up here."

He stopped well away from us, shrugged, and drop-kicked the bucket in Lucy's direction. It landed and bounced, rolling well outside of her reach.

"Not my problem," he said. He sauntered toward Lucy. "How you doing, darling?" he asked.

She clenched her free hand around her knees and hid her head.

"Cat got your tongue?" he asked, crouching in front of her.

She remained silent and he grabbed her chin, twisting her face up so she was forced to look at him.

"See you later, sweetheart," he said. "I'll be back as soon as my shift is over."

Lucy's face contorted with fright.

"Hey, leave her alone," I shouted.

"Can't wait," he said to her, ignoring me.

"Hey," I shouted again. "Asshole."

He spun on his heels, stood, and faced me.

"What did you say?" he asked.

"I said, 'asshole'. Asshole," I repeated for good measure. "You," I said, chinning in his direction. "Leave. Her. Alone."

I didn't even see it coming. The flat of his palm hit my cheek and my head snapped to the right. The room spun. Then, he grabbed my hair and pulled my head back, bringing his face close to mine. His eyes burned. "I'll be back," he said. "Soon. And you'll have to watch."

He dropped my chin, strode to the door, exited the room, and slammed the door shut.

"Shit," I muttered.

I slid to the floor and leaned my head back. I could feel blood pooling in the back of my mouth. I spat. A tooth wiggled.

"You okay, Lucy?" I asked.

She didn't say anything, and I wasn't sure if my display of bravado had helped us or if I'd just plunged us into an even more tenuous situation.

I rattled my handcuffs against the pole in frustration.

And then, I decided to scream. I took a deep breath, held it in my lungs as if I was going to swim underwater, and then screamed as loudly and as shrilly as I had in the car. If there was anyone nearby, they would certainly hear it. I stopped for a breath, inhaled, and let loose again.

When I stopped to take another breath, I said, "Lucy, do it. Scream with me."

Together, we shrieked, screamed, wailed, yelled, hollered, screeched. But there was no response. Lucy gave up, and after my throat started to hurt, I sank back into silence, thinking.

For the life of me, I couldn't figure out what this pole was for. Water? Sewage? Wires? With the flimsy fitting at the top of the pole, I doubted it was structural. Would it move? I positioned my spine against the pole and pushed backward.

I felt the pole give, just the tiniest bit.

I shoved again.

Now, I distinctly felt the pole wiggle.

With my feet right against my butt, I pulled my wrists taut around the pole, so tightly that the handcuffs were cutting into my wrists. I swayed, back and forth. Once I found my rhythm, I put energy into it, yanking hard on the forward motion and shoving on the backward. All I needed was to crack the plastic fitting at the top of the pole or loosen the metal collar by my feet. I leaned back and pushed with my legs until my shoulders were burning and my legs cramped up. I continued to rock back and forth and felt the pole give again. I scooted into it with renewed energy.

The pole gave, the tiniest bit. I stood, jammed my feet against the base of the pole, and leaned forward. All my weight was positioned on the chain between my wrists. I bent at my waist, pulling with every ounce of my strength. Keeping one foot at the base of the pole, I stepped forward into a lunge, grunting with the effort.

And then, something snapped.

"Lucy," I hissed, "Watch out. Cover your head."

As if in slow motion, the long pole swayed. Bits of plastic cascaded down from the ceiling. The fitting had cracked, and the pole listed to the left toward the middle of the room. It stopped at about a sixty-degree angle, the metal collar on the floor keeping the pole upright. I quickly stood up and baby-stepped the length of the pole, pulling it down as I walked. Eventually, the pole cracked at the bottom, leaving a jagged end.

I heard Lucy gasp.

I was free.

Then, I stepped over the cuffs, so that my hands were in front of me. The pain in my shoulders immediately eased. Holding the jagged edge of the pole, I stomped on it, wrenching it up and toward me in an L-shape. The plastic fractured, leaving another sharp end. Perfect.

With a weapon available, I felt much more confident. I hoped Lucy would also.

I crouched next to Lucy and handed her the pipe. "Hold this," I said.

I slipped my feet over the hard surface, looking for a small metal shim with which to pry open the lock on the handcuffs. Without light, this would be tricky, but I had learned the technique in my week-long police academy course many years ago. I was so proud when I was one of the few students able to unlock the cuffs with a bobby pin. Unfortunately, I didn't have a bobby pin now; I needed something like that or a paper clip: a flexible, strong, short length of wire.

I slid across the floor quietly. It was poured concrete flooring, a slab sanded to what once might have been a shine. I knew these things; my father had been a concrete contractor, and he'd schooled my brother and I in the various applications of cement. Interiors: slabs, stairs, ramps, flooring, countertops, foundations. Exteriors: patios, driveways, walkways, pizza ovens, firepits. My foot rolled over something small, and I leaned down to pick it up. It was a nail — too big for the tiny keyhole on the handcuffs. But it might be useful later, so I put it in my pocket. I continued sliding my feet across the floor, heading for the sink.

Once at the sink, I ran my hands along the rim and felt in the basin. The sink was empty. I felt along the edge and underneath the freestanding tub. Nothing. I lifted my hands up, leaning over the sink to examine the wooden shelf. I started at the left side and worked my way to the right, feeling along the join where the shelf was bracketed to the wall. I slowly ran my fingers over the rough, unfinished surface, praying for a miracle.

And my prayer was answered.

The end of a wire poked out between the middle bracket and the edge of the shelf. I reached for it, grasped the end, and wiggled it. Seconds later, I'd extracted a three-inch long piece of wire. I thought back to that workshop. We'd had bright lights, instructors, and all the time in the world. Here, I had no light, no instructor, and no time. I scurried back to Lucy, slid down next to her, and waved the wire in front of her face.

"Got something," I hissed.

"What is it?" she whispered. "I can't see a thing."

"Piece of wire," I said. "I remember you bend it near the tip, insert it and bend it backwards, and wiggle it around. Let's see how it works. I'll try it on you first."

I twisted the wire into a ninety-degree angle, felt the smooth flange of the handcuff, and located the small lock. I inserted the end of the wire into the small keyhole at the bottom of the lock and bent it backwards, forming another ninety-degree angle. Then, I positioned the wire in the hole so that it was at a ninety-degree angle to the keyhole and started wiggling it around. And presto, bingo, after five minutes of patient, delicate, wiggling, feeling the wire hit the various parts of the lock, I felt the lock give. It popped open.

Lucy placed her hand to her lap, rubbing her shoulder. "Wow, that smarts," she whispered. "Pins and needles up and down my arm." I started to insert the wire into my cuffs on my wrists, but she said, "Give it to me. I can do this."

Her work was much quicker than mine. Within a minute, she'd freed me.

We both stood. I picked up the PVC pipe and hefted it from one hand to the other. "Let's go," I said as I started across the room.

Lucy stopped me, saying, "Hang on." She reached over and scooped up both sets of handcuffs. "These might be useful. You have a way to carry these?"

I nodded and slipped them into the pockets of my jacket. "Listen, Lucy. I got your back. We're in this together. But if we find a way to exit this building, and you want to go, just go. Run. I have unfinished business here and I need to figure it out."

Lucy replied. "It's okay, Shelby. I have unfinished business also."

42

LUCY FOLLOWED ME ACROSS THE ROOM. I unlocked the deadbolt and opened the door. We slipped into the hallway and carefully shut the door behind us. Lights housed in small metal casings flickered on and off. Three steel doors lined both sides of the corridor. We'd been locked in a room on the right side, at the end of the hall, by the alarmed emergency exit. We hurried toward the heavy fire door at the other end of the hallway. I slowly opened it, revealing a short flight of steps that ended in a small landing.

Cautiously, we tiptoed up the stairs to the landing, turned, and found five more steps that would take us to the next floor and another reinforced fire door. I signaled to Lucy to stay put and crept up the stairs, holding my PVC pipe like a bat. I eased up to the door, staying low, and lifted my head to peer out of the small window, placed at chest height. I saw a brightly lit, empty, corridor. I pushed the door open, bracing for an alarm or siren. But it was silent.

The hall was lined with closed doors, with a badge reader attached to the side of each one. To my right, a set of double doors opened into what must be a lobby area. A second fire door, with a reader attached to the wall, was at the other end of the hall.

I slipped back into the stairwell and quietly shut the fire door. "What should we do?" I whispered. "We're not going to be able to get anywhere. There's a badge reader on every door."

"Should we head back downstairs and hide? Or do some more exploring downstairs?"

If we were downstairs, hiding, freed from our handcuffs, we'd at least have the element of surprise on our side when someone came back. "Good idea," I said. "Let's go."

We tiptoed back down the stairs and quietly entered the hallway. I tried the door on the left, Lucy tried the one on the right. Locked. Both middle doors were locked. The last door on the right, the door to our prison, was still unlocked. Gesturing for Lucy to wait, I slipped into the room. The door swung shut behind me. I dropped the PVC pipe on the floor and ran across the room to investigate the stack of boxes. I pawed through them, looking for anything that would serve as a weapon. They were empty. I ran back to the door, picked up my pipe, and eased the door open. But the hallway was empty.

"Lucy?" I hissed. "Lucy? Where are you?"

No answer.

I clutched the pipe in my left hand and rattled the handle of the door across the hall. It was locked. I slid down the hall, trying the other doors. All locked.

"Lucy?" I hissed again. I wanted to shout, but I didn't dare. I didn't want to announce myself.

Then, I heard a click. The fire door at the top of the stairs.

I sprinted down the hall and yanked open the door at the bottom of the stairs. I took the steps two at a time, twisted around the landing, and ran up the remaining five steps to reach the top of the staircase. I slowly opened the heavy fire door. It swung out into an empty hallway.

Where had the person gone? And where was Lucy?

I jogged back down the stairs, frantic.

Where had she gone?

I tried all the doors again. All locked, save for the last one on the right.

Then, I stood quietly, listening.

And I heard a faint tapping. It was coming from the door across the hall from our prison.

I banged on the door; the tapping grew more rapid.

Lucy was in there.

I rattled the door handle, but the door, a solid floor to ceiling steel door, didn't budge.

I'd have to find a key.

"Lucy," I whispered, having no idea if she could hear me. "I'll be back. I need a key."

I ran back down the hall to the fire door, pushed it open, and leapt up the stairs.

I pulled open the door to the first floor and peeked out into the hallway, wondering what to do.

Then, I heard a woman's voice call, "See you later," followed by the swishing sound of a set of double doors closing. I slowly slid the fire door closed as a woman entered the hallway, walking slowly. After she passed the door, I quickly yanked it back open and wedged my plastic pipe in the door frame to prevent the door from swinging shut.

I exploded into the hall. I took two long strides and reached the woman, shoving her from behind. She stumbled. I shoved her again and she crumpled. I rolled her over and sat on her, scissoring her legs between my knees and clamping her arms straight at her sides. Her eyes were wide and she was opening her mouth as if to scream. I slapped my left hand over her mouth and shook my head.

"Where am I?" I whispered.

I slid my hand to the left, leaving her a little room to speak, but she shook her head quickly. Loyal or just plain terrified?

"What happens in this place?" I asked. "Something to do with genetics? Babies? Does the name Boyd ring a bell? Brannon?"

Again, she shook her head, her eyes wide.

"Look," I said. "You get one more chance. Where am I?"

This time, a clear look of fear slid across her face.

Holding her down with my left hand, I lifted my right, and curled it into a fist, leaving her mouth unprotected. But she didn't scream or yell or draw attention to herself. She clenched her eyes shut, fisted her hands. It was almost as if being knocked out was her best option, the way out.

I decked her. I had to; I couldn't leave her there, in the hallway, unattended. I had no idea how long she'd be out. I had to hide her. Quickly, before someone else walked into the hallway, I opened the door to the staircase and dragged her into the stairwell, kicking the PVC pipe out of the way so I could shut the door. I laid her down. She was about my height and size, and wore a white knee-length lab coat over her slacks and shirt. She wore comfy shoes, but her feet were much smaller than mine. I turned her on her back and rifled through her pockets. Empty. But a badge hung around her neck on a lanyard and I grabbed it, holding it up. The name "Brittany T" was printed below her picture in a large black font. I slung it around my neck.

Then, I squeezed the PVC pipe under my arm and lifted her under her armpits. Her head lolled forward, reminding me of the time I'd dragged Megan this way, across a meadow, to help. I bumped the woman down the stairs, turned at the landing, dragged her down the next set of stairs and then pushed the door at the bottom of the stairs open with my hip. I maneuvered into the hall. It was completely quiet. I was going to deposit this woman in the room where Lucy and I had been imprisoned. I could use her badge to find a set of keys and free Lucy.

I backstepped down the hall, dragging my prisoner. When I reached the last door on the right, I grabbed the door handle, and slowly opened it. I dropped the PVC pipe, lugged Brittany across the room, propped her up, and stripped off her lab coat. I took a pair of handcuffs out of my pocket, snapped one cuff to her arm, and the other to the pipe. I heard something clank and assumed Brittany was waking up, rattling her chain.

I didn't have time to waste. As I pulled the lab coat over my fleece jacket, I gave the woman a silent word of thanks, resolving to get back here as quickly as I could. Then, I exited the room, closing the door behind me. Armed with a badge and a lab coat, my confidence grew.

I jogged quickly down the hall, up the stairs, and opened the fire door leading into the corridor on what I assumed was the first floor. I strode purposefully to the opposite door. I waved the badge in front of the reader, but it flashed red. I moved down the hall, holding the badge in front of each reader. But I was denied access. I wondered how long it would be before a security guard barged down the hallway wondering why Brittany was trying to get access to restricted rooms.

Finally, the small light on the badge reader attached to the door closest to the fire door at the end of the hall flashed green. The door clicked. Taking a breath, I pushed down on the handle and opened the door.

I stepped into the room.

43

T HE ROOM I ENTERED WAS DIM, lit by a faint greenish glow. Three hospital beds sat against the opposite wall. Banks of monitors covered a long table on my right. The wall to my left was bisected by a heavy interior door, flanked by a flock of IV poles. I moved across the room and stopped at the middle bed, staring. The head of the bed was angled upright with the covers thrown back, as if someone had just slipped out to use the restroom. A paperback was face down on the pillow. I could see the title, *The Last Guest House.* I slipped around the side of the bed and picked it up. It was open to page 124. The cover was branded with a gold circle medallion, the logo for Hello Sunshine, Reese Witherspoon's book club.

I set it back down. There was nothing unusual about the bed itself — it was a standard hospital bed with crisp white sheets and a polyester fill blanket topped with a white bedspread. Three plump pillows had been tossed to the foot of the bed. The bed to my right sported similar bedding, with an upside-down *People* magazine on the pillows. The third bed was also made up with identical bedding: white sheets, three inviting pillows, a blanket, and a white bedspread. This bed was messier, with the blanket kicked down to the end of the bed and the bedspread falling to the floor. *Where the Crawdads Sing* was closed and lay faceup on the sheet. No bookmark, as far as I could tell. Another Hello Sunshine pick. An articulating swivel-mounted tray was attached to the side rail of each bed, allowing the patient to pivot the tray and eat while sitting in the bed.

Where were the patients? And who were they?

I continued to examine the room, walking over to the desk to check out the equipment. One of the monitors was a slim Apple computer; I hit the attached keyboard, but the screen flashed to a password field and I knew I was out of luck. I checked the other equipment on the table. Rubber hoses, test tubes in a rack, syringes, cotton balls, Band-aids. A blood draw station.

Next to that, an ultrasound that could wheel right to a patient's bed. I knew why that was here.

But I didn't find any communication devices. There were no phones — neither a cell phone nor a landline. No tablets. No computers I could access. No Alexa or Google devices. No walkie-talkies. No radio or Bluetooth speaker. Each bed did have a TV on a swing arm, with a remote dangling from a cord, but other than that, the room was designed to prevent the occupants from having any contact with the outside world.

Nor did I find a set of keys. I checked drawers, cabinets, shelves. Not a single key in the entire room. I'd have to keep looking. I thought about Lucy locked up downstairs behind one of those steel doors. I needed to open that door. I needed to rescue her.

Just as I was about to slip back out of the room, into the hallway, I heard voices.

I looked around for a place to hide. A black double-sided wardrobe sat across the room next to the door. I opened it. The right side held clothes hanging on a rod. I pawed through them: ten blue hospital gowns and three pink bathrobes hung from plastic hangers. Slippers of varying sizes lined the bottom of the wardrobe. Shelves and drawers lined the other side. The shelves were stacked with white towels and washcloths, adult diapers, and adult-sized wipes. One of the drawers at the bottom of the wardrobe was stuffed with wadded hospital socks in bright pinks and reds, the non-skid kind with rubber on the bottom. Another drawer held women's nylon underwear, running the size chart from large to huge.

I shoved the slippers aside, crouched on the floor of the wardrobe, and shut the door.

"Ladies," I heard. A man's voice. For a second, I thought it might belong to the man who'd hit me. Who'd threatened Lucy and who might have her prisoner now. I wished this standing closet was one of the antique variety, with a keyhole that I could peek through, but this was a solid, modern piece of furniture, where the edges of the doors fit together with precision.

I heard the shuffle of feet sliding across the floor, then the creak of beds as bodies settled in.

The man's voice was smooth, modulated. "All set?" he asked.

I tensed, listening carefully.

"I'll be back in a minute," he said, "with breakfast."

Despite the similarity in tones, I realized this wasn't the man who'd tormented us.

I had to figure out where I was, find keys to the doors downstairs, and free Lucy.

A woman spoke. "That guy is such an asshole," she said. "I hate the way he looks at me."

Another woman, her voice lower, replied. "I know. Every damn day."

The occupant of the third bed chimed in, "Not every day, Ellen. Just most of them." I put my ear to the door. She sounded like Crystal, with that sassy edge, but it was likely just my imagination.

The second woman laughed, "You're such an optimist."

The first woman asked, "What do you think we'll get for breakfast?"

The second woman said, "Eggs?" in a lilting question, and the three of them all broke into laughter.

I shivered. What was this place? Why were they laughing? Was there a hysterical edge to it?

"I wish I could have coffee," said the second woman.

"I know," agreed the first. "I sure miss my Starbucks white chocolate mocha with a shot of peppermint, double whip."

"Wow," said the second woman. "You used to drink those? That must have cost a fortune."

"Ah well, I had some help."

The women were quiet. If I was going to do something before the man returned with breakfast, I needed to do it now. Slowly I pushed the door to the cupboard open, stuck out one leg, then the other. I slid out of the wardrobe. Someone had turned on the lights and the room was now bathed in a cheery white light.

"Who the hell are you?" the woman in the middle bed questioned, while from the bed on the right, the bed where I'd seen the *People* magazine, I heard a sharp intake of breath and a "What the …?" before it petered out into a small gasp. At the same time, the woman in the right-most bed said, "Jesus Christ. What are you doing here?"

I turned. My eyes opened wide.

Crystal?

44

P UTTING MY FINGER TO MY LIPS, I kept my focus on the woman in the bed on the right side of the room. Her hair was cut short, close to her scalp, as if it had been shorn with a man's razor. But her blue eyes were wide and open, and she regarded me with an expression of disbelief.

"Shelby?" she asked. "How did you get here? Why did you just come out of that closet?"

"I could ask the same thing," I whispered, my heart hammering. "How did you end up here? And where is here?" I circled my finger in the air, taking in the hospital beds, the trays and TVs, the medical equipment. I leaned in. "Where are we? And what the hell is this?" My voice had an edge and I had to work hard to modulate my tone.

Crystal explained, excited. "Shelby, I'm making history. I'm a surrogate. I'm part of a study where they're testing new techniques in fertility." She gestured to the other two women. "We're all surrogates. And we're all making a bundle of money. I'm going to be able to send my grandparents on that cruise they've been talking about."

I flashed back to what Crystal had told her mother. Buckets of money.

"But, Shelby, Walt is going to come back with our breakfast in a second. He watches us to make sure we eat everything and we're not sharing. After that we're left on our own until lunch. In the afternoon, a technician comes to run tests.

"Go hide," she said, swinging her legs out of the bed. "Hurry up." She pointed at the wardrobe, then turned to the other women and put her finger to her lips.

I glanced at the three women and scurried across the room. As I slipped into the wardrobe and pulled the door shut, I saw Crystal wink and wave at me. Seconds later, I heard the rattle of a cart followed by Walt's upbeat voice. "Ladies, your breakfast is ready."

I heard clattering and I could visualize Walt placing plastic trays of steaming food on the tray tables. The odor of bacon and toast wafted into my cramped quarters. I thought about what I'd seen. Three pregnant women. The woman in the bed on the left: long blonde hair, clear-skinned, tough demeanor. The woman occupying the middle bed: short dark hair, round face, agreeable. And Crystal.

Then, I thought about Lucy, locked in a dark room.

I could barely contain myself. I was just sitting here. I needed to do something. Find keys.

But for now, all I could do was wait. Keep my fidgeting to a minimum.

Fifteen long minutes later, Walt bussed the trays and the room was quiet again. I heard a loud hiss, "You can come out now."

Cautiously, I slid out of my hiding place and walked to Crystal's bed, aware that the other two women were eyeing me with suspicion.

"Tell me again. What are you doing?" I asked as I leaned over to hug her. "I need to get you out of here. I also need to find keys. Have you seen any keys? Does the guy watching you have keys?"

Crystal shrugged and shook her head as she reached up to hug me in return. Her long-sleeved pajama top slipped down her shoulder and I could see her tattoo, the fantastical creatures given new meaning in this prison-like environment.

"I've been doing this since right after graduation," Crystal said as I sat down on the foot of the bed. "Almost four months now. I'm two and a half months pregnant. Ellen, over there," she pointed to the woman in the far bed, "is almost due, and Charise, right there, is due in about three months. So we're on a three-month rotation." Ellen and Charise nodded and waved.

"You've been here since you disappeared?" I asked. "But I heard you were in Vegas."

Crystal shook her head. "Vegas? I was never in Vegas."

I stared at her. "You didn't send your grandparents a postcard from Vegas?"

"No," she insisted, "I never went there."

I searched her face. "Why would someone send a postcard saying you were in Vegas?"

Crystal leaned forward. "I don't know. What did they say?"

"They made it sound like you were fine. That you were waitressing and had a place to live. Your grandfather hired me to go to Vegas to look for you. Of course, I didn't find you."

Crystal shook her head and put up her hand, palm out. "Scout's honor. I never went to Vegas."

I filed that away for later. It explained the San Jose cancellation on the postcard, which must have been sent to reassure Stu and Marilyn. To let them know that their beloved granddaughter was alive and well. The person sending that card never thought it would encourage Stu to continue looking for Crystal.

"Do you know if there were other women here before you?" I asked.

Crystal shrugged.

Just like I'd been at her age, all she could see was what was right in front of her. A growing belly and the dollar signs.

But Ellen piped up, "Yes, there was another girl here. I can't remember her name. Jasmine? Jessamine? Something like that. She left just before Charise came. She was pregnant with twins. I wonder how much she got for that," the woman said wistfully. "She wouldn't say. And she never came back."

"What's going on, Crys?" I asked. "This isn't normal."

Crystal shrugged. "Shelby, I'm getting paid a lot of money to be here and stay pregnant. As far as I'm concerned, being stuck in this room is just an inconvenience, nothing more."

I twisted around on the bed. "What about you two?"

"Same here," piped up Ellen.

Charise chimed in with, "Me too."

"How did you get here?" I asked.

"I replied to an online ad for surrogates," said Ellen.

Charise chimed in, "Same here."

Crystal said, with pride in her voice, "They came to me. They recruited me."

I turned back to Crystal. "Crystal, this isn't normal," I repeated. "Your grandparents are very worried about you."

Crystal looked down. "I figured they would be," she said. "I feel badly about that. But once I get out of here, I'm going to be with them all the time and go to college. They believe in me."

I eyed her, saddened. If my guess was correct, she wouldn't get out of here once her time was up. That was not part of the deal. The remains of Jasmine or Jessamine, whatever her name had been, were likely somewhere nearby. Her babies, a genetically engineered set of twins, just like Justin and Justine Boyd, were probably in another room in this building. That wad of cash, dangling in front of these women like a carrot, was just an illusion.

Besides, I was going to get all three of these women out of here, one way or another. The cash, if it had ever existed, was officially off the table. The government would be monitoring the women once we escaped. But I knew I wasn't going to have their support in any escape plan I came up with. They were pregnant and bedridden. They'd been confined to this small room for months. They would be unable to move quickly, if at all.

I stared at Crystal. Her face was open and guileless, and I really believed she thought she was doing the right thing. "Tell me what happened," I said.

"I met a guy. When I was working at the cafe last year. He told me about this opportunity. He told me that someone had selected me, out of hundreds of young women, for this work. How they'd been watching me. How my efforts will help millions of women across the world. Once he explained that all I had to do was be a surrogate, I signed on the dotted line right away. That must have been in April or May. I signed a confidentiality agreement and a non-disclosure agreement and right then, he gave me one thousand dollars in cash. A signing bonus, just like that." She snapped her fingers and waved her arm. Her hospital gown slid down to reveal her tattoo. "That's what I did with it."

Crystal continued. "The day after graduation, I just left. I felt bad for disappearing like that, but part of the agreement was complete secrecy. It was for the best. My mom and stepdad were going to kick me out anyway. I took the train to San Francisco where my friend met me. He took me to a building in an industrial park south of the city and I stayed there for a month. They did a bunch of tests and I got a lot of shots. Then, they did one round of IVF and three days later implanted the eggs. Two weeks later, I had a pregnancy test, and, when it was positive, they brought me here."

She looked at me pleadingly. "I thought about you, Shelby. I did. I knew what happened to you. I knew about those babies, those twins. But my friend was so sincere. And everyone was so nice. I asked him if there would be any tinkering with genes and all. He swore that it was nothing like that."

"Your grandfather has been frantic with worry," I said. "He thinks you're in a ditch somewhere."

Crystal covered her mouth with her hand. "Oh that's awful. I'm so sorry."

"He was so relieved to get that postcard. That's why he sent me to Vegas to find you." I stared at her. I remembered how earnest and impressionable she'd been when I'd first met her. How eager to learn. How trusting.

"You're not going to tell anyone about us, are you?" She pointed to herself, and then to her colleagues. "We need this money. We're earning this money. Right? Ellen? Char?" She tried to enlist their support, but they seemed to have dozed off.

Their food must have had something in it to put them to sleep. Whoever was keeping them here, and I had an idea about that, was drugging them. What were these women taking? And how could a nine-month course of tranquilizers or sedatives or whatever they were on possibly be good for an unborn child? But I knew the answer to that, too.

Crystal's eyes fluttered, and rather than try and rouse her, I let her head loll back onto the pillow. Too late, I wondered if this room was full of hidden cameras and I realized that it must be. I guessed that Walt's job was to monitor the video feed and I hoped he was too busy washing dishes to pay attention.

45

I opened the door to the hall and stuck my head out. Empty. I slid across the hall, wondering which room would hold a set of keys for the basement. I held Brittany's badge up to the reader next to the door directly across the hall. It flickered red: no go. I tried all the doors in turn on that side of the hall. The badge I had wouldn't open any of them.

I ran to the end of the hall, slapped the badge to the reader, and was flabbergasted when the door buzzed open. I found another set of stairs and took them two at a time. A second badge reader was attached to the wall by the door at the top of the stairs.

This was my last chance; if I couldn't get past this door, I had two choices: exit through the double doors down the stairs at the far end of the hall and take my chances. I could also make my way back to the basement and wait. Neither scenario was optimum. The double doors probably led to a lobby with a security guard. Waiting downstairs, out in the open, with no weapon was just plain foolish.

I needed this door to open. I needed to find a weapon. I needed to find a key for the door downstairs so I could rescue Lucy.

Holding my breath, I held the badge against the reader. Nothing. I rubbed it against my pants and lifted it again, pressing it to the reader.

This time, the light flicked green.

I pushed the door open.

I stood at the entrance to a full-scale, windowless hospital nursery — a bright room of subdued yellows and pale greens. Tall office-style cubicle walls of mauve fabric divided the opposite side of the room into six bays. Each bay held a sturdy plastic crib surrounded by a thicket of equipment, including monitors, IV poles, tubes, and wires. Tightly coiled hoses dangled from the ceiling. Cameras on swivel poles were positioned by each crib. Utilitarian metal shelves stood on the wall next to the door, along with three sinks and drying racks. Every bay also held a standing desk, which contained a laptop, camera, headphones, paper, and pen.

Four of the bays were empty. But two of the bays were bathed in a warm light.

I moved to the bay at the far end of the room. A baby, cocooned in a pink blanket and wearing a pink cap, lay on her back in the crib. Above her, a black and white mobile twisted slowly in the current, catching the light. Reflecting shadow, brightness; shadow, brightness. I took another step. Slowly, so as not to disturb her.

Up close, I could see her wide-open eyes, alert, moving, following the contrasting black and white patterns fluttering above her. Already, her eyes had developed those tell-tale rings of color: the amber, brown, gray, green, and hazel bands that circled a yellow-brown pupil. Just like Justin and Justine Boyd's eyes.

"They're learning," said a voice from across the room. "You can see their eyes tracking. When we measure brain activity, it's off the charts."

I knew that voice. I'd recognize it anywhere.

"Impressed?"

I swiveled, placing one hand on the side of the crib to steady myself. With the other, I grabbed an IV pole.

Dr. Helen Brannon, older now, but still recognizable, stepped from the shadowy corner of the room into the light. She was pointing a small handgun at me.

"Hello, Shelby," she said. "Nice to see you again." She gestured with the gun. "Move. Get away from the baby."

But I didn't move. I couldn't move. I was looking at the woman I'd punched into oblivion in my boxing class. The woman who'd stolen my fertility. The woman who was likely poisoning the three women downstairs, as she'd done with countless others. Including me. The woman who was responsible for all my miscarriages.

The woman who had sold my eggs to fund her plan.

She was responsible for the child my mother had found on *Ancestry*.

She was the reason my marriage had failed.

She had caused my life to fall apart.

And she'd lured Crystal, my impressionable and naive friend, into her trap.

I would not move. I would not do anything she said.

She leveled the gun at me. "Move," she said.

I stared at her until my vision darkened to a pinhole. My heart raced. My breath came quick.

"Shelby," she said. "Don't make me use this."

Hearing her say my name infuriated me. She had no right.

A roar burst from my chest.

Rage fueled me.

I exploded from my stationary position, crashing into a rolling cart.

I grabbed it by the handle, leaned into it, and bulldozed forward.

The cart banged into one of the cubicle walls. It fell over with a crash onto a desk.

A baby wailed, a long shriek that descended into a hiccupping sob. The other joined in, howling.

I continued to run, shoving the cart in front of me.

I ran as if my life depended on it.

I ran, certain that everything I'd done over the last ten years had been careening toward this moment.

Toward this moment of revenge.

Adrenaline shot through me as I came closer to my enemy, toward her trembling outstretched arm. Toward the barrel of the shiny black handgun pointed at me.

She'd placed all her faith in that weapon, thinking it could protect her.

She had no idea.

Then suddenly, I stopped short. Something caught my attention. Another black and white mobile circled lazily above a crib. Another baby in a second crib, this one wrapped in a blue blanket. A wiggling, clearly angry infant, shaking his head back and forth, with his small mouth open as far as possible, emitting a piercing shriek.

I leaned over the crib, cooing. The infant's eyes were closed and his face was growing redder and redder as he screamed. I glanced toward the doctor, still yards away. Still aiming her gun at me.

"Well, aren't you a dear? You sweet thing," I said as I placed my hand on the baby's chest.

"What's your IQ?" I whispered as I reached for him.

Helen Brannon's voice was loud and stern as she ordered, "Do not touch that child. Do not pick him up."

"And who's going to stop me?" I asked as I swung him out of the crib and lifted him to my shoulder. I nuzzled his cheek and kissed his head. I nodded at Helen, at the gun. "I'd put that down if I were you," I said.

I squeezed the baby close.

"Put the gun down," I repeated.

She leaned over and placed the gun down on the floor.

"Push it over here."

As she kicked it, she said, "This room will be swarming soon."

I shook my head. "Uh-uh," I stated. "That's not going to happen. If you trip any alarm, open any doors, I toss the baby." I lifted the baby up and down, swinging him in my arms. His weight was a comfort. "He's hefty," I said. "Fifteen, sixteen pounds? Three months old now?"

"It's already done," she said. "I hit the silent alarm when I saw you come in."

"You didn't," I countered. "If you had, someone would already be here. Besides, you wanted to see me again. Just as much as I wanted to find you, you wanted me to find you. Why else would you lure Crystal?

"You wanted to show me what you'd done. You wanted to rub my face in it." I swung the infant toward the middle of the room. "Over there," I gestured. "Face me. We're going to talk."

She held her hands up as she edged by me. She was dressed as she had been the last time I'd seen her. Plain blue skirt with a pleat down the middle. A button-down white blouse with a severe collar. Sensible round-toed black shoes. Hose. Her hair was shorter, whiter. Her glasses were different. But it was her, all the same.

The woman who left human wreckage in her wake. The woman who'd proven, over and over again, that she wouldn't let anything — family, compassion, ethics, international or U.S. law — get in the way of her evil goal: to create a new species of humans.

Still cradling the baby and keeping Helen Brannon in my sights, I bent down for the gun. I picked it up, checked the safety, and held it loosely in my right hand.

"He's ruined now," Helen said. "We raise them without any human contact. No skin time, no breast feeding, no snuggling. They seem to do better that way. Less human connection seems to work better in the long run." She paused, adding, "They aren't human after all."

I pointed the gun at her.

"Where are we?" I asked in as conversational a tone as possible.

She shrugged.

"Where?" I demanded.

"Doesn't matter if you shoot me. My work is all over the world now. Everywhere. My legacy is established."

"I'm not going to shoot you," I said. "I'm going to make sure you go to jail this time."

"Impossible," she said.

Still as arrogant as ever.

"What happened after we parted company last time? When you abandoned your son?"

She smiled. "I had my other identities," she said. "Like I told you, scientists all across the world revere me. I was welcomed in China and Russia." I must have looked skeptical, for she continued, "All very hush-hush. They couldn't say anything. Remember the Crispr babies, born in China in 2018?"

I kept my face blank as she goaded me, waiting for my reaction.

"They didn't do that on their own. I was there, every step of the way." She sniffed. "It was a pointless application of the technology, but the Chinese government wanted to be the first country in the world to announce gene-edited babies."

When I didn't react, she continued. "I know, I know. Xi Jinping, the Chinese president, claimed to know nothing and denounced the scientist, but of course they were behind it all the way. Nothing happens in China on that level without government approval. And then I got an offer to come here." She spread her arms out. "So here I am."

"An offer from a Mr. Little?"

She nodded slightly, as if she were royalty granting her subject a small favor.

"That other lab? The one outside of Vegas?"

"Research," she said.

"And the photo of Justin and Justine taped to a shelf?"

"Inspiration," she replied. And then she sniffed.

Something about that gesture, that aloof, cavalier, cocky display of entitlement and power and disregard for the people she was damaging — that infuriated me.

She stared at me, smiling.

In one lightning-swift motion, without thinking, for if I thought about it, I'd stop myself, I pointed the gun at her. I wanted to kill her. I wanted to show her I was in charge now. I wanted revenge.

I felt my finger tremble on the trigger. Any more weight on the delicate device would fire the gun. A blast would fill the cavernous room. Bright red would bloom through her clothing, spreading into a Rorschach inkblot, a blot I would spend the rest of my life trying to decipher.

I stared at her, breathing hard.

Then, I removed my finger from the trigger, feeling the spring settle back into place.

"Can't do it, can you?" she asked. "Ruthlessness was one characteristic that no one in your family tree carried," she said. "It's a good quality. One I've honed to perfection."

Visions of all the lives she'd sacrificed in her quest passed through my mind — all the infants she'd sold to parents who couldn't adopt through normal channels. The infants sold for their tiny organs. The infants trafficked into the sex trade. The birth mothers whose lives were shattered once they'd realized what had happened to their babies.

I crouched and placed the baby on the floor. His enraged howls tore through the room. I snapped the gun safety back on and tucked the small handgun into the waistband of my pants, against the small of my back.

Then, I attacked.

I hit her square on the jaw. She dropped to the ground, hard. I leaned over; smacked her in the cheek. She rolled to her side and spit blood on the floor, followed by a tooth. She put her hands on the floor and tried to push herself up, but I kicked her in her side, watching in satisfaction as she collapsed.

She lay there, immobile and silent. I kicked her again, just because I could. My bare foot thumped into her lower back and she shifted, wheezing. I raised my leg to kick her another time. One more, for good measure.

But she rolled to her side and curled into a ball, with her hands around her head.

I crouched down next to her. I shoved her onto her back and grabbed her chin, leaning in. Blood dripped from her nose. Abrasions covered her cheeks and forehead. Her lip was split, and the skin around her eyes was already starting to puff up.

Just like I'd imagined.

Her eyes fluttered. She stared at me for an instant, with a puzzled expression on her face.

Then, she slipped into unconsciousness.

Both babies were crying, their indignant shrieks rising and falling like a chorus.

46

I STOOD AND SURVEYED THE ROOM, looking for something to tie her up with. Anything. A rope, a length of wire, a sash, a belt, an electrical cord. I jogged to the shelves along the wall and rifled through, shoving beakers, vials, boxes, and books aside as I searched. A stack of diapers ended up on the floor, followed by a box of latex gloves. I passed over a shelf of manuals and notebooks. I reached up to the top shelf, my fingers touching glassware and plasticware. Nothing useful.

Then, I remembered the handcuffs I'd put in my pocket earlier. I'd used one set to cuff Britany to the pipe. I still had the other set. I reached into my pocket, but it was empty. I patted the other pocket; also empty. With a sinking feeling, I remembered that clank I'd heard when I'd cuffed Brittany earlier. The woman wasn't testing her handcuff. What I'd heard was the other set as it fell from my pocket to the floor.

The babies were still crying; the pitch just on the edge of hysteria, their tone demanding attention. But I couldn't do anything for them. Yet.

I whirled around and ran to one of the empty bays. A plastic bag on a length of rubber tube dangled from an IV pole. I jerked on the tube. It came free and the pole clattered to the floor. I returned to Helen and rolled her to her side, shoving her so that both arms were behind her. I grasped the tube and stretched it, then wrapped it around her wrists, securing it with three square knots. It only had to hold for five minutes, tops.

Then, I ran to the sink, grabbed a plastic basin and filled it. Water sloshed as I hurried back to Helen.

I tipped the basin and dumped the water on her head.

Helen thrashed to life. She opened her eyes, sputtered, tried to sit up, and swore.

I grabbed the gun from my waistband and pointed it at her.

"Up. Get up." I gestured with the gun, up and down. "Up, up."

Helen fishtailed her feet, trying to find purchase. Trying to obey.

I didn't lean over to help. Given the chance, she would spit on me or bite me. I was sure of it.

"Up. Now." My voice was loud.

"I'm trying," she muttered.

Her feet came into contact with the wall and she was able to stabilize herself, maneuver to her knees, lean into the wall, and stand. She swayed as she stood, then slumped against the hard surface.

"Aren't you going to do anything to stop that racket?" She looked at the infant on the ground, still on his back. The blue blanket had fallen away and his arms were jerking, the tiny hands spasming as he shrieked.

Ignoring her, I said, "Keys. Where are all the keys to this building?"

She pointed with her head, then winced. "Over there."

Keeping the gun trained on her, I said, "Show me."

Helen shuffled, half-leaning into the wall for support, half under her own steam.

"Why do you want the keys?" she asked. "You already have a badge."

"Get me the keys," I ordered.

We reached the far wall. She angled her head in the direction of a small gray electrical panel. "In there," she said.

I circled her, giving her a wide berth, and kept my gaze on her as I approached. "No tricks," I said.

Helen nodded her head, as if in defeat. But I knew better.

Keeping my eyes trained on her, I reached for the panel and found a small latch. I pulled it open and quickly glanced in. A monster set of keys hung on a lanyard. Perfect. I grabbed it and draped it around my neck, tucking it inside my zipped fleece jacket so it would stay out of the way.

"Let's go," I said. "Walk."

She turned around and leaned into the wall again. I could see her shoulders tense. In a flash, I was on her, the small circle of the barrel pressed against her lower back. I grabbed her left elbow, saying, "Don't try anything. Get away from the wall." I released her, giving her a small shove.

When she took a cautious step away from the wall, I ran back to the baby boy and picked him up, adjusting the blanket to cover him. His crying stopped abruptly. Within seconds, the baby girl stopped also, as if, despite the physical distance between them, they remained connected on a cellular, fundamental, level.

The sudden silence was a welcome relief, a balm in the midst of this chaos.

I shifted the weight of the infant to my left hip, keeping my arm circled around him. His neck was strong already and he held his head up, looking, staring. I angled the gun toward Helen. "Walk over to the door."

Head down, she dragged her feet and slowly moved across the room. I was behind her, on full alert, unable to tell if her speed was a function of resistance while trying to figure out how to overpower me, or a function of the physical damage I'd inflicted.

As she walked, I stashed the baby back in his crib, on his back, covering him with the blanket. I slipped the blue hat off his head and stuffed it in my pocket. Proof, I thought. Just in case the babies had been moved by the time I returned, I'd have proof that an infant had been here. I briefly thought about leaving Helen and taking one of the babies instead, but I couldn't do it. I could not let her get away this time.

She stopped at the door, turned, and gazed at the crib where the tiny baby girl lay. As if she'd read my mind, she said, "You should take her for insurance. She doesn't weigh as much as he does. And no one is going to believe you if there aren't any babies here later on."

I replied, "They both stay here. Law enforcement will be here soon enough."

Helen stared at me. "You think you've got me this time, don't you?" she asked. "You don't," she announced. "I've got my backup plan."

"So do I," I said. "And I'm about to put it into place."

While holding the gun to Helen's side, I reached around her and lifted my badge to the reader. The door clicked open and I shoved her into the stairwell. The gun at her back was an impressive motivator.

The stairwell was empty and silent. I had expected some trick: a keening alarm, a dozen armed guards, an attack dog. I nudged her down the steps with the gun, and she complied, one slow dragging step after the next. At the bottom of the staircase, I gestured for her to move to the side so I could badge the door open.

As soon as the door clicked, Helen leaned into it, shoving it open. She screamed, an all-out shriek, a horror-movie scream, a hair-raising howl. It reverberated through the hallway, echoing off the walls, sliding under closed doors, seeming to grow louder and louder. I flinched, pressed the gun hard into her back, and muttered, "Shut up. Shut up. Shut up."

Helen screamed again. I grabbed the baby hat from my pocket and shoved it into her mouth, stifling her. Her eyes grew wide and I could sense fear. I had done something she hadn't expected.

I pushed her out into the hallway. And to my surprise, no one appeared. None of the doors along the hallway flew open. No one came running from what I assumed was the lobby. I dragged her down the hall, pressing the gun to her side. We passed the door that led to the maternity ward, where Crystal and the other two women were likely slumbering. When we reached the fire door to the lower floor, I stuck the gun in my pocket while I held Helen with one hand and badged the door open with my other hand. I slipped my right foot in between the door frame and the door to keep it ajar.

As if sensing this was her last chance, Helen flung herself against the door. Her full weight slammed the door closed, squeezing my bare foot against the unyielding door frame. I felt a bone crack. A fiery pain shot up my leg. I twisted, lifted the pistol, and coldcocked her with the butt of the gun. She dropped and slumped against the door.

My breath quickened and sweat poured down my forehead. My vision blurred. I felt like I was about to faint. I steadied myself against the door frame and pulled on the door to move it just the tiniest bit so I could wiggle my foot out. But Helen's weight held the door closed.

I could feel myself fading. The pain was overwhelming.

But I was so close. So close.

I needed to try the keys on the door downstairs.

Lucy needed me.

I shook my head to clear it, braced myself, put all my weight on my non-injured foot, and tugged at the doorknob. Helen shifted enough so I could open the door a crack and shimmy my foot out. I stared at it. It was already red and puffy. I could see a raised red welt where the door had squeezed the middle of my foot, across the arch.

I hopped on my left, putting as little weight on my right foot as possible, and reached Helen, slumped in the hallway against the now-closed door. I needed to move her out of the way so I could open the door. Listing to the left as I stood, I rolled Helen onto her back, leaned over, placed my hands under her shoulders, and tugged. I moved her an inch. My breath came in ragged, short bursts. I tugged on her again and again, inching her out of the way.

Finally, I had her where I needed her. I leaned into the side of the door, held the badge against the reader, heard it click, and opened it. I squirmed through, then turned around to drag Helen in after me. Her head hit the hard floor as I pulled and her hands tied underneath her were as effective as a brake.

But I managed.

Just as the door clicked behind me, I heard voices in the hallway. I fell to my knees and grabbed the gun, straight-arming it at the door. But the people continued down the hallway.

I didn't have much time.

47

HELEN LAY AT THE TOP OF THE STAIRS on her side, her arms still bound behind her. I stuck the gun back in my waistband, leaned over, and placed my fingers on her neck. A pulse. Thready, but a pulse all the same. I stared down the steps, remembering how I'd dragged Bethany, the lab worker I'd jumped in the hallway, down this staircase not so long ago. Five steps, the landing, then five more steps. It had been difficult then; now, with my right foot just about out of commission, it would be nearly impossible.

I debated leaving her here. With a gag and her hands tied, and in her unconscious state, she might stay hidden for a while. But that wasn't good enough. I needed her somewhere safe. Someplace where I could guarantee she'd stay put.

I leaned on the bannister, took my weight off my right foot, and carefully worked my way down one step. Then another. I turned around and reached for Helen, rolling her onto her back, and grabbing her under her arms. I yanked. She didn't budge. I yanked again. No movement. I didn't have the right angle.

As I hopped back up the two steps, the toes of my right foot brushed the riser. Pain rippled deep in my foot. I swore. I maneuvered myself behind Helen, squeezing in between her body and the door. Then, just like I'd done before, I took a deep breath, planted my injured foot flat on the ground, leaned over, and pushed.

Helen moved. I shoved again, noting in satisfaction that I'd moved her closer to the top step. I lifted my right foot and hopped forward, leaning against the wall for support. I steadied my weight on my left foot, leaned over, and shoved. At the lip of the staircase, her form hesitated for an instant, then reached the tipping point. She rolled down the stairs, her legs and head banging against the carpet.

Just as I was sure the noise would amplify through the building, bringing in the cavalry, a siren erupted, a rising and falling claxon. Through the small window in the fire door, I could see flashes of red, the emergency lighting, pulsing in time to the rise and fall of the alarm.

I limped down the stairs as fast as I could, keeping as much weight as possible on my heel. Concentrating on how my right foot hit the floor helped me ignore the pain.

Helen lay sprawled across the landing, with her head toward the wall and her feet toward me. When I reached her, I leaned over and put my finger under her nose. Still breathing. I didn't have time to assess any additional damage. I shoved her around the turn in the landing, so she couldn't be seen by anyone looking through the window in the door at the top of the stairs.

Then, I left her and stumbled down the stairs, through the door at the bottom of the staircase, into the hallway where I'd last seen Lucy. Sirens split the air here too and I felt like I was standing right next to a police car. Red alarm lights flashed up and down the corridor. I couldn't see. I couldn't think. I wouldn't know if someone burst through the door at the bottom of the stairs. I had to hurry.

I yanked the lanyard holding the keys off my neck, held them close to my eyes. I prayed that one of them would open the door to Lucy's prison. I rifled through the gold and silver pieces of metal. Several smaller sets were attached to the monster set on small rings. Green twist ties, like grocery bag ties, identified the sets: "1", "2", "3". Could it be that easy?

The set labeled with the number "1" was small, consisting of six keys. One for each door on this floor. I lurched to the door where I'd heard the tapping. I grasped the small key ring, and tried one of the keys in the lock. It fit, but wouldn't turn. I tried the second. It didn't fit. I fished through the keys again, picking another one. This one fit and I was able to twist the key in the lock.

The deadbolt turned and I pushed the door open.

Someone started shouting.

I stumbled in and fumbled along the wall for the light switch.

"Lucy?" I yelled, trying to make my voice heard over the sirens. "Lucy?"

As the overhead light flicked on, a shadowy figure emerged, running at full tilt from the deep shadows across the room.

"Lucy," I yelled. "Lucy."

I waved my arms.

Just as she was about to crash into me and bowl me over, possibly doing more damage to my injured foot, she skidded to a halt. She put her hands on her knees, leaned over, and inhaled.

Then, she looked at me with a half-smile and gave me a thumbs up.

Taking my hand, she pulled me to the door, then lifted my hand to touch it. The surface of the door was smooth. There was no door handle or deadbolt. She'd been locked in.

I nodded to show I understood, then reached for her, putting my hands on her shoulders.

"Lucy," I yelled, leaning in so she could hear me. "Lucy."

She cocked her head and put her hand behind her ear.

I gestured toward my injured foot; Lucy drew in a breath and looked horrified. Then, I waved my hand, indicating she should follow me. The sound of the siren was overpowering, rising and falling; it would be impossible to tell her my plan. I needed to show her.

Out in the hallway, the noise was deafening. I took Lucy's hand and placed it on the small of my back, where the pistol was securely tucked into my waistband. She nodded in understanding and followed me to the fire door. I pulled it open and pointed to Helen, still lying in a crumpled heap on the landing. I frantically mimicked pulling Helen down the hallway to the room at the end on the right.

Lucy ran up to the landing, rolled Helen over, grabbed her under the arms, and dragged her. Within seconds Lucy reached me. Holding the fire door open with my right hand, I pointed down the hall with my left. When we reached the end of the hall, I pushed open the heavy steel door and turned on the light. Brittany was where I'd left her, handcuffed to the pipe in the wall, just where Lucy had been chained, hours earlier. The bluish light from a cell phone screen glowed on Brittany's lap. In my haste, I'd missed that when I'd locked her in here.

The handcuffs that I'd expected to find in my pocket were on the floor next to Brittany. I pointed to the phone and the handcuffs. Lucy bobbed her head, clearly understanding what I planned. She quickly pulled Helen over to the wall by Brittany.

But I hadn't given Brittany enough credit. With her free hand, she reached down and picked up the handcuffs, throwing them across the room where they clattered to the floor. Just as Lucy was about to snatch the cell phone, Brittany tossed it, obviously hoping that she'd render the device unusable. Then, she reached out and grabbed Lucy's hair, holding on to it as Lucy tried to twist away. She wouldn't let go. In return, Lucy stomped her ribcage and was able to slide out of Brittany's grasp.

I picked up the handcuffs and held them out. Lucy grabbed them, and like a practiced expert, snapped one cuff on Helen's wrist and the other around the pipe. Helen laid perpendicular to the pipe, with her arm up, behind her head, now slumped on her chest. Brittany started yelling something, but we couldn't hear her over the sirens.

I pointed to the phone. Lucy ran over to pick it up, tapped it, and returned to me, holding out the phone with the lock screen. It expected a pattern. I gestured to Brittany. She shook her head. Lucy waved the phone in front of her. Brittany shook her head again, screaming something; swear words, threats, curses? I would never know. I pulled the gun out of my waistband, trained it on her, and held up the phone again.

Now, Brittany snapped her mouth shut. She reached for the phone. I shook my head, waving my finger in the air, tracing a pattern. Brittany shook her head. Lucy grabbed the gun from me, and in two swift steps, reached Brittany. She put the gun to the woman's temple. And Brittany held up her finger and drew a pattern. A simple "Z".

Moving as quickly as we could, we left the room and slammed the door shut behind us. The hallway was still empty. I pointed at the emergency exit, knowing that any alarm on that door would be completely eclipsed by the wail of the sirens encapsulating the building.

Lucy pushed the rocker bar on the emergency exit door to open it. I followed her out, limping into a foggy and damp morning.

48

W E FOUND OURSELVES in a half-filled parking lot enclosed by a chain link fence topped with circles of razor wire. Across from us, a group of farmworkers, wearing sunhats, bandanas, long-sleeved work shirts and jeans, were standing by a truck, staring in our direction. The driver of the truck was leaning out of the vehicle, yelling something. Seagulls wheeled overhead.

I slumped down behind the nearest car and jerked Lucy down next to me. My foot was throbbing now, the pain surging in great crests, like ocean waves. Suddenly the sirens stopped, the blare ceasing abruptly, leaving a hollow ringing in my ears. The sound was replaced by someone shouting and it took a few seconds to realize that two men were talking: "Do you see anyone?" "No, no one." "You sure something happened in there?" "I don't know. Head of security told me to check out the parking lot and I brought you along."

I could see their legs as they ran across the gap between the parked cars: two sets of khakis, black work boots. The barrel of a black pistol swung from a man's hand. A radio crackled, followed by squawking static and someone yelling, "See anything?"

I heard the response: "No sir."

Another second of static, followed by, "You are looking for two females."

"Roger that." The voice faded as the guards continued to jog across the lot.

Lucy pointed to the phone. I handed it to her, leaning over to whisper, "Call 911 and say you're Lucy Flores kidnapped from Santa Cruz. Sheriff will be here in an instant."

Nodding, Lucy gestured to the parking lot, the building, the farmworkers, the fence. "Where are we?" Her voice was low.

"No idea," I said. "Open the phone. We can figure it out that way."

Lucy traced the zig-zag pattern that Brittany had sketched in the air. A left-to-right, diagonal down, right-to-left pattern. A "Z". Assuming that Brittany had traced the pattern from her left to her right. But the lock screen didn't change.

"Try it the other way," I urged.

Changing the direction of the pattern didn't unlock the phone.

"Shit," Lucy said. "She lied to us."

I put up my finger and closed my eyes for a second, trying to remember what the woman had outlined. "Give me the phone," I said. "I want to try something." Lucy handed me the phone and leaned in. I traced the pattern again, but followed the "Z" shape with a vertical upward swipe. No luck. I tried it again, with a diagonal upward swipe.

This time, the screen brightened.

"Oh, thank god," Lucy said, almost crying. "Thank god."

"Here," I whispered. "Take it. Call."

With shaking hands, Lucy took the phone, pressed the dial icon, and tapped 911.

Lucy looked at me as she whispered. "My name is Lucy Flores," she said. "I was kidnapped yesterday morning. I managed to get away. Please come and get me. Please. Shelby McDougall, another kidnapping victim, is also here."

"Where are you?" the dispatcher asked. Her voice seemed loud.

"Shh," I hissed, while Lucy whispered, "I don't know." Her voice was shaky and her hands were trembling. Now that the ordeal was almost over, she was starting to crash.

I gestured for the phone. "Hang on," I said to dispatch. "Let me look at the location." I almost dropped the phone as I fiddled with the slick screen, searching for the map app, trying to figure out where I was. When I found the teardrop-shaped icon, I almost cried in relief. I tapped it. The map opened to Google Maps, with a blue dot on my location.

"We're by the beach," I stammered. "In south Santa Cruz county. San Andreas Road, near Dairy Road. We are hiding at the side of the building, behind cars in the parking lot. We think there may be a gate. We just saw a security guard with a gun. Hurry."

"I'm alerting the Sheriff's department now," dispatch said. "Stay on the line, please."

I leaned back against the building. My right leg was stretched out underneath the car in front of me, a white low-to-the-ground sedan. Next to me, Lucy pulled her knees to her chest. She was rocking back and forth. I transferred the phone to my right hand and put my left on her shoulder. She flinched.

"You okay?"

She shrugged, keeping her head hidden. I could hear her sniffling.

I rubbed her back, and she sat up, wiped her eyes defiantly, and pointed to my foot. "What happened?" she hissed.

"Long story," I whispered.

I stiffened as I heard the sound of a radio crackling. The guards were on their way back. I put my finger to my lips as I simultaneously muted the phone. She pointed at my leg as if to ask, "Should we move?"

They'd missed our hiding spot on their first pass through the parking lot. Now, they might decide to check behind the parked cars.

But I couldn't go anywhere. I wouldn't be able to stand. The pain overwhelmed my ability to think.

I leaned close to her so that my mouth was right against her ear. "You go," I said. "You take the phone and the gun. Go to the back. There's bound to be a trailer or a shed you can hide behind."

She twisted. Her eyes searched mine. She pointed to me, thumbed her chest, then intertwined her hands. "Together," she seemed to be saying. "We should stick together."

I had a different plan. "Go," I ordered, my voice low. "If they find me, they'll be busy. I'll yell so you'll know. The cops will be here soon enough." I prodded her with the phone, urging her to take it. I opened her hand and placed the gun in it.

Realizing I wouldn't take "no" for an answer, Lucy grabbed the items, stepped carefully over me, and crouched, moving quickly between the row of parked cars and the side of the building. The sun broke through as she reached the corner. As she turned back to give me one last look, light winked off the phone screen.

I pressed my back against the wall and drew my left leg up to my chest, keeping my right leg straight out in front of me. I couldn't see my foot. I knew it was swollen. I assumed that many of the delicate bones were broken and that it would be many months before I'd be walking without a limp. But I couldn't think about that now.

The crackling static from the radio grew closer. The two guards were talking to each other. "I wonder what happened," muttered one of them. The other replied, "Dunno. Let's finish this sweep and get back inside."

The voices grew louder. One of the guards said, "We better check under all the cars. You start there." My stomach clenched as I assumed he pointed to the end of the row of parked cars. "I'll start at the other end and work back."

They would find me.

I had to get up. A monster truck sat two cars over, to my right. I could hide behind one of the massive front tires, and, if they were looking head on, they might not see me.

Leaning forward, I reached for the grill of the sedan, grabbing the lip of the bumper. I hauled myself forward. Then, I lifted my injured leg with both hands, sliding it to the left, twisting my body at the same time. When I was parallel to the front of the car, I put both hands on the ground below me, rocked until my left leg was underneath me, and tried to stand.

But I couldn't. Just when I was at the tipping point, when I could either stand or fall, I crashed. I landed on the hood of the sedan with a clatter and, in an instant, I had a guard on either side of me, with weapons drawn.

"Up, up," snarled one of the guards. He was a short, stocky, fireplug of a man. He gestured rapidly with the gun. "Up, up," he repeated.

"I can't," I grunted as pain, like electrical shocks, coursed through me. "My foot is messed up."

He leaned over cautiously, as if I were trying to trick him.

The second guard approached, saw my puffy and swollen foot, and said, "It's true, boss. She's not going anywhere."

The first guard barked at me. "Where's the other one?"

I gave him a confused look. "Other one?"

"The other woman who broke in here with you."

I shook my head. "Just me. And I didn't break in. I was brought here. Kidnapped."

The guard said, "Bullshit. You broke in."

I pointed behind me, at the building. "How could I possibly break in there? How could I even get in here?" I raised my voice, hoping Lucy could hear me. I gestured at the razor wire topping the chain link. "I don't even know where I am."

"Shut up." The guard levelled his gun at me. "Help her up." He pointed at the other guard, who clipped his gun into the holster at his side and reached for me.

At that moment, the unmistakable whoop of sirens split the air. The guards cornering me turned toward the front of the building, confused.

I reached for the bumper and scooched under the car. When the cop cars tore through the gate, I didn't want to be anywhere visible.

49

TWELVE HOURS LATER, I lay on my back staring at the white ceiling tiles above me; my right foot encased in a boot up to my knee and elevated. Pain medication blurred my thoughts. I tried to remember how events had unfolded earlier in the day, but all that came to mind was sheer and utter pandemonium. Tires squealing against pavement. The thump as the guard who'd been reaching for me hit the ground, with blood squirting from his knee. His grunts and moans as he'd twisted in pain. Heavy footsteps as the other guard turned tail and ran. Bullhorns squawking. Sirens splitting the air. People screaming and yelling. The sharp retort of shots fired. The acrid smell of blood.

I'd lain under the car for what seemed like hours, motionless. Emerge or stay hidden? With my foot the way it was and my mobility severely limited, I opted for staying hidden. I knew Lucy would come for me as soon as she could.

On my back, staring at the mud-spattered engine block above me, I had to depend on my hearing. But sounds were muffled and indistinct, as if from far away. I wondered if the pain had become so consuming I was losing touch. Fading in and out.

"Shelby." I heard someone, close by, saying my name. "Shelby. Wake up." Someone shook my shoulder. "You can come out now."

Slowly, I rolled to my side. Lucy was crouched next to me, offering her hand.

I put my palms flat on the tarmac and slowly inched out. I winced as my injured foot dragged against the pavement. It had swollen considerably as I'd lain there and seemed as big and heavy as a large, ripe watermelon. Lucy helped me up and I tried to stand using only my left foot. But I lost my balance and I reflexively put down my right leg, landing square on the ball of my foot. Sharp pain whipped up my calf, overpowering the constant throbbing. I gasped as I twisted and swayed to keep upright, before collapsing into Lucy's arms. The last thing I heard was her frantic "Help, help. I need help."

Everything went black. Slices of memory came to me, like vignettes from a movie. A masked paramedic holding an oxygen tank to my face. A gloved hand flicking a needle of clear liquid. The swish of the ambulance's tires on the road. The occasional blast of the siren. The static of the radio. Blue sky as I was transferred from the ambulance to a gurney and wheeled into a hospital. The whiff of coffee overlaid with cleaning fluid. More still images: IV poles, X-ray machines. A drip that turned my insides to ice, countered by a warm blanket that put me right to sleep.

And finally, a doctor talking to me, explaining that bones in my midfoot had been broken when the door crushed my foot. It looked like confetti in there, he'd told me. I remembered he said I had a long recovery ahead of me, but knew I was up to it, because I could obviously kick ass. I laughed and wished I had someone to share that with.

But no one was with me. Because of the pandemic, no visitors were allowed in the hospital. As far as I knew, no one had called me either. I was sure someone had to know I was here. I pulled the TV over, and twisted to pick up the remote from the nearby tray. I clicked it on, then pressed the channel button, flicking past advertisements, the shopping channel, a rerun of *Law and Order*. My phone rang. Eagerly, I reached over to pick it up.

"Shelby," the woman's voice was faint, reedy. "Oh my god, you're alive. How are you? I've been trying to reach you all day. I've been sick with worry. We're all worried. Are you okay? What happened?"

"Erica?" I fought back a tear. "Erica?"

"What happened?" she repeated.

I shook my head. "I don't know. It's so complicated." I took a breath, the room suddenly swimming around me. I thought about when I'd last seen Erica, tied up on the bed upstairs in her house. "How are you?"

"I'll recover," she said, her voice matter of fact. "I'm trying to just forget about it. I'm sure years of therapy lie ahead, but for now, I'm really okay. I wasn't raped. I liked the guy well enough, even though he was kind of creepy, until he turned into a monster." She stifled what sounded to me like a hysterical giggle. She continued, "In any case, I'm not going back to the house just yet. And I definitely can't go back inside until I do some kind of cleansing ceremony."

"Makes sense to me," I said, trying to wrap my head around what I was hearing. She must still be in shock.

"When are they letting you out?" she asked.

"I have no idea." I squeezed my eyes, trying to concentrate as the room was blurring into soft edges around me. "You're the first person I've talked to."

"Not Dexter or Megan? Lucy?"

"No one." A tear squeezed out from my right eye. "No one," I repeated.

"I've been on the phone with them all day." She stopped and said, "Don't worry. We've got you covered. Dexter will come get you when you are released. As soon as we're off the phone, I'll call everyone and let them know I talked to you."

"Thank you," I said. "Thank you."

"By the way," Erica's voice grew high-pitched, "you and Lucy are all over the TV."

"What?" I was stunned. Celebrity status had haunted me before in my career and it had not been the kind of publicity that I wanted. "Why?"

"Jeez, Shelby. GMO designer babies? Really? Right here in Santa Cruz County? Brought down by Shelby McDougall and Lucy Flores of

Shelby McDougall Investigations? You two are famous. You are the lead story. They're talking about your past while standing in front of your office building. National news is starting to pick it up. I had no idea. My housemate is one tough cookie." She paused. "Besides, that's the only thing keeping me upright. Thinking of my small part as a pawn to lure you in. Though I hope that doesn't get in the news," she added.

"Wow," I said. "Wow. Wait. Did they say anything about Helen Brannon?"

"Who?"

"The scientist behind it all. The woman who created these creatures."

"I don't think so," Erica said slowly. "Is she important?"

"If she's not caught, she'll just do it again," I said. "And again. And again." I dropped the phone. I needed to get out of here. I needed to find her and stop her. I tried to get out of bed, yanking my free arm across my body in order to lever myself up. But my hand was connected to an IV pole. An alarm started beeping.

"Shelby?" I heard through the line. "Are you okay?"

A nurse, dressed in blue scrubs, hurried in. "Ms. McDougall." She put her hand on my shoulder. "You need to stay in bed. Please. You can't put any weight on that foot yet." She removed the phone from my hand, spoke into the receiver, and placed the handset back in the cradle. "Please lie back down." She reached across me, fiddled with the tube in the IV drip, and turned off the alarm.

As she helped me settle back in bed, she nodded toward the door and called, "Come on in."

A familiar figure filled the door to the room and my heart skipped. Cody.

His face was covered by a mask, his hands were encased in latex gloves, and he wore paper booties on his feet. He was dressed in his uniform and gear, complete with duty belt sporting his pistol and taser. He stood a few feet from the bed.

"I heard what happened."

My eyes grew wide as I asked, "Were you there?"

He shook his head. "I was way up in North County on a domestic. I didn't arrive until after you were gone."

I reached my hand out, but Cody shook his head again. "Sorry, I can't. I'm under strict orders not to touch you. Not to touch anything in this whole place. I'm allowed just a few minutes."

"How's Lucy?" I asked.

"I talked to her. She's at home with her parents. She seemed shook up, scared, but okay all the same."

"Dexter?"

"He said he'd pick you up when you get released. You'll be staying with him for at least ten days until your first post-surgery appointment."

I swallowed. The pain meds were making me fuzzy. "Helen Brannon?"

Cody bowed. "You'll be happy to know that she has been apprehended by the Santa Cruz County Sheriff's Department and will not be seeing the outside of a jail cell for the rest of her life."

"Thank god," I said. "Thank god." I leaned my head back and closed my eyes. It was over. Truly over. Helen Brannon had been caught. My life's goal, met.

I looked at Cody and he smiled above his mask. "I'm really impressed, Shelby," he said. "Wow. You wouldn't give up. You wouldn't let it go. And you caught her. It's amazing. You're amazing."

I smiled back at him, feeling happy. Elated even, yet curiously hollow and shaky at the same time. All those pain meds and not enough food, I guessed. I picked up the sheet and wiped my eyes.

Cody continued, "I should let you know that Crystal is okay too. The county is trying to figure out what to do with those three women and the two babies. For now, they're all in a secure ward at a hospital in Salinas. I imagine the Feds will swoop in and take over. But they're safe. Stu and Marilyn will be able to see her soon." He paused. "The main reason I was allowed in was to tell you that a detective will be by to interview you tomorrow. Do you want me to be here?"

I nodded eagerly, not caring if he would be here as a friend, a witness, law enforcement personnel, or a spouse. He would be here for me.

Cody glanced at his watch. "I gotta go," he said. "But I did bring you something." He reached into his pocket and pulled out a bright yellow packet decorated with dancing M&Ms. "Your favorite."

He tossed it toward me and it landed on my stomach. A treat we used to share as a reward for a long day spent on home improvement projects.

"Bye, Shelby," he said.

"Bye," I replied, the yellow packaging blurring as tears streamed down my cheeks.

50

T HE ELEVATOR DOORS SLID OPEN and a nurse pushed my wheelchair into the hallway. My injured foot stuck out straight in front of me and my orders were clear: stay off the foot for ten days until the post-surgical visit. Only get up to use the commode. Keep the foot elevated. Keep the ice packs on. And no shower.

She wheeled me slowly down a hallway to the hospital lobby, where whimsical oversized sculptures were lit by the bright sunlight streaming in through the floor-to-ceiling windows. I could see people outside, pressed up to the glass.

"You ready for this?" the nurse asked. "I understand there's quite a crowd out here."

"I think so," I said. When Dexter had called to tell me he'd be picking me up in the afternoon, he'd also warned me. "There are going to be reporters, Shelby," he'd added. "Lots of them. Megan will wait in the car. I'll be at the door. We'll just whisk you over to the car, put you in, and drive off."

"Has anyone found your house yet?" I'd asked.

"For now, we have cops at the gate. We can't stop the reporters congregating on the sidewalk, but it's the best we've got."

Now, I knew what he meant by "lots of them." Reporters mobbed my chair, ignoring Dexter's pleas to back off and give the injured woman some room. One particularly pesky reporter, with a Fox News decal on her microphone, wearing a lime green mask, planted herself in front of the wheelchair, shoving the microphone into my face. She leaned over too far and grazed the boot protecting my foot. A zip of pain, like sweets on a bad tooth, caused me to gasp in surprise. I almost told her off, but Dexter expertly slipped himself between us, and managed to bark, "No comment."

Reporters pressed in as I transferred from the wheelchair to Dexter's Corolla, awkwardly scooting backward across the seat. Dexter stood in front of the car door, blocking reporters, photographers, and camera operators. Once I heard the locks engage, I sighed in relief, and leaned against the door.

"Thank you," I said. "How many of them are at your house?" I asked as we circled the rotunda by the hospital lobby. The crowd was breaking up, with reporters scrambling to their respective vans to file stories.

"Not as many as yesterday, but there will be plenty by the time we get back. We'll drop you at home and then go out and pick up your prescriptions. Annie gave up her bed for you," he continued, twisting around in his seat to look at me. "She'll squeeze in with Max. Her room is closest to the bathroom."

I brushed a tear from my eye. "That is really nice. Where are the kids now?"

"Home," Megan answered, as she flicked the signal and accelerated into the turn. "Someone's staying with them. We'll have a full house for a while," she said.

Dexter leaned over to confer with Megan, so quietly I couldn't hear. She nodded and then Dexter shifted back around to face me.

"Mom came," he said. "As soon as I called her, mid-morning yesterday, she got in her car. 'Virus be damned,' she said. She arrived well after midnight last night. She's staying in Ashley's bedroom."

"Oh," I said, surprised by the multiple emotions swirling inside me. Excitement that I'd be seeing my mom, dread that I'd have to confront the issue of the found child, and worry that she'd driven almost seven hundred miles in one sitting, risking coronavirus infection at every gas station and rest stop. After a beat, I asked, "How are we going to manage the social distancing?"

As Megan launched into a bathroom cleaning protocol that everyone would follow and an explanation of how we'd handle meals, she also reminded me of my orders: complete bed rest. They'd squeezed a commode into the bedroom. Anyone who entered the room would be wearing a mask and gloves. Once I'd had my post-surgery checkup, Mom and I would head to Bonny Doon. Mom would be at my beck and call, as she'd be living in the guest room directly across the hall from me. Megan, the super-organizer that she was, had already cleared this with Erica.

I was too tired and fuzzy to argue. I knew I couldn't stay with Dexter and Megan forever, but somehow I thought I'd be able to manage on my own once I went home. But I knew that driving would be out of the question, for at least six weeks. And managing the stairs in Bonny Doon to reach the kitchen would prove impossible for some time. Mom and I would have plenty of time to work things out.

Once we reached Dexter's house and I hobbled past the gauntlet of reporters, up the three steps to the porch, and down the hallway to Annie's room, I collapsed on the bed, lifting my right leg with both hands. My entire leg throbbed, from big toe to thigh. An equal level of discomfort coursed up and down my left leg. After I adjusted the pillows behind me, I surveyed the room. I could tell that Megan and Annie had de-cluttered and cleaned. The floor was free of toys, books, and clothes. The top of the dresser was empty save for two rolls of toilet paper and a pack of wipes. A commode squatted in the center of the room, in the space between the bed and the door. I stared at it with distaste.

"I'll empty it for you," a familiar voice said. I turned toward the doorway. Mom stood framed there, the black mask covering her face making her look old, severe, and tired.

"Thanks, Mom," I said, my voice soft. "Thank you so much for coming."

"I was so worried about you," she replied. Her white hair fell almost to her shoulders; she hadn't gotten a haircut in six months, since the pre-COVID days. She held it back with a forest green bandana. "I'm glad to be here," she added. "Glad we could work it out."

I reached for her. "Me too," I said.

But Mom shook her head, and wiped her eyes. "No touching. I don't have my gloves on." She lifted her bare hands. "You've been in a hospital, so we all have to be super careful. Dexter said I could come only if I followed his rules."

"Thanks," I replied, sniffling, surprised at the emotion welling up inside me. Maybe my time with her wouldn't be so hard after all.

I dozed then, waking up only when Mom brought me a cup of broth and pain pills. Dexter, Megan, Annie, and Max, all wearing masks, stood in my doorway at some point to wish me goodnight. I slept fitfully, waking sometime in the night when Megan brought me my next dose of pain meds. And then again, in the early morning.

By Monday, the fourth day post-surgery, my head was a bit clearer. We'd developed a routine in the house. Dexter and Megan would leave early for work, with Megan dropping Max off at preschool. Annie would log into online school for three hours. She'd already made a new friend who lived nearby, and the problems she'd had just a few weeks ago seemed a distant memory. Annie's tutor would arrive at noon, help Annie with schoolwork for a few hours, then pick up Max in the early afternoon. Dexter and Megan would arrive home after five, and I'd listen for Max's excited footsteps as he raced to see his dad and mom. During the day, Mom would bring me my meals, make sure I stayed on top of my antibiotics and pain meds, and keep me entertained. I'd drift off into an uneasy sleep around seven or eight.

Cody called me every day. In my fuzzy state of mind, I couldn't tell if he was doing this out of obligation or as my worried spouse. He'd been with me for my first interview with the detective, and promised he'd be there for any subsequent ones. But our conversations were always brief, and I was at a loss as to what he was thinking.

51

T HE BLUE SKY ARCHED ABOVE as Mom made the turn from Pine Flat Road onto the driveway that led home. I noticed two orange cones at the intersection that Erica must have used to keep the reporters at bay. Luckily, they'd all moved on to other stories by now.

I rolled down the window, inhaling the sharp scent of campfire. It looked like Erica had started hacking away at some of the charred vegetation herself instead of waiting for the tree service. Six five-foot tall piles of blackened shrubs lined the driveway.

"Shelby?" Mom turned to look at me. Her voice was muffled behind her mask. "You okay?"

I nodded. "Glad to be getting home." And I was. I was surprised I wasn't experiencing flashbacks or chills or other physical symptoms. I just wanted to see the house and hug Erica, who I knew would be here, waiting for me. I wanted to sleep in my own bed. I wanted my laptop. I wanted my own toiletries, my own clothes, my own sheets and blankets. My own pillow. And a phone. I'd ordered a new one; the night I'd been taken, I'd dropped mine as I'd stormed through the house looking for Erica.

A few cars I didn't recognize were parked by the house when we pulled in. My Prius was just where I'd left it that night. When Mom parked, I opened the door, savoring the breeze, in spite of the smoky smell. Once I got upstairs, I knew I wouldn't be coming back down for a while. I could open the window in my room, but it wouldn't be quite the same.

I waited until Mom hurried around to the passenger door before attempting to extract myself. We'd worked out a system: Mom would hold the door steady while I levered myself out, using the door and my crutch to stand. Just as I was hauling myself upward, I heard a loud, "Shelby," and saw a blur as Erica flew down the porch steps, her face covered with a bright yellow mask emblazoned with a smile. She stopped, watching me, wincing, as I carefully balanced on my left foot and stood, transferring my weight from the door to the crutch in one careful move.

"That's impressive," she said.

"It's because we've had a lot of practice," I replied. I smiled, happy to see her. She'd come to Dexter's several times to visit, standing in the backyard by Annie's window on her phone, while I was on the inside, sitting in a chair by the window, on my mom's phone. We'd talked about everything but what had happened. She'd been so excited to tell me about her pots, the ritual cleansing of her room, how she'd hired someone to redo the upstairs.

"Can you manage the stairs?" Erica pointed toward the front porch and the three steps leading up to it.

"Absolutely," I said. Mom pulled the other crutch from the car and I swung it under my left arm. After ten days of mandated flat-on-my-back rest, I'd quickly become an expert with my crutches. Not that using them felt at all natural, but I was now able to navigate in and out of a car without finding myself sweating, trembling, and exhausted.

"Have you met?" I pointed from my mom to Erica. "Mom, I mean Denise, meet Erica. Erica, meet my mom, Denise."

Erica laughed. "We sure have. We'd chat in the backyard after I visited with you through the window."

"Oh right," I said as I shuffled over to the porch steps. I eyed them and then handed the crutches to Erica. I leaned into the bannister and hopped up the stairs, collapsing into one of the Adirondack chairs on the porch.

"Don't get too comfortable," Erica said as she slipped into the nearby chair. "I have something to show you."

"What's that?" I asked.

"Come on," she nodded toward the door. "It's just inside."

She stood and hurried to the door, obviously unable to contain her excitement.

I used the wide arms to pull myself to the lip of the chair, then reached for the porch railing. But it was too far away and I needed help. "Where'd Mom go?" I asked.

Erica turned toward me. "I'm not sure. Maybe she took some stuff upstairs already?"

"I need help," I said. "I'm stuck."

"Uh-oh," Erica said. "Let me help."

"Not supposed to," I said, as I wiggled forward. "Masks and all that. I just went to the doctor's yesterday, and just in case …" My voice trailed off as Erica approached me and put her hand out. "We'll be okay. We're going to be living together, right?"

"Better wash our hands after," I said smiling, as I took her hand. Her hand was cool, the skin rough and dry from all those years of throwing clay.

She pulled me up and I grabbed the crutches, moving quickly to the open front door. I followed her inside, the room as dim as ever. As best as I could tell, the room looked exactly the same: table lamps, sofa, comfy chairs, coffee table. Erica lifted a squirt bottle of hand sanitizer and offered it to me. As I balanced on my crutches and rubbed the liquid into my hands, she gave her hands a spritz and then stood proudly, expectantly, like a new mom waiting for a compliment. "What?" I asked. "What am I missing?"

Erica leaned her head to the right, toward the stairs. "Look," she pointed. "Look."

I leaned onto my crutches and stared. I was looking at a small chair, complete with a footrest, attached to the bottom of the staircase.

"What is that?" I turned to look at her, then back at the chair, then back at Erica.

"A stair lift," she said. "I had it put in last week. It's perfect, isn't it?"

I sagged into my crutches, speechless. Fighting back tears, I said, "That's one of the nicest things anyone has ever done for me."

She smiled. "I knew you'd like it. Dexter thought it was extravagant, but I thought, 'why not'? Besides, once you don't need it anymore, it's going to be super-handy for carting your laundry up and down the stairs."

"Thank you," I said. "Thank you."

"Now," she continued, "I have some snacks ready in the back patio. It's such a nice day, I thought we'd sit outside for a bit. I want to catch up, okay?"

I nodded in agreement. We did need to catch up. Our visits through the window of Annie's room hadn't offered the right moment. I needed to apologize. In person. I needed to apologize to Erica for how she'd been used to lure me in. I needed to apologize to her for not being aware enough to see what was happening. I needed to apologize for her humiliation. I had a lot to apologize for. And I was ready to do it.

Erica turned and walked through the house toward the kitchen. Before following her, I yelled up the stairs, "Mom? Are you up there?"

But no one answered. Maybe she was already in the guest room, unpacking her things. Maybe she needed to use the restroom.

I watched as Erica stopped in the kitchen to pick up a tray sitting on the kitchen table. It looked like it had at least a half-dozen glasses on it as well as a glass pitcher. As I slowly navigated through the living room, past the wood stove, I paused, thinking about the fireplace tongs I'd grabbed for a weapon. It was laughable in retrospect — as if a set of tongs would have been able to protect me from all the violence that lay ahead.

"Shelby," I heard Erica call. "Come on."

"Coming," I replied. "Is Mom out there?"

"I don't know where she is," Erica called back.

I continued through the dining room and under the archway separating the dining room from the kitchen. At the back door, I reached for the knob, twisted it, and pushed.

The door swung open an inch and then was yanked wide open to a chorus of people yelling "Surprise, surprise." I stood, fixed in place. As my eyes adjusted to the light, I could see a group of people on the patio. Erica and Mom. Dexter, Megan, and the kids. Kathleen and Lucy. And Stu and Marilyn, Crystal's grandparents.

Annie and Max were jumping up and down in excitement. "Surprise, Aunt Shelby. Surprise." Everyone was laughing, smiling, taking pictures.

A huge grin plastered my face. I knew it was radiating out from under my mask, beaming through the cloth, crinkling my eyes in delight, appreciation, love. "I had no idea," I exclaimed. "No idea at all." Looking at Annie and Max, I asked, "How did you keep it a secret?"

Four-year-old Max looked at me solemnly and said, "Me and Annie are really good at keeping secrets." Annie nodded in agreement, while Megan laughed and said, "Uh-oh."

Annie handed Max an envelope. "Take this to her," she said.

Max grabbed it and skipped over to me, yelling, "Open it, open it."

I leaned over as far as I could on my crutches, took the envelope, and slit it open. I pulled out a 'Get Well Soon' card, signed by everyone here, plus Cody, my surgeon, the anesthesiologist, the physician's assistant, and every single nurse who'd taken care of me.

I looked up. "Thank you. Thank you so much. I can't believe you're all here. Thank you." I stood in the afternoon light, feeling the warm sun caress me, reveling in the love and joy that surrounded me. Happy to be alive. Happy to be home.

52

ERICA POINTED TO A CHAIR in the middle of the patio under an umbrella. A stool had been placed in front of it. As I sat down, Erica handed me a pillow. "Put this under your foot. Elevate. I'll bring your ice pack."

Gratefully, I gave Erica a thumbs up. Megan dragged over a small wooden side table and Annie handed me a glass of lemonade. "Do you want anything to eat?" she asked. She counted on her fingers as she said, "We have cheese and crackers and chips and veggies and dip and cookies."

I laughed. "Did you help prepare the food?"

She nodded. "Yes."

"How did you do that?"

She gave a sly grin. "Well, you were lying down all the time in my bed. It wasn't too hard. Granny and I did the shopping yesterday and then while you were getting ready to go this morning, we put it all together."

"Thank you," I said. "And thanks for the lemonade. That's going to hit the spot." I removed my mask, reached for the drink, took a long sip, then faced Annie. "I think I need a little bit of everything," I said.

When Annie scampered off to bring me a plate of food, Lucy pulled up a chair next to me. "Hey boss," she said, keeping her mask on. "How are you?"

"I'll recover," I replied. "How about you?" My eyes searched hers. Her brow furrowed the tiniest bit and then she answered, "Truthfully? It might take a while. But I know I'll recover. It helps that the perp is in custody and that I was immediately taken to the hospital for an exam." She paused, collecting her thoughts. "Having studied this in college, and knowing what to expect …" Her voice trailed off, and I sat in silence, waiting for her to pick up the thread. "Kathleen was with me the entire time, which helped a lot."

Just then, Annie returned with a plate heaped with food: everything she'd recited before, plus a few monster strawberries, small circles of green melon, and a cluster of grapes.

"Thank you," I said.

She put the plate down and ran over to Max, setting up a Hot Wheels track on the far side of the patio.

"I'm so sorry," I said. "You only got caught up in this because of me."

Lucy put her hand up. "It's okay, Shelby. Really it is. I'm thinking of changing careers because of it. Law enforcement with a specialty in sexual assault crimes. Now that I've had this experience, as horrible as it was, I know I can help others. I know I can make a difference. Thanks to Kathleen and my parents and my therapist, I will get through this." Her face saddened and she looked down at her feet. "I'm not there yet. It will take time. But I will get through it." Then, she lifted her chin. "I'm not sure yet if I'll be able to return to the office. I don't know if I can go back in there."

I reached out to take her hand, but stopped myself. Not only because of COVID and social distancing, but also because I didn't want to appear patronizing or dismissive. Instead, I said, "I understand. Take all the time you need to decide."

"Thanks, Shelby," she replied. "Thank you."

Kathleen wandered by then, and stopped in front of us.

"Pull up a chair," I said.

Kathleen nodded, grabbed a nearby chair, and wrestled it across the patio. "Thanks." She sat down, saying, "How are you two?"

"I guess we've both decided that we'll recover," I said.

Lucy chimed in, "Yes. We will. Thank you."

"When did you get to the lab?" I asked. I was still unclear about all the events that had taken place that day. My lengthy interviews with law enforcement had helped and Cody had filled in some of the gaps.

"Cody called me as soon as he learned what was happening. I arrived just about the same time he did, around noon. You both were long gone by then. Once I learned what had happened to Lucy, I thought she'd need some support."

"How were you able to get into the hospital with her?" I asked.

"Lucy was taken to the hospital in Santa Cruz, where there's a sexual assault nurse examiner. Who I happen to know from my volunteer work at one of the womens' shelters. She authorized me."

"It was a miracle," Lucy said. "I don't know how I would have managed otherwise."

"It was so great that I was also able to talk to your parents," Kathleen pointed out, turning toward Lucy, then back at me. "I could tell them how long she'd be there, when she could go home, and what they could expect. Otherwise, they would have just been sitting in their car, waiting. Wondering what was going on."

"Kathleen helped me so much," Lucy added.

"I was so glad to be there," Kathleen replied. "And please call me anytime. Whenever you need to talk, okay? No matter if it's two in the morning. Call me."

Lucy nodded, wiping a tear from her eye.

Kathleen leaned over to me. "How's Erica doing?"

"She seems fine," I said. "Maybe she's having a delayed reaction, but what she's put together here is amazing. And the stair lift to the second floor? Above and beyond." I stopped for a second, collecting my thoughts. "I owe her an apology, getting her dragged into this." I gestured half-heartedly toward Lucy. "People who get close to me seem to end up hurt."

Kathleen grabbed my wrist, hard. "Don't you ever think that, Shelby. Put that thought right out of your mind. Now. That's poison."

Lucy added. "That's right, Shelby. That is not true."

But I knew it was true. Megan had been the first to get hurt, eight years earlier in 2012. Now Lucy and Erica. I shook my head. "Well, I'll have a lot of time to work it out with her."

"When are you going back to work?" Kathleen asked.

I shrugged. "I'm not sure," I said. "I'm going to take at least a few more weeks off. Maybe until I can drive. In the meantime, I have a few things to finish up."

Kathleen said, "I'd be happy to help."

I smiled, saying "Thank you. I could use it." I leaned in. "Did you know that our offices were bugged?" I asked.

Lucy's eyes grew wide and she said, "You're kidding. A bug? How? Where?"

Kathleen said, "Well, that explains a lot. Everything." I could see her eyes moving as if she were working to piece it all together.

"Brannon was stalking me," I said. "I'm sure of it. She had our offices bugged from the get-go. Maybe even when we were over at the harbor."

Lucy stood up, fists at her side. "Our offices were bugged? How could I have missed that?" She looked at me and then slumped back in the chair. "Oh wow, Shelby. I can't believe that."

I added, "I also found a GPS tracker on my car."

"I'm so sorry," Lucy said.

Kathleen asked. "It sure makes sense that it would have been Helen Brannon. But without proof, it's just a theory," she pointed out.

Lucy and I laughed. With Helen Brannon behind bars, listening devices, timelines, trackers, spyware — none of it seemed to matter.

Stu and Marilyn approached, and I could sense Lucy shift in her chair, getting ready to stand up. She did, offering her chair to Marilyn, who thanked her and sat down. Kathleen stood too and the two women slowly walked to another table, deep in conversation.

"Shelby, we can't thank you enough," Stu began as he slid into the chair Kathleen had occupied, but Marilyn interrupted, "You found our girl. Thank you. What can we do for you?"

"Nothing," I smiled. "Absolutely nothing." Truth be told, stumbling across Crystal had been a complete luck of the draw. I was convinced that the boyfriend her co-worker had told me about was a sexual predator. I had been unable to see the few clues that might have pointed me in the right direction: her comment to her mother that soon she'd have enough money to do whatever she wanted and the expensive full-sleeve tattoo that seemingly appeared overnight. "How is she?" I asked.

"She appears to be fine," Stu said. "She's still in the hospital in Salinas. There's a guard posted outside the room. But she can walk up and down the halls. They've taken her off whatever drugs she was being given. She's worried she'll have a miscarriage or a still birth." He leaned in and tugged the brim of his Salinas Rodeo cap. "Between the three of us," he pointed to me, Marilyn and himself, "seeing as what's happened with those Boyd twins, maybe that would be for the best."

He sat back. "Thank you again for bringing our grandbaby back home."

Marilyn, a thin, wan woman, pulled a tissue from her pocket and wiped her eyes. "Thank you."

Stu put his hands on his thighs, and stood. "We just wanted to come and show our support, Shelby. We'll let you get back to your family now," he said.

I looked up at him and smiled. "Please stay. After all we've been through, you are family."

He held out his hand to Marilyn as she stood. "Thank you."

As soon as Stu and Marilyn moved away, Mom came over. She looked tired, and I could only imagine that her busy schedule had been wearing on her. Full time caregiving would do that to a person.

"Need anything, darling?" she asked.

I shook my head. "No thanks, Mom. I'm okay. I do need to get up and use the bathroom, though." I eyed the distance between where I sat and the back door. And the additional distance from the door to the half-bath on the ground floor. "I better get moving before I embarrass myself." Mom watched while I gently lifted my leg off the stool and wiggled myself to the edge of the chair. She handed me the crutches, saying, "Here you are."

"Thanks," I said. Once I was standing, I sagged into the crutches, catching my breath. I could feel a deep ache in my foot and leg. "When did I last take a pain pill, Mom?" I asked.

Just like a kid, she picked her phone out of her back pocket, tapped it, and said, "You get another one in thirty minutes. I have an alarm set. Every four hours." She looked at me. "Are you going to make it?"

"Yes," I replied. "I think so."

Dexter was waiting for me when I returned. He helped me get settled, offered me more snacks, then said, "You going to be okay up here? You're more than welcome to stay with us longer, you know."

I turned to look at him. "You and Megan have been amazing, putting me up. And Mom too. But I think we'll be okay here. Give you all your house back."

"Keep it in mind. Especially if things go south with Mom." I glanced at him. He was smiling. "That was a joke, Shelby. Just a joke." Sometimes jokes were just that. Jokes. But sometimes they weren't.

I decided to let it go. "Thanks, Dexter." Changing the subject, I asked, "Did you know that Erica was putting in the stair lift?"

"Yes," he replied. "She called me about it, to ask if it was too extravagant. We talked about it. She really wanted to do it. I mean, really wanted to do it." He took a sip of his lemonade. "We talked for about an hour, right after all this happened. I think in a weird way, she's grateful it all happened. She said it opened her eyes to what she was doing. She said she was going to be more careful now with men. That she was better than hook-ups." He looked at me. "She was into hook-ups?" he asked.

I shrugged. "She was out a lot at night," I admitted. "But other than that, I don't know. I didn't meet many of them. That lift …" I started to say, but emotion overcame me, and I tried not to cry. "That lift; that was so thoughtful. She must have thought about it right away. When she was processing what had just happened."

"Sometimes," Dexter said, "the way to work through pain is to do something for someone else."

I nodded, thinking of Cody. I always came back to Cody. I hadn't worked through the pain yet and I couldn't remember the last time I'd done something for someone, just to be nice. Out of pure kindness. One of my grandpa's sayings came to me: "Always be kinder than you need to be."

As if reading my mind, Dexter said, "Too bad Cody couldn't come today. He had to work."

I nodded. "It's okay. I talk to him just about every day. He's been so helpful. He drove me to the sheriff's office for the second interview, got me to the right room, stayed with me during the entire thing, and then explained some things to me after. He swears that Helen will be behind bars forever. He's sure she'll be charged with kidnapping, several times over. That's a federal crime. Possibly murder. There's also a federal ban against genetically modifying embryos. She'll be charged with that too."

"What about the people who worked there?"

"I don't know. It seems like some of them at least, would have had to have known what was going on."

"The surrogates?"

"Crystal said she signed a piece of paper saying she was becoming a surrogate by choice. Nothing about designer babies, of course."

Dexter nodded, then stood and lifted his glass. "Hey everyone," he called. A few heads turned toward him. He said it again, his voice louder. "Hey, everyone." People quieted. Dexter raised his glass even higher. "A toast. A toast to Shelby Emma Sterns McDougall, the best sister in the entire world. The bravest, most stubborn, most persistent, and smartest sister I could ever ask for."

I blushed as the chorus of "Hear, hear!"s and "To Shelby!"s surrounded me.

"Speech, speech," Erica shouted, and the refrain was picked up by Megan, Lucy, and Kathleen.

Continuing to sit, I raised my hands in a shrug. "No speech. Just a heartfelt thank you. This is amazing. So wonderful to see everyone all in one place. Thank you."

Dexter raised his glass again, saying, "To Shelby." I raised my now-empty glass and smiled, taking it all in: Kathleen, Megan, Erica, and Lucy sitting around a table across the patio under an umbrella, chatting happily. My mother standing next to Stu and Marilyn, a three-person tableau. Max absorbed in a Hot Wheels track. Annie lying flat on a lounge chair, reading. The table of snacks, the glass pitcher of lemonade, the stack of brightly colored napkins. And Dexter toasting me.

A sense of contentment washed over me. I hadn't been this happy in a long, long time.

53

T HE PARTY BROKE UP SHORTLY AFTER THAT. I staggered inside, anxious for my next pain pill, which my mother offered me as soon as I sank down onto the sofa. Erica walked in from the kitchen, wiping her hands on a dishtowel.

"You want to try the lift?" Erica asked.

I nodded. "Sure," I replied. "I'm ready for a nap."

"While you're napping," Mom said, "I'll run to the store for groceries. I'll be back in a couple of hours." She stood. "Anything else for the list?"

"I think it's pretty complete," I said, adding, "I'm sorry you're having to do this second trip."

"It's okay," she said. "It'll be good to get it out of the way. We'll be set for the week. I'm going to get takeout for dinner if that's okay. I'm beat."

"Sure," I agreed. "Not Mexican food though," I added, remembering my trip for burritos the night I'd been kidnapped.

"No," Erica added. "Not burritos."

We discussed which restaurant would be the quickest and easiest, and finally decided on the Thai restaurant across the street from the grocery store.

"Thank you, Mom," I said.

"Yes," Erica added. "Let me give you some money."

"No, no," Mom said. "This is on me. Please."

Erica and I sat for a minute as soon as my mom left. "Thank you, Erica," I said. "For the party. For the lift. I am so grateful."

"You're welcome," she replied. Just as I was about to offer my apologies, to start a deeper conversation, she stood, effectively silencing me. "Come on, let's try the lift. I've done it plenty of times," she called over her shoulder. "It's fun. It's like a Boardwalk ride."

As I stood, I realized how much my leg was hurting. Definitely time to lie down. "Oh, can you grab an ice pack? I think Mom put a bunch of them in the freezer."

"Sure." Erica hurried past me back to the kitchen, while I hobbled over to the lift. The small seat snapped down when I gave it a good shove. I leaned my crutches against the wall and slid onto the chair, holding my right leg out in front of me.

Erica returned and picked up my crutches. "Looking good, Shelby," she said. "See this?" She pointed to a switch on the handle of the lift. "Just press it, and you'll go up."

I did. The chair moved slowly, smoothly, and quietly up the track. I laughed in delight. Erica followed me up the stairs. Once I pushed myself out of the chair, she handed me the crutches and followed me as I made my way down the hall. She stopped by the door to the guest room, and I gave her a questioning look. "Open it," she said.

I reached for the door and twisted the knob, watching as the door slowly swung open. It took me a minute to process the change. The room had been completely redone. The walls were now a cheerful yellow. The double bed had been replaced by a twin. The dresser was new, a solid classic with ample drawer space. Photographs of redwoods and mountain streams graced the walls. A white desk sat in the corner of the room, tucked into the corner under the windows. Bright yellow and white check curtains and a multi-color large rag rug on the floor completed the makeover. Mom's suitcase sat on the floor by the dresser.

"Wow," I said. "You've been busy. This is lovely."

"The only way I could move back into the house was to completely redecorate this room. I also got myself a new bed and rearranged my room. And you know about the smudge cleansing ceremony." She sat down on the window seat at the end of the hall, adjusting the cushion under her. "I also had this reupholstered," she said. "And I put up new artwork on the walls here."

I turned, surprised I hadn't noticed. More nature photos lined the walls. Close-up shots of flowers, exuberantly colored; sunsets streaked with pinks and golds; a maple tree in full fall foliage. "They're beautiful. Who took them?"

"A friend," Erica said. I looked at her. "Not that kind of friend," she said. "I'm done with that kind of friend. I learned my lesson the hard way. You may have figured out, long before me, that I'm not the best judge of men. So, I'm taking a break. I'm working on myself. And on you."

"Me?" I pointed to myself. "Me?" I repeated, laughing.

"Yes, you," she replied. "More yoga," she said as she stood and pointed to my door. "Look. I hope you don't mind. I kind of got carried away."

She opened the door. I caught my breath, taking it all in. The walls in my room were now a pale peach instead of a robin's egg blue. The second-hand desk, dresser, chair, and nightstand had been replaced with a matching set. Not the Ikea variety, but something that appeared more solid and was definitely one-of-a-kind. The rag rugs on the floor complemented the light lace curtains tied back against the windows. She'd added a set of louvers for complete privacy.

"Do you like it?" she asked.

"It's beautiful," I said. "I love it. How did you manage this, what with contractors all booked up?"

"I have friends," Erica said coyly, laughing. "Anyway, I put your phone over there." She pointed to the desk.

"Thanks," I said. "I'll get to that later. Much later."

"Sit," she pointed to the easy chair with a matching oversized stool, a new piece of furniture next to the desk under the windows. "I am also getting an alarm put in," she said. "And motion sensitive lights. Not that either of those would have prevented what happened, but since I'm up here alone a lot of the time, I thought it would be a good idea." She stared at me. "I'm so sorry for that text, the one that took you to Pericos and brought you up here. He made me do it."

I stared back at her, surprised. She felt as guilty as I did. "But I need to apologize to you. If it wasn't for me, you would have never met the guy. That's all on me."

"Shelby," Erica said, "it's okay. Let's just say I knew the guy was off and I still went out with him. And look what happened." She shook her head and gazed out the window. "I was in the habit of being unable to stop myself. If someone showed an interest, no matter how unhealthy I knew it would be for me, I had to go for it. I couldn't say no. But now," she turned to me, "let's just say I'm in therapy two times a week. I reached out to the therapist I went to after my divorce. It's really helping. We're trying to figure out if I'm a sex addict." She made a face. "My pottery helps. Having you back home will really help. And I love your mom. She can stay as long as she wants," Erica added.

I put up my hand. "Not quite that long," I said.

We both laughed.

Erica continued. "Anyway, you should sit down. Or lie down. Get off that leg. You must be exhausted. Here's the ice pack. Do you need anything else?"

"Maybe a glass of water."

"Be back in a second." Erica's footsteps receded down the hall.

Getting into bed was my top priority. I sat on the edge of the bed, wiggled backward, and hauled my leg up, adjusting the extra pillow so my foot would be elevated. I laid back and turned to face the window, gazing at the view of the meadow and the burned forest rimming the far edge. A pair of crows harassed a red-tail hawk, dive-bombing the bird as it landed in a treetop. I wondered if it was the same pair I'd seen a few weeks ago. I wondered what the hawk was eating now; it seemed like any prey would have been obliterated by the fire. The enormous bird fluffed its wings and shrieked as it settled onto the branch, while the crows squawked in return. The larger bird seemed to simply ignore the hecklers.

Erica returned with a glass of water and set it on the desk. "Should I take the boot off?"

"Sure," I said. "But please leave it here on the bed. I'm not supposed to move around without it."

After making sure I was comfortable, Erica said, "Have a good nap. See you later."

"Thank you," I said. "I'll be down in a while." I adjusted the quilt that Erica had pulled over me and fell into a deep sleep.

54

T HE ROOM WAS DARK WHEN I WOKE and, for a few minutes, I was disoriented, confused. I felt fuzzy and I had a headache. Then, I remembered. Home. The party. The remodeled bedrooms. I shifted and slowly sat up, gasping when I saw a shadowy figure in the easy chair across the room. My heart went into overdrive, and I was just about to yell for help, when the person stood.

Cody.

"Hey," I said. "What are you doing here?" Not the most friendly of welcomes, I realized after it slipped out.

"I couldn't come to the party, but I wanted to see you. Erica said I could come up and see if you were awake. You were out cold, so I just decided to wait." He sat back down. "I hope I didn't wake you."

"What time is it?" I asked.

"Around seven," he said. After a beat, he said, "Shelby, I have something I want to talk to you about."

I wiggled further upright and moved the pillows behind me until I was comfortable, trying to ignore the sudden anxiety that gripped me.

"What's up?" I asked.

"I've been such an ass these last few months. I want to apologize. I want to know if we can reset. When I got back to the station that day and found out what had happened, I almost died inside. No one could report on your status and I didn't know." His voice caught. "I didn't know if you were dead or alive. I didn't know anything." He looked at me. "And I realized how much I missed you. What an idiot I've been. I realized how much I want to be with you and how sorry I am."

I stayed quiet, not wanting to move a muscle.

He continued, "I couldn't tell you when you were at Dexter's. Too public. And it wasn't right over the phone. So here I am. I'm not asking for an answer now. I just want to sit here and be with you."

"I'd like that," I said. "I'd like that a lot."

We sat in silence for a few minutes. It was too dim to make out Cody's features, but I could see him in my mind's eye. His expression, which you could think was stern, until you knew him and knew he was just thinking. His kind brown eyes, which could seem severe when confronted with an injustice. His even jaw and picture-perfect smile.

"There's something else," he added. "More on the case."

"Okay," I said slowly. I was bracing myself for the worst. That Helen Brannon had been let out on bail. That all charges had been dropped.

"The detective said she'd call you tomorrow, so you'll find out soon enough. But I wanted to be first."

I sat up as he shifted his gaze toward me.

"Just don't let on that I told you. I could lose my job."

Now, he had my full attention.

"When the forensics team went into the lab, they found a freezer in one of the rooms. An industrial freezer set to a subzero temperature. As part of the forensics work dismantling this lab, the FBI contracted with a fertility specialist who would be able to identify each piece of equipment and figure out where it might have been purchased, so they could then do accounting research to see who paid for it."

My eyes were fixed on Cody. Where was this going?

"When the fertility specialist, along with FBI agents, opened this freezer, they found vials and vials of human eggs. At least fifty vials. Each vial was labelled with a woman's first name, last initial, and a date. They're being cataloged now. And kept frozen. The fertility specialist was adamant about that."

Cody leaned toward me. "Shelby, one of the last vials to be removed, from the back corner of the thing, had your name on it. With a date of February, 2007."

"What?" I realized that I was clutching the edge of the quilt. "What?"

"My guess is that Helen Brannon harvested extra eggs from every woman she used as a surrogate. Maybe those eggs were her trophies. Kind of like those trophies that Diane kept from all the birth mothers she'd swindled."

An image flashed through my mind of a storage shed, filled with boxes of baby quilts and blankets, hand-knit hats and sweaters.

"Shelby?" Cody asked. His voice was gentle.

"There are some of my eggs?" I stared at him. "You're sure?"

Cody nodded. "I am. I talked to the specialist myself."

"But how?"

"I went out to the lab this afternoon. The sheriff's department is responsible for securing the property. So my buddy, who put his job on the line for me, gave me permission to go in. I found the specialist, a Dr. Ruskowsky, in the hallway and asked him a few questions. First off, they are just starting to catalog all the eggs. I asked if he'd found a vial with your name on it. He said yes, then he requested that I only ask yes/no questions. So I asked him if the eggs, in general, looked like they were still viable. He nodded. I asked him if he could tell if the eggs had had their genetic material altered. He shrugged, so I paraphrased and asked if he would be able to tell with tests. He nodded again."

Cody stood and approached the bed, kneeling beside me. He reached for my hand and touched my wedding ring, twisting it around and around. I looked at him, with an ache so fierce I thought I was about to cry. Cody took a breath. "Anyway, here I am. With a crazy plan." He smiled as he looked into my eyes. "I want to get back together. I want to get your eggs tested. If they check out, I want us to use those eggs to have a child with a surrogate. If it doesn't work, I want to adopt. I want a family with you. With *you*, Shelby."

He squeezed my hand, his eyes searching mine. Then, he rose up, reached for me, pulled me close, and kissed me, a long, deep kiss.

When he released me, I held his face in my hands and studied him, holding back tears.

"I love you Cody Wilson," I said. "I've always loved you. I never stopped."

I leaned into him, holding him tight. "Let's stay like this forever," I whispered in his ear. "Forever."

EPILOGUE

Y EYES BLURRED AS I PICKED UP THE PIECE OF PAPER from the desk. The attorney had already filled in names and addresses, dates, the *'whereto …'*s and *'whereas …'*s. For the amount of money exchanging hands, it was only to be expected. I handed the paper to Cody, who removed a pen from the front pocket of his blazer. He placed the document on the table and set the pen on top of it.

I pulled out my phone to get a picture. The attorney's office, on the 32cnd floor of San Francisco's Transamerica Pyramid, was understated, up-scale, and reeking of money. I wanted a photo of Cody, with the contract, framed by the view. We'd done our research and had chosen the very best. We knew it was extravagant, but it was worth every penny. Our journey had brought us to this point, and I wanted a picture so I could slow down the moment. Remember it. Savor it.

Savoring life came more easily to me now. After our conversation that night of the party, Cody and I had become inseparable. Once I could drive again, after six weeks, Mom returned to Portland and Cody moved in. He and I lived upstairs. And the house became a home. We shared chores with Erica. We ate meals with her. We worked the land together, marveling in the spring as tender green shoots sprouted from the scorched earth. We went on hikes and watched movies and binged TV shows. Over time, we'd become a family.

I ditched the boxing classes and took up trail running with Cody. Though smashing a small ball was great for my upper arms, it wasn't so good for my psyche anymore. Boxing had served its purpose. We could easily slip out our back door, and within minutes, be on a quiet trail through a slowly regenerating redwood forest. Early morning was best, when the forest was quiet, the light was filtering through what was left of the canopy, and the birds were calling, starting their day. We often saw deer in the meadow or coyotes trotting on the trail in front of us.

Once a vaccine was available, the pandemic receded into our collective and cultural pasts. The United States was hit hard. Just about everyone knew someone who had died from the novel coronavirus. My mother had passed away during the long winter of 2020-2021; the vaccine had arrived too late for her. Dexter and I weren't allowed to see her in her last days, but we were both so grateful she'd been with us in the fall. When her time came, I hoped she wasn't scared, and that she had seen my father's open arms as she slipped into unconsciousness.

The promise of Helen Brannon spending the remainder of her life in prison helped me heal. She was charged with assault, kidnapping, attempted murder, theft. The detectives were trying to find evidence that would connect her to murder: the skeletal remains of two women had been discovered in the fields around the lab. She was also being charged with breaking federal law banning development of genetically altered human embryos.

The babies I'd found in the lab had been scooped up by the government and now lived in Reston, Virginia, with the Boyd twins. Crystal, as well as the two other pregnant women, had eventually given birth to non-human children. Those babies were also under government care and guarded day and night. I was sure there were other synthetic children out in the world, but so far, Helen hadn't revealed their location. It was her bargaining chip, I supposed.

The fertility doctor who Cody had spoken to, Dr. Ruskowsky, had been one of the principal investigators into what was called "the designer baby project". As Cody had guessed, the vials in the freezer held eggs likely harvested from every woman who'd signed on to be a surrogate during all the years Helen Brannon had been doing her research. My vial held three eggs. The DNA had been tested, and it came up clean; unaltered.

The three eggs were what remained of the dozen or so eggs Helen Brannon had harvested from me all those years ago. Some of those eggs, likely three or four, had been sold to the mother of the found child, the *Ancestry.com* discovery that had started this quest. That left five to six eggs unaccounted for. Had they been tinkered with and implanted in some other unsuspecting subject? Had they been sold, resulting in other genetic progeny? I didn't want to know.

Now, Cody and I were here, in a high-priced fertility attorney's office, signing a contract to hire a twenty-eight-year-old woman named Melinda to be our surrogate. Melinda was a happily married mother of two who loved being pregnant. We'd get just one try. If it was meant to be, so be it. If not, we were at peace with that also.

"Shelby? Cody?" An assistant eyed us cautiously. "Are you ready to sign?"

I nodded. Cody picked up the pen, wrote his name, then handed it to me. I signed on the line next to his, writing my full name, "Shelby Emma Sterns McDougall". I dated it. The assistant picked up the stack of papers and leafed through them, double-checking.

"I think that's it," she said, as she reached across the desk to shake our hands.

We shook hers in return, then walked through the door as she held it open.

ABOUT THE AUTHOR

Nancy Wood grew up in various locations on the East Coast and now calls Central California home. Recently retired, she spent thirty-five years as a technical writer, translating engineer-speak into words and sentences. She likens it to translating ancient Greek — when you're not too familiar with the Greek part.

Since retiring, she and her husband have been traveling the world. So far, they've visited France, Spain, England, Sri Lanka, New Zealand, Belgium, the Netherlands, India, and Vietnam. They are not anywhere close to done and have many more trips planned. Nancy is also a passionate photographer, focusing on macro photography and blur.

For more information about the world and works of Nancy Wood, visit *nancywoodbooks.com*.

BOOKS BY NANCY WOOD

DUE DATE

Surrogate mother Shelby McDougall just fell for the biggest con of all: a scam that risks her life ... and the lives of her unborn twins.

THE STORK

It's been five and a half years, and Shelby McDougall is finally on track. But a late-night phone call puts Shelby's perfectly ordered life into a tailspin.

THE FOUND CHILD

Private Investigator Shelby McDougall is out for revenge.

TREASURE HUNT

When ten-year-old Tyler signs up for a Saturday afternoon treasure hunt sponsored by the city's Parks department, he discovers much more than he bargained for.

Available from Paper Angel Press in
hardcover, trade paperback, digital, and audio editions
paperangelpress.com